CAPTUR
WEST TEXAS

BARB HAN

STALKED THROUGH
THE MIST

CARLA CASSIDY

MILLS & BOON

First Published in Great Britain 2025
by Mills & Boon, an imprint of HarperCollins*Publishers* Ltd
1 London Bridge Street, London, SE1 9GF

www.harpercollins.co.uk

HarperCollins*Publishers*
Macken House, 39/40 Mayor Street Upper,
Dublin 1, D01 C9W8, Ireland

Captured in West Texas © 2025 Barb Han
Stalked Through the Mist © 2025 Carla Bracale

ISBN: 978-0-263-39702-4

0325

This book contains FSC™ certified paper and other controlled sources to ensure responsible forest management.

For more information visit: www.harpercollins.co.uk/green

Printed and Bound in the UK using 100% Renewable Electricity at CPI Group (UK) Ltd, Croydon, CR0 4YY

CAPTURED IN
WEST TEXAS

BARB HAN

All my love to Brandon, Jacob and Tori, my three greatest loves. To Samantha, welcome to the family officially. Happy first anniversary. I love you all more than words!

To Babe, my hero, for being my best friend, my greatest love and my place to call home. I love you with everything that I am.

And, last but certainly not least, to Oliver and Birgit Pohl for a rare and beautiful friendship.

Chapter One

Abilene Remington, Abi to everyone who knew her, cursed her family tree as she squeezed the piercing pinch in her side and tried to catch her breath. Genetics had given her five feet two inches of height, which meant she had short legs. She was fast, like soccer players gunning down the pitch about to score fast, but short. Also, she hated running. She'd never liked it. Never wanted to be a runner despite Mesa Point High School coach David McGeary's burning desire to put her on the team. But running was as much part of a US marshal's job as sharpshooting. Felons who were about to be sentenced to life in prison or worse didn't have a whole lot to lose. So they ran, or they fired a weapon, or both, sometimes at the same time.

Reynosa the Reprehensible, the felon she'd chased to the abandoned strip mall, was a runner.

Typical.

Maybe she should change his name to Reynosa the Runner instead.

Abi could think of dozens of better things to do at ten o'clock on a Saturday morning in late October than go for a run, but it would be worth it if the tip was correct, this was actually Reprehensible, and she could take a serial killer off the streets.

Lungs clawing for air, Abi almost skidded to a dead stop in front of an opened industrial AC unit vent. *Are you kidding me?*

Since Abi could keep up with the best of them, she almost always got to places before her colleagues, who were other marshals, deputies or cops. Depending on the case, they might be from one of those other alphabet agencies while on joint task forces. Being short, tiny and small-boned, she also got to be the one to follow perps into tight spaces.

Lucky her.

Abi didn't have time to wait for Agent Grayson Chisolm to catch up. Not if she was going to keep Reynosa the Reprehensible within reach. Catching the bastard was the only way to stop the senseless murders. This twisted offender had cut short the lives of five college kids already and counting. According to the FBI profiler from Quantico assigned to the case, this young male wouldn't stop until he was caught or dead.

Climbing into the abandoned warehouse's AC vent, she took a deep breath to steel her resolve and make herself slim enough to fit into the tiny shaft. The opening wasn't large enough for her to crawl into: she had to go belly down as she stretched her arms out in front of her.

Teeth clenched, Abi did what she'd been hired to do. She climbed inside and went after the felon, hoping to catch him before he got away.

Despite Halloween coming up in a couple of days and the fact the sun hadn't yet reached its peak, the metal vent was stuffy and unusually hot. Dust caused her to sneeze almost immediately. There hadn't been any air circulating in this sucker for a long time. Would she even be able to breathe as she wriggled her way toward Reprehensible? He was too far ahead to grab. There was at least a slight chance another law enforcement officer or agent would make it around the building to greet him on the other side. The thought kept her pushing him toward the exit.

"Surrender," she commanded in her most authoritative voice. Perps like these rarely listened to her but it was worth a shot. Plus, it was protocol to identify herself. Her voice bounced off the tin walls. She tried to shout above the shuffling noises that made her ears hurt. "My name is Marshal Remington, of the US Marshals Service. I'm ordering you to stop. *Now!*"

What? Nothing? Her sarcasm wouldn't exactly win her any originality awards but amused her in stressful times. Staying calm and keeping her focus was critical in clutch situations. Developing a sense of humor about her job kept her from burnout, which had taken a lot of great marshals down before and during her time, her grandfather included. But his heart had always been in the paint horse ranch he'd built from nothing. Sadness at the thought of her grandparent threatened to crack her focus.

At twenty-eight years old, she wasn't ready to throw in the towel in her current profession. In some ways, she was just getting started.

The feeling of a dozen fire ants crawling underneath her skin jacked her pulse through the roof. Being this close to pure evil always affected her in more ways than one. Her skin crawled and bile churned in her stomach. Adrenaline thumped through her veins, pushing her forward and turning her into what her supervisor called Ramped-up Abi. It was her on steroids. Her stubborn streak caused her to dig in her heels. Her version of fast became hyper speed. And when she locked onto a target, she was better than military-grade precision weapons. Her laser-like focus amped up too. Wonder Woman had nothing on Abi when she was this close to catching a creep.

Senses on high alert, she also heard claws against the metal scurrying ahead of her. Mice? Rats?

Oh, please don't let it be rats this time. They might be intelligent critters and some folks might enjoy keeping them as pets, but they gave Abi the heebie-jeebies. Every time. Her body rocked an involuntary shudder at the thought of sharing space with them.

"Marshal Remington, you in there?" FBI Agent Grayson Chisolm's deep timbre came through the radio in a low whisper, echoing inside the hollow container. Well, almost hollow. There were two humans army-crawling as fast as they could go, blocking sound's ability to travel to the opposite end. There were critters too, but she forced those out of her mind, or all forward progress would be lost, and she'd end up stuck. Trust her, it happened.

At least Agent Chisolm had finally arrived on the scene. He wasn't as fast a runner as Abi, but the man had arms built like a bodybuilder's and he had a reputation for being the best. This was the first joint task force she'd worked on with him, and she refused to be intimidated by his legendary status.

At the risk of giving her location away again, she whispered a response, "Yes." Then again, climbing through the shaft wasn't exactly quiet. Taking in air through her nose and blowing it out her mouth long and slow was a vain attempt to calm her rapid heartbeat. Swallowing dust and God knew what else in pursuit of Reprehensible wasn't exactly her ideal way of starting her day. Losing him would be much worse, so she doubled down on the army crawls.

There was truly little wiggle room in that air vent. Arms tucked to her sides with barely enough room to crawl, she pressed on. The perp's loud movement up ahead combined with his heavy breathing should hopefully mask most of the noise she was making.

In this tight space it would be next to impossible for him to look back. The longer it took for him to realize she was gaining on him, the better. No matter how fast she went, though, he would reach the opposite end before her. Guaranteed.

At least the space was tight enough to ensure he wouldn't be able to get off a shot while they were both inside, if he had a weapon. Otherwise, she'd be a goner already, because she was directly behind him with nowhere to go. Once he made it out the other end, though…

Too soon, Abi saw a hint of light in front of her, which meant the perp was getting close to the exit. On her belly like a worm, she inched her way toward him, determined not to let him get away. In front of her was nothing but darkness except for the occasional peek of light.

The perp, based on her earlier glimpse of him from a hundred yards away where it was hard to judge, couldn't be a large man. Although, the dark, baggy clothes made it difficult to define his shape. There was no way someone the size of a linebacker would fit in the vent. Agent Chisolm would definitely not be able to squeeze into this tight space.

This man could fit into the vent with Abi, which made him even smaller than the size the FBI profiler who'd been assigned to do a case study had originally believed him to be. These profiles, she'd learned, were always being refined when new information came in.

The perp couldn't be much wider than her. Taller, yes. But not broader. She was almost shoulder to shoulder with the walls.

Abi made mental notes to report back to the team in case this thing went south, and he got away.

This bastard has to be caught. Period.

She clawed her way closer to him, but he was still too far out of reach. If only she could close the distance faster.

The first hint he wasn't physically as strong as someone like Chisolm was the fact Reprehensible drugged his victims before torturing and eventually killing them. The murderer didn't rely on brute strength, which had been noted by the profiler. The bodies of all the five college kids he'd already killed had been found in shallow graves in the border town of Reynosa, Mexico, since the semester began late August. All five had brown hair and were reported as last being seen at a party. All victims had been given bowl cuts despite their sex. There'd been two female and three male victims to date. In two months, this bastard had taken five lives, with no sign of slowing down or stopping. The sixth attempt—on nineteen-year-old Max Hague—was the reason the task force believed they had a location on the perp and Abi was presently crawling through this damn vent.

The last thing Max remembered before being drugged was being at a party and drinking. He had managed to escape a structure—he'd said the size of roughly a two-car garage—and run while half-dazed and almost naked to flag down a motorist.

And then a call came in that someone had broken into a detached garage of a boarded-up home five blocks away from the party where Max last remembered being. Max fit the kind of victim Reprehensible thrived on finding. If this was Reprehensible, they had another detail to add to the case file. He took his victims to a secondary location, possibly for days before killing them.

Light filled the vent shaft. Abi tensed, waiting for the crack of a bullet.

Nothing came.

The perp was gone.

Could Abi at least get through fast enough to get a direction before he disappeared?

THE LAST MINUTES of morning were ticking by. At this rate, the perp would be long gone by the time Grayson Chisolm made it around the long strip mall on foot. At forty years old, he was the most experienced member on the joint task force, which also consisted of a US marshal, a sheriff and a deputy from the border town of McAllen, plus members from Texas State University campus PD, University of Texas at Austin campus PD, as well as Austin PD. Including him, the number came up to seven. Sheriff Benton and Deputy Carlson were on the team. It was a decent-sized team that had been formed a few days ago in order to catch the serial killer dubbed Reynosa the Reprehensible by the media.

Grayson wasn't a fan of giving this sonofabitch a name, especially so early in the process. Two months since his killing spree had started, and the body count was already racking up. Giving him a name might inflate his ego, which in turn could ramp up his killing streak.

The perp must have some tie to Reynosa, Mexico, since the bodies were found there, but that didn't mean he was born there, lived there, or worked there like a couple of the task force members had decided. The location might be a convenient place to dump a body since it was across the border from a small Texas town.

Marshal Remington kept an open mind. She'd argued against using the media dub to name the file, same as him. They'd lost on that one, but he was relieved to have someone who thought like him on the team. It was important to size everyone up on a task force like this, to find allies for when the time came to make critical decisions. Having one person on his side had tipped the scale in his favor more than once, if not this time.

Grayson had been on the job long enough to trust his instincts—instincts honed by years of experience. The good thing about a task force was being able to pull from everyone's jurisdiction in order to chase a criminal or make an arrest. A US marshal gave them international networks to draw on. Grayson's FBI background gave them access to the US. And then involving a sheriff, campus police, and Austin PD ensured cooperation and gave them instant local resources.

All of which came in handy when they zeroed in on a perp. It made all the difference in the world when getting close to an arrest of a dangerous criminal and making the charges stick.

Grayson pushed his legs faster. Marshal Remington had outrun him. He could admit he was no Tom Brady despite passing his annual department physical at the top of his age group.

Running wasn't his favorite activity. What he didn't have in speed, he made up for in strength.

Panting, he could only hope the perp had made it out the other end and would make the mistake of running around to the front of the strip mall center, playing into his hands.

Grayson tucked his chin to his chest and pushed his legs harder, pumping his arms to give him the little bit of extra momentum in his sprint.

He wasn't even around the first corner yet. There was a patch of trees behind the building. The parking lot was cracked from the relentless Texas summers.

They'd received a tip this might be the guy they were looking for and had acted on it fast. As luck would have it, both he and the marshal were within driving distance of the location where the perp was believed to be hiding. Grayson had been farther away than the marshal, so they'd waited for him, keeping an eye on the garage at a distance they'd deemed safe until the deputy walked out in the open in uniform. The perp had caught on and made a run for it.

This perp was going to be slippery. The ones good at killing always were. Otherwise, they would be caught after the first attempt. The general public had no idea how many would-be serial killers out there were caught during the first attempt or immediately after their first murder. It was probably for the best that way. He, for one, knew he didn't want his almost-five-year-old kid walking around scared of the world even though it could be cruel and harsh. It could also be the most amazing place. Grayson had learned those les-

sons firsthand. The same world that had taken his wife during childbirth had given him a perfectly healthy baby boy.

The world took and the world gave. It wasn't biased. It
did the take-give dance with everyone in equal measure.

On the surface, it might seem like some folks got away
with gaining and rarely ever had anything taken. But that
was a mirage, like water in the middle of the desert. Every
person, good or bad, was dealt wins and losses.

Grayson didn't make the rules, because he sure as hell
would have done things differently. That was just how it
worked. He'd learned the hard way after finding the love
of his life in Michelle and then being married only eighteen months before she'd died giving birth to their baby
boy, Collin.

She'd named their son, smiled up at Grayson with the
most beautiful glow before closing her eyes and bleeding
out.

Collin got his mother's sandy-blond hair and blue eyes.
He got her bad vision too. Grayson almost chuckled out loud
at the thought. Michelle had called herself blind as a bat. She
wasn't too far off and had the shin bruises to verify it from
being so sure she knew the way to the bathroom without her
glasses on when she got up in the middle of the night. The
ouches and swear words that would have made his grandmother wash her mouth out with soap as she banged into
the end of the bed proved she'd overestimated her abilities.

Then again, that was Michelle. She was always leaping
before she looked. Her spontaneous spirit was one of the
things he'd loved most about her. The decision to have a
baby at all had been spur of the moment. Grayson hadn't

thought he would be a good father, based on his own family history.

He'd believed in Michelle's ability to be an amazing mother, though. In the end, that was the reason he'd agreed to go for it.

Collin looked so much like his mother Grayson's heart squeezed every time he looked at his son. His boy had not only inherited his mother's terrible vision but had somehow managed to get her overactive imagination as well.

As he turned the corner, Grayson's blood ran cold. The perp they'd been chasing was at the mouth of the vent where he'd exited and Marshal Remington would come out, and he was hiding behind a trash bin.

Chapter Two

Pepper spray?

Getting a shot of the fiery liquid right in the face took a second to register. What the hell just happened? Her face burned. The moment of disbelief was immediately followed by the feeling of Abi's eyeballs being wrapped in barbed wire while invisible hands played tug-of-war from opposite sides of her.

Forget about her contacts. They were gone after this. Forget about seeing. Her vision was gone too. She climbed back inside the vent in case the perp decided to take advantage of her weakness.

"Halt!" Agent Chisolm shouted.

Then came the sounds of footsteps, of running.

If not for the FBI agent there would have been a blow to the head coming. Abi was as certain of it as next summer being as brutally hot as this past one.

As if she wasn't in enough discomfort already by the tug-of-war game scratching her eyeballs, the mucus came. Pretty much all the mucus her body could possibly produce came flooding out. The tsunami of tacky syrup flooded every orifice. Trying to see or breathe was punishment.

Now that her mucous membranes were activated and it felt like a bomb had gone off in her sinuses, her eyes reacted by starting to swell shut.

At this point, all she could do was remind herself life would get a whole lot better in about an hour, when the spray started wearing off. Because feeling like she was swallowing soup every time she tried to breathe was panic-inducing.

The effects might be temporary, but they were hell on wheels while they lasted. Give her a Taser any day of the week over being pepper sprayed. Abi had been misted before during training to be shown what it felt like. Twice in real life. There was no amount of preparation that would get her used to burning corneas or the feeling of choking on thick mucus. Your body wasn't supposed to turn into a weapon against you, but it did when faced with pepper spray.

The sounds of someone's beating feet reminded her the killer was getting away and there wasn't squat she could do about it. There was a patch of woods behind the strip mall. Could he get lost inside? Escape? Could Agent Chisolm catch him? His voice had sounded far away. Was he too far to catch up to the bastard?

This guy had been a fast runner. Then again, a burst of adrenaline could give that extra oomph to reach normally impossible speeds.

Abi forced herself to move to the mouth of the vent where she could listen better to hear if Agent Chisolm was more successful than she'd been.

There wasn't much she could do as she popped out her contacts, one by one, while she could still force her eyelids open. She jammed her fist inside her pants pocket and released the useless pieces of plastic. They were done, so there was no hope of flushing those babies out and popping them back in at some point. There was also no hope of seeing anytime soon either. Everything was a blur.

"Stop or I'll fire," Agent Chisolm warned in the kind of deep, authoritative voice that left no room for argument.

Abi stayed close to the temporary shelter to protect herself while in a vulnerable state. She could no longer hear the perp's footsteps as aggravation settled in. She'd been so close to catching this monster she could almost taste the sweet reward of slapping cuffs on him.

Now?

She was back to square one. Or at the very least, relying on someone else to do the job she should have been able to close.

An engine, a motorcycle engine, revved in the distance. The noise trailed off in the distance a few seconds later. Abi released a string of swear words her grandparents would disapprove of as she listened for Agent Chisolm's footsteps.

"Marshal." His deep timbre, the kind that washed over her and through her like warm, rushing water, broke through her coughing fit.

"Did it have to be pepper spray?" She would almost rather take a bullet in a place she didn't need so much, like nicking her arm or thigh. There'd be a scratch and a little blood but not enough of either to require a hospital stay.

Agent Chisolm's footsteps and heavy breathing alerted her to the fact he was close to her. He wouldn't leave her vulnerable to go after the perp, who must have disappeared in the tree line before hopping on that motorcycle. Plus, it wasn't like he could outrun a bike when he couldn't outrun her.

"Hold on," he said as he called in the motorcycle and location. "Sheriff has a deputy nearby. Said he would dispatch him immediately."

Abi could only hope the deputy could do what she hadn't…catch the bastard.

"How are you doing?" Agent Chisolm asked.

"I'm good," she lied. It fell into the little lie category. She would be good. That much was truth. And she was willing herself to be good right now.

"You sure about that?" he asked, still panting.

"I'm not planning to drive home if that's what you're asking," she quipped before she could reel it in. They probably hadn't worked together long enough for her to whip out her sarcastic side. Frustration did that to her.

"Good," he said without missing a beat. "I heard you're a horrible driver anyway. The streets will be safer this way."

Abi laughed. She couldn't help herself.

At almost that exact moment, sirens pierced the air. Had the deputy caught the perp?

Abi waited with bated breath. Her pulse kicked up a few notches as minutes passed. A cell phone buzzed. Since hers was back inside her vehicle, it had to be the agent's.

"The deputy can't find him," Grayson said. "He's coming to get more information from us while the sheriff puts out a BOLO in this area."

As she leaned her head against the brick, a sense of failure wrapped long, lean tentacles around Abi.

The sounds of tires spitting gravel came around the back of the building a few minutes after their location had been relayed over the radio.

"Looks like the deputy is here, Marshal Remington."

"If we're going to work together much longer, and from the looks of it we are, I'd rather you call me Abi," she said, hearing the disappointment and frustration in her own voice. Her attitude could get out in front of her. What could she say? As the youngest of three siblings, she'd turned out to be the most spirited. Not unlike the paint horses on her grandparents' ranch. In fact, she'd been compared to the feistier ones more than once.

"Okay, Abi," he said, his voice threatening to crack through her carefully constructed walls—walls that kept everyone out, especially coworkers.

Her grandparents. Abi had to force thoughts of them out of her mind so she could maintain focus on the case. As she plopped her backside down on the concrete, she absently fingered the St. Michael pendant they'd given her when she took this job. The sun blaring in her eyes made everything worse.

"He led us here because he had a plan to escape," she said, praying her eyes would stop watering and knowing they were just getting started as her body instinctively rejected the foreign substance. At least all her parts were working, physically speaking. The defense her body launched was top-notch.

"I know," Agent Chisolm agreed. "Call me Grayson if you want me to call you Abi, by the way. Deal?"

She nodded as help arrived a little too late to catch the perp.

Deputy Thad Carlson's voice replaced the once-wailing siren. A car door opened and closed. "I have an unopened bottle of water that might not make the sting go away altogether but it'll help."

"I'd be grateful for anything right now to be honest," Abi said. Truer words had never been spoken.

"Okay," the deputy said. As she heard him approach, a blurry figure came into view. "Tilt your head back."

Normally, Abi would say, *Hell no*, to such a request. The neck was the most vulnerable part of the body. A female wolf will position herself under her mate when threatened just to protect his neck. In this case, Abi would happily make the move if it meant getting some relief from the burning that made her want to literally scratch her eyes out.

The cool liquid spread over her left eye first, followed by her right.

"That's good," she said with a slow exhale. "Amazing, actually." It wasn't as healing as she was letting on, but she wanted to believe it worked so badly she refused to say anything less.

"Hang in there," Deputy Carlson said as he must have emptied the bottle on her face. She'd never known how much skin could burn without having acid thrown on it until she met pepper spray. "The worst of it doesn't last forever."

"Thank the heavens for small miracles," she quipped, once again willing her words to be true.

"Did you, by chance, get a description of the perp?" Deputy Carlson asked.

She shook her head. "Afraid not. Although, since he fit into this vent, we know he can't be as broad-shouldered as Agent Chisolm. He'll be built more like me."

"Taller, though," Grayson added. "And I would have given one to the sheriff when I called him if we'd gotten anything more concrete."

Abi paused, blinking. With her bad eyesight, she wouldn't

be able to see well without her contacts anyway. The spray only made her vision marginally worse. At least her eyes weren't swollen completely shut. Still, the effects generally got worse before they improved. Pepper Spray was a long game. "Yes, taller."

"What about you, Agent Chisolm?" Deputy Carlson asked as though Grayson hadn't just made the comment a few seconds ago. Carlson's voice had an air of superiority in it that didn't sit well with Abi. She didn't like having anyone on the task force who believed they were better than anyone else.

"I have nothing to add," Grayson said. "Abi ran a lot faster than I did. By the time I got here, the perp had been waiting at the vent for Abi to come out. He sprayed her and then bolted. I went through the usual steps, gave chase, came up empty."

Deputy Carlson's chuckle fired Abi up. What? Because she was a woman, she couldn't outrun a male counterpart?

GRAYSON SAW ABI'S shoulders bristle at the deputy's slight. She opened her mouth to speak and then clamped it shut again, seeming to think better of whatever comment sat on her lips—lips that he'd noticed had a naturally rose-colored tint. They were full, too. And he didn't need to notice either fact.

"What can I say? Abi should have run track in high school whereas I was more of a power lifter." His urge to defend her honor overtook logic. "Why? Do you have a problem with that?"

"Me? No," Deputy Carlson responded but his tone said otherwise. Was he one of those macho guys whose attitude came from a bygone era? Here was a news flash: women were strong. They were fast runners, sometimes the fastest in the group. He'd seen it play out plenty of times during his years of training and at the gym. Guess what? Some women could out-bench-press all their peers, including men. His Michelle was a case in point. She'd been the smarter one of the two of them: he was one hundred percent certain of the fact. She didn't have an ego that made her want to prove it all the time. Grayson was no slouch. His IQ test had come back top of his class. Of course, he wouldn't have that bragging right if Michelle had been in the room.

A stab of pain pierced him in the middle of the chest. It happened every time he thought about his dead wife. Almost five years had passed, and the pain made it feel like he'd lost her yesterday. Grief was strange, more roller coaster than straight line.

Since the three of them needed to work together and Abi was perfectly capable of taking care of herself, Grayson decided not to split hairs over the deputy's tone. If the guy thought he was winning points with the young and beautiful marshal, he was dead wrong, based on the look on her face.

And, yes, Abi had the kind of looks that people said would stop traffic. Grayson wouldn't disagree. She had the kind of long dark hair with big brown eyes that reminded him of Liv Tyler when she was close to Abi's age, which he believed was twenty-eight years old. Twelve years his junior, but her maturity gave the impression she had a lot more years in law enforcement under her belt.

Grayson hadn't seen instincts like hers in a very long time. But then he'd probably stopped noticing a whole lot of things after losing Michelle within hours of Collin making his appearance in the world.

"I'm guessing you both need a ride," Deputy Carlson offered, unfazed by Abi's physical reaction to his words a few moments ago. Was he unable to read her body language?

Grayson would step in if the deputy crossed a nonnegotiable line, like hitting on Abi while on the job. There was a time and a place for everything. Grayson prized his professionalism. Based on what he'd witnessed so far in the short time the task force had been together, Abi held herself to a high standard. Good. They would get along just fine.

Plus, everyone needed to use all their focus to find the bastard who'd gotten away.

"That's correct," Grayson answered as Abi tried to blink her eyes open again. The swelling wouldn't go down for another half hour or so, he knew from experience. Even then, her vision wouldn't return to normal for much longer than that. She was in for a rough ride.

"All right, if the two of you are ready, we can head out now," Deputy Carlson announced. His momentary act of chivalry with the water was overshadowed by his machismo. *Time and place, dude.*

Grayson took a couple of steps toward Abi to close the distance between them, effectively shutting off Deputy Carlson with the move. "Need a hand up?"

She reached for him as she nodded but came up short considering her vision wouldn't return for a while. He found her hand and pulled her to standing with her help.

"My contacts are gone, and I don't keep a spare in my vehicle, not that it would matter today," she said.

"I'll take you to a motel where both of you have been set

up by the department for the night," Deputy Carlson said, jumping on the opening.

"I got this," Grayson stated, after asking for keys. "If we're staying at the same motel, it wouldn't make sense for you to go out of your way." He paused, waiting for a retort. When none came, he continued. "Do you mind taking us to my service vehicle near the garage where this all started?" He gave directions to where he'd parked before heading out on foot.

"Will do," Deputy Carlson conceded with the enthusiasm of a little boy who'd just had a piece of candy stripped from his hands.

"I appreciate it," Grayson offered, figuring they needed to maintain a professional relationship.

"What about Marshal Remington's vehicle?" the deputy asked.

"I'll stay with her until she's able to see again and then bring her to retrieve it once she can," Grayson said, solving the problem and leaving no room for alternate ideas. His hunch said Deputy Carlson was looking for an "in" with Abi. Based on her expression, the man would be shot down.

Since Abi didn't give off the impression of being unprofessional, Grayson had no doubt she would be tactful about the rejection. However, she shouldn't have to deal with it after what she'd been through today.

She deserved a "Calgon, Take Me Away" moment like in the commercials his mother used to watch on what felt like repeat.

Deputy Carlson locked in on Abi. "Is that what *you* want?"

"I'm good with whatever," she responded, deflating some

of Grayson's bravado. "But it probably makes more sense for Agent Chisolm to take me back to the place we're both staying. It'll save you a trip back and forth when I can see again and can pick up my car."

Deputy Carlson shrugged. "Suit yourself."

Grayson was almost certain he caught a wink from Abi that was aimed in his direction as the deputy puffed up his chest and then turned to walk toward his idling vehicle. Then again, she might have just been trying to blink.

Was he seeing something he wanted to rather than something that was there?

Chapter Three

"I can't believe he outran and outsmarted me," Abi said to Grayson once they'd been dropped off at his vehicle and Deputy Carlson pulled away after a quick wave. The deputy had said someone would meet them at the motel off the highway with keys. They only had to text a number when they arrived, no need to go to the front desk.

Abi had seen the same dynamic between the deputy and Grayson in other male colleagues. Deputy Carlson had been beating his chest like a silverback gorilla back there, trying to establish dominance.

Having grown up with a brother and two male cousins, she got it. Although she couldn't imagine her family members pulling anything like what she'd just witnessed. To Grayson's credit, he hadn't played along. He'd remained calm and focused while Deputy Carlson tried to one-up him. Seriously, though, did he think she was some kind of prize to be won?

Grayson was a professional. She appreciated him for stepping up to offer assistance, considering she couldn't see for squat right now without her contacts and her eyes still burning like wildfires. Working with a legendary FBI agent like Grayson rattled her nerves more than she wanted to admit. It also made her want to rise to his level and be the best at her job.

Of course, he had more than career achievements working for him. The term *easy on the eyes* came to mind. Along with *superhot* and *hotness on a stick*. He had that whole rugged-mature-gorgeous look down. Don't even get her started on his carved from granite jawline or literal bod of the gods.

"You'll have to be my eyes," she said to Grayson as they stood next to his vehicle. "Who is here and what's going on?"

He provided a quick rundown. The sheriff, accompanied by a pair of deputies, was at the scene of the garage. Activity around the garage said they would be in the way if they stuck around. Plus, her vision was so poor she would only get in the way.

"I keep an overnight bag in my service vehicle along with my handbag," she said, fishing the key fob out of her pocket before clicking it to open the trunk. "Do you mind grabbing them?"

"Not a problem," Grayson said before circling back to her earlier statement and pointing out the perp had a sizable head start or they would be having a different conversation right now.

Right, she forgot to mention just how intelligent Grayson was and how much common sense he possessed. Men who looked like him weren't usually so down-to-earth. There was a sad, almost hollow quality too. An old soul who'd lost someone, maybe. She couldn't quite put her finger on it but still felt a soul-deep connection to it, to him, for reasons she had yet to explain. Since she knew him from work, she would leave the thought there, where it belonged, and walk away, figuratively speaking.

"I'll be right back," he said, leaving the car running as he hopped out to grab her belongings.

Not that she could see him right now, with all the mucus oozing out of her pores.

"That shouldn't have mattered as much as it did," she argued when Grayson returned to the driver's seat. She was still angry the perp was out there, able to kill again.

"We have an escaped victim and a secondary location, which is more than we had to work with before," he said, using more of that practical logic while she was busy beating herself up.

"A witness who was already drunk before being drugged and can't give us a description of the man who spiked his Heineken." Being this close without gaining any useful information was beyond frustrating.

"There were others at the party who might be able to do a better job," Grayson said with a confidence she didn't come close to feeling. "We're figuring out more about the guy's methods. We didn't know he used a secondary location before. The sheriff might find something inside the garage that leads us directly to him. We'll catch him. It's only a matter of time at this point."

"I hope that's true, and I pray it happens before any more lives are lost."

"Agreed," Grayson said. He was a man of few words. She'd noticed how he studied the room a week ago when the task force was first put together.

"I didn't even get close enough to get a good description of the guy, unless you count the back of his head," she continued. The term *beating a dead horse* came to mind on this topic, but she couldn't let it go.

"You outran me," Grayson said. She could hear the slight amusement in his voice.

She could feel her cheeks flush.

"Everyone in law enforcement in the area knows to look out for a male on a motorcycle," he added. "It might not feel like progress yet, but we're moving forward. We've never been this close to the sonofa—"

He caught himself and didn't finish the word, but the same one had been on her mind when it came to this perp.

"What I'm trying to say is don't beat yourself up," he continued. "It's easy to get caught in the trap of always wanting to be perfect. Perfect doesn't arrest criminals any faster. Believe me, I've tried. I've been in your shoes."

"Really? What's different now?" she asked.

"I don't have the energy to waste on being frustrated with myself, so I stopped," he explained. "All my brain power goes to my next move and gleaning any piece of knowledge I can out of what just happened. And we got information. That's successful. Of course, I want to stop someone before any other lives are lost but I can't let emotion cloud my judgment. I'm better at my job when I stay focused. In the long run, fewer people die that way. I have to take the wins as they come."

Those words sounded like they came from hard-knock experience. She could relate on many levels. Abi wasn't just hard on herself for her career moves so she could receive accolades or move up the ladder. She wanted to wrap this case up as quickly as possible for more reasons than the obvious saving lives part. At this very moment, her grandparents were lying in hospital beds fighting for their lives. The folks who'd taken her in and raised her, who'd given her unconditional love, were both in a coma. Where was she?

Not at their sides.

So, yeah, she wanted to wrap this baby up to save the lives of future victims and so she could request a short leave of absence to go home to Mesa Point. She wouldn't say where she belonged because she'd shaken the dust of that town off her boots and moved a day after graduation. After two years at Austin Community College, she'd transferred to the state's prized school, University of Texas at Austin, to finish her bachelor's degree in criminal justice. She'd worked to put herself through school in a total of three years. She'd casually dated during that time but hadn't found anyone interesting enough to consider having a relationship with.

Here she was now at twenty-eight living her dream job. Her second thought was how empty her townhouse seemed without anyone to share her day with, but that was the frustration mixed with pepper spray talking. Right?

Because right now, thinking about her life, it seemed empty in a way it never had before. She had her sister, brother and cousins. They gave her all the support she needed.

It dawned on her thinking about losing her grandparents was creating a hole in her heart. In her life? Or was it pointing out something she never had?

Abi blinked a few times and gave herself a mental headshake. She was hardcore overthinking her life. Besides, she was getting a chance to work with a legend. Instead of being hard on herself for what she didn't do today, maybe she could pick his brain instead. That sounded a whole lot more productive.

Before she could formulate her first question, he pulled into the parking lot of the motel where they were both staying off the highway. Grayson fired off a text to let the front desk know they'd arrived.

"Are you hungry?" he asked.

"I'd like to circle back and interview the victim, once he's released from the hospital before I think about food," she said.

"How about after we read the sheriff's report, and you can see again?" he asked. "Maybe get some food down. It's lunchtime."

His suggestions were logical. "Okay, then. I could eat," she admitted. At least a half hour had passed since the pepper spray incident. By the time they figured out where to go, secured food and sat somewhere to take it down, she would be mostly clear of the effects. Or at the very least close. "Maybe not right this hot minute but this...party—" she made a sweeping motion around her face, with emphasis on her eyes "—will wear off at some point. Or at the very least become manageable enough to get some food down without choking."

She could have sworn she heard the normally cool and casual agent mumble an apology along with a curse underneath his breath. Was that for not being the one to get there first?

"The guy we're looking for is familiar with the area and mapped out backup plans in case things went south," Grayson finally said after a few moments of silence.

"The motorcycle," she said .

"I think we both know he didn't accidentally find one in those woods," he stated. "He'd stashed it there, possibly when he first came to town."

"The vent had to have been opened or else he knew how to open it fast," she said. "It's not hard to find a party in a small college town. My guess is that he arrived last weekend to check out the scene."

"He could have relatives spread around Texas," Grayson surmised. "They could work at or near colleges."

"The secondary location would make sense if he was trying to hide his activities from them, which obviously he would," Abi pointed out. "The guy didn't miss a beat."

One of the deputies on the scene would stay back to take pictures and dust for prints. Even in an expedited case like this one, it could take weeks to get forensic results. Real law enforcement work wasn't like in the movies or on TV shows. Investigations took time.

In the span of a few weeks, there could easily be two or three new graves. Of course, Reprehensible was "hot" now after leaving a witness and his secondary location. The Mexican government had offered their full cooperation, so that poured on more heat. It was impossible to have agents or officers covering every square inch of university parties, this area, and along both borders. Extra help was always appreciated, especially when they might have to cross a border to make an arrest or follow the criminal.

Under the circumstances, it was highly possible the creep would find another spot to bury his victims, especially after today. But government cooperation was a good place to start.

"The attendant is here with keys," Grayson said as a blurry figure came into view.

"Do you mind if we go inside my room for a few minutes to see if this spray will wear off enough for me to put a fresh pair of contacts in and maybe change clothes?" she asked, thinking she might have a backup pair of glasses in her overnight bag. Abi regretted the question almost the second it left her mouth. The thought of being alone in her room with the handsome FBI agent sent a sensual shiver skittering across her skin. Her body's reaction was every shade of embarrassing.

She'd glanced at the third finger on his left hand at the first task force meeting. No wedding band, which didn't mean he wasn't married. It just meant he didn't wear a ring. Not uncommon for folks in her line of work, males and females. Some officers preferred to keep their personal life secret. The less a perp figured out, the better.

Was it dangerous to be alone in a motel room with this man?

Abi's heart argued it was and yet she barely knew the agent. Should she listen to emotion or logic? Because her practical mind said she would never be so unprofessional as to fall for someone she worked with. Could she trust it?

GRAYSON CLEARED HIS throat as his cell buzzed. He checked the screen and saw his sitter's number. "Will you excuse me? I need to return a call."

"Yes, of course," Abi said, suddenly looking uncomfortable.

"I'll meet you inside," he reassured after retrieving her bag and purse. He handed them over. "Give me five-ten minutes."

"All right." She reached for the door handle.

"Can you get yourself inside and settled okay?"

"Yeah, sure, no problem," she responded as she felt her way out of the vehicle. She didn't stumble as she walked, which was a good sign she had her balance back. His wife had been half-blind without her glasses, so he could relate to Abi's situation. He didn't want her banging into a door, bruising herself or worse. Once, Michelle had broken a toe on the bedframe. Talk about pain. She'd hopped around the bedroom, in the dark, screaming and holding onto her foot until she crashed into the dresser. Unfortunately, a flat-screen TV sat on that dresser. The bang caused the TV to fall forward, onto her. She knocked it away.

By the time Grayson had turned on the light, the bedroom resembled a junkyard.

Now he could smile at the memory. It hadn't been so funny at the time. Strange how it was the trivial things like that he missed most of all. The way his wife used to sway back and forth to music when she helped him cook. The way she would grab his hand and tug until he relented and danced with her in the kitchen on a random night, dinner be damned.

Michelle made food taste better. She made music sound better. She made the world better.

Now his kid was stuck with one parent. If he had to be trapped with one parent, it should have been his mother. She would know how to handle the bumps and bruises of childhood. She would know how to handle the kids at pre-K who'd made fun of Collin for his glasses. She would know what to bring for the fundraiser bake sales. She certainly wouldn't buy cookies at the store and get busted trying to pass them off as homemade.

Grayson would have traded places with his wife in a heartbeat if it meant his kid got to grow up knowing a woman whose heart was bigger than the Texas sky. Talk about life being unfair. It had dealt a blow to a kid who was only hours old, sticking him with the worst of his two parents.

The only reason Grayson believed he could do the whole "have a kid" at all was because of Michelle. He would have been happy as a lark if they'd limited their family to two, not that he regretted Collin once he was born. But if it had been up to Grayson, his wife would still be alive.

But then, Collin was the best thing that had ever happened to Grayson despite the trials of bringing up a kid on his own and there'd been plenty of those. As a matter of fact, the trials were still racking up.

Grayson's worst fear was that he was doing a terrible job with the kid, who deserved so much better than the dad he got stuck with. Collin was smart for his age. He wasn't athletic in the least. Sports had been Grayson's home turf. He'd made most of his school friends while sweating and battling it out together on the sports field.

Collin's brains came from his mother. She would have known what to do with a brainy, nonathletic kid who had the face of an angel and bottleneck glasses too big for that face. Collin liked to play with figurines or on computer keyboards. Grayson wasn't so sure it was healthy for an almost-five-year-old to stay inside as much as his kid did.

Then again, Grayson didn't have to worry about Collin suffering sports injuries. Unseen benefit?

Despite the challenges and their differences, Grayson

couldn't have asked for a better kid. He couldn't love his son more than he did for all those quirks that made him Collin and not a carbon copy of Grayson. He loved his kid for how much he reminded Grayson of Michelle.

He hoped love was enough when it came to bringing up good kids, because it was all Grayson had in his bag of tricks. That and, he hoped, being a good role model.

Grayson called his babysitter. Martha Hope was her name. She was a great aunt to three young adults, with no children of her own. She and Hank, her husband, had taught school together and traveled. He'd taught history and she'd taught math, both working in the same middle school. Martha had lost Hank to a brain tumor six months before Collin was born. Retired, she'd approached Grayson about helping out with Collin a week after they lost Michelle. Michelle and Martha, as it turned out, had become close while Michelle was stuck on bedrest.

Martha, being an amazing human and great neighbor, needed something to take her mind off losing Hank. She didn't speak the words out loud, but she'd lost Michelle too. All within a brief time period.

Grayson wasn't good with people like his wife had been, but he'd known he was in over his head with a newborn and welcomed the help.

He returned to his vehicle and palmed his cell. Ever since losing Michelle, a dark cloud hung over Grayson's head, and he expected the worst. Every time he got a call from Martha, his chest squeezed like he was waiting for the other shoe to drop.

Taking in a deep breath, he counted backward from five and hit Martha's name on his "missed calls" screen.

Martha answered on the first ring.

"Did something happen to Collin?" Grayson asked, his heart in his throat.

Chapter Four

Abi managed to step inside motel room number three without face-planting. No small miracle. Since Grayson had asked for privacy with his call, she assumed he was married or in a relationship at the very least. Disappointment stabbed.

When she'd casually glanced at his wedding ring finger first day on the task force, a little spark of excitement had filled her at the realization there was no band and no tan line. Then again, many in law enforcement didn't wear them.

She fell into that camp too. Keeping her personal life private was one of many reasons she didn't do social media outside of work purposes or helping post for the paint horse ranch her grandparents owned and operated since before she was born. *Until now.*

Stubbing her toe on the bedframe, Abi hopped around on one foot in the small space after tossing her bag on top of the bed. Narrowly missing the dresser, she braced herself with a hand on the laminate piece. From here, two steps would get her to the first of two full-size beds and her overnight bag. After losing the perp, she might be on the road again soon.

The couple of steps went off without incident despite having to hop as her toe screamed in pain from connecting with the frame a few seconds ago. She sat down on the edge of the bed and pulled her overnight bag toward her, cursing the fact they'd anticipated the perp making a move at the nearby university and had been spot-on with their assumption but still hadn't managed to arrest him.

Everyone in the task force had gone in different directions. Spreading out, everyone reasoned, was their best chance to nab the bastard. According to his profile, he was believed to have suffered abuse at the hands of an authority figure. For instance, a mother, father, stepfather, uncle, or possibly a babysitter. In the babysitter scenario, the profiler linked the perp to a college student to explain why he targeted them specifically. Another scenario had the perp in a relationship—male or female since he didn't discriminate based on sex—in which he'd suffered a perceived loss of control or had suffered abuse, be it physical or emotional.

Today reinforced the theory that even though he'd killed five times since the semester began in August, he plotted and planned, making several escape routes before he struck.

Was it even possible to hold a full-time job with this much activity?

Did he target college students for a reason other than possibly having an abusive babysitter who was in college? Or was there another, even simpler reason?

Many young people at that age were looking to party and, therefore, easy prey?

Could it be that simple? Or was there a more sinister explanation?

One thing was certain, the perp targeted a look, which

narrowed the suspect list to males and females with brown hair. All five, now six, targets were young students who had been lured away from crowded parties where alcohol was present. Music festivals, frat parties were all fair game for this killer who moved in and around Austin and San Marcos like a ghost. Ketamine had been found in each of his victims' systems. Lab results would be sent out for intended victim number six, who was presently in the ER, but Abi would put money on it coming back positive for the common date-rape drug along with an alcohol content in his blood.

As she fumbled in the bag for her glasses, a couple of knocks sounded before the door cracked open.

"Okay if I come inside?" Grayson asked, his deep timbre sending another round of useless goose bumps up and down her arms. Useless because he was clearly attached. Useless because he was a coworker. Useless because they might never see each other again once this case was over. Abi tried to convince herself it wouldn't matter anyway since she didn't date people she worked with, but the all-knowing voice in the back of her mind laughed. For Grayson, would she make an exception?

"Sure," she said as she slipped on glasses that suddenly embarrassed her. She'd been called all the names on the playground. Four Eyes was the most common and the least appreciated. At least Tommy Gardner had come up with *Cryptoptila immersana* in sixth grade. She'd had to perform an internet search to figure out what he referenced. A moth, as it had turned out, with black dots that looked like eyes running down its back. Tommy got points for originality.

She still felt like a dork without her contacts.

"Nice glasses, by the way," Grayson said after entering.

"Ha ha," she quipped, feeling more self-conscious than she cared to admit.

What she could see of his face twisted. The blurriness was calming down at least. "I happen to like glasses in case you thought that was a joke."

"How's home?" she asked, figuring a change in subject would stave off some of the embarrassment at being wrong. Now that she could see his face more clearly, he'd been serious about the compliment. Why was it easier to believe the opposite was true?

Grayson shot her a warning look. "Good."

"Ready to go?" she asked, figuring they could discuss the case over lunch.

"Did you decide what you wanted to eat?"

Abi shrugged. "My eyes are still burning. Mind if you check to see what our options are? I doubt I could focus on my phone's screen."

Grayson nodded, taking a seat on the end of the bed next to hers. His response to her asking about his home life had caught her off guard. It was normal to keep personal information from perps but they were in a motel room with the door closed. They were coworkers as long as this task force existed. She hadn't expected him to become so defensive about a basic question like the one she'd asked.

Fine, she decided. They didn't need to be chummy on a personal level to be an effective team. Knowing a little about each other could build trust and talking could help pass the time in between the action but Abi reasoned that everyone worked differently. With more years of experience under his belt, Grayson must prefer to stick to the job and then move on once it was over. She wouldn't make the mistake of asking more questions of a personal nature.

Grayson studied his phone. "Tex-Mex, home cooking diner, or tacos?"

"A diner sounds good to me," she said.

"Let's roll."

After locking up the room, which Abi liked, she moved to the passenger side. Grayson surprised her by following her and then opening the door for her.

"Next time, I got it," she said to him before sliding into the leatherette seat of the four-door sedan. At this point, she regretted telling him to call her by her first name instead of Marshal Remington. Abi knew how to keep a relationship professional, dammit.

She folded her arms across her chest and waited for Grayson to claim his seat on the driver's side. Give her another hour or so and she'd be more than ready to be dropped off at her vehicle.

The ride to the diner was spent in silence. It gave Abi time to collect her thoughts.

Grayson parked but didn't get out of the vehicle. "Everything is fine at home. Thanks for asking."

"Okay," she commented before exiting the sedan. What was she supposed to do with that?

Grayson took a minute before following suit. He pocketed his cell phone and keys before saying, "Lead the way inside."

This time, he didn't attempt to open the door to the restaurant. The move meant he'd heard her loud and clear. Abi exhaled slowly. She'd worked with female colleagues who refused to let a male colleague open a door or extend a courtesy. If they were in the heat of a chase, there was no time for those pleasantries, but Abi appreciated the gestures if they were going out for food, which in this case was lunch.

"I overreacted earlier," she said to him as he followed her inside. "If you want to open a door, it's fine with me." Her grandparents' situation had her on edge but that was too personal to explain to someone who'd drawn a clear boundary.

"You reacted to me snapping at you," he said as the hostess greeted them at the stand that was nothing more than a sign that read Please Wait to Be Seated.

"Hello there," the smiling, twentyish blonde said to Grayson. Her gaze barely touched Abi before returning to the gorgeous man standing behind her. "Is it two?"

"Yes," Abi answered for Grayson. The hostess needed to know Abi had a voice too. Grayson's might be deeper and cause an ache to well up from deep inside but that didn't mean he was the only one who could speak for the two of them.

"Okay, then. Follow me." The bubbly hostess in pink hot pants and a polka dotted silk button-down shirt wore a nametag that read Izzy.

Abi did as requested after Izzy grabbed a pair of laminated menus and then led the way. So much for the barcode that had become the norm in recent years. It seemed as though most places had reverted back to handing out hard copies again.

After being seated, she set the menu that had been handed to her down and caught Grayson's gaze. Her thoughts had drifted back to the case on the walk over to the table. "In your professional opinion, how long do you figure we have until he goes for number seven?"

"MY FEAR IS not long and it won't be in this town," Grayson admitted as he glanced around the room. The diner was small and had a cozy feel. It was the kind of place that Grayson would expect to end up on one of those popular shows that featured diners and drive-ins. Booths lined the walls. The place had an overall everything-pink feel. As long as the food was good, he didn't care what color the vinyl bench seats were. The gravy could be pink for all he cared as long as it tasted the same smothered over chicken fried steak.

This meal, though, he was going for a salad with steak strips. Michelle had always given him a hard time about his diet. Now that he was Collin's primary—and only—parent, he took her advice not to clog his arteries to heart. Literally and figuratively. Before losing his wife, he would have thought nothing of smothering a piece of fried meat with gravy.

He picked up a packet of sugar, flipped it around his fingers. It was a habit he picked up when he focused.

"Mine too," she admitted. "Evidence points to the fact he could strike in a matter of days, but I keep wondering how he'd have time to do the research."

"The guy is a planner," Grayson reasoned. "That might mean he has a master plan behind all of this."

"Certain campuses that he's aiming toward?" Abi compressed her lips and frowned. She did that when she was thinking along the same lines as him. He'd noticed her little tics in the short time they'd been working together. Observing, knowing could mean the different between life and death in a critical moment. Memorizing her habits and facial expressions would tell him when she was in panic mode or in trouble but couldn't say the words outright. Remembering the exact details of her tone would allow him to pick up on nuances that could, once again, mean the difference between action and staying put.

It was all part of the job.

"Exactly my thoughts," Grayson answered after a thoughtful pause.

This place had a retro feel of something that came out of the 1950s. There were vinyl records hung on the walls as decor. The hot pink uniforms and waitresses with their hair tied up in ponytails were also dead giveaways. At this rate, he half expected Richie Cunningham and The Fonz to come waltzing in the front door. And here he'd left his leather jacket at home.

Speaking of home, leaving Collin to go out in the field was getting more and more difficult as his son got older. Kindergarten was on the horizon next year. As much as Grayson hated the idea of becoming a pencil pusher, he had to consider what was best for his family.

The idea of sitting behind a desk made him want to loosen his collar. He was made for the outdoors. One of the many perks of his line of work was travel. Another came in the form of no two days looking the same. But there were dangers too. Grayson could admit that putting his life on the line kept him feeling alive. He'd been stabbed several times, shot twice, and punched more times than he cared to count. His forty-year-old body reminded him that he wasn't in his twenties or thirties anymore. Muscles ached more. Joints hurt when he got out of bed. He was beginning to feel like a football player must after game day.

This, however, was the only job he knew. He'd worked in law enforcement his entire career. As a single parent, though, he couldn't stop the growing feeling that he was being selfish staying with it. He'd thrown out all the usual excuses to keep from changing careers. *People get killed driving their car in traffic every day. No one ever knew when they were going to die. You could get killed walking into the grocery store, or the bank, or a shopping center.* Were they cop-outs because he didn't want to face the truth? He placed his life on the line every time he went after a dangerous felon. Period.

He didn't know when the end would come. But an argument could be made that he was increasing his chances of it coming sooner rather than later.

A desk job waited, and he might as well seriously consider taking it. Once this case was over, he could…

Grayson stopped himself right there. How many times had he seen a "one last case" scenario go south? Too many.

Realizing he'd been lost in thought while working the sugar packet, he lifted his gaze to find Abi studying him.

"Everything okay?" she asked.

"I should be asking you the same question," he deflected.

"All right," she conceded. "I can see now, so that's a plus. Your turn."

Abi was observant and wise beyond her years, assets that would aid her moving up the career ladder. Studying her now, he could perceive there was something going on with her. She'd come highly recommended for the task force, so he doubted it was professional. Personal? Boyfriend trouble? It occurred to him Abi could be married and not wearing a ring. The deputy who'd hit on her back at the strip mall should be embarrassed if that was the case. Hell, he should be embarrassed by his unprofessional actions either way.

A waitress bebopped on over.

The real monster was still on the loose, possibly moving onto his next victim. Could their interview with the latest victim provide a clue as to where the bastard might strike next? Grayson glanced at his cell as the waitress took Abi's order.

A summary from the deputy's interview with the couple who'd been driving the vehicle flagged down by the victim had arrived in his inbox two minutes ago.

The waitress finished up with him, and then promised to put their orders in before heading back toward the kitchen.

"We got something," Grayson said to Abi. Would it be enough to get them back on track before the trail went cold?

Chapter Five

Abi leaned forward, clasping her hands on top of the table. "I'm listening." The twinge of hope the perp wouldn't get away was premature.

Grayson tapped on his phone's screen. "It's an email with a summary from the couple flagged down by Max Hague."

Her heart went out to the nineteen-year-old whose life would change forever after experiencing a trauma like this one. She recalled several stories, one of which had stuck out in her mind despite not being involved with the case. One of a pair of survivors of Jeffrey Dahmer, who couldn't escape the trauma from nearly being killed at the hands of a monster. He ended up abusing alcohol and drugs. He lived on the streets, unable to work. There'd been multiple arrests for criminal activity. The damage had been lifelong. She thought about the story and others a lot. They provided motivation to keep going on the toughest and most dangerous cases. If she could stop one person from suffering, putting her life on the line was worth it.

"The young couple only saw Max Hague running down the street, waving his arms in the air," Grayson supplied. Her chest deflated at the no-news. He rattled off their names and ages, thirty and thirty-two years old. "They almost didn't stop because they thought he was on drugs and might hurt them."

"Does it say why they changed their minds?" she asked.

"The man said he couldn't ignore the desperate pleas for help. He stopped as his girlfriend called 911. The male witness then took off his sweater to give to the naked victim. The female witness helped wrap a picnic blanket around Mr. Hague, who they realized had had bindings on his wrists."

Kind people, she decided. Max Hague might be alive because of them. She'd take whatever luck she could get in this case. "Unfortunately, we already knew this."

Grayson compressed his lips in a frown as he nodded. Abi forced her gaze away from those thick lips of his. What they did was none of her business.

"I wish there was more to the eyewitness account," he conceded. "But that's all we have other than the fact Max Hague was released from the hospital a half hour ago."

"Do we have an address for him?" she continued.

"He's in a dorm on campus," he supplied, then gave the building and room number. That should be easy enough to find.

"Are we authorized to interview the witness?" she asked, not wanting to step on anyone's toes on the task force.

"We need to submit a reason," Grayson said. "I can ask based on the need to verify the profiler's assumptions. That should be enough to get the green light." He fired off an email.

Abi was already on tentative ground with the deputy after she had rebutted his advances, and Grayson's position was worse after their exchange. One person working against them on the task force wasn't the end of the world. Carlson shouldn't be enough to hold them back.

Abi's turkey burger and sweet potato fries arrived along with Grayson's steak salad.

She picked hers up as he finished typing the request. "Looks like a heart-stopping meal you've got there."

"This?" Grayson asked, switching gears with a smile. "I'm as healthy as a horse."

She shot him a look before taking a bite of her turkey burger.

"What?"

"Nothing," she responded after chewing. At least they could kill time by eating while they waited for the go-ahead to interview the witness. Working with a task force had its disadvantages and benefits. Multiple interviews with a victim could traumatize the person further, so most of the time teams did their best to minimize the number. For Abi, she excelled at witness interviews, so it was difficult to trust anyone else's.

"Do you have a problem with me saying I'm as healthy as a horse?" he asked after a bite of salad. He motioned to his plate as if to say, *Case in point.*

"What do you know about horses?" she asked. The subject gave her mixed feelings. One the one hand, she'd loved growing up on a horse ranch. But she couldn't think of them without her mind snapping to the picture of her beloved grandparents in the hospital fighting for their lives.

"Not much, to be honest," he said.

"I could tell," she quipped, trying to shake the sadness that came with thinking about them.

"How is that?" he continued.

Giving up a few details of her background wouldn't exactly qualify as getting personal. "I grew up on a paint horse ranch."

"I didn't know that," Grayson said.

"Why would you?" She cocked an eyebrow at him as she tossed a fry in her mouth. The food here wouldn't make up for the awful day she'd been having so far but at least she was able to get a quality meal. It was small, but something. In the worst of situations, Abi tried to find one positive thing to focus on if only for a few moments. When it came to her grandparents, though, she couldn't. Their lives were in limbo. Waking from their comas was not guaranteed.

Grayson shrugged. "Good point. I guess we don't know much about each other's backgrounds."

"No need to," she qualified.

"What was it like?" he continued. "Growing up on a horse ranch. I imagine it's every little kid's dream."

She involuntary shivered at the word *kid*.

Grayson cleared his throat. A look flashed behind his eyes that she couldn't quite pinpoint. What did he care if she didn't like kids?

"It's as great as everyone assumes it would be," she conceded, biting down on her bottom lip after returning to the original conversation. "I loved every minute of being outside with the horses, learning how to break them so they could be sold. I loved exercising them." Moisture gathered in her eyes at the memories, catching her off guard. Abi turned to face the wall before sniffing tears back. "Sorry."

He set a couple of napkins on her side of the table. "I've seen tears before, Abi. It's not a big deal."

"It's probably just leftover pepper spray," she insisted. "My tear ducts are overreacting." She took the napkins and patted the corners of her eyes underneath her glasses. "I'm good."

"Like I said before, I like those glasses on you better than contacts," Grayson said after another bite of food.

"Yeah, funny," she said. Now he was just being nice out of sympathy.

"I mean it." He set down his fork and studied her. "The color of the frames compliments your eyes."

"Oh," she said, realizing he actually meant those words. "Thank you."

"And you're probably right about the pepper spray still reacting."

Now he really was just being kind. Either way, she would take the out. Crying while on the job wasn't something she'd ever done before and had no plans to do again. Emotion had been building since hearing the news back home and she'd been holding everything in. It shouldn't be a surprise some of it found a way to leak out.

They finished their meals and paid the bill. Abi managed to make it through the rest of her turkey burger without another wet droplet from her eyes. She did, however, make a mental note to call her sister later this evening for an update. Crystal had taken leave from work to hold vigil at the hospital. It would be Abi's turn next. Their brother, Duke, had taken the first round.

Grayson's cell phone dinged as they returned to his vehicle. "We got permission to interview the victim."

Abi put her worries about her grandparents aside. Right now, all her focus had to be on interviewing Max Hague.

GRAYSON TOOK THE driver's seat after opening Abi's door for her. This time, she thanked him and smiled, lighting a half a dozen campfires inside him. They drove to the small campus of West Texas College and to the dorm parking lot aptly named Residence Hall. There was no missing the three-story redbrick building, considering it was the only dorm on campus according to the map Abi had pulled up on her phone on the way over. Easy enough.

They walked to the Hall and stood at the glass-and-metal door where a security pad was mounted on the red bricks. A pair of male students came walking out almost immediately, so Abi, who might be perceived as the less threatening of the two of them, grabbed the door before it closed again. She smiled at the pair of young students. They nodded while keeping their conversation going. Something about a hard test and a professor who pulled questions from the test bank.

Grayson held the door open. "After you."

Abi walked in first and quickly located an elevator. The traditional building was on the newer side. Inside, the tile floors were scuffed and there were mud tracks from recent rain. A pegboard with pins held announcements and advertisements.

"What's the number?" Abi asked after pushing the up button.

"Two-twenty-one," he supplied.

Abi pushed the number two once inside. They probably could have walked up the stairs, but the elevator was closer. Metal doors closed and the elevator surged. Abi reached for Grayson to steady herself, grabbing a fistful of his shirt in the process.

"Whoa!" she said.

A ding sounded and the elevator jolted to a stop.

"Remind me to take the stairs back down," she said as the doors opened again.

Grayson cracked a smile. "One flight doesn't seem so bad compared to that antiquated metal box."

"No, it doesn't," she agreed before straightening her shirt and flicking lint from her pants. Even disheveled, she would look amazing.

Grayson wiped the smile from his face as they approached Max's room. A flurry of voices sounded on the other side of the door.

Abi took a deep breath, glanced over at him, and seemed to get the response she wanted, because she knocked twice before opening the door.

Two young men met them at the door, blocking the view inside. The Asian man was tall and had the build of a football player. The Caucasian male next to him was a full head shorter and much thinner but filled the rest of the doorframe. He looked like what most folks decided a gamer should— skinny with glasses and not a lot of muscle. That was the general stereotype Grayson came across. He could see over the young man's head.

"Can we help you?" Football guy asked, sizing them both up.

"My name is Marshal Abi Remington," Abi started, her voice soft enough to recite a lullaby. She produced her badge from the belt holding up her slacks. "My partner Agent Chisolm and I have a few questions for Max Hague." In a classy move, she maintained eye contact with the Football guy rather than crane her neck to see if Max was hiding in the room. "Is he here?"

"Yes, ma'am," Football guy said without budging. He turned his head to one side and then asked, "Are you up to talking to anyone, Max?"

"Okay," came the unsteady voice.

"Mind if we stay?" Football guy asked.

"If it will make everyone more comfortable," Abi conceded. Her gracefulness with victims was up there with the best Grayson had ever witnessed.

Football guy stepped aside and then took a seat on the bunk across from Max's. Gamer guy followed suit as though a shadow, giving a view to Max who was seated on the floor. Grayson had to hand it to the young men: they were ready to stand up and defend their friend from unwanted guests. He had a lot of respect for that.

"We're sorry to intrude," Abi said calmly to Max.

"My parents are on their way from El Paso," Max stated as he stuffed a trunk with books and laundry that he picked up piece by piece on the floor and shoved inside. "I'm leaving school. Finishing the rest of the semester remotely." He barely glanced at Abi and Grayson as they stood just inside the door.

Abi's shoulders were relaxed as she leaned against the frame. She tented her fingers together, indicating she was the one in charge in the room.

Max wasn't taller than five feet seven inches. He wore baggy sweatpants and an oversize hoodie. His brown eyes were wild when he focused on Abi. "I can't stay here anymore after what…"

"You've been through a traumatic experience," Abi said with the kind of compassion that made Max stop long enough to move to his bed and then plop down. He tilted his face toward the ceiling as he closed his eyes and took in a deep breath.

"We're here to help you, Max. Going through the details of what happened isn't going to be easy," Abi said. As she crossed the room, one of Max's friends stood up. No doubt, he would place himself between her and Max. Abi put a hand out to stop the young man from intervening, and in a surprise move, he froze. "But it will be worth it once we stop this monster." She paused, letting those words sink in. "Can you help us, Max?"

Max opened his eyes the second she got within five feet of him. Abi slowed, making eye contact the whole time. She had a gentle, calming tone like the one he imagined a horse whisperer would use. Growing up on a horse ranch might have honed those skills.

She crouched down in front of Max when she made it to within a foot of him. The nonthreatening position allowed Max to feel in charge. "There's a very bad man out there, Max. I know it. You know it. My partner and I want to stop him before he moves on to the next victim."

Max started to open up but then clamped his mouth shut. Young people were usually afraid to talk when they'd done something wrong in the process.

"I'm not here to give you a hard time about underage drinking." Her soft but determined tone resonated with Max. "All I'm after is the truth about what happened so this horrible person can be stopped. Any information you can provide will help. I promise."

Max nodded as he gathered courage. His gaze flicked over her head, to his friends.

"I can ask them to leave the room if that makes it easier

for you to talk about it," Abi said, her voice as soothing as honey on a sore throat.

"Yeah, man, we can wait in the hallway if you want," Football guy offered. "Either way, bro."

Max gave a tentative nod.

"We'll be right outside that door," Football guy said as he and the other friend stood.

"Promise you won't leave?" Max's voice was small and vulnerable.

"I'm not going anywhere, man."

"We can keep the door open if that helps," Abi offered, keeping her compassionate gaze steady on Max.

"Okay," Max said before the pair exited into the hallway.

Grayson might have been in this business longer than Abi, but he was witnessing a master at work. Her special touch had Max's shoulders relaxing and his breathing almost back to normal. It wasn't uncommon for a victim's heart to race when law enforcement arrived even though they weren't guilty of anything. The stress of the event flooded them, and in many cases involving young people, they worried they'd done something wrong.

Once the others were gone, Abi sat down on the floor, crisscrossing her legs.

"Start whenever you're ready," she said to Max.

Chapter Six

Max Hague took in a deep breath. He exhaled slowly, brought up his right foot to rest his ankle on his left thigh. He clasped his hands around his right knee as it shook. "My parents don't know about me." His gaze shot from Abi to Grayson and back. "About my lifestyle."

"We have no judgment on how you live your life and no reason to discuss your lifestyle with your parents," Abi reassured. "You are a college student. The rest is up to you to tell them when and if you're ever ready." Half the battle in getting good information from a victim was making them comfortable in your presence. It was the reason she sat on the floor while Max stayed on the edge of the bed. He'd been victimized, almost killed. He felt helpless. Having him sit taller than Abi gave some of his power back. It was a psychological trick she'd picked up early in her career from working with several young victims about to go into the WITSEC program. Plus, her heart really did go out to Max. The kid would likely have trust issues for years to come, if not the rest of his life.

Abi might have an aversion to kids, but she didn't mind teenagers. Most people thought she had it flipped. Except that she had no idea what to do with a crying baby or a toddler in the middle of a temper tantrum. They looked demon-possessed and scared the bejesus out of her. By fifteen years old, though, they had opinions of their own. She'd had lively conversations with teenagers. Plus, they could go to the bathroom on their own and wipe their own backsides. No need to change any stinky diapers. So that was a huge plus.

Max gave another tentative nod. "I don't remember much."

The brain often blocked out details of a traumatic event, not to mention the effects of ketamine.

"Anything you can give us will be helpful," she continued. Grayson took to the background on this one, letting her take the lead. In this case, it was best. Logic said he would most likely be more suspicious of men. A woman's presence, however, could have the opposite effect. Grayson didn't seem to mind playing the odds on this one and the strategy seemed to be working. On a human side, she didn't want to inflict more pain on a victim. They deserved to be treated with compassion, which clearly was her strength.

Max kept his eyes closed as Abi told him to start from the beginning and take his time with the details.

"It's hazy," Max said. "One minute, I'm at a party having a great time, dancing and talking with friends. The next, I'm in someone's car." He paused. "The next thing I know, I'm in the back seat. Someone is on top of me, holding me down." His bottom lip quivered.

"It's okay," Abi soothed. "You're doing great, and we can stop at any time if you need a break."

Max closed his eyes and gave a slight nod.

"What do you remember about that moment?" Abi asked.

"The feel of plastic gloves against my skin, like at the doctor's," he said before opening his eyes. "I didn't remember that before, but he had on gloves like he was going into surgery or something. Purple. They were purple."

"Can you recall what else he wore?" she asked, wondering if the car part was true or if he'd confused it for the garage. Then again, there could be a bench seat in the garage. She would have to read the sheriff's report once it was sent to the group.

Max shook his head. "I already told the deputy who visited me at the hospital this part is fuzzy." The date rape drug would cloud his memory. It was one of the reasons that ketamine or similar drugs were so popular aside from the ease of slipping them inside someone's drink. "All I know is the person was strong." It could have been the drug that had made Max compliant, more than the perp's arm strength. Perception was skewed with those drugs. Then again, the perp had to be somewhat strong in order to handle his victims.

"Would you say he was tall? Heavy?" she asked.

"Tall, I think," Max said. "When you're my height, it's not hard to beat."

"Heavy?"

"I don't know," Max said on a sharp sigh. "The clothes he had on were loose, baggy. Made it impossible to tell."

"In the back seat of the vehicle, were you facing up, to the side, or down?" she asked.

"Down."

"And then what happened?" she continued.

"The pressure on me ended, and then I was told to strip off my clothes," he said with an involuntary shiver at the memory. "I did what he said. Then the guy disappeared for a little while. Or I passed out. I'd been drinking all night, so…" The perp must have wanted to strip Max to make it more difficult for him to run, or more scared to make a wrong move.

"Did he threaten you?" she asked.

"Said he would kill me if I didn't listen." Max nodded as he rubbed his wrists. "He put some kind of restraints on my wrists, though. But honestly, I don't remember much of that. I just noticed it after I ran."

Face down on whatever seat was in the garage, arms tied presumably behind his back, Max would be easier to subdue. Sadly, Reprehensible's other vics had marks on their wrists too. The forensic report on the first vic had confirmed some type of plastic was used. A zip tie came to mind. They could be purchased at hardware stores or any of those big-box DIY places.

"Do you have a guess as to what kind of material was used?" she asked but she could read the report to find the answer. This was a way to check facts. She didn't believe Max would lie about his experience. He had no reason to. His answers would tell her how lucid he'd been and how reliable the information might be.

"No," Max admitted. "All I know is it cut into my wrists." He held them out for inspection. They resembled burn marks. Abi scooted closer, careful not to invade his personal space. The red marks could have come from a zip tie or rope. They were probably too thin for rope burns, though. Could be plastic or wire, based on the cuts. If plastic had been confirmed on vic number one, she would put money on the perp using the same material here too.

"Before the vehicle, can you tell me anything you remember from the party?" she asked, hoping to backtrack.

"Not really," Max said. "It was in someone's backyard." He flashed eyes at her. "We were drinking and there was music, the usual stuff. The neighbors were there, so no one was worried about the cops being called." He seemed to catch himself as guilt flashed over his features. He was telling someone in law enforcement that he'd broken the law with underage drinking. "People were partying, you know, so mingling and dancing."

"Did you stay outside the entire time or go into the house?" she asked.

"Yeah, we were all banned from using the house," he said, looking up and to the right, a sign of recall. "No one was allowed inside after the last party when Micky dropped a bottle of tequila in the living room. Aiden said the place still reeked. We couldn't even use the bathroom. He told us to go behind the bushes." It was possible Max had been watched.

"What about recreational drugs?" Abi asked but Max was already shaking his head.

"I don't do those," he said emphatically. Could she believe him? Admitting to drinking had been difficult enough. Alcohol was legal for those old enough to consume it. Drugs were a different ball game. "I would never take anything. All I do is drink on the weekends." His demeanor changed and guilt flashed across his features, which probably meant he'd experimented at the very least. But he wasn't willing to own up to it and she wouldn't know for certain until toxicology reports came back. A drug screening panel would have been run in the hospital, but those didn't cover all drugs, just the main culprits.

"What about pictures?" she asked. "Social media?"

"I mean someone always pulls out their phone to take pictures, but we have a rule about nothing being posted on social," Max said. "It's an easy way to get kicked out of the university since there's a hard rule against underage drinking."

The sheriff had already requested partygoers come in voluntarily and bring their phones. She had no idea how many young people would take him up on the request. Many would guard their pictures with their lives if they thought someone would get into trouble with the law. A few would come forward, though. Some people would do the right thing after news got out. On a small campus, it wouldn't take long for word to spread.

"Did you ever lose track of your drink at any point in the party?" Abi continued.

"No, I…well, actually, there was an outdoor bar near the back fence. I may have set it down a few times while grooving," he admitted. "I didn't remember that before either. Now that I think about it, though, I'm sure I set my cup down multiple times to dance. Or even just to talk to someone."

Women were warned about date rape drugs and told how to protect themselves. Information was out there for everyone. However, she wondered how many guys actually paid attention to flyers or warning ads, thinking it would never happen to them.

"Anyone at the party could have had access to your cup, then," she said. She and Grayson could get the house resident's full name and the address easily enough from the report. She already had the names Micky and Aiden. She wouldn't dig deeper into those questions with Max when the information would be readily available in the report.

"I'm afraid so," he said after he thought about it for a few seconds. It was obvious from the dilation of his eyes that he was still in at least a mild state of shock. The drug he'd been given last night would have lingering effects. It had only been fifteen hours, give or take. Not to mention the massive hangover from all the drinking. But he mostly came across as frightened of his own shadow. There was a bandage over a cotton pad on the inside of his left arm. The hospital would have taken blood for testing and most likely rehydrated him with an IV. "We all drank out of those red Solo cups. I'm pretty sure I picked up the wrong one after getting a mouthful of tequila at one point. Someone was drinking it straight up with no mixer." Max's face twisted. Then he shook his head. "I get sick off anything but beer."

Abi didn't want to think about the hangover that a drink such as straight tequila in a Solo cup would bring on. And that was after possibly throwing up. College kids and binge drinking seemed to go hand in hand. She realized that didn't apply to all college students, just to note that it was still common when young people got their freedom for the first time.

It also sounded like someone else might have been the target, except that Max fit the physical description of Reprehensible's prior victims.

"I'm sure you gave the deputy a list of names of the attendees at the party," Abi said.

"I did," Max stated.

She wouldn't trouble him twice since the list would be in the deputy's report—a report he was most likely putting together right now.

From roughly 1:30 in the morning to 7:30 a.m. when Max flagged down the couple, Reprehensible could have done anything he wanted. Max was compliant due to the drugs in his system.

"Was it a big party?" she asked.

Max nodded. "Could have easily been a hundred people or more in the couple of hours I was there. It's not unusual to hop from party to party."

There weren't enough resources to interview every individual.

"How frequent are the parties?" she asked, wondering if the same core group traveled from place to place. If she could narrow the number down, it would be worthwhile to interview a handful of young people. Then again, waste too much time here and Reynosa might already be on to his next vic.

"There's something going on every weekend," Max said, dropping his leg, stretching both and crossing them at the ankles. "At least, usually. Plus, there's not much else to do in a small town except get-togethers." His hand trembled as he bit his thumbnail.

"I know you've been asked this question multiple times but is there anything else you remember about the person who did this to you?" Abi asked.

Max sat quiet for a long moment. "His voice sounded like he was talking through a fan. You know how that sounds. Like it's some kind of effect."

The perp didn't want anyone to be able to pinpoint him from his voice, she noted. Having a living witness made her wonder if the perp would try to circle back and murder Max. His parents must be thinking along the same lines, which could be one of the reasons they were pulling him from school. That, and the fact he'd just been through a horribly traumatic event and needed time to recover.

"Oh," Max said, brightening up. "I think he has a mole on his neck. It was dark. Big."

"I thought it was dark outside and he was clothed to the hilt," Abi said.

"It was and he was," Max confirmed. "But I remember a flash of light and then seeing it." He frowned. "At least, I think so." His shoulders deflated before he straightened up and stood. "I could be confusing memories, mixing them up. I've been woozy ever since it happened. The brain fog is real. At the time, it felt like I was going in and out of a dream. None of it felt real. It still doesn't."

"I understand," was all Abi could say. They had something more…a neck mole.

But not much else.

"Does anything else stand out in your mind that you might have forgotten to mention earlier?" she asked.

He sat there for a long moment. At nineteen, he was part adult, part child. His current expression was all kid.

"Thank you for your time, Max," she said, figuring this conversation was over. He'd already stood up and returned to packing.

"You're welcome," he said, his hand still trembling. "Will you tell the guys they can come back in?"

On the way out, she did just that after providing her contact information to Max and asking if he'd be more comfortable if they waited around until his parents arrived before taking off. He gave them the okay to go since his buddies were nearby. Abi was relieved Max had such devoted friends. He would need them in the coming days and weeks. If he was to have any chance of recovering from the psychological effects of a crime like the one he'd survived, he would need a strong support network from here on out.

"GOOD JOB IN THERE," Grayson said once they reached the elevators. The doors opened. An older couple came rushing out. The panicked look on the older woman's face said she was Max's mother. His father, an older version of Max, was so distracted that he ran into Grayson's chest.

"Sorry," the senior Max said before rushing down the hallway in the direction of his son's room.

A knot tightened in Grayson's chest as they walked to the stairs. His mind immediately snapped to his little boy, who was presently home with a babysitter instead of a parent.

An almost debilitating wave of guilt stabbed Grayson in the center of the chest at the thought of letting Michelle down, his son down. During their eighteen-month marriage, they'd never once talked about the possibility of him not coming home from work. Two years of dating beforehand, they hadn't broached the subject. Michelle knew his job was dangerous. She'd been fully aware of the risks while they were dating. Both had been superstitious about bringing up the subject, though. They'd agreed not to discuss what could go wrong in life, talking around the topic. Instead, they'd focused on what could go right. At least, Michelle had. Her belief in him knew no bounds. Coming home to her had made him want to be a better person.

The thought of his wife being the one to die had been unimaginable. She'd given up her career as a wedding photographer after Collin's birth to stay home with him full-time. Michelle had wanted at least two kids. Grayson had countered they should see if they were any good with one.

He would have given her anything she wanted.

After heading down one flight, they exited the building.

"Hey," Abi said, her voice breaking through his reverie.

Grayson cleared his throat in an attempt to dislodge the emotion stuck there. "Good interview, by the way."

"Thanks, but you already said that," she said, confusion in her voice.

He needed to steer the conversation to the case before she could ask him where he'd gone just now. He'd accepted the fact his wife was gone. Revisiting their past only came about when he thought about the disservice he was doing to her by not being home for Collin. Then again, they'd had no contingency plan. They'd never spoken about what her wishes would be if—heaven forbid—one of them died before their son reached his eighteenth birthday, let alone after his birth. Since Michelle was gone, Grayson needed to figure it out on his own. In addition to Abi's other good qualities, she was kind and intelligent. She knew when to push and when to pull back.

He shook off the temptation to talk about his personal life with a coworker. *Temporary coworker,* that same voice pointed out.

"What are your takeaways after speaking to Max directly?" he asked, getting the conversation back to the case.

"That he is still in shock and trying to process," she said. "We didn't get as much as I would have liked."

"The possible mole is interesting," he pointed out.

"Thanks," Abi said. "True about the mole, except his brain is so jumbled. Plus, with alcohol consumption, he admitted to not knowing if he could trust what he was saying, let alone us use it to move forward."

"All good information for the report," he said. It was something. Progress might be a game of inches right now, but he believed he could find more clues.

They didn't have time to discuss their personal lives. Although, after seeing her way with Max, Grayson wondered if he could bounce a few ideas off her as a friend instead of coworker. Friends had been in short supply lately. And they wouldn't be coworkers for long.

Could he forge a friendship with Abi?

Chapter Seven

"I thought about making a short list of young people who visited the parties regularly, but the deputy most likely did that," Grayson said to Abi after reclaiming the driver's seat. She leaned back in the seat and pinched the bridge of her nose. A raging headache threatened. It was late. She wanted a warm shower and a comfortable bed.

"Same here," she said, sitting up a little straighter. "I need to go back to my room and make a supplemental victim interview report. Do you want to join me? We could wait for the other reports to be uploaded. Go over them together."

"It couldn't hurt to go over the details of the deputy's summary," he agreed. Her heart gave a little flip at spending more time together. Abi reminded herself being in the same room would benefit the case. Two heads were better than one. Plus, Grayson was a seasoned agent. She wouldn't mind picking his brain.

Also, by now, reports might be uploaded. They could stay in and order pizza for dinner while they broke everything down. Once they had names and addresses, they could go out together to interview witnesses. She also wanted to go to the scene of the party at night to see how easy it would be to watch the backyard activities.

"He's moved on," she said, tapping her forehead, trying to distract herself from the dull ache. Ibuprofen only lasted so long and hers had run out. At least for tonight, they would be better served going over the information.

"I know," Grayson responded. "There's no way he would stick around here after almost getting caught. I'm assuming he's already ditched the motorcycle by now too. It might have been stolen. Or at the very least he might have switched the plates so it couldn't be traced back to him."

"Right. Makes sense." She paused. "Based on your years of experience, how long do you think we have before he strikes again?" The part of her that wanted to rest didn't want to know the answer to that question. Because she knew in her bones it would be soon. Too soon. The effects of the pepper spray might have worn off but that didn't mean she wasn't worn out. Today had been one for the books and it was still going. She glanced at the clock on the dashboard: 5:55. Some people saw it as a good omen when you looked at a clock and all the numbers matched. She would take whatever luck she could get in this case.

"We got close to catching him this time," Grayson said. "While most serial killers would wait, I believe this one will strike soon because it's the last thing we'd expect."

"Logic says pull back and make certain the coast is clear," she said.

"His pattern has been cutting the time in between kills rather than the other way around," he said. "He's not regrouping after he strikes…"

"He's moving on to the next," she said. "Considering the time in between kills shortens, he mapped this out beforehand."

"Not the individuals, though," Grayson said. "Those, I believe at least, he takes at an opportune time."

"It would be easy enough to have locations scouted, even parties. They occur on a regular basis on and around college campuses." Repeating those last words as she'd done many times during this case wasn't providing the breakthrough she'd been hoping for. Sometimes, repetition helped. Not today. The headache was making it more difficult to concentrate too. A shower and fresh, clean clothes might wake her up. If not, she could down a shot of espresso. Or whatever coffee the motel stocked. "I need more ibuprofen if I'm going to use my brain much more."

"He'll strike soon, but not tonight," Grayson predicted. "If you want to write and submit the report, we can always swing back by the house for a quick look after dinner. Then, start fresh early in the morning."

"As much as I hate to admit it, that might not be a bad idea," she said. "Sometimes, when I'm too focused on a case, the answers move further away. Maybe we should talk about something else for the rest of the ride back."

"Your cousin Julie has been getting word out to every college in Texas to make sure faculty and students are aware of the situation," Grayson said. Abi's cousin was also a US marshal. "That's as much as can be done anyway."

"I know you don't discuss your personal life—"

"Any chance you'll let me edit that statement?" he interrupted.

"Depends on the edit," she said, turning to look at him. Abi considered herself good at reading people. Grayson had definitely just stepped out of his comfort zone.

"I don't normally discuss my personal life with coworkers but I'm not against gaining a new friend," he said. "What do you think?"

Abi wasn't sure what changed his mind, but she liked Grayson. He was honest and genuine. She could easily shelve the unwanted attraction she felt toward him. Maybe not *easily*. But she could set it aside, ignore it. "I'm good with being friends." She could use one considering everything going on at the ranch while she was on this case.

"What's your opinion about kids?" he asked.

"Not for me," she said. "But I guess they're fine for other people."

"You don't want to have children?" His question was loaded with shock. Enough to catch her off guard. Was he one of those people who thought every woman wanted 2.5 kids and a white picket fence?

"I don't like them enough to want to have one," she quipped.

Grayson laughed.

"What? I'm supposed to want them because I have ovaries?" she asked, more than a little indignant.

"No, it's not that," he said. "I was looking for advice but you're not the right person to ask."

"*You* want to have kids?" she asked, confused.

"No," he corrected. "I *have* a kid. The call I took earlier was from my babysitter."

"Wouldn't you want to talk to your wife about your kid?" Abi asked.

"That's the rub," he said with the kind of sadness in his voice that said he'd been through something terrible. "She died almost five years ago."

"I'm so sorry, Grayson," she said and meant every word. "I had no idea. That must have been awful."

"It was, but I've had time to get used to it," he said. "Five years is a long time. I appreciate your sympathy, though."

"Of course," she stated. "How old is your kid?"

"Almost five years old."

"Oh." Abi didn't know what to say, so she reached over and touched his forearm.

"It happened during childbirth," he continued.

Her heart went out to the man. She couldn't imagine finding the love of her life and then losing them so quickly. And immediately after starting a family.

"I used to have the same reaction about having kids as you just did," he said.

"What changed your mind?"

"Michelle," he said. "That was her name."

"It's a lovely name," Abi said.

"Thank you." He paused for a few moments. Was he catching his breath? "She was confident I'd be a good father."

"But you weren't," Abi surmised.

"Not in the least," he admitted.

Losing the person you loved most in the world would put the haunted look in his eyes. She'd never spent time with anyone who made her think about having a future together but if she had, she would have wanted it to be someone like Grayson. She would have wanted it to be with someone who loved her like he must have loved Michelle.

She also realized that anyone else he might be in a relationship with in the future would be competing with a ghost.

ABI HAD A way with people. Her words soothed him in places that had been encased in a hard shell for almost five years now. It was the reason he could keep going. "This job is dangerous."

"True," she said, cocking her head to one side. "But we knew that when we signed up, right?"

"That was before I was a single parent," he pointed out.

"What's changed?" she asked. "You've been on your own for quite a few years now. I assume everything has been going well."

"Collin is about to go into kindergarten," Grayson continued.

"And so?"

"He's starting school next year," he said. "Who will help him with his homework every night?"

"I don't know much about kids to be perfectly honest, but I don't remember having a whole lot of homework in kindergarten," she said. "I'm pretty sure we sang a lot of songs, held hands and played tag on the playground."

"He needs stability," he said.

"How are you not providing that?" she asked. "You have a job that requires you to be away. No different than a businessman who travels for work. Don't you agree?"

"Well, yeah, but last time I checked businessmen didn't have bullets flying past their heads."

"Good point," she admitted. "But doesn't working in your dream job make you a better parent? Doesn't it teach your kid to be happy and do the kind of work you love?"

He didn't immediately speak. He'd loved his job at one time. Did he still?

"When you love it, that's true," he said as he drove past the crime scene on the way to the motel.

At the four-way stop, he glanced over at Abi, who nodded her head and pursed her lips. "My grandfather was a US marshal a long time ago."

"I thought you said he owned a horse ranch or is this your grandfather on the other side of the family?"

"Same one," she reassured. "He worked the job when he was young but got burned out on it after a few years. He didn't like being away from my grandmother so much."

Grayson felt that statement in his bones about being away from Collin.

"He squirreled away every penny to scrape up enough money to buy land and then fix up the home there," she said with a wistful quality to her tone as she turned her face away from him, toward the passenger window.

Did he hear her sniffle?

"I'm guessing he left his job after building his horse business," he said. Being outside sounded damn good to Grayson right now. Being on the land. Watching the sunrise in the mornings with a cup of coffee in his hand. Collin having room to run around a big yard. Grayson dialed back his enthusiasm. Not only was his kid not athletic but he was allergic to grass. Grass and almost everything else in the environment too.

"That's right," she confirmed. Then came the sniff before she took in a deep breath.

"Doesn't sound like a bad life to me," Grayson admitted. "Is that what you want?"

"I'm qualified to sit behind a desk for the rest of my career," he said. "Which sounds like hell to me." Then he turned the tables. "Have you ever wanted to do anything else other than work for the Marshals Service?"

"Wanted to be a cowgirl on the rodeo circuit when I was eight," she said with a laugh that was almost musical. "Does that count?"

"Only if by age ten you wanted to be a vet," he retorted.

"Most definitely," she said. "I can tell you one thing. I was never one of those girls who sat around and played with dolls or dressed up in high heels or experimented with makeup. Those things never appealed to me when I was young."

"You were busy living most kids' dream of growing up on a horse ranch," he interjected.

"Well, that's true enough. I was mucking stalls in overalls before school two mornings a week," she said.

"Lucky kids who got to sit next to you in class," he quipped.

Abi laughed. The break in tension was good. Talking about his personal life had never appealed to him before. Was he missing having friends? Rather than hit happy hour after office work or after shooting range practice, he headed home to Collin. During the time he wasn't in the field, the least he could do was be home for his kid. So he didn't date. At least, not traditionally. While Collin was in preschool, Grayson had gone out to a few lunches here and there. It had taken a couple of years to get out there again. If someone passed the lunch test, Grayson would invite her over for a late dinner or a movie at his place once his kid went to bed.

It wasn't much, he realized, but he was dipping his toe back in the dating waters and had been for the past three years. No one had sparked his interest enough to date anything more than casually.

The women he'd dated didn't stick around for long once they realized he didn't have anything to offer them other than a night here and there. Most thought him staying home to be there for his kid was adorable in the beginning, until they wanted to be taken out to a restaurant during dinner hours and he had to say that wasn't possible. Quite a few left in a huff, saying something about him being emotionally unavailable. He'd served the line *It isn't you, it's me* enough times to know it was truth.

"Okay, hotshot," she began, "What would you do if you didn't work for the FBI at all?" She didn't seem to mind putting him on the spot, but he'd asked for it. Her honesty was refreshing, though.

"I have never given it much thought," he admitted.

"Maybe it's time to consider a complete overhaul," she pointed out.

Grayson pulled into the parking lot of the motel and parked in front of their doors. Their rooms were next to each other. He cut the ignition off and turned to her. "Your grandfather...did he have any regrets for leaving it all behind?"

"Not one," she said as a small smile upturned the corners of her lips.

Grayson wanted to know what that smile was about.

Chapter Eight

Grayson came around to the passenger door and opened it for Abi. She thanked him and then waited as he grabbed his own overnight bag from the trunk of his service-issued sedan. "I probably could have picked up my car when we drove past the crime scene a few minutes ago."

"It'll still be there in the morning," Grayson pointed out. "Or if we get back out to interview witnesses for ourselves."

"I was thinking we could go back to the party house once it's dark," she said. "Take a look at the possible angles where Max could have put down his drink. See if we can uncover how it all might have gone down. It's helpful for me to walk through it. But I can't stay up until one or two o'clock in the morning to do it."

"We can do that and we don't have to wait up that late," he said. "I usually do the same thing before too much of the dust settles around a scene."

"Really?" she asked, figuring if a legend like Grayson had similar habits, then she was on the right track in her career.

The sun was beginning its descent. It felt like lunch had been eons ago but it had only been a couple of hours. Time ticked as the day began to disappear into night.

"Yes," he confirmed as he closed his trunk and followed her to her room.

Once inside, he set up his laptop at the small table with a pair of chairs. Now that Abi could see clearly, the room reminded her of her grandparents' home. Floral curtains in purple and pink hues matched the bedspreads. Beige carpet led to a tiled bathroom. The place even smelled of rose petals. It had that warm, cozy feeling that made her half expect someone's grandmother to show up holding a plate of warm cookies. "What do you think about ordering pizza while we go over the files?"

"Sounds like a winner to me," he said.

"Do you mind?" she asked. "I need to shower and change into something more comfortable."

"No problem," he said but there was a husky quality to his voice that hadn't been there a few seconds ago.

Abi grabbed her overnight bag and headed into the bathroom, suddenly aware she was going to be naked in the next room. She was relieved her back was turned so Grayson couldn't see her cheeks flame three shades past red.

The bathroom was just as cozy as the other room, with its scented bath soaps and thick towels. There was a small basket filled with everything she might need, including a toothbrush wrapped in plastic with a tiny tube of toothpaste. This place couldn't be more adorable. Focusing on the details instead of her attraction to her coworker helped douse the flame. It had been too long since she'd been on an interesting date or in a relationship that lasted more than a couple of months.

Grayson was a father, which was the equivalent of a bucket of water on the burning embers. Abi repelled young kids. Her sister, Crystal, could handle them much better. Not Abi. Her sister would tease her if she knew about Abi's attraction to a single dad. Crystal would laugh under normal circumstances. Abi doubted her sister would find much funny while keeping bedside vigil with their grandparents.

She slipped out of her shoulder holster and then removed her button-down shirt. The slacks came off next after she set her glasses down on the counter. She would need those for the next twenty-four hours at least while she gave her retinas time to heal. The last thing she wanted to do was pop in new contacts. After removing her undergarments, she turned on the water and then slipped into its warmth.

Fifteen minutes later, she turned the knob and wrapped herself in a towel. She'd packed sweatpants and a sweatshirt, so she grabbed those along with a sports bra and a fresh pair of cotton underwear before dressing. She spent the next ten minutes drying her hair before digging around for a hair clip that would keep it off her face and neck.

After twisting her hair and clipping it, she put on her glasses and then gathered up her dirty clothes. She placed those in the small laundry bag she had tucked in the zippered pocket. Once those were put away, she headed into the next room.

The smell of pizza wafted, causing her stomach to growl.

"I was just about to give you a shout to let you know food arrived," Grayson said as he set up paper plates and set a pair of Coke cans out. "Wasn't sure what you wanted to drink, so I got water and Coke."

"Caffeine sounds good if I'm going to stay awake long enough to check out the scene," she said on a yawn.

Grayson's shoulder holster was hooked onto the back of

one of the chairs, his shirt unbuttoned. A man shouldn't look as sexy as he did with so little skin showing.

"I'm starved," Abi said, redirecting. She took a seat across from him and filled her plate with a couple of slices. "How did you know I liked every vegetable known to man on my pizza?"

"Took a guess," he stated. "We shared a meal already. It wasn't hard to figure out your preferences once you picked apart the menu." He brought his gaze up to hers for a split second and smiled. The temperature in the room heated up several degrees without either one touching the thermostat. "I hope Italian sausage is okay. I've never been a big fan of pepperoni."

"Well, that's it," she quipped in dramatic fashion. "I can't eat this. This is awful."

A mix of concern and disbelief flashed across his face.

"I'm just kidding," she added quickly. She hadn't meant to stress the poor man out. "I can literally eat anything on my pizza, but this is perfection."

Grayson shook his head and laughed. "I should have known. Who needs sriracha when you have that kind of spice around?"

They both laughed. Hard.

He was giving new meaning to words *dad joke.*

"That was bad," she finally said when she could stop laughing.

"The worst," he added. The man didn't mind making fun of himself. Add another amazing trait to the long and growing list.

If Abi dated coworkers, she would want it to be Grayson. Except for the kid part. She couldn't talk to anyone below the age of fifteen. Really. Plus, at twenty-eight years old, she would have been twenty-threeish when the kid was born. At that age, she'd been too focused on figuring herself out, which still applied. She'd finally gotten somewhat comfortable in her career.

"Did you ever think about the dangers of the job before you got married?" she asked Grayson.

"No," he admitted. "You?"

"I never even considered them," she responded. "Didn't then and don't now. But I also don't have anything to go home to like you do." Her life suddenly sounded empty, felt empty when she thought about it in those terms. This conversation triggered a deeper one that had been simmering underneath the surface for a while now. Abi's career was on track, but she couldn't keep a houseplant alive. The dead fern on the kitchen windowsill could attest to the fact. Her former boyfriends would also complain that she didn't "water" their relationship, to keep the metaphor running. She finished chewing the bite of pizza she'd taken while getting lost in thought, then asked, "Can I ask you something?"

"Shoot," he said.

"Don't take this the wrong way, but do you regret having a family?"

He picked his cell phone up from the table and then tapped the screen a couple of times before sharing. The picture of a dark-haired kid with short, spiky hair that had too much gel in it, and a small face and big glasses with red frames tugged at her heartstrings in a way no other kid had.

Looking at Collin made her ovaries ache, and more shockingly made her think she might be missing out on something big.

A WARM SMILE morphed the normally serious and sometimes sarcastic marshal's face. Abi was even more beautiful when she smiled. "Your son may be the cutest kid I've ever seen."

"Thank you. He's one of a kind." Her words and her smile warmed places in him that had been encased in ice far too long. If he went home and took a desk job, would that release some of the guilt that kept his dating life on ice too?

The annoying voice in the back of his mind said it was time to move on, get into a rhythm with his son's schedule. Be home for the kid. Teach him how to throw a ball if Collin ever decided to play sports. Or—and this scenario was more likely—Collin could teach his dad how to use all the tech gadgets. Grayson had always been an outdoor person. He knew the basics of using his phone and laptop. The agency had provided enough training for him to use those tools effectively for his job, which carried over into his private life. He had the basics covered.

And, hey, if his son wanted to play computer games instead of sports, Grayson wouldn't complain. All he cared about was having a healthy kid. Some outdoor time was necessary. Collin just hadn't found the right activity.

"Tell me more about him," Abi said but she was probably just being nice. She'd admitted to not being able to stand little kids. He now noticed a twinkle in her eyes that he hadn't seen before that was more like a longing, but he was most likely misreading her. When someone told you they didn't like something, experience had taught him that it was always best to believe them.

Setting aside the growing piece of him that wanted Abi to like his son, he decided to keep it short and sweet. "He likes pretty much all the Marvel characters. But the Hulk is his current favorite." Did his affection for the brainy scientist Bruce Banner, who turned into a big green hulk of a man when he got angry, have anything to do with Collin being picked on by some of his bigger, rowdier classmates?

"That's adorable," Abi said with a sigh. "I got picked on mercilessly for wearing glasses. Turns out kids can be ruthless with each other."

"He's had his fair share of insults hurled at him," Grayson admitted with a frustrated sigh.

"Makes me want to have a stern conversation with the parents of those bullies," Abi said with the kind of overprotectiveness usually reserved for parents. In Abi's case, she could relate on a personal level and tie it back to the harshness she'd suffered. Her reaction had nothing to do with Collin specifically. It was important to make that mental note because for a second, Grayson felt an intense connection to Abi that ran deeper than the sparks that flew between them when he stood too close.

"Makes me want to take those little twerps out back and give them a dressing down boot camp style," he couldn't help but say.

"You served in the military?" Abi asked.

"I did four years, which is how I got my degree," he said. The change in topic was good because he'd been known to overthink the bully situation with his kid, which in turn made him want to act on it.

"Thank you for your service," she said almost immediately.

"My pleasure."

"You want to know what I would do if I had a kid like yours and a job that required this much field work?"

He was surprised she was ready to offer an opinion, but he figured he knew what she was about to say, based on her earlier shock that he would consider changing his job. "Shoot."

Abi motioned toward his phone. "That face is worth staying home for. I get it now. Earlier, I was speaking from a place of not having a tie back home. No one needs me like he needs you. And, believe me, after being on the receiving end of being picked on, I know firsthand how much he needs you. I also know he's probably too embarrassed to tell you how much it hurts his feelings. And he might not even know the effects words like that have in the long run. You're doing the right thing in thinking about making a change." She flashed eyes at him. "Of course, what that change turns out to be is up to you. You need to be a desk jockey for a few years to be there for your kid. There's no shame in that. You can always get an adrenaline rush from jumping out of airplanes for fun."

He laughed.

"Funny to think that's actually safer than the jobs we do," he said. "If I was younger, I doubt I'd be having any of these thoughts of taking a step back. I'm forty years old. I've accomplished as much as I need to as a field agent."

"You're only ten years out from a pension," Abi pointed out. "I'm guessing you're beyond the twenty-year mark at that point." You had to work for the agency for twenty years and reach the age of fifty in order to receive a pension.

"Yes, I would be," he noted. "A decade is a long time."

"That's true," she said with a sneaky grin. "I'll be pushing forty by then."

"You'll be so old," he said after laughing.

"Ancient," she quipped, the spark returning to her eyes.

"In all seriousness, Collin would be just shy of fifteen at that point," Grayson said. He'd done the math. He knew the policy.

"You'd only have three years with him before he went off to college," she surmised with a look of pity. "I see the struggle you have there." And then she added, "Having a family worth staying home for is a good problem to have, though." The statement caught him off guard as much as the look in her eyes when she said it.

"I may have been looking at this from the wrong perspective all along," he admitted.

Abi's cell buzzed. She finished the last bite of pizza on her plate as she checked the screen. "It's the sheriff. He wants to know if we can come to his office. He has a war room set up with volunteers looking through cell phone data."

Before he could respond, she said, "I'll tell him that we'll be there in twenty minutes."

Chapter Nine

Abi changed into jeans, a blouse and a blazer before heading out to the sheriff's office. At least they'd had a break from thinking about the case for an hour while she showered and they ate. She was feeling refreshed and ready to dive back into the case.

The picture of Grayson's kid also reminded her why she did this job in the first place, to keep innocent people safe and lock up the bastards who would prey on others.

"We can pick up my car on the way back from the sheriff's office," she said to Grayson, who'd also shifted back into serious work mode.

"Easy enough," he said as she navigated them to the sheriff's office using the map feature on her phone.

The parking lot had a minimum of twenty-five vehicles parked in it. Grayson found a spot near the exit. The office itself was a small nondescript brown brick building, one-story. There was a larger building not twenty yards behind it, a jail.

A metal door opened to a lobby that looked like something out of the 1970s. Wood chairs and benches, beige patches of carpet, and a desk completed the room.

"You must be Marshal Remington and Agent Chisolm," an older lady who had stacked her gray hairs in a loose bun on top of her head said, standing up the minute they stepped into the room. "Sheriff Benton said to expect you." The older woman glanced at her watch. "You two are right on time."

Abi nodded and then shook the outstretched hand before Grayson did the same.

"I'm Inez," she said. "Pleasure to meet you." Inez had a sense of urgency about her kind and weathered blue eyes along with energy usually reserved for people half her age. "I'm Sheriff Benton's aunt. We run a small but tight ship around here."

Abi smiled at the beaming Inez.

"If you'll both follow me, I'll take you to the war room and let my neph…the sheriff know you arrived." Inez was a dear. She oozed small-town charm. Being related to the sheriff made sense as to why someone who looked like they should be a school librarian worked the sheriff's lobby instead.

The place had its charms and plants that were still alive.

Abi followed Inez down the hall to a conference room that had white boards on the walls and fold-up chairs around a conference table. There were tables lining the walls as well, with more fold-up chairs and folks studying screens, sometimes in pairs. She had to hand it to Inez: the place was quiet and organized. Maybe Inez missed her calling, considering she'd set the place up like a library.

"I'll alert Sheriff Benton of your arrival," Inez practically beamed before turning more serious. "Folks volunteered as soon as they heard about what happened." She had one of those time-worn faces that gave her an air of experience and intellect. "We're a good community here. When something happens to one of our own, we stick together." She lowered her voice. "Do you think he'll come back?"

"Only time will tell," Abi said honestly. "But we're going to do everything in our power to keep your citizens safe."

"We appreciate it," Inez said on a sigh. "It's just terrible what happened to that college boy."

Abi couldn't agree more. Inez excused herself and was off much like a tornado that touches down, spins around for a few seconds, and then bounces up and disappears. Of course, Inez didn't leave a destructive path in her wake.

Abi studied the walls. There wasn't much on them.

"Hey," a familiar voice came up from behind. "Looks like you two aren't afraid to roll your sleeves up and do some of the dirty work."

Abi turned around in time to catch Thad Carlson's sneer when he glanced at the back of Grayson's head. Seriously? Did the deputy not have better things to do than try to stir up more of his toxic masculinity?

"We're here to collaborate," Abi said before Grayson could respond. She expected him to turn and shoot a retort at the deputy. Instead, Grayson surprised her by leaning against the wall and folding his arms.

"Good to see you again, Deputy," Grayson said without a hint of sarcasm in his voice. The man was calm. The deputy was obviously feeling in his home turf here.

"Carlson, I told you to get out of here ten minutes ago to interview neighbors," Sheriff Benton said as he walked in, irritated.

"A lot of folks will be going to bed about now," the deputy countered. "Wouldn't it be better to swing by first thing in the morning?"

"You're almost guaranteed to catch them home right now," Sheriff Benton stated. "I don't care if they are wearing their pajamas or make you wait so they can dress. I asked you to canvass while information is still fresh in folks' minds."

"Yes, sir," came the deflated response. Deputy Carlson came across as someone who didn't want to be told what to do. He also seemed to have a problem with anyone who outranked him, unless of course you counted Abi. Did he see women as automatically beneath him?

Abi would be glad when they wrapped up the investigation here in town and moved on. The sheriff seemed fine, but Carlson was as a jerk and a creep. She'd come across her fair share of good old boys while working in rural towns. Thankfully, they weren't the norm any longer.

Carlson took off as the sheriff apologized for keeping them waiting.

"Was there something specific you wanted to show us?" Grayson asked.

"As a matter of fact," he said, glancing around and seeming to think better of having a conversation out in the open where his volunteer citizens could hear. "Would you mind following me?"

They did. The sheriff led them to the end of the hallway, to his office. It resembled the lobby but with leather couches, chairs and a better-quality oak desk that was massive. Behind the desk, the executive chair was flanked by a Texas flag on one side and an American flag on the other. Dead center was a picture of the governor. The office resembled many others she'd seen in her career.

The sheriff walked behind his desk and motioned for them to come with him. Abi and Grayson complied. She noticed her coworker was quietly taking everything in. He rarely spoke first. Even when provoked, he maintained a cool head.

Abi could learn a lot from the senior agent. It would be a shame for his agency to lose him, but after seeing the angelic, smiling face in the picture, she was certain Grayson needed to leave fieldwork. He would be an asset to any team with his experience. Sitting behind a desk might put him out of the action but he would still be contributing to putting perps behind bars. Wasn't that the ultimate goal anyway? Keep citizens safe from those who would prey on them?

The sheriff sat down and then entered a password before his screen came to life. "We got some pictures that might be of help. They're blurry when I blow them up, but we have someone working on filling in the pixels or whatever it is these computer wizards do."

That summed it up well enough for Abi's computer abilities.

"I thought it might give you a snapshot of the perp's movements, which is why I wanted to show these to you," Sheriff Benton said.

"We appreciate being brought in, Sheriff," Abi stated, which seemed to please the sheriff. He was tall, six feet one-inch at a minimum if she had to guess, and big-boned. The sheriff was probably in his early-to-midfifties, had a full head of white hair and plenty of sunspots on his leathery face and neck to indicate he didn't believe in breaking out the sunscreen. Inez was his aunt and was probably in her early seventies. If the sheriff inherited half of her energy, he would be just fine.

She also noted he was at the retirement age that would provide a retirement and pension for Grayson to be home with his kid.

The sheriff started bringing up pictures, one by one.

"See here," he said, going back and pointing to the first. Blown up, the images were blurry, but a good computer guy should be able to fill some of that in. "There's a hooded figure moving along the fence on the east side of the property."

"I see him," Abi reassured. Too bad he never showed his face as the sheriff clicked through the pictures. There were photos of Max, looking inebriated as he talked to friends. Another showed him dancing. The red Solo cup was in his hand at one point as he held it up in the air while dancing on the edge of the yard near the fence. This corroborated Max's story about his activities last night. "Hold on." She saw something in one of the pictures with Max in the background holding his drink up. "Go back."

"Where? To this one?" the sheriff asked.

"Yes," Abi stated as Grayson leaned in. This close, she couldn't help but notice his unique, spicy scent. "Look at that." She pointed to the right of the screen. The picture was blurry. Whoever took it was most likely dancing themselves.

"I'll be darned," the sheriff said.

A hand hovered over Max's cup as he held it in the air. A gloved hand.

"The purple surgical glove," Grayson stated.

"You saw that too, didn't you?" she asked. "When the picture first clicked onto the screen, you tensed."

"I did," Grayson said. "It was blurry, so I wanted to see the others first, but this is a good find."

"We know the perp hung around in the background," she continued. "He wore clothing so dark that he blended in with the night."

"I'm guessing he either kept his gloved hands hidden in his pockets or put the gloves on last minute," Grayson said.

She wished they had something more to go on. "I haven't had a chance to write up my interview with the victim, but he remembered something after he spoke to you," she said to the sheriff.

"Oh," Sheriff Benton said.

"His mind is still foggy, and his memories can't exactly be depended on, but he believed that he saw a mole on the perp's neck," Abi said.

"The perp could have been circulating around the party at some point during the night," Grayson added. "Do you mind asking your volunteers to check for pictures of a male with a distinct mole on his neck?"

"Did he say where?" the sheriff asked.

Abi motioned to the spot. "The victim said it was noticeable." She also realized the kid was drunk.

"His blood-alcohol content was 0.18 percent," the sheriff informed them.

"Jesus," Abi muttered under her breath. That was seriously impaired to the point of the term *drunken stupor* to apply. This alone could cause Max to feel confused. Add a drug to it, and she was surprised he didn't pass out altogether right there on the lawn, making a spectacle of himself and dead weight for anyone who tried to carry him.

"I uploaded several reports to the shared folder about an hour ago," the sheriff continued.

Abi was still thinking about how the perp knew to act at just the right moment to get Max to walk away from the party.

"WE WERE JUST about to go over the documents when you texted," Grayson confirmed. "If you see any pictures of Max leaving, will you upload them to the shared folder?"

"Will do," said the sheriff.

"Thank you for contacting us right away," Grayson added. "It might be best if we took off so we can acquaint ourselves with everything in the files tonight."

"Yes, sir," the sheriff stated. Grayson appreciated the level of respect in the lawman's voice, especially after the conduct of his deputy. There had to be a story as to why Thad Carlson had a job. But that was a conversation for a later date and time, if at all.

The sheriff walked them out to the lobby and a smiling, waiting Inez.

"I appreciate you both for getting here so fast," he said after offering a handshake to Abi first and then Grayson. The man had a firm handshake and an honest disposition.

"Take care and if you need anything, give me a call," Inez said. "Even if it's just a recommendation for food."

"We will," Abi promised before heading out to the car with Grayson.

Once inside he started the engine and asked, "Did you notice what Max was wearing in the pictures?"

"A T-shirt and jeans," she said.

"A bright yellow T-shirt," he added as he navigated out of the parking lot. "That made him stand out."

"That's true," she stated. "We don't know what the other victims were wearing because they were found in just their underclothes."

"Which initially led us to believe they might have been sexually assaulted but that hasn't been the case so far," he added.

"I thought that was strange." Abi issued a pause. "In cases like these, sexual assault usually comes into play."

"Because the perp himself was victimized at some point in his life and acts out revenge on others," he continued. "But this guy isn't assaulting them even though they are compliant."

Abi snapped her fingers. "The bowl cuts. He's acting out some type of fantasy that has nothing to do with sex." Max had escaped before the haircut.

"And everything to do with losing his power in some way." Grayson thought about the other victims. "I wonder if we can find a way to figure out if they wore some type of bright clothing that caught his attention."

"The team has been struggling to find a link between the victims other than the obvious ones of height, weight and hair color," she said. "This might be it."

Grayson might be digging here, but a small detail could lead to a trail that could find a killer. It sometimes came down to the little things in an investigation.

"It wasn't difficult for the perp to move around in the group," Abi observed. "And I checked time stamps on the pictures. There was no sign of him in anyone's pictures until long past midnight."

"Makes sense to go to a party that's already rocking," he pointed out. "Easier not to get noticed that way since, based on the pictures, this was a drinking crowd."

"There had to be someone sober at the party," she said.

"We can check the reports to see if anyone came forward as a designated driver last night," he mentioned as they reached the neighborhood. "At least we can retrace part of the perp's steps."

"What about the home's occupants?" she asked. "We should knock first. You never know when someone will sneak up on you with a shotgun in a small town like this."

"True," he said. "Keep your badge visible too."

"It's clipped on my belt, as usual," she stated. "But that's a good point. The faster we can identify ourselves as law enforcement, the better." She paused for a minute. "You don't think he'd come back to the site, do you?"

"The perp had to take off in a hurry," Grayson stated. "Which means he might have left something behind."

"The deputies on the scene would have collected any evidence," she reasoned. "We probably should have asked to see it."

"There will be pictures in the files," Grayson said. "We can get our bearings before we ask for anything individually."

"Good point," she said on a sigh. "But this guy is smart. He has already killed five times and my guess is that he's getting smarter each time, not the other way around. There's more attention on campuses now but I wonder how much that will stop him. Or if it will at all." She paused as a thought seemed to be bubbling up to the surface. "What if he hid something nearby?"

"Good logic right there," Grayson said, impressed. "He might have tucked a bag behind the garage or even in a neighbor's yard."

"Then he would have had to have scouted out the area a little bit to make certain there were no dogs that could alert folks to his presence," she continued along with the line of thinking.

Which meant he was most likely at his next location, starting the process all over again.

Chapter Ten

Abi pulled her badge from her belt clip and palmed it as Grayson knocked on the door at 365 Armstrong Court. The small home had empty beer cans strewn in the fenced-in front yard. There was a trash can that overflowed to one side of the concrete porch. Grayson stepped back so Abi would be seen first. Everything Grayson did was deliberate, she'd noticed, so this move was meant to disarm the person on the other side of that door. Make them feel more at ease. Being tiny had its bonuses when it came to putting others at ease. Unfortunately, perps underestimated her, which meant they were more likely to fight.

A young man answered on the second round of knocks. His wide-eyed gaze immediately snapped to Abi's badge.

"We're sorry to bother you this late in the evening," Abi started. "I'm Marshal Remington and this is Agent Chisolm."

"Aiden Harker," the young man said, keeping the door cracked. He looked to be in his early twenties. His curly brown hair was a little too long. He stood maybe five feet nine inches and had a small build. He wore a wrinkled T-shirt and baggy sweatpants. His panicked expression said he was likely still reeling after what had happened in his backyard.

"We realize other law enforcement officials have been here, but we'd like to request permission to be on your property to assess the situation for ourselves," Abi stated.

"You can do whatever you want," Aiden responded without hesitation. "Just please find this person."

"That's what we're working on," Abi said. "We shouldn't take more than fifteen to twenty minutes."

"Do you want me to come outside?" he asked.

"No," Abi answered. "We're okay working by ourselves." She thanked the polite kid before stepping off the porch, turning on her cell's flashlight app, and walking through the front yard in search of anything out of the ordinary. "There's nothing here."

"No, there isn't," Grayson stated as he moved around with his own light.

"Local law enforcement would have walked all over the backyard, so footprints won't help us," she stated.

"It's still helpful for me to put myself into the mindset of the perp," Grayson explained.

She nodded, thinking the same thing. It was the way she liked to work. And she lacked confidence the reports would tell them much because she would have received a text or phone call if something important had turned up. Reading them later was solely about digging for nuggets of gold that might have been overlooked. Some things didn't mean much in isolation but put them together with other things and a picture emerged.

Being out in the field, examining the scene and every possible piece of evidence had always given her an edge.

Interviewing Aiden was unnecessary because he'd been just as drunk as everyone else. He has been interviewed this morning not long after Max had been found and the young man remembered nothing. He'd granted access to his pictures immediately. His house was a regular party spot and he, as host, supplied alcohol to minors. Local law enforcement would have to figure out how they wanted to deal with him. Much of his cooperation most likely came out of guilt for Max and to save his own skin with law enforcement who could prosecute if they desired.

That, however, wasn't Abi's concern. Her only focus was finding the bastard who was looking to make someone his seventh target.

She and Grayson walked along the chain-link fence around to the backyard. Unsurprisingly, no dogs barked as the two of them made their way around the area. Abi crouched low to study the backyard. There was a wooden bar that looked like someone had made it from scratch. It was old and the wood wasn't in great condition after being exposed to the elements for years, but it was sturdy enough.

Based on her memory of the photos, she envisioned a yard bustling with young people who were dancing, spilling drinks all over themselves and others while others stood on the edges of the makeshift dance area and talked over the music. She retraced the steps of the killer, best as she could, based on the evidence they had so far. And then reenacted the chilling moment where a gloved hand come up and hovered over Max's drink—a drink that was raised in the air.

From here, the perp must have been watching for…how long? A minute? Two? The bright yellow shirt could have made Max a target. Aiden could have easily been the target with his dark hair and height. She wondered how much he'd been told about the situation and if he knew how easily this could have been him instead of Max? Black hair, or some variation thereof, made up more than 80 percent of Americans. Brown was the next most popular, coming in at roughly 11 percent. If those numbers held and there was a hundred people here in this yard last night, there would have been eleven candidates. Narrow that down based on height and the number would shrink.

Aiden would have been just as likely a target, so why Max?

The bright yellow shirt?

By his own admission, he kept to the perimeter of the party. Was Aiden in the center of it all? In the house? He'd banned everyone from coming inside due to carelessness with their drinks.

Was Aiden inside at the time the perp was out here picking his prey? An icy chill ran up her spine. This seemed like a good time to remind herself that going into the mind of a serial killer would always be creepy. It would always make her stomach turn and her skin cold. But there was a reason she put herself through it—to save lives. She switched gears to remind herself of the college students who were blowing off steam, making memories here. Their smiling faces, the group dancing was a way of connecting and dealing with the demands of tests and sometimes difficult classes or professors. Of course, in her mind's scenario they were all of legal drinking age. Not the case in reality, considering Max and many of the others who looked barely out of high school in the pictures.

Why college students?

"At some point, Max must have talked to the perp," Abi said to Grayson. "Right?"

"I was just thinking along the same lines," he admitted. "We should ask Aiden where he spent most of the party because he was just as good of a candidate as Max based on looks."

"Agreed," Abi said, moving back toward the front yard. She'd seen all she could out here. The homes on either side had the college-student decor of trash cans filled with empty beer cans and bottles along with kegs.

This whole street was most likely inhabited by college students, who were all part of the party scene. There was one way to find out, though. Go door-to-door.

Another thought struck. If the perp had ridden into town on a motorcycle, wouldn't someone have seen him?

Not necessarily. Gas stations were pay at the pump. A helmet could have kept all of his head and most of his face hidden. He could have worn leather, which was common among the motorcycle set. It was chilly enough to get away with a leather jacket. So it was entirely possible he swooped into town unseen and without having to interact with anyone.

What about food?

If he stayed here very long, wouldn't he have to eat? Would he pack something and leave it on his motorcycle? He could have strapped something to the back. Also, some motorcycles had compartments.

A frustrated sigh slipped out.

Grayson reached out and placed a hand on her shoulder. His touch sent rockets of electricity firing throughout her body as warmth settled over her with the force of a tsunami.

This man's touch impacted her entire nervous system, and her body wasn't exactly being subtle about its reaction.

"We'll find him," Grayson reassured her. The man had a sixth sense when it came to saying what Abi needed to hear in a particular moment.

She had no plans to give up before the bastard was behind bars. But would they find him before another life was lost?

GRAYSON KNOCKED AT Aiden's door one more time. The door opened almost immediately.

"We have a quick question for you," Grayson said to Aiden now that the young man seemed to have calmed down a notch.

"Okay," Aiden said. "I'm more than willing to cooperate. Ask me anything."

"This might seem like an odd question," Grayson started.

Aiden's lips compressed into a frown as he nodded.

"Can you show us the shirt you wore at the party last night?" Grayson asked.

"Yes," Aiden said, his face twisting in confusion. "I-uh-yes, I remember now." He disappeared before returning with a classic gray Old Navy T-shirt.

"Thank you," Grayson said. "That's a big help."

Abi stepped forward. "One more thing, would you mind walking us through where you were during the party?"

"The backyard," Aiden supplied.

"Can you be more specific?" Abi continued.

"Do you mean actually walk you through where I stood every moment because I had been drinking and I might not remember every step I took," he stated, crossing his arms over his chest to stave off the chill as he stood with the door open.

"If you could just give us the general area, that would be sufficient," Abi clarified.

"Do you want to come in and walk through the inside?" Aiden asked.

"That would be fine," Grayson answered.

The door opened wider, and Aiden backed away to allow space for them to walk inside. Abi walked inside first. Grayson followed into the living room. Wood floors creaked. Nails stuck up at odd angles from the old flooring that hadn't been attended to in far too many years. If these walls could talk, Grayson figured they would have plenty of stories to tell considering this place had the look—barely any furniture and he wouldn't dare sit down on the stained sofa—and the smell—stale pizza and beer—of a place that was rented solely to college students. The flooring was sloped. The living space small. A desk in one corner had a laptop on it and not much else. Notebooks like the ones he'd had to use were a thing of the past, replaced by technology. It made for less clutter, he had to give it that.

The kitchen had a fridge, an ancient stove with pots stacked on top of it, a sink with very little counter space. A small table with folding chairs sat to one side of the room.

Aiden led them straight to the yard and onto the concrete porch out back. He didn't bother to put on a jacket as he shivered, crossing his arms over his chest once again the minute he stepped outside.

"I mostly sat here." He pointed to the edge of the small concrete porch that was nearest the keg. "I was guarding the back door so no one slipped past me and destroyed the inside. I'd like to get my deposit back when I move at the end of this year."

"Did you find a new place?" Abi asked.

"Graduating," he offered. "If I can pass all my classes and don't get kicked out after this happened." A look of embarrassment crossed his features. "That makes me sound like a jerk. Max is a friend and I hate what happened to him, especially since it was here." He involuntarily shivered. "This whole thing creeps me out." His gaze darted around the fence line.

It was possible Aiden could have been in the perp's sights. He fit the general description the killer normally went for. He was the home's resident. Reynosa could have watched him come and go for days without Aiden realizing.

The perp was smart for changing up his location every kill. No one knew which campus he'd move on to next. There were more than 140 four-year colleges in Texas. Almost 500 options if you counted community colleges and trade schools. Given the location where the bodies had been buried, the assumption was that the perp only targeted campuses in west Texas. Only time would tell if the assumption was correct. So far, the northeastern Texas colleges had been safe. How long would the sanctuary last?

"Did you stay here the entire time?" Grayson asked. "Or circulate?"

"I didn't go far," Aiden admitted. "Couldn't trust people not to sneak in the house." He shook his head. "I knew I should stop throwing these parties. It's senior year and I'm too close to graduating to mess up my life."

There was a chance he was saying this because he was trying to get out of being arrested for allowing underage drinking to occur. But there was a sincerity to this young man's voice that was laced with regret. Grayson believed Aiden would probably blame himself for a very long time. It could have been so much worse.

"What happened here wasn't your fault," Grayson said reassuringly. "I'm not saying that you have no responsibility for the underage drinking. That is between you and local law enforcement."

"I deserve to go to jail," Aiden said. "My parents told me not to say anything until they sent a lawyer, but I didn't listen to them."

"What do your parents do for a living?" Grayson asked.

"They're lawyers," Aiden supplied. "I should know better." He waved a hand around the yard. "Right?"

"You're young, Aiden," Grayson pointed out. "This won't be the last mistake you make in life. But what happened to Max is not your fault."

"He could have died," Aiden argued. "I read the news…"

His voice trailed off like he couldn't find the words. Grayson wondered how much local law enforcement had condemned Aiden for the party. *Don't have the party and there wouldn't have been a crime* couldn't have been more off the mark but he could see someone like Thad Carlson making the statement.

"Still not your fault," Grayson said, a little more sternly this time. "You couldn't have known what was going on. Kids host parties around college campuses all the time. I'm not encouraging you to bring underage drinkers here." Grayson put his hand on Aiden's shoulder. "We've all done things we look back on and wonder what we were thinking. What happened here, though, is like lightning striking on a sunny day in New Hampshire. It's not typical and there is no way you could have predicted it."

Aiden's nod was slow, which meant at least some of Grayson's words were sinking in.

"I've been doing this job for a long time, Aiden. Believe me when I say there's nothing you could have done to stop someone in this town from becoming a target," he continued.

"He's right," Abi piped in. Grayson appreciated the show of support. "Don't blame yourself for what happened to Max. There are so many factors outside your control that led to what happened to him."

The argument was taking hold as Aiden's jaw relaxed some of its tension.

No one would know without interviewing the perp if Aiden might have been the original target. The bright yellow shirt Max had worn along with the fact Aiden never left the area right around the porch could have been factors in the perp's decision. As sly as this one was, Grayson doubted the perp would expose himself by leaving the perimeter.

"Did you meet anyone, by chance, who had a visible mole on their neck?" Abi asked as the conversation was winding down.

"No," Aiden confirmed after a quick headshake. "Not that I can remember anyway."

"If you should talk to anyone, especially a man with a mole, in the next few days, would you give me a call?" Abi asked.

"Yes, of course," Aiden stated. "Let me grab my cell so I can get your information."

He disappeared into the kitchen, returning a few moments

later as Grayson looked out into the darkness. There were lights strung in a V, coming from the structure over the small back porch extending to the back fence where poles kept the lights high enough in the air not to interfere with the makeshift sixteen-by-sixteen dance floor.

As Aiden and Abi exchanged information, Grayson asked the young man to flip on the lights. He still hadn't figured out how the perp managed to talk Max into leaving. So far, there were no pictures of anyone being carried out.

The lights came on, brightening the backyard significantly.

"How well do you know Max?" Grayson asked Aiden.

"As well as anyone can know a freshie," Aiden said, then corrected, "freshman."

"Was he a frequent partygoer?" Abi asked, catching on.

"I'd say he was a regular," Aiden stated.

"How about drug use?" Grayson continued.

"I don't know," Aiden said as though trying to recall. "Drugs are banned at my parties because I'm not into that." Grayson believed the young man. When someone lied, there was usually a tell. Aiden would have to be an experienced liar not to give himself away or at least cause some doubt in Grayson's mind. "I can't recall ever hearing anything about him asking for drugs and I definitely don't remember him showing up looking high."

Drugs would have been an easy explanation for how someone could pull Max into the shadows. Plus, Max had been evading the truth when Abi had asked him about drug use.

Could a drug deal be the way the perp lured his targets out of the party once he dropped a drug—unbeknownst to them—into their drinks?

Chapter Eleven

Frustration niggled at the back of Abi's mind. What was she missing?

After reassuring Aiden that what had happened to Max wasn't his fault, she thanked him for the information and asked him to get in touch with her if he saw a male with a neck mole around town.

Local law enforcement hadn't located anyone on a motorcycle in the area, and the perp was most likely long gone by now. Tension mounted with each passing hour because the bastard was already working on his next target. Abi knew it to be true and could feel it in her bones.

As they walked to Grayson's vehicle, she bit back a yawn and said, "It's late and we still need to stop by the garage."

"What about going back to grab a few hours of sleep?" Grayson asked, studying her as he walked her over to her vehicle. "I'll follow you back to the motel."

Abi bit down on her bottom lip, then scraped her teeth across it. Sleep sounded good right now. Her ability to think would be impaired if she kept pushing to stay awake. The killer would need time to regroup anyway. "Go ahead back to the motel." From the corner of her eye, she saw movement across the street from behind the houses leading in the direction of the garage.

With his back to the garage, Grayson must have read her based on her expression, because he turned so fast it made her head spin. Issuing a curse, he took off running. Abi easily passed him before they managed to cross the street.

Pushing her legs, she bolted toward the spot where she'd last seen the figure in between two houses. Pumping her arms, she ran as fast as she could, a burst of adrenaline aiding in her stride.

The dark figure easily hopped fences. He was four houses down, then five before she knew it and he kept going. From this distance, it was impossible to get a sense of height and weight, especially with the baggy clothes he wore. He was a runner, though. No mistaking that.

Their assumptions that the killer had left the area were blown out of the water if this was him. It made sense that he'd be back if he'd left something near the garage. Or was one of those animals who liked to hang around his crime scene. Some even joined a search for the missing person they'd killed. It was one of the reasons pictures or videos were requested by law enforcement at large gatherings or parks where youth sports were played, when a crime occurred. A perp could come across like someone who wanted to help.

It made Abi's stomach turn.

The runner hopped a back fence, heading in between a pair of houses. At this rate, he would disappear before she could reach him. Instead of following, she made a left and hopped the back fence. If she could see which direction he went, she had a hope of catching up to him.

Grayson's heavy breathing meant he was coming up from behind. Good. She wouldn't run off half-cocked without her backup this time. *Fool me once, shame on you. Fool me twice, shame on me.*

With Grayson close enough behind her, Abi rounded the house and turned to her right. Cars lined the street, but the perp was nowhere to be seen.

Had she lost him?

Half a dozen curse words fought for center stage as she ran into the middle of the street, scanning both sides. She pulled her weapon from her holster as Grayson reached her. With one look at her and a quick glance, he was caught up to the situation.

Grayson motioned toward the right-hand side of the street and then waited. He wanted to take that side. Abi gave him a thumbs-up, then she moved to the left. As near to the vehicles as they could be, they started walking. The road was eerily quiet. Abi didn't like this one bit. This kind of situation was dangerous. The perp could be anywhere, including inside a vehicle.

He wouldn't be this close, though. No, he wouldn't circle back toward them. Would he?

Other than a streetlamp clear at the end of the street, it was dark. No porch lights were on. A few of the houses had windows boarded up. There was enough of a chill in the wind to remind her this was late October, and she could do with a coat. Without one, however, it was easier to run.

Step by step, she and Grayson made their way toward the streetlamp. The perp had cut through the houses about halfway, whereas she and Grayson were only roughly one third of the way up the street.

The ease with which this person lost them made her think he might be local. Or someone who grew up here. Spent time here at some point in his life. Could he have gone to college here?

Another car down, tension pulled Abi's muscles taut as she took another step closer. The perp could have gone inside one of the homes. He might be looking out a crack right now.

Steady.

Considering the possibilities had kept her alive this long. She and Grayson would have to call for backup before going inside one of the boarded-up homes. Taking time to make the call right now would give away her location and allow the assailant to move farther away if he was still on the street.

She and Grayson could work this together. Once they reached the streetlamp, she would call it in if there was no progress. The thought of this perp getting away tightened the tension.

As Abi took a step, a figure jumped out in front of her roughly ten cars ahead and pointed a weapon.

"US marshal, halt," she shouted with authority.

The perp fired a shot.

Abi didn't have her Kevlar on. A second later, she felt cold liquid on her left shoulder. She'd been hit? Her brain denied reality.

Ducking behind a vehicle for cover, Grayson identified them as law enforcement before firing a shot.

"Stop! Help!" The frightened voice belonged to a teenager. There was no way this could be the person they were looking for.

"Put your hands up where I can see them," Grayson instructed. His training dictated he defuse the situation. He wouldn't run to his wounded partner.

Abi checked her shoulder. Shouldn't she feel different? Wasn't she losing blood? Instinct had her touching the spot where she'd felt impact. There was liquid all right. But unless she'd started bleeding green blood, the person who shot her hadn't used a real gun.

"It's a paint gun," Abi shouted. "I'm fine."

She peered around the vehicle in time to see the kid step out from in between two cars, hands high in the air.

Grayson had to treat the situation as if the gun was real. "Slowly, and I mean slowly, lower the weapon until it's on the ground."

The kid did. "I'm sorry. I didn't know. I thought you were someone else." He bent down and set the weapon down.

"Kick it far away from you," Grayson stated, moving closer with his gun still drawn. This wasn't the time to take chances.

Abi never understood why paint gun makers made them look so real. It was impossible to tell them from an actual weapon. Not all teens were smart enough to realize a law enforcement officer wouldn't be able to tell the difference. In her own hometown, a thirteen-year-old boy had been shot by a deputy after aiming a realistic-looking paint gun at the law enforcement official. She'd been in high school when the tragedy happened.

Grayson had the kid bent over a vehicle and was patting him down to ensure he had no hidden weapons. Abi took that moment to call the sheriff and report the encounter.

Sheriff Benton promised to have a deputy on the scene in ten minutes or less.

Abi joined Grayson when they were certain any threat had been neutralized. "What do you think you're doing out here shooting at a US marshal?"

"I'm sorry," the boy who looked to be fifteen years old said as tears streaked his cheeks. "I wasn't trying to hurt anybody. Just having a little fun."

On the hood of the vehicle, there was a knife and a small bag of weed along with a pipe and lighter. The kid had dug a deep hole and Abi wasn't buying the tears. He might be sorry he got caught but he wasn't truly sorry.

"What are you doing out here at this hour?" Grayson asked. It was getting late, exhaustion was settling in as adrenaline faded, and Abi felt bone-tired.

"Hanging out," the teen said. He was face down on the vehicle with his hands clasped behind his back.

"What's your name?" Grayson asked as Abi inspected her shoulder. Sure enough, it was green paint.

She retrieved the paint gun for evidence. The kid was in more trouble than he realized. Or maybe he knew based on the way he was pleading.

"Riley," he supplied.

"Do you have a last name, Riley?" Grayson continued.

"Kline," Riley stated with a shaky voice.

"Do you know how much trouble you're in?" Grayson bit out.

"No, sir," Kline said. He wore baggy sweatpants and sweatshirt. He had on a black ball cap that he wore backwards.

"Do you think any of this is funny?" Grayson asked.

"No, sir," came the response.

"A deputy is on his way right now," Abi stated. "Soon enough your parents will be called in."

The threat was meant to score a direct hit. Instead, Riley's mouth twisted.

"Good luck finding my mom," he said.

This wasn't going well.

"SOMEONE WILL HAVE to pick you up from lockup," Grayson stated, holding his frustration back. He had no idea what would possess a young person to pull a stunt like this one, especially since shootings like this made the news. Grayson might have ended this kid's life over a paint gun. Naturally, he thought about his own son. Would Collin miss his mother so much that he turned out like Riley? Grayson wouldn't be able to stand himself if that happened. Collin was a good boy with a big heart. Didn't that mean he would end up a good teenager? "You need to tell us what you're doing out here."

"I was curious," Riley said. "About the…thing."

"Attempted murder isn't a *thing* to be casually thrown around," Abi said sternly. She had an air of authority that demanded respect and an intelligent, calm demeanor that said she deserved it.

"No, ma'am."

"Then, what? Why would you come sneaking around here this late at night with no one else around?" she continued.

"I just… I guess… I wanted to see it for myself," he managed to get out. His voice shook. He was nervous. Innocent?

"You do realize you fit the description of the kind of person the killer likes to target," Grayson ground out. This kid could end up a victim, creeping around to get a look at a crime scene.

Riley drew in a sharp breath. "No way."

"Yes," Abi reinforced. "Brown hair. Around your height. Would you like me to tell you what he does to his victims before he kills them?" Abi was intentionally providing information to bring a dose of reality to the kid in the hopes he wouldn't pull another stunt like this one again. He needed a wake-up call, especially if he didn't respect his parents. Not that all parents deserved respect. Grayson hadn't met Riley's, so he couldn't make a determination there. Many perps had a bad start in life. It wasn't an excuse. Plenty of folks had a rough beginning and still didn't end up on the wrong side of the law. But every hardcore criminal he'd arrested had a story of abuse or neglect that dated way back to childhood.

The more Grayson thought about it, the more he realized this needed to be his last case. He should probably pull himself off now that he realized what he had to do. But he couldn't abandon Abi.

"Coming out here alone could get you hurt in other ways too," Abi continued. "Possibly shot. You should know there are plenty of people who sleep with a shotgun next to their beds. If any one of them saw a dark figure lurking around, they could shoot. Everyone's nerves are on edge since last night." Abi might be coming down hard, but he was sure she wanted to make an impression on the kid. Grayson would be doing the same if she wasn't, in the hopes they could save this teen from doing something that could get him seriously injured or worse.

"I'm sorry," the teen whined, sounding more like a child than a teenager. Was it an act?

Grayson once heard from a former CIA agent who specialized in deception detection that every time a teenager opened his or her mouth, they were lying. The audience had laughed. He imagined many had teenagers of their own or at the very least experiences with them. Looking ahead to Collin's teenage years, which he'd heard would come faster than he realized, he couldn't imagine the sweet, innocent child morphing into someone he didn't recognize.

A deputy arrived, lights and sirens off, as the teen started to beg to be released.

"I identified myself as law enforcement and you still fired a weapon," Abi said. "You won't get off easy for that."

All innocence drained from the teen's face, replaced with bitterness. "Bitch."

Grayson's hands clenched at his sides. Abi's jaw tightened.

The deputy exited the driver's seat and joined them, breaking some of the tension. Abi gave a statement followed by Grayson. The deputy handcuffed Riley as he spewed more venom. All signs of the innocent teen were gone.

"That kid should get an Academy award for acting so innocent when he initially got caught," Abi stated as she checked the paint on her shoulder. Thankfully, it wasn't anything more than a large green splotch. But it could have been so much worse. Would she have survived? Absolutely.

Still.

"Are you good?" he asked her.

"Yes," she said a little too quickly. "It's just paint."

An incident like this one could shake up an agent or, in

her case, marshal. Grayson had seen more than one decide to work desk duty after taking a bullet or coming close to one. Becoming aware of one's vulnerability could do interesting things to the mind, and mindset was everything while staring down danger.

"We can ride back to the motel in my car, if you would rather not drive," he offered. "We'll be back first thing in the morning anyway."

"Okay," she said. "We'll be joined at the hip."

If Grayson was going to think about the future and about the possibility of actually dating again, he would like to find someone intelligent, thoughtful, funny and beautiful. Someone like Abi.

Shoving the unproductive thought aside, he walked back to the sedan alongside Abi.

The drive back was quiet. Abi leaned her head back on the headrest and closed her eyes. It was past midnight on what had been a very long day.

"Let's go over the files," she said the minute he cut off the engine. "My room okay?"

He nodded.

"I just need a few minutes to grab a shower in—"

"You can do that in my room so we can keep the conversation going," she said. "It'll be more efficient time-wise."

"Then, I'll grab my bag and head over." If this day was going to keep going, he needed to wake up. Best way to do that was a cold shower.

"I'll keep my door unlocked."

Grayson made a beeline for his room, grabbed his bag and then paused at his door to look at his cell phone. There was a text from Martha with a sleepy pic of Collin that tugged at Grayson's heartstrings. After tonight, he wanted to hang on to all that innocence for as long as possible.

Knocking once on Abi's door, he got the go-ahead to come inside.

"Shower is all yours," she said. She'd washed her face, pulled her hair back, and changed into the sweatpants and shirt she'd had on before the sheriff's text. She was sitting on the bed closest to the door with her laptop in front of her.

"Give me ten minutes," he said before heading into the bathroom.

True to his word, ten minutes later, he emerged showered, with brushed teeth, and wearing sweats.

Abi's head was back, her eyes were closed, and her steady, even breathing said she was asleep.

Not wanting to wake her but also not wanting her to wake with a crick in her neck, he set his bag down and helped her underneath the covers. He put the laptop on the table where they'd eaten dinner and then took the second bed next to the bathroom, wanting to be here in case she woke up at three o'clock in the morning and wanted to get back to work.

Being here with Abi felt like the most natural thing in the world. He hadn't had this feeling since Michelle. Even then, it hadn't been this feeling of rightness.

Grayson couldn't risk falling for someone who didn't like kids. Collin had to be the priority.

This attraction had to stop here.

"Stay with me," Abi's sleepy voice shouldn't be sexy as hell. She patted the bed next to her.

Against better judgment, Grayson joined her.

Chapter Twelve

Abi woke to the sun peeking through the floral curtains and a sense of peace like she'd never known. She blinked her eyes open. Grayson was there. She was nestled into the crook of his arm, her right leg hitched over his left. Two layers of thick cotton kept them from touching bare naked skin to bare naked skin. But the heat pulsing between them caused the air to come alive, crackling with electrical current.

Reality was a hard bite because they weren't a couple and couldn't stay this way forever no matter how much her body craved more of his touch. An ache filled Abi's chest as she slid out from underneath the covers. She had a fuzzy recollection of asking him to join her last night after one helluva day.

Clothes on, no inappropriate boundaries had been crossed.

After freshening up in the bathroom, she put on coffee and grabbed a power bar from her overnight bag to put something in her stomach. She cleaned off the table following last night's pizza dinner. There were no leftovers, but the box wasn't the most pleasant smell first thing in the morning. Luckily, it was soon replaced with coffee. Much better.

Abi removed the box, taking it to the outside trash to get rid of the odor.

The sun was bright and the air crisp. All in all, the weather was shaping up to make it a beautiful day. In dark cases like this one, it was important to take a moment here and there to breathe fresh air and take in the warmth on her face. It was surprising how those little things could boost the spirit. Keeping up morale was important. Keeping a clear mind helped her come up with creative solutions. Staying away from a dark rabbit hole kept her sane and allowed her to do her job in the best way.

Between this case and the situation with her grandparents, she needed to find as many little moments as possible to get her through each day.

Speaking of her grandparents, she texted her sister for an update. The response came back immediately: No change.

No change meant they weren't getting worse. No change meant they weren't coding again. No change meant there was still a possibility of them waking up. What it didn't mean was they would have a meaningful recovery.

Abi thanked her sister for the update and then opened her laptop. She vaguely remembered falling asleep moments after she performed this same thing last night. The first update was on Riley from last night, who turned out to be fourteen years old, which was even younger than he looked. She could only hope he would wake up before he continued down a path that would lead him to jail down the road. Given his attitude, she feared the worst. Shame.

Next, she filtered through several reports that didn't tell

her anything she didn't already know about the case. Then, she opened a document and started taking notes to filter through the important details, like the bright yellow shirt and the order of the campuses that had already been hit in search of a pattern.

A report from Julie said she'd called all campuses and had sent flyers. Most had agreed to pin them up in prominent spots on campus. It was something.

Julie had had no luck with finding out if any of the other victims had been wearing bright-colored clothing.

"Good morning," Grayson said as he sat up and stretched. His sleepy voice stirred a place deep inside her that didn't need to be stirred with a coworker.

Abi smiled and did her best to force down the attraction that had a mind of its own. "Morning."

"When did you get up?" Grayson asked. "I didn't hear you."

"You were out," she said. "I haven't been up long, though. I didn't want to disturb you."

"Give me five minutes and I'll get up to speed," he stated as he threw the covers off and then headed toward the bathroom. Being here with Grayson felt a lot like stepping into the sunshine after weeks of cloudy skies.

She got up and fixed him a cup of coffee while the sink ran in the bathroom. By the time he emerged, she had a cup ready to go. "Here you are."

Grayson looked taken back. "You didn't have to do that."

"I didn't mind," she said as he took the offering. "I can't believe I fell asleep." She shook her head. "There's an extra power bar in my bag if you're interested."

He thanked her for the coffee and then laughed. Reaching inside his bag, he pulled out a power bar. "Like minds."

Abi smiled. She didn't want to notice how in sync they were. Leaving Grayson once this case was over was already going to be difficult enough.

Grayson studied her after joining her at the table and polishing off his bar. He took a sip of coffee. "You look rested."

"I was running on empty last night," she said. "Thanks, by the way, for tucking me in and staying with me." She'd never needed that before from anyone, so she was certain it wouldn't happen again.

"Not a problem," he said but his husky voice told a slightly different story. Was he as affected by her as she was by him? There'd been a few signs here and there, but she almost convinced herself she was reading too much into them. Maybe even seeing what she wanted to see versus what was there. But the sound of his voice and the look in his said the attraction was mutual.

Not that it mattered. They lived in different cities. He had a kid. They had different lives. And after this case, they would have no reason to talk.

Or, could they be friends? Stay in touch at least on a surface level? She cared about whether or not Grayson decided to move on or stay in law enforcement. She cared about his kid and the bullying. As a matter of fact, once this case was over, she would like to meet Collin and tell him that he was going to be fine. She wanted to tell him the bullying wouldn't last forever and that it might even motivate him to find something he was good at and loved doing. She wanted to tell him that it was okay to stand up for himself.

Glancing up from her screen, she realized Grayson was still studying her.

"A whole conversation just played out across your face," he said. "Want to talk it out with me?" He must believe the conversation had to do with the case.

"I'm just forming thoughts," she said, definitely not wanting to share what had just happened in her brain. "It's just flashes, really. Nothing to discuss yet." She moved on by giving him a quick update on Julie. "She's doing everything she can from behind a desk."

"It's a huge help," he said. "We don't have time or resources enough to visit each campus in person. Sounds like she's covering a lot of ground."

"Part of me wishes we had time to educate these young people on the dangers of binge drinking after looking at some of those party photos," she stated.

"Did you party in college?" he asked.

"I went to a couple, but the scene wasn't for me," she admitted. "Plus, I was trying to graduate in three years since I'd taken a lot of college-level classes in high school. I didn't want to drag out getting my degree."

"Driven and beautiful," he said before catching himself. "No offense."

"Did you just apologize for saying I was beautiful?" she asked with a smirk.

"I did but I'm usually more professional than that," he stated, straightening broad shoulders.

"Can friends say something like that to each other?" she asked. "Because we decided to cross that line yesterday."

"Friends can absolutely remind a friend that she's beautiful," he said, returning the smile now. "It's only unprofessional for coworkers to cross a line like that with a compliment."

"Good," she said. "Because I need more friends, not co-workers."

He closed his laptop. "What do you want to talk about?"

"CAN WE SHIFT gears from the case for a few minutes?" Abi asked.

Grayson didn't mind. "We don't have any new information to go on and I don't fully wake up until my second cup of coffee. It's a good time to think about something else."

"Now that we're friends, I just wanted to say thank-you on a personal level," she stated. "You trusted me enough to talk to me about your son and your career."

"You're smart, Abi. I knew you'd offer a good perspective."

"And you trusted me despite the fact I have way less experience on the job and in life," she said.

"Doesn't mean you're not beyond your years," he countered. A slight flush to her cheeks made her even more attractive. "Don't doubt it for a second. Some law enforcement personnel that you'll end up working with the longer you stay in the business will treat you like you don't have a brain because of your looks. Don't let them get inside your head. Your instincts are sharper than anyone else I've worked with in my long and storied career. You might not have as many years on the job, but you understand what it takes better than most."

She gave a slight nod. Did she believe him? Or still have doubts?

Or was he on the wrong track?

"Can I tell you something about your son?" she asked, switching gears.

"Yes," he said. He'd already told her that he trusted her judgment.

"I've never been a parent and, honestly, can't say that I ever thought I would want to be one," she admitted before quickly adding, "I'm sure your son is amazing, though."

"He is."

"Keeping in mind that I have no experience with parenting, I still believe that Collin is going to be fine no matter what you decided about your job," she surmised.

"What makes you so certain?" he asked.

"He has you," she said. "And you're an amazing dad."

The statement shocked Grayson speechless. It took a couple of minutes for him to gather his thoughts enough to form words.

"When it comes to my job, I know I'm good at what I do," he started. "But parenting is a whole different ball game. Some days it feels like I'm swinging at every pitch trying to get it right. Others, the bat connects and I make it to a base or two. And then there are those days where I'm striking out at every pitch." He paused. "Does that make any sense?"

"I get the sports references," she said with a reassuring smile. "I guess I just wish you could see this from an outsider's perspective. Take, for instance, my parents. My mom also died during childbirth."

Those words were an arrow to the heart. "I'm sorry, Abi. I've been talking about my wife and how she died in the same manner without knowing how that might impact you. If I'd known—"

"There's a reason I didn't tell you before," she explained.

"I don't remember anything about my own mother but hearing about Collin's, about how much she must have wanted him to be here, makes me think that maybe I'm not to blame for my mother's death. I didn't even realize I'd been carrying around that guilt until now." She took a sip of coffee before continuing. "But let me tell you, my father is nothing like you."

Grayson cocked his head to one side, wishing there was something he could say.

"He ditched us after Mom died and dumped us on our grandparents," she said.

"That's awful," Grayson said, his protective instincts jumping into action. "I honestly can't imagine any father doing that after he held his own child."

"Neither can any of us," she continued. "I'm the youngest of three children, in case I haven't mentioned that."

"I knew you had a brother, sister and cousins," he said. "I just wasn't sure how many of each."

"There's six of us in total," Abi revealed. "My sister is the oldest and I'm the baby. We have a brother, Duke, in between." She studied the rim of her cup. "Anyway, our father believed bringing up kids was too much work, so he took off and didn't visit. He didn't stay in touch by phone. We just suddenly didn't exist to him."

"The pain of losing a wife doesn't excuse shutting out those who need you most," he said as frustration any father could do that seethed.

"That's what I'm talking about, Grayson." She bit down on her bottom lip before continuing. "Your first instinct was to protect your son. You figured the best way to give him stability was to provide for him financially. Now that he's getting older and you feel like he might be missing you more or needing you more, you're contemplating quitting the job you love in order to be physically present for him. That's pretty damn amazing in my book."

Grayson had never thought about his situation in those terms. "Why is it so easy to focus on the areas where we feel like we're failing?"

"I don't know," she said, "but I can certainly relate."

"You deserve a better dad than the one you got," he said after a thoughtful pause.

"He has another family now," she said on a sharp sigh before lifting her gaze to meet his. "And I have no desire to speak to the man again. I did hear that he called to sniff around about any possible inheritance after the accident."

Grayson flinched. "What a jerk."

"Truer words have never been spoken," she agreed. "But we had our grandparents, each other, and our cousins. I had the best childhood growing up on a paint horse ranch. As far as reasons to complain go, I got a bum dad. The other people in my life more than made up for it." She took another sip of coffee. "Collin has you. And you care about that little boy more than anything else in the world. He'll be more than okay in life."

Those words caused emotion to well in the center of his chest, forming a knot. "I hope you're right because he deserves the world."

"A kid that adorable deserves you."

Some of the weight on Grayson's shoulders eased. "If it's any consolation, I'm willing to wager your mother loved you more than you will ever know."

"From what I've heard from others in the family, she

was an amazing person," Abi said, her eyes glistening with moisture.

"Then the apple didn't fall far from the tree," he pointed out.

"I hope I'm like her," she beamed.

"Based on what I've heard so far, you must have received your good qualities from her." He meant every word. "Your father is the one who is missing out, by the way. If your siblings are anything like you, he lost big-time."

Abi finished off her coffee after making eyes at him that said she agreed. Then came, "Do you think I could meet your son someday? It sounds like we have a lot in common and he seems like a great kid."

Grayson opened his mouth to speak but shock gave no words. His heart squeezed as an ache formed in his chest—a dangerous ache. One he couldn't afford to give in to while working on a case.

Abi had already been shot by a paintball. What if that had been the real thing?

Once a law enforcement officer saw the end of his or her career, sticking around put everyone in the vicinity in danger. Was Grayson a bad omen for this case?

Chapter Thirteen

Abi had never once considered what she would do if she was shot in the line of duty. So, the line of thinking was throwing her off now. "You said you and Michelle never discussed the possibility of you being injured or worse on the job. Why do you think that is?"

"Superstition, for one," Grayson admitted. "Michelle said she got into a wreck after waking up one morning worried about driving when she'd just received her license. She had to block those thoughts out to get behind the wheel again despite the wreck not being her fault. It drove home a superstition, though."

"After one time?" she asked. "I mean, we all had those concerns when we first started driving."

"Her mom didn't help matters," he said. "She told me that she had a premonition about Michelle's death. She refused to see the baby for weeks, saying that he brought on a bad omen."

"She sounds like a piece of work," Abi stated.

"Her intentions weren't bad, but the woman was afraid of her own shadow," he said. "She always made predictions that didn't come to pass."

"Throw a hundred theories out randomly and one or two are bound to stick," Abi reasoned. "I guess I get it, but I've never been one to hide and superstition feels like hiding."

"How so?"

"It's a way of not facing what might happen," she said. "Not that I want to stay awake nights dreaming up scenarios about how I might meet my end on this job, but ignoring the possibility isn't realistic to me. Facing it, to me at least, is more of a *I see you, risk, and I'm taking you anyway because that will make me train harder and become better at what I do.*"

Grayson paused. A slow nod came as he processed. "I like it. It's logical. Avoiding a problem never made it go away in my experience. I just didn't talk to Michelle about it because it made her uncomfortable. But this makes a lot of sense to me."

"The paintball could be a real bullet next time," she said. "I have to face that fact and also acknowledge that I made a mistake not wearing my Kevlar."

"The paintball is the reason I've decided to change careers," he said.

"Ride a desk?"

"Or something like that," he said. "I have a little money saved up. I might have to be a desk jockey for a short time, but I don't see myself doing that for a decade. Hearing about your grandfather's business got me thinking about starting something of my own."

"What would you do?"

"I don't know," he admitted with a chuckle. Chuckles shouldn't be so sexy on anyone. "But it's time to face the fact that I don't want to travel anymore, and I don't want to go to a job I can't stand longer than I have to. I might have to do that for a little while until I figure out the rest, but I have other talents."

"Sounds like you're headed in the right direction," she said with more than a hint of pride in her voice. "Doing something you love is important considering we spend so much of our lives at work."

"Exactly," he agreed. "Being assigned to this case has been good for me in ways I never could have anticipated."

"And you found a new friend in the process," she said.

"The friend is the reason the case has been good for me," he said so quietly she almost didn't hear.

Rather than get inside her head about the implications of a statement like that one, she refocused on the laptop screen in front of her. They needed to shift focus anyway.

After a few quiet moments where Grayson set up his laptop and made a second round of coffee, Abi asked, "What are we missing?"

"I wish I knew," he said.

"There's no pattern to the murders," she said after studying the locations and their order. "One minute he's to the south, the other, he's to the west. And then he stayed sort of in that area before striking again."

"I'm not picking up on anything either," Grayson admitted. "There are no new pictures with the perp in the background from the volunteers. No new statements. We've already gone over the ones we have."

"Sitting around waiting for him to strike again is the worst feeling," Abi said, issuing a frustrated sigh. "We should get dressed and head over to the garage. See what we can find there that might have been missed."

"I just closed the folder with the pictures from the deputy on the scene," Grayson stated. "It's a small space but the report wasn't as thorough as I would have liked."

"Let's do this," she said, closing her laptop. And this time, she wouldn't be caught unaware. She intended to wear her vest.

THE WINDOWS OF the oversize single-car garage had been boarded up. Jagged glass stuck up from the sill. Abi followed Grayson past the yellow crime scene tape, wondering if the teen from last night had gone inside too. A move like that could implicate him in a crime. Maybe not this one since he couldn't have gone to all the campuses or carried the bodies. Would he know about ketamine? The internet made it easy for kids to learn way too much, way too early. Not all information was good to have for young minds.

The cold cement floor was stained with motor oil. Was there any on Max's clothing? Where was Max's clothing anyway? They knew his shirt was bright yellow because of the pictures, not because the clothing had been found.

An old convertible that looked to have been pieced out for parts sat on one side of the garage. This must be where Max remembered being in the back seat. "Why didn't the deputy take pictures of this?"

"Your guess is as good as mine," Grayson said, shaking his head. Shoddy work allowed far too many criminals to run free. Every law enforcement officer came to their job with different talents. Being good at details, however, should be a job requirement.

"He mainly covered the outside," she continued. "I didn't see this vehicle in his inventory list in the report either."

"That tells us everything we need to know about his level of detail and training," Grayson said with more than a hint of condemnation in his tone.

Small-town law enforcement had a reputation for being lazy but that wasn't fair to most in Abi's experience. Did some need more training? She would definitely say yes to that. Were they downright lazy? Not usually. There was the occasional Thad Carlson who seemed to skate by for reasons she had yet to figure out but most, as far as she knew, were eager to do a good job and liked having the chance to work with larger agencies. Thad was a piece of work. He wasn't the last chauvinist she would come across. Abi knew how to handle herself with jerks like him. The problem was they got in the way of a good investigation sometimes.

That was unacceptable.

"Thad's signature is on the inventory report," she said after checking the file on her phone.

"Figures," Grayson stated with more of that disdain. "He probably headed here after you turned him down for a ride to the motel."

"A guy like him likes to insert himself where he does more harm than good," she said. "Wonder why the sheriff puts up with him."

"Could be a relative who needed a job," Grayson reasoned. "Sheriffs are elected, and we already know Benton hired his aunt to work in the office."

"True." She walked through the mostly empty space, checking for other items not listed on the report. In actuality, very little was listed. Did Thad miss these items out of laziness or negligence?

Grayson dropped down on all fours, checking underneath

the vehicle that was up on blocks. "Do you think the perp would've stayed here after Max escaped or gone after him?"

"Gone after him," she suggested. "I wish we knew how Max got away from him."

"Could have swung at the guy, connected, knocked him off of him and ran this way." Grayson reenacted the scene without getting inside the car.

Abi moved to where the perp would have fallen. Sure enough, a bucket that was tipped on its side looked like it had been knocked across the floor by someone. She got out her camera and started taking her own images. "Go through those motions again for the camera."

Grayson did as she stared at the screen to ensure she got a good video. A figure moved past one of the larger cracks.

"Grayson, someone is out there," she said to him before motioning.

He immediately pivoted toward the door and raced outside.

The squawk of a radio met her as she stepped into the cool air. Abi stopped cold. "Deputy Carlson, we were just talking about your report."

GRAYSON TOOK A step back, ready to watch a pro at work. Abi was a force to be reckoned with and he had a feeling Thad Carlson was about to be on her bad side.

The deputy's defenses came up as he practically sneered at Abi. *Wrong move, buddy.*

"What about it?" Deputy Carlson asked in practically a growl.

"I'm curious as to why a lot of inventory was left off the list," she stated. Abi spread her feet in an athletic stance as she seemed to stand taller than her roughly five feet two inches. Grayson smirked. He couldn't help it.

"I didn't see the relevance of some of the items," Deputy Carlson defended. "When I do inventory, I only mark what is important to the case." He spread his feet, mimicking her movements. Was he trying to establish dominance? *You are so lost right now, dude.*

Abi issued a grunt, but otherwise came across as unbothered. "What makes you think you know what is and isn't relevant to a case this early in the game?"

"Maybe your brain is still fuzzy from taking a face full of pepper spray," Deputy Carlson started. "So, I'll go easy on you, little lady. But you need to learn your place before—"

"Care to enlighten me?" Abi asked, maintaining her cool despite Deputy Carlson trying to bait her into an argument. "Exactly what will you do, Deputy? Because last time I checked, keeping an item off an inventory list that could be sold or used personally meant interfering with a federal officer's investigation." She took a step closer but didn't raise her voice. "Have you met my partner, Federal Bureau of Investigations Agent Grayson Chisolm?"

Deputy Carlson's cheeks turned a shade of red equivalent to a wildfire. The heat radiating from his glare matched the intensity of his expression. "Look here, little lady. I'm not about to—"

"What, Deputy? Have to explain yourself to an entity that you don't have an inside line on?" she quipped. "We already know about your special in with the sheriff. Do you really think the US Marshals Service cares the two of you are related? Or the federal government? Blood only gets you so far when you abuse your position."

Carlson's face turned pale. His jaw dropped. The man wasn't very good at hiding his reaction when he got called out.

Abi took another step toward him until they were two feet apart. Not close enough to be in his face but enough to let him know she meant business. Fists clenched at her sides, she was a ball of energy that could explode on the deputy at any second. Her voice, however, was a study in calm.

"Well, now, hold on there," Deputy Carlson's disposition flipped on a dime. Abi's dime. "Let's not get our panties in a bunch."

Abi leaned back like a cobra about to strike. "Word of advice, Deputy?"

Carlson nodded as sweat formed on his brow. His pulse must've kicked up, because he was breathing like he'd just sprinted across the street instead of walking slowly like he usually did. He started blinking rapidly, another telltale sign of guilt. Abi had hit on something that made the deputy uncomfortable. Nepotism? Squirreling away evidence on a crime scene instead of reporting it so it could be sold later? Used for personal gain? Or just used personally?

"Go on," Deputy Carlson said to Abi. His body language told a different story as he touched his belt for the third time in less than a minute.

"Look me in the face when you talk to me because my mouth isn't down here." She motioned to her chest area. "Drop the words *little lady* out of your vocabulary or you'll be brought up on sexual harassment charges. And, finally, never mention my undergarments when you address me. My name to you is Marshal Remington or ma'am. If you don't respect me or the badge, have a little respect for yourself.

Speaking down to a female colleague or making derogatory statements isn't flattering and could be cause for you to be forced to turn in your own badge. Now, you need to ask yourself an important question. Do you really want to take on the US Marshals Service or the Federal Bureau of Investigations?

The deputy's jaw dropped. He wasn't used to speaking to a female colleague who could hold her own. He closed his mouth with an audible snap. "Are you intending to make a report, ma'am?"

"About the evidence missing from the initial report? Absolutely. As far as the rest goes, mind your p's and q's and I'll consider giving you the benefit of the doubt this time." She stood her ground. "Be on notice that if I hear one more demeaning statement, I fully intend to file every possible complaint against you and your department. Understood?"

Deputy Carlson stood at attention. "Yes, ma'am."

"Now, do you want to clue us in as to why you left the items off the report?" she asked.

He leaned back on his heels. "Didn't think they were relevant," he said as he touched his belt again.

The man had just lied.

Chapter Fourteen

"What else didn't you 'think' was relevant?" Abi asked the man who'd tried to push every one of her buttons. His reaction to her line of questions, however, told her that he was lying. At this point, she needed to make certain he wasn't covering anyone else's tracks.

Did he have any links to the towns where the other murders occurred? Abi made a mental note to find out.

"Just what you saw there," Deputy Carlson stated. His demeanor changed and he treated her in a professional manner now. If nothing else, that was a win. Men like him were relics left over from a different time—and that time was up.

Was he involved in negligence or criminal activity?

One had a little more relevance to the case.

"Here's a suggestion," Abi started. "Why don't you go back through the garage and catalog every item? Then file an amended report to include the items you missed on the first go round?"

"Yes, ma'am. I'll do that right now." At least the deputy knew better than to argue at this point.

He waited for her to give the go-ahead before walking away and entering the garage.

Grayson moved next to her and said in barely a whisper, "Well done."

It meant a lot to hear him say those words. "Thank you."

"No one should have to put up with that kind of bias," he continued as they walked away from the garage. "I feel confident he'll watch his words moving forward. Future women will have you to thank."

"He was lying, though," she pointed out.

"I caught that too."

"Do you have a guess as to the reason?" she asked.

"Since you and I think along the same lines, I doubt I have anything more to contribute than you've already figured out," he conceded. "I went with covering someone's tracks, being too sloppy with his work, and wanting to use or sell the items off the list. Mainly the vehicle. Old cars like that can be sold for parts."

"And if there's no record of the vehicle, no one can trace it back to him," she said before issuing another grunt. "It's deputies like him that give small-town law enforcement a bad reputation."

"Couldn't agree more." Grayson pulled out his cell and typed in *Carlson* along with the name of the town. "I got a hit. Check this out." He tilted the screen so she could read it better.

Carlson Auto Repair.

"Hell's bells," Abi said. "Guess it didn't take a whole lot of detective work to figure out what the 'good' deputy intended to do with the convertible parts."

"It's big business to find out-of-stock parts for old vehicles," he pointed out.

"I'm guessing Carlson gets a cut on the back end," she said with a tsk. "He just gave us no choice but to report him."

"My thoughts exactly," Grayson said. "I'd offer to write up the report myself, but I think you'd enjoy it more."

"There's no room for criminals in law enforcement," she stated. Period.

"A small few sure make our jobs difficult as hell," he said on a frustrated sigh as they circled the perimeter of the garage outside of earshot.

"If we dig a little deeper, my guess is that we'll find out that the sheriff and the deputy are related." Abi didn't like nepotism. Too many times the relationship was taken advantage of by one of the parties. In this case, her money was on the deputy. She usually got a feel for people. The sheriff came across as honest. The fact wouldn't stop her from looking into his background to make certain.

As she surveyed the area, a bright yellow fabric dot caught her eye. "I might have spotted something." Before she finished speaking, she was already making her way toward the dot as Grayson walked by her side.

The dot led them to the back of an abandoned doghouse tucked in the back of the neighbor's yard next to a tall mesquite tree. This was the reason she always investigated a crime scene for herself. In the moment, it was too easy for a law enforcement officer to miss a critical piece of potential evidence. The shock of a crime like this happening could throw a decent deputy off. Having someone like Carlson around didn't help matters as he probably volunteered to take what he would consider the easiest job of walking the perimeter in search of clues.

The doghouse was in poor repair. Meant for a large dog,

it stood five feet high and had a shingled roof. It also had a few flaps at the door like most dog doors in homes did. The flaps were black rather than clear, which would keep out the sun but also made it difficult to get a look inside without touching them.

Abi pulled a pair of gloves from her back pocket and slipped them on while Grayson looked around on the ground for something to use to open the flaps.

He located a stick and then flipped on his flashlight app.

Abi crouched down and checked behind the doghouse. She took the bright yellow fabric piece—fabric was notorious for not holding prints so she wasn't worried about touching it—and then reached behind. "There's a large hole in the back of the doghouse. And the chain-link fence has a hole big enough to fit a box or bag through."

"Can you determine if the fence cuts are recent?" he asked, kneeling beside her.

"No," she admitted. Either the perp had cut the fence, or it was already there, and he'd taken advantage of it. "Coming from the back like this wouldn't leave obvious tracks in front. Most deputies would skim the area looking for the obvious." It was a smart move on the perp's part to come from behind, if that was the case.

"What about the fabric?" Grayson asked.

She held it out on her palm. "Not much more than a swatch." The piece covered her palm. It was ripped, not cut with scissors. Hastily?

"Souvenir?" he asked the second she thought it.

"I'll check the front," he said as she trailed a step behind.

Using his phone, Grayson turned the flashlight app on. The sun was high in the sky at this point but inside the doghouse would be dark based on the size of the opening and location of the sun overhead. Plus he wouldn't be able to see far without additional light. He crouched down and pulled the flaps back.

"Bingo," he said almost immediately.

"What did you find?" she asked. She'd been unwilling to stick her hand in the dog shelter from the back, considering all the spiders and who knew what else that might be crawling around inside.

"Hold on," he said as she joined him up front. He had to lean in so far that his torso disappeared. He came out with a beaten up camo lunch-type bag, using a stick so that he didn't get any fingerprints on the straps.

"We need something else to pry it open with," Abi said, immediately searching the ground for another stick to use. Even gloved, she didn't want to risk the possibility of wiping away any fingerprints that might be on the strap or bag.

The usual adrenaline rush that came moments before a big case might break wide open slammed into her. Pulse racing, she located a stick and controlled her breathing to slow, measured breaths to stop her hands from shaking.

Grayson caught her gaze. "Brilliant work so far, Abi." The way her name rolled off his tongue sent goose bumps up and down her arms, radiating through her body. The compliment from a seasoned agent meant the world.

"Thank you," she said. "Now let's see if we can find something inside this bag to stop the bastard before he kills again."

A meticulous killer like Reprehensible wasn't likely to leave an obvious trail. Not even now. Could they find a trace that could point them in the right direction? The tip line had been flooded with calls, according to one of the reports Abi read this morning. Not uncommon in a high-profile case like this one. Sorting through them to find a nugget of gold wouldn't be easy.

Could they catch a break here?

"Ready?" she asked Grayson.

"Let's do this," came the quick response.

Each used their stick to pry open the opening of the bag using opposing force.

Abi used her gloved finger to expand the opening. The triangle approach gave them a view to the contents.

Five fabric swatches of varying bright colors were the first things she noticed. "Souvenirs," she said under her breath.

"That's something we didn't know before this case," Grayson stated. "The bright colored shirt theory was on point."

"True," she agreed. "Should we dump the rest onto the ground?"

"Carefully," he said with a nod after making eye contact. "Since this was your find, why don't you do the honors?"

Abi took hold of the bottom of the bag before shaking it out gently. A small horde of protein bars fell out, all stuffed inside Ziploc bags. An unopened water bottle tumbled out from the bottom of the bag.

Abi turned the bag over. They opened it again with the sticks. A piece of paper stuck to the bottom of the bag, caught in the seam. She didn't dare assign too much meaning to it. "Could be nothing."

She made eye contact with Grayson. The look on his face made words unnecessary.

"I know," she agreed because they both knew one little object like this could be the puzzle piece they'd been searching for. Using the sticks as chopsticks, Abi pulled the paper out with the kind of precision used when someone was scared they might topple a Jenga puzzle over, causing all the pieces of wood to come crashing down around them.

With the makeshift chopsticks, Abi was able to pull the piece of paper out. It was an article from the *Daily Texan*.

Abi set the crinkled-up page on the ground. Using the sticks, she and Grayson flattened the paper out so they could read it.

"It's about him," she said with an eerie feeling. "What do you think the odds are that he's going to strike at UT Austin based on this?"

"I'd say it's time to check out of our motel, notify our supervisors and get on the road to Austin."

"UT is known for being a party school," she pointed out. "Even if we get there in time, how on earth will we figure out where he'll strike?"

"We can brainstorm ideas on the road," Grayson said as they meticulously placed evidence back inside the bag.

"Who do we trust with this?" Abi asked.

"No one here," Grayson decided. "We'll call this in once we get on the road to Austin and see who we can get to either meet us or tell us where a good drop spot would be. I don't trust anyone in this department to handle evidence properly after what we saw in the garage."

"Agreed," Abi said as they pushed to standing. With the stick looped through the bag's strap, they made a beeline toward their vehicles. "I'll follow you back to the motel."

"Sounds good," Grayson said. "You take the evidence since this was your find."

Pride brought a smile to her face that faded too quickly. It was a shame Grayson was leaving fieldwork. She could learn a lot from someone like him, not to mention the fact they made a good team.

Friends would have to be enough.

Abi reached her vehicle, and then pulled out an evidence bag so as not to taint anything. After placing it inside with the kind of care usually reserved for handling expensive and breakable artwork, she set it down on the floorboard of the passenger side.

She tried to start her engine, but nothing happened. *What the...?*

Abi hopped out of her vehicle after hitting the button to pop the hood. She exited as Grayson caught on, joining her.

One look inside had him swearing.

"What is it?" Abi asked, scanning under the hood. And then she saw it too.

Chapter Fifteen

"Your battery cables have been cut," Grayson said to Abi.

"What the actual hell?" she asked. The question was directed to no one in particular. "I'll send a text to the sheriff and see if he can lean on the teenager from last night. Riley might have pulled something like this."

"He was my first thought too, but to what end?" Grayson asked.

"Other than being a twit and not realizing the consequences of his actions?" she asked. Her frustration made her cheeks flush. Anger did that to her the same as embarrassment, he'd noticed.

His first thought might have been Riley but how would the kid know which car was hers? "Find out where he lives, would you?"

Abi already had the sheriff on the line. She asked for Riley's home address then rattled it off to Grayson. He pulled up the map feature on his phone and input the address from memory. The place was several blocks away. It would have been impossible for him to watch the investigation unfold from inside a window as Grayson suspected might have happened.

Deputy Carlson stepped out of the garage. He glanced over, stopped. Then, must have decided it was worth the walk over to find out what was going on. "Everything all right over here?"

"Marshal Remington is having car trouble," Grayson supplied, wondering if her car would be towed to his relative's repair shop.

"I know a guy who can help," the deputy said.

"Any chance this person is a relative of yours?" Grayson asked.

"My cousin owns a place," Deputy Carlson stated. "He can tow the vehicle and fix the li… Marshal Remington right up. No charge."

"The Marshals Service would cover any cost associated with the repair," Grayson pointed out. "Your offer to help is much appreciated, though." Was the man trying to redeem himself because he'd been called out over his shoddy work? Was he trying to butter them up? On a hunch—a hunch honed by years of field experience—Grayson asked, "You didn't happen to see any suspicious person or persons around Marshal Remington's vehicle while working out here, did you? I know it's a long shot but just in case."

Deputy Carlson touched his belt. "No, sir. I did not."

Damn liar.

Was the deputy trying to force Abi to use him for a ride? Was he that desperate to get her inside his car for some alone time? Did he think this was appropriate?

Grayson already had the answer to that question. When it came to the opposite sex, the deputy had no idea how to treat them as equals. He didn't view women as colleagues.

And, based on his actions so far, thought all he had to do was get Abi alone for five minutes to charm her.

Carlson walked a narcissistic line bordering on criminal. Then again, his actions so far said he wasn't afraid to bend the rules for his own gain.

Going by the narcissistic line of thinking, Deputy Carlson could have cut the battery cables himself to punish Abi for not taking him up on his offer. This was the type of guy they were looking for if pushed to an extreme. Reprehensible didn't differentiate between sexes, though. He was looking for a type. He was looking for bright clothing.

This thing with Deputy Carlson needed to be shelved for the moment so as to be not distracted from the case. Studying the man right now, Grayson had his answer. Carlson had either cut the lines or had had them cut to get back at Abi. Plain and simple.

Grayson would call the sheriff on the road to get a feel as to whether he knew what kind of deputy he'd employed. If the sheriff was in on it, which Grayson doubted, he'd ensure the department underwent an extensive federal investigation. For the moment, however, he would feel out the sheriff.

Walking away without reporting Deputy Carlson's actions wasn't an option.

Shifting gears for the moment, Grayson thought about the motorcycle. Since he'd been in town, he'd counted half a dozen. Most were easy rider types. He hadn't seen any crotch rocket types.

If he had time, he would stick around and interview anyone who lived near the highway. He would check in with businesses too, just to see if anyone saw a male on a motorcycle. Pulling records to find out how many Class C licenses belonged to males in Texas would be like looking for a needle in a haystack. It would waste precious time—time that was running out with each tick or tock of the clock.

"Don't worry about Abi's vehicle," he finally said to Carlson. "I'm sure the Marshals Service will send a tow." He made a mental note to remind Abi to tell her supervisor not to allow her vehicle to be picked up by Carlson Auto Repair.

"Let me know if there's anything I can do to help," Deputy Carlson said.

"An amended inventory list is a good place to start," Grayson stated.

"I'll get that filed first thing," the deputy promised.

Abi had made two calls in the duration of Grayson's conversation with the deputy. The first had been to the sheriff. The second had been to her supervisor.

"How much of my conversation did you overhear?" Grayson asked.

"Pretty much all of it," Abi admitted. "The lying bastard."

"My thoughts exactly," Grayson agreed. "We'll deal with him later. In the meantime, what does your supervisor want you to do?"

"I asked if I could catch a ride with you to Austin," she informed. "Hope you don't mind."

"I'd prefer it," he said. "Makes it easier for us to talk on the road."

"I'll just grab my things out of here and then we can swing by the motel." She closed the hood and then started toward the driver's side. "By the way, I believe the sheriff has no idea what he's dealing with." She tilted her head toward Deputy Carlson, who'd slipped into the garage.

"I get the same impression," Grayson said.

"My supervisor is having a tow pick up my vehicle to have it repaired in a bigger city," she added.

"Good."

Grayson helped remove the last of the items from Abi's vehicle before she emptied the trunk. There was an arsenal of weapons back there including a shotgun and enough ammunition to last a week in a shootout.

"Ready to roll?" he asked once her vehicle was emptied and locked.

"Let's do this," she said, echoing one of his most used lines. The knot in his chest tightened at the thought of not working a case with Abi.

Or being able to talk to her on a whim.

Grayson realized he was in trouble when it came to the dark-haired, feisty beauty. He just didn't know how much until now.

FORTY-FIVE MINUTES AFTER climbing into Grayson's passenger seat to drive back to the motel, Abi claimed it once again for the next leg of their trip. The drive to Austin on US 87 S and State Highway 71 would take a little less than five and a half hours.

"How hungry are you?" Grayson asked once they'd been on the road twenty minutes.

"I could eat my shoe, but my stomach will kick back another power bar," Abi admitted with a laugh.

"Do you want to check for the nearest fast-food chain?" he asked.

Abi pulled out her cell, then muttered a curse. "How did I miss this?" A missed call from Crystal sent Abi's stomach churning. She immediately called back, noticing the call had come in more than fifteen minutes ago.

Crystal picked up on the first ring. "Hey."

"Good news or bad?" Abi immediately asked.

"Grandma Lacy opened her eyes and squeezed my hand," Crystal reported. "I immediately hit the nurse's button but by the time the doctor showed five minutes later, Gran was unresponsive again."

"What does that mean?" Abi asked.

"That this is going to be a roller coaster," Crystal stated on a heavy sigh. "The doctor explained that ups and downs like this one are not surprising. Recovery is generally not a linear proposition."

"Was this a good sign at least?" Abi asked, trying to find a positive thread to hang to on to.

"It's not a bad one," Crystal said. Clearly, her sister didn't want to set up false hope. Then came, "I'm sorry that I don't have better news. We're all hoping to get some kind of sign at this point."

"Sounds like we have reason not to give up hope," Abi said, trying to lift her sister's spirits. "Wish I was there."

"There's literally nothing you can do," Crystal pointed out.

"I could keep you company," Abi countered.

"Wade's been a rock," Crystal said. How had Abi so easily forgotten her sister was no longer alone? She'd been so stuck in her own head, in the investigation that she'd almost forgotten about her sister's fiancé.

A stab of jealousy mixed with happiness that Crystal had found the one.

"Wade sounds like a great person," Abi managed to say

with forced enthusiasm. She couldn't be happier for Crystal and Wade, but she would like to meet her future brother-in-law face-to-face at some point.

When this case is over.

"I think you're going to love him," Crystal said.

"Probably not as much as you," Abi said, forcing a smile she didn't feel. She wanted to be happy for her sister and she was, but most of her couldn't get past the stress of not being at the hospital. Guilt stabbed at the thought she could so easily block out everything but the case until she was reminded of it by her sibling.

"He's special to me," Crystal said. From the sounds of it, she was just as guilty of pretending not to be down about their grandparents.

"I'm glad the two of you found each other," Abi added. "You deserve a great partner, Crys."

"So do you," Crystal said, then quickly added, "Don't feel guilty about not being here right now. Okay. I was in the same shoes as you not long ago and I know how difficult a position you're in. Give yourself a break. Okay, Abs?"

Only her sister ever got away with calling her that. Vice versa, she was the only one who called her sister Crys.

Moisture gathered in her eyes at the thought of ending the call with her sister. Abi was not usually the emotional type, so they caught her off guard.

"Thank you for being at the hospital, by the way," Abi said, hoping her sister knew how much having Crystal there made it easier for Abi to focus on doing her job.

"I hope you catch the bastard you're after soon," Crystal said. "And not just because I want you home. Though I do."

Abi understood completely what her sister was saying.

They were both US marshals. Hell, the whole family worked for the Marshals Service. They all most likely had their grandfather to thank for that.

"He called again," Crystal said. The note of anger in her voice clued Abi in.

"Dad?"

"Yes," Crystal confirmed.

"What did he want?" Abi asked with a sour taste in her mouth.

"He's acting like he's concerned but I think Duke was right about the man fishing around to see if there's going to be an inheritance," Crystal said.

"That's up to our grandparents but the man doesn't deserve the time of day if you ask me," Abi said.

"He called Duke, not me," Crystal stated. "I'm with you on that one. If he called me, I would hit that block feature so fast his head would spin."

"We're on the same page there," Abi agreed. People could be real jerks. She thought about what Grayson had said when she told him about her dad. His reaction restored her hope in humanity.

But then Grayson was just good. His list of positive qualities grew by the minute.

"I better go," Crystal said. "Wade just walked into the lobby with lunch."

Food. Abi's stomach must've heard because it picked that moment to growl. "Eat. Rest. Take care of yourself." As stressed as Abi was by the situation, the case was a distraction. Crystal was in the thick of it. Caregiver stress was real.

"Which one of us is the big sister here?" Crystal teased. The words were meant to be playful but the undertone to her voice spoke volumes. Abi's sister was exhausted. "I'm supposed to be looking out for you. Remember?"

"I'll keep that in mind," Abi teased back. Her heart wasn't in the lightheartedness, and neither was Crystal's, but they were paddling hard, trying not to get sucked under by the gravity of their grandparents' long-term health concerns.

"I'll talk to you soon," Crystal said before exchanging goodbyes and ending the call.

"I couldn't help but overhear the conversation," Grayson said after a couple of minutes ticked by.

"I am right here," she responded with a small smile. It faded too quickly.

"I'm an only child," Grayson started. "The product of divorced parents who couldn't agree the sky was blue let alone any decision that had to do with me. My mom got so frustrated that she gave up fighting my dad. She gave him custody and I only saw her summers and holidays. She put on a brave face, but I could tell she never quite recovered from the divorce. It wasn't until years later that she told her side of the story. She was in her sophomore year of college when she got pregnant with me. She and my dad decided she would quit school to be a stay-at-home mom. It was harder than she realized. She felt isolated. They didn't have money while he finished school so she did everything she could to help. Nothing she tried took off, so she gave up and decided to be the best wife and mother. She put her heart and soul into being the 'model' wife and never felt so alone in her life. When she caught Dad cheating with the community college student they'd hired to babysit me for their date nights, Mom broke down. She put all her energy into fighting him for custody, which put her in the hole. Dad ended up marrying and divorcing my babysitter. They lasted a couple of years until she talked about expanding their family. For Dad, one kid was more than enough."

She noticed his grip tightened on the steering wheel when he mentioned his father.

"The reason I'm telling you this is because I just got to witness family when it works," he said, his voice had a raspy edge to it like a cloud filled with emotion that was about to burst into a rain shower. "Believe me when I say that I'm taking notes because that's the kind of unconditional love and support that I want for Collin."

Abi had to fight to hold back tears that were like race-horses lined up at the starting gate on race day.

Abi wasn't a crier.

And yet, tears spilled out anyway, streaking her cheeks.

"I'm sorry if I said something to upset you," Grayson immediately chimed in.

"That was the most beautiful compliment that I could ever receive," she said. "I guess I'm not used to it."

"You should be, Abi. You deserve the world."

Could Grayson give it to her when he seemed determined to move on with his life? Would he shut her out in the process?

Chapter Sixteen

Grayson reached across the console and took Abi's hand in his. One-handed steering was no problem on this stretch of highway, and that was easily accomplished with his left hand. The only concern was fighting the wind gusts. With a low-profile vehicle that was less of a problem. He'd done this stretch in a van once while interviewing a prisoner who was being transferred. That trip had him reaching for the van walls, praying they wouldn't end up in a death roll.

"The only gift of not having parents was having each other and our grandparents," Abi said.

"That makes me wonder who Collin has other than me," Grayson said.

"You're an amazing father, Grayson," she pointed out. "You're being too hard on yourself."

"Maybe," he conceded, not yet ready to agree.

"Look at Aiden," she continued. "That kid has it bad. He'd said his lawyer parents didn't care about him. They were more concerned with keeping him above the law than meeting his needs. When you're not thinking about this case, your mind is always with your son. The fact that you think about him at all in terms of his needs beats both of our fathers."

"I can't argue there," he said.

"Plus, you have us now too," she stated with a hitch in her voice. "We're friends, remember?"

The word *friends* was wholly inadequate to describe the mix of emotion swirling around in his chest like a dust storm. But it was a place to start.

"Your friendship means the world, Abi." He gave her hand a little squeeze, ignoring the electrical impulses shooting up his arm seeking an outlet as they exploded in his chest. He cracked a smile. He couldn't help it. The effect Abi had on him was something out of this world. As much as he wanted to hang on to it and see where it could go, he knew their time together would end. Then what? The occasional phone call? He was lousy at texting and even worse at keeping in touch if someone wasn't sitting right in front of him.

Could he change his ways for Abi?

Because she would be worth trying for.

AUSTIN TRAFFIC WAS a beast, as usual. While Grayson met up with his contact to hand off evidence from the crime scene, Abi figured this was as good a time as any to make a courtesy call to the sheriff before filing her report. She checked to see if the addendum had been filed by Deputy Carlson and found that it had.

"Sheriff Benton," he said, answering on the first ring.

Abi needed to feel him out first before dropping the bombs about his deputy. "Sheriff, Marshal Remington here."

"Yes, ma'am," he said, not sounding one bit the wiser about what went down at the garage. "How can I help you?"

"I visited the crime scene this morning and noticed there were many items left off Deputy Carlson's report," she said, throwing out the first piece of bait to fish around for what he knew.

"Carlson informed me that he realized he'd left important evidence off the initial report," Sheriff Benton said, an air of question marks in his tone as if to say, *why are you telling me this*.

"Sir, did he mention why he'd had the change of heart about what to include in the list?" she continued, not ready to give up her hand.

"Said he missed cataloging a few important items in the heat of the moment but circled back to make sure he'd done a good job since he knew this was an important case," the sheriff responded.

"He didn't mention running into me and Agent Chisolm?"

"No, ma'am. He did not."

"Or the fact that we were the ones who noticed the missing items?" she continued.

"No, ma'am." Now the sheriff sounded frustrated. "I apologize for my deputy's actions. He's not a bad pers—"

"I'm guessing he also didn't mention that one of the pieces of evidence he forgot to mention was an old convertible," she said, cutting him off. Deputy Carlson wasn't a good person. At a minimum, he was lazy.

"No, ma'am."

"I'm sure you're aware of the auto repair shop owner, who shares the last name Carlson," she said.

"I am," Sheriff Benton said as it seemed to dawn on him where she was going with this.

"Are you further aware of how much money can be made from selling rare automobile parts piece by piece or restoring an old vehicle?" she pressed.

The line went dead quiet.

"I'm calling to inform you because I didn't want to surprise you with the report I'm about to write up," she explained. "If Deputy Carlson had been honest with you about what happened this morning, I'd have more confidence he was trying to do the right thing."

Again, the line was quiet.

Then came, "This report you said you were writing up, will it contain all the information you just shared with me?"

"Yes, sir. It will."

"All right then," the sheriff said. "I'll place Deputy Carlson on administrative leave pending an investigation into this and past cases." He issued a sharp sigh. "Carlson has been requesting to work auto thefts for years."

"There's a pattern," she said.

"I appreciate your courtesy in calling before you filed the report," Sheriff Benton said. The man came across as trying to do a good job. Did he hire relatives? Yes. One of whom was fencing parts under the sheriff's nose? Yes. Was he too trusting? Probably.

He could have blown up at her or tried to flip the script. Instead, he owned up to the possibility he had a problem on his staff, and that was always a good sign.

"No problem," Abi responded. "You deserve a heads-up before this goes into the system."

"I'll take care of Deputy Carlson on my end," he committed. "He'll be handing over his badge and weapon in a matter of minutes."

"Just so you're aware, I could be filing sexual harassment charges on the deputy," she stated.

"My wife will string him up by his ears when she hears this," Sheriff Benton promised.

"I'll add a few of his remarks to the report and leave you to handle it how you deem necessary," she stated.

"After this conversation, I'll put him through the firing process and let the committee decide if criminal charges apply," the sheriff said. "Conduct unbecoming a law enforcement officer while involved with a cooperative agency is unprofessional. Deputy Carlson's actions won't be tolerated by anyone in this administration."

"I have every confidence you'll take appropriate action, sir."

They exchanged goodbyes before ending the call. Abi had a good read on the sheriff. Deputy Carlson was taking advantage of working for a relative. Distant cousin on his wife's side? Either way, judgment day was on the horizon for the deputy. She wondered how much more the sheriff would find once the committee started digging into Carlson's work.

Abi hit Send on the report at the exact moment Grayson showed up holding two coffees in his hands. She hit the button to roll down the window and took them both. The man was part angel.

He claimed the driver's seat. Before he started the engine, she gave him the quick and dirty rundown on her conversation with the sheriff and the fact she'd just sent the report.

"I believe Sheriff Benton isn't involved in Carlson's dealings," she said.

Grayson nodded after taking a sip of fresh brew. "Same here."

Abi was reassured by the fact she and Grayson were on the same page. His years of experience outnumbered hers by a decade. It gave her confidence she was on the right track with her career.

Or were they just twin flames?

Abi squashed the thought.

"I'd like to meet Collin," she surprised herself in saying as Grayson started the engine.

He sat there for a long moment, engine idling, not responding.

Meanwhile, Abi's heart pounded a drum solo inside her rib cage.

"I think Collin would like that very much," he finally said, causing her to release the breath she'd been holding. "Besides, you know more about me and my family than anyone else. You might as well take a front-row seat to our chaos." He cracked a smile that could melt Texas roads during a February ice storm.

"We might be close-knit, but I think you'll find just as much havoc in my family," she said with a laugh.

"Challenge accepted," he quipped.

"Good," she said. "Because I'd also very much like the rest of my family to meet you."

Abi held her breath again, waiting for a response.

"I'd like that," Grayson said without hesitation this time.

"Good," she said. "It's settled."

"I know your family is going through a tough time with

your grandparents," he interjected, killing the light mood. Was he about to let her down softly? "So, no rush on trying to schedule any get-togethers."

Yep. The air was being let out of the balloon. She didn't want to give herself away as to just how deflated the comment made her feel. "Yeah, sure. Of course. Nothing in the immediate future. We do have a lot on our plates."

"First things first," he said. "Let's find and arrest this bastard so we can get you home."

Why did Abi feel a wall come up between them when they'd been doing nothing but using a sledgehammer against one all day?

Had she been reading too much into their conversations? Because she felt an intimacy with Grayson that she'd never known with anyone else.

He was right about one thing, though. It was time to shift all focus to the investigation now that they were in Austin, fed and caffeinated themselves.

"What do I owe you for this?" she asked, holding up her latte.

"Nothing," he said, his tone steady and calm like he hadn't just jammed a safety pin in her balloon. "It's on the house."

"Well, I'm keeping a running total because I don't want to owe you anything once this case wraps up," she stated. "Next one is on me."

Grayson was quiet for a long moment. Contemplating?

She hoped he got the message because she wasn't kidding. Abi survived fine on her own. She didn't need anyone else's charity.

Period.

GRAYSON HAD NO idea what had just happened to shift the air in the cab of his sedan, but he made a mental note to circle back and ask about it later. "Either our perp plans to strike in Austin next or he is starting to save clippings of his notoriety."

"Agreed," came the one-word response.

"There are more colleges than UT in Austin," he said.

"The parties should cross over," she stated. "I've heard of kids driving down from Waco to attend a party at UT."

"Right," he said. "There will be a lot of ground to cover."

"I sent a text to Julie, asking her to alert administrations of an increased threat," she said. Her voice held no emotion when she spoke now, save for the cold chill to it. She was in all-business mode. It was probably good for the case even though he missed the warmth that had been radiating from her a few minutes ago. Being near Abi when she smiled was like stepping into the sun. If the sun was also sexy as hell.

"Here's hoping college kids listen," he said.

"She responded that UT promised to send an emergency alert text to its students about increased threats at parties," she said. "If I had to guess, he will target UT based on the evidence we have so far."

He didn't point out the fact Carlson's shoddy work could have caused them to lose pieces of evidence that could point them in a new direction. The article was their best bet, though.

"Are you surprised the perp didn't circle back to retrieve his belongings?" Abi asked.

"Not really," he said. "The area was too hot. I believe he will circle back at some point, though."

"It might be a good idea to see if the sheriff can reach

out to the property owners to see if he can place a camera there," she stated.

"Can't hurt," he said.

Abi picked up her cell and tapped the screen before sending a text. "Done." She leaned her head back and pinched the bridge of her nose. "Now what else can we do to prevent this bastard from being successful with his next target?"

"Austin PD is on alert, I'm assuming," he said.

"Julie would have thought to give them a heads-up," Abi informed him.

"With their cooperation along with campus security and university administration, we have a lot of eyes and ears in Austin."

Was it enough?

Chapter Seventeen

"Do you want to grab an early dinner?"

Abi wasn't in the mood to spend more time with the gorgeous, kind agent when she needed a nap. Plus, separation from Grayson would help her hit the reset button on her attraction. They had hours to kill before parties started rocking and rolling. All the other agencies had been notified of the heightened risk. And there wasn't much else they could do at this point. Besides, she could use the break before emotion tried to overtake logic again and convince her they had some kind of future together beyond casual friendship. "No, thanks. I'll just order room service." She held her room key in her hand as they stood at the elevator bank.

A flash of defeat crossed Grayson's features before he pulled it together and brought back his neutral expression. "I should check in at home. Make sure all is well with Collin and the babysitter." He hit the button to call the elevator. They were on the same floor with adjoining rooms. Abi intended to keep all doors locked this time.

"What time should we meet up again?" she asked as the elevator dinged.

The doors opened and they stepped inside.

"How does eight o'clock sound?" he asked as she pushed the button to the seventh floor. The hotel was rated four stars. The check-in person was appropriately accommodating. And the beds were hailed as the most comfortable in downtown Austin. Somehow, she doubted that was true, but a soft bed and warm covers were all she needed at this point.

"Good for me," she responded.

The seventh floor arrived smoothly. She got out first and headed to room number 714. Grayson stood in front of 712, his room, long enough to indicate he was lingering for a reason. Did he have something to say?

Abi wasn't in the right frame of mind to discuss anything but the case right now. She sure as hell didn't need him to "let her down easy" if that was what he was winding up to say.

In a preempt, she flashed the hotel card key at the receiving box and immediately stepped inside without so much as a glance in Grayson's direction. There was no need to punish herself by looking at him and she sure as hell didn't need him to feel sorry for her.

Standing on the other side of her door after closing it, she could have sworn she heard his footsteps in the hallway, heading toward her room. Rather than go down that path, she headed to the bathroom, stripped and grabbed a quick shower. She might be facing a long night ahead and had no idea when she'd have this opportunity again. Despite being early on in her career by comparison, she'd learned to take advantage of these moments.

After showering, she threw on a hotel bathrobe, closed the blackout curtains and set an alarm. Three hours should be enough sleep to keep her going and fresh all night if needed. And then Abi climbed underneath the covers and closed her eyes.

GRAYSON WAS IN new territory. He'd never once in his career fallen for a coworker or task force member. Abi might have said nice things about Collin, but she'd been clear about not liking young children. Grayson couldn't date someone who couldn't accept Collin. The relationship wouldn't go anywhere, and he was long past casual flings.

He thought she was being polite by inviting him and Collin to meet her family, but the response he'd gotten from her when he tried to let her off easy caught him off guard. She'd seemed genuinely hurt.

And now?

She didn't want to be in the same room with him. Sleeping in the same bed with her last night had been the most intimate he'd been with someone since Michelle. And their clothes had stayed on the entire night. It had been enough to have Abi curled around him. Not having sex had never been sexier.

Abi was sexy. Intelligence was sexy. Strength was sexy. She had those traits in spades and even more than he cared to count. The list would be too long.

There was another bigger problem with their friendship. He didn't want to be friends with Abi. He wanted more and he picked up on the fact she did too. Except their lives were moving in different directions and he had a kid. Their schedules could be overcome with the right strategy. The kid was nonnegotiable.

Plus, what if Collin met Abi and liked her? What then?

She would be a temporary fixture in Collin's life, which couldn't be good for him. If Abi met Collin, it should be as Grayson's girlfriend.

Hold on there. Was this a case of putting the cart before the horse?

In order for Abi to become Grayson's girlfriend she would have to reciprocate his feelings. Their mutual attraction couldn't be denied. Making the decision to act on that attraction was a different ball game.

That was tricky, given their lives and careers.

Abi was a field agent who loved her job. Grayson was on the verge of leaving the Bureau after taking a desk jockey position for a while until he figured out his next move. He was about to devote himself to dad duty. Not exactly the recipe for starting a new relationship with someone who didn't live in the same city, was married to her job, and didn't like kids.

If he'd met Abi before Michelle, he might have had a different life and a possibility to be in a relationship with her. Even through the pain of losing his wife, he couldn't regret Collin. That kid was an angel walking on earth. Or, should he say, an angel playing with Thor and Iron Man figurines.

Grayson's heart said Abi would fall in love with Collin and change her mind about kids, but logic warned him against it. And the question ended up being: how much was Grayson willing to risk to find out?

Because Grayson could handle the pain of loving and losing but would it break Collin?

Slouched in the chair next to the window, he was jerked out of his reverie when his cell buzzed. Abi?

He fished it out of his pocket and checked the screen. Panic gripped him when he saw Martha's name.

"Everything okay?" he immediately asked. Part of the curse of losing the woman he'd loved in tragic fashion meant he was always waiting for another shoe to drop.

"Collin has a tiny fever," Martha explained. Her calm voice should settle his nerves but that wasn't the way the curse worked. It took a nugget of information and worked it in the back of his mind for hours, sometimes days, until torturing him with several worst-case scenarios.

When he was with Abi, however, the curse held at bay, and he could finally let his guard down and breathe.

How was that for doubling down on the curse? You get to find a woman you could truly love but she won't like kids.

"What qualifies as tiny?" Grayson immediately asked.

"It's a hundred and one," she replied, the information causing Grayson's pulse to rise.

"How long has this been going on?" Grayson fired. *The Wiggles* sounded in the background. If someone had told a young Grayson he would be able to sing half their songs before his thirty-eighth birthday, he would have laughed.

"I called the minute it started," Martha calmly replied. "He's right here on my lap."

Of the two of them, Martha was probably the better choice to take care of Collin while he was sick. But it wrecked Grayson to be away from his kid when he needed him most. It took a moment like this to confirm what Grayson already knew…his time in the field was up.

Part of him was ready to wrap up this case for more than just the obvious reason, to get the murdering bastard off the street. It was crystal clear to him now that he needed to be available for his boy. The other part of him wasn't ready to wrap up his time with Abi. That was the selfish part—the part that wanted to consider a future with her once this case was over.

Unrealistic as it might be, his heart had spoken.

"Did you call Dr. Frank?" Grayson asked.

"No reason to yet," Martha said. "I'll keep monitoring him, though. I gave him medicine, which should start working in the next ten minutes or so. If it doesn't bring the fever down, I'll give the pediatrician's office a call and see where we are. It's after hours, so he'll probably ask me if I've given Collin anything for the fever before he sends us to be looked at."

Martha was covering all the bases. She had far more experience at keeping kids alive than Grayson. He trusted her judgment and experience.

And yet, everything inside him wanted to rush home right now and see that Collin was okay with his own eyes. Since he would probably only stress his son out in the process, he decided it was best to let Martha handle the situation.

The other issue pressing hard on him at the moment was the need to save a life. If he didn't put 100 percent of his focus on the case, someone could die tonight.

The slap of reality made his next move crystal clear.

"Thank you for calling, Martha," Grayson said, meaning every word. "I have no idea if I tell you how much you mean to this family nearly enough, but we're damn lucky to have you."

"It's a beautiful family you have here, Grayson," she said, and he could almost feel her smiling in those words. "I'm the lucky one."

"Not sure about that," he said, thinking he would bring home a box of those doughnuts she loved when he could put this case behind him. "This is going to be my last case in the field."

"Oh?"

"I'm missing too much at home," he said. "Which means I'll probably need you even more in the near future but I'm certain desk work is the right move for me while Collin is still young."

"You love him, Grayson," she reminded in the grandmotherly tone that wrapped you in a hug. "Either way, he's a lucky boy."

"You'll stick around and show me the ropes, right? Because I wouldn't have gotten through these past years without you."

"I'm always next door," Martha said. "And I have no plans to go anywhere." She hesitated, which was uncharacteristic of her.

"Are you okay?" he asked.

"Yes, fine," she said a little too quickly. Something was up but he wouldn't force her to talk about it before she was ready.

"Once I get home, maybe we can go out to breakfast or coffee after dropping Collin off at preschool," he said, offering her an option to talk about whatever was on her mind.

"I'd like that," she said, sounding satisfied. "In the meantime, I'll keep you posted on Collin."

"Maybe the medicine will bring down his temperature," Grayson said.

"I hope so," she said. "He's still taking sips from his juice box. That'll help keep him hydrated."

Martha had things under control. She would alert him if the fever persisted. Still, the dark cloud returned.

"Sounds good," he said, not feeling one bit of those words.

They ended the call, and he made a cup of coffee. He missed the days when hotels had small pots that made two cups at a time. Everything changed. Change was in the air for him too.

And he hoped he hadn't just cursed the case by announcing to Martha that it would be his last.

ABI TOSSED AND turned for three hours. Instead of getting out of bed rested, she had to drag herself out from underneath the covers. *Coffee.*

Logic said food first, so she grabbed the room service menu, ordered a quinoa bowl with tuna, and then made a cup of fresh brew. It was quiet next door but then she'd placed a towel underneath the connecting doors to keep out light before going to bed a while ago.

Food arrived five minutes after she freshened up and got dressed. The coffee was cold by the time she picked up the cup, so she placed a few ice cubes inside and downed it like a shot anyway. It was a means to an end at this point.

The meal was decent, the room nice, but it was time to get dressed and out onto the party scene. Abi made certain to put on her Kevlar vest underneath her button-down shirt. Next came her shoulder holster before her blazer.

To keep hair off her face, she pulled hers into a low bun and then used just enough makeup to keep her from looking like the walking dead.

It was strange how much she missed being with Grayson, considering she barely knew the man. But did she barely know him? Because part of her felt like they'd known each other her whole life. Twin flames?

She was beginning to believe it was possible.

"Hey," Grayson said after joining her at the elevator bank.

"Did you sleep?" she asked, searching for something neutral to say.

"Not much. You?"

"I got to power down," she admitted. "But no real sleep."

"We can stop off for coffee since we'll be patrolling until we see something or receive word."

"Sounds good," she said. They were searching for a needle in a haystack.

Two cups of coffee and three hours later, they sat downtown with no idea of where to go next and no solid leads. The tip line was getting plenty of action, but nothing was panning out so far.

Frustration ate away at Abi as they navigated the one-way streets downtown.

A phone call had Grayson pulling over. After a few *uh-huhs* and *I-sees*, he locked gazes. "My son's fever has spiked. I don't live that far from here. I can drop you off anywhere you want but I have to check on him." The panic in his voice got her heart racing too.

"Don't let me hold you up," she said without hesitation. "Let's go."

Not two seconds later, they were racing toward his home.

Chapter Eighteen

"Everything okay?" Abi asked once Grayson met her in the living room where she stood at the door.

"It's late and there isn't anything else we can do tonight," Grayson said to Abi. "I can't leave until I make sure Collin's fever is down in the morning. It's the only way I'll be able to focus on the case."

"Makes sense. I can grab a motel room nearby," she said, feeling more at home the minute she stepped into his house than in her own townhouse. The feeling should scare her, but she was so damn tired of fighting it. So she didn't.

"There's a guest room," he quickly stated. "You might be more comfortable here than at a random motel."

"Lead me to it," she said.

"I'll grab your bag from the car first," he said with a spark in his eyes that was another big red-flag type warning signal. Again, she was too tired to struggle against the current washing over her and through her, pulling her toward the man she knew better than to fall in love with. Abi cracked a smile. Since when did her stubborn heart listen to logic?

Could she compete with a ghost?

Grayson disappeared into the garage, returning a few moments later as she studied the pictures of Michelle. Surprisingly, Abi felt didn't feel a shred of jealousy as she looked at the smiling woman who seemed so happy. Instead, she felt sorry for Collin, who would never know his mother.

"It's good that you have pictures of her around," Abi stated.

"Really?" Grayson asked. "Because I almost took them down. They broke my heart to look at them in those first few months. Hell, years."

"It's good for Collin to see how happy his mother was," she pointed out. "We never talked about my mom, and I always wondered what she was like." It occurred to her that she might never be able to ask her grandparents now.

"You didn't ask?"

"No," she said. "Somewhere in the back of my mind, I thought my grandparents might be offended in some way if I asked about her. Like I was saying they weren't enough."

"I never thought about it in those terms," Grayson said after a thoughtful pause.

"You should tell Collin stories about her now while he's young," she said. "It'll make it easier for him to ask questions later. Otherwise, he might get it in his head the subject is taboo, like I did."

Grayson stood so close that his spicy male scent filled her senses. Before she got lost in him, she took her bag so she could head into the guest quarters. Unfortunately, their fingers grazed during the transfer. Abi was unprepared for the jolt of electricity that coursed through her. It was a force. One that made the earth tilt on its axis and made her fight the urge to lean toward him, push up to her tiptoes and kiss him.

The air crackled with electricity in between them, heating the room several degrees.

Abi had to get away or risk crossing a professional line—a line that she refused to cross with anyone. Even Grayson.

"I...um...have to...bathroom." She shook her head in an attempt to shake off the fog that was all Grayson. "That's not right...shower."

With that, she pulled on every last ounce of strength she had. Like a planet pulling out of its orbit, with effort, she managed to drum up enough power to walk away.

Since Abi had never felt anything that came close with anyone else, she could only imagine what a kiss would feel like. Would it catch her on fire? Consume her? Her lips burned to explore his. An ache the size of a canyon formed in her chest for this man.

After placing her bag inside the guest room, she immediately hit the shower. As much as she tried to refocus her attention, it was impossible. So she stopped fighting that too. There was power in surrender.

When it came to Grayson, she had no choice but to give in to her feelings. While they worked a case together, however, she refused to act on them.

Shower. Bed. Sleep.

Those three things reset just about anything in Abi's experience.

THE SUN PEEKED through the slats of the mini blinds, waking Abi after a deep sleep. She glanced at the clock and realized she'd gotten a solid seven hours. Not bad during the heat of a case.

After freshening up in the bathroom and then throwing on borrowed sweats and sweatshirt, she moved toward the kitchen in search of food and caffeine, not necessarily in that order.

Sounds coming from the living room stopped her cold in the hallway. Cartoons?

Was that a good sign Collin was feeling better?

Abi was way out of her league when it came to kiddos. Was that the curse of being the youngest of the family? She'd grown up around foals but no human kids younger than her. How different could they be?

Did she just compare babies to foals? Yep. Definitely not winning this morning.

To get to the kitchen, Abi had to cross the living room. The sudden urge to sneak out a window, circle the house and come in through the back door struck. Okay, now she was really losing it. *It's just a kid, Abi. A human. How hard can it be to say hello and then get breakfast?*

Taking in a breath to fortify herself, Abi squared her shoulders and marched toward the living room. All she had to do was cross over to the kitchen without making eye contact and she'd be fine. While in the office, she walked with purpose so no one would talk to her. The same strategy could work now, right?

Two steps into the living room and she froze.

"Are you my daddy's friend?" the little boy with glasses too big for his angelic face asked.

"That's right," she confirmed. "You must be Collin." Why was her pulse racing like she'd just sprinted across a football field chasing a perp? *Calm down, Abi. It's just a kid.*

Collin's wide smile cracked what was left of her heart in two.

"Want to watch *Iron Man* with me?" he practically beamed.

"Yes," she said before thinking her answer through. The thought of disappointing that face shredded her. No way could she have refused.

So she sat down next to him on the carpet flooring and crisscrossed her legs. He immediately climbed onto her lap. It was a good thing the kid's back was to her so he didn't see her reaction. Her jaw dropped open as every muscle in her body tensed. How could he become comfortable with her this quick? Did she have a hidden talent? Child whisperer?

Whoa, there! Don't be too pleased with yourself. You stayed one night, not forever. The kid climbed in your lap. He didn't call you Mommy.

One thing was abundantly clear. The kid had wriggled his way into Abi's heart in a matter of minutes.

"What's your name?" Collin asked.

"Abi," she supplied.

"How old are you?" he asked, eyes glued to the show even though his attention seemed to be split between her and the TV.

Meanwhile, Abi—ever astute being that she was—couldn't for the life of her figure out what to do with her hands. Should she hug him? No. That didn't sound right.

Leaning back, she put her flat palms on the carpet to brace herself. The kid, however, made himself right at home. He seemed unbothered by physical contact.

She could do this. She could be easy-breezy. No problem.

"I'm twenty-eight years old," she said.

"Wow," Collin responded. "I'm this many." He held up

four fingers. "My birthday's in three weeks." He proudly extended fingers and thumb. "I'll be this many."

"Five?" she asked, unsure what to say to that. "Do you go to school?"

"I'm sick," Collin said, not sounding terribly disappointed about missing school.

"Do you like school?" she asked, figuring she might as well throw herself into the conversation.

"Not really," he said. She could hear a frown in his voice.

"Why not?" she asked. "Don't you like the teacher?"

"Ms. Brown is nice." Collin perked up.

"What do you do in school?" she continued.

"Learn stuff," he answered.

She might as well go all-in at this point. "Don't you like to learn stuff?"

He craned his neck around to face her. "Learning makes me smart."

"Then, why don't you like school?"

He shrugged.

The reason dawned on her. "Do you have friends?"

"Michael is my best friend," Collin supplied. "Kids say mean things to him too."

Suddenly, Abi was right back in grade school, being picked on for wearing glasses. "Kids used to say mean things to me because I wore glasses."

"But you're pretty," Collin said like it was as obvious as the nose on her face.

"Mean kids say mean things to everyone," she said. "And it's okay to stick up for yourself when they do or tell the teacher."

"Teacher says we're not supposed to be tattle tales," Collin said.

Grayson needed to have a discussion with Ms. Brown or move Collin to a preschool that didn't put up with bullying. How Ms. Brown could not defend a sweet kid like Collin was beyond her.

"There's tattling to get someone in trouble and then there's another thing called letting a teacher know when someone is acting bad," Abi said.

Collin cocked his head to one side. His face scrunched in serious thought.

"The teacher wants to know when someone is acting bad," Abi continued, hoping that clarified things. "So she can help them act better."

"Will they get in trouble?" he asked.

"Sometimes," Abi said. "Other times, they'll be sent over to say they are sorry."

"Rupert would never do that," Collin exclaimed, shaking his head in the process.

At least they had a name. She could tell Grayson so he could reach out to Rupert's parents. Maybe stop by on the way to work this morning. Or they could swing by and have a conversation with Ms. Brown.

Either way, the bullying needed to stop.

"Hold on a second," Abi said. She picked Collin up and set him down next to her before getting up. "I'll be right back."

She popped out her contacts and then put her glasses on.

When she returned to the living room, Collin's face lit up. He clapped and beamed at her.

"You have glasses too?" It was more excited statement than question.

"That's right," she said. "And I think yours are pretty cool."

She sat down and he immediately crawled in her lap again.

He twisted half his body around when he looked up at her this time. "Can you be my new Mommy?"

If words were bullets, those were the equivalent of being sprayed with an AR-15s.

"Hey," Grayson said from the kitchen before she could find the words to come up with an answer. His voice cracked on the word, which gave the impression he'd been standing there long enough to hear the question that had rocked Abi's world.

Was it strange that she'd only known the kid for a matter of minutes but would jump at the chance to be his Mommy? Abi! Someone who never wanted the white picket fence or the 2.5 kids running around. Abi! Who never saw herself in a Cinderella ball gown wedding dress or any other white dress for that matter. Abi! Who used to think of kids as not much more than an annoyance on airplanes.

Boy, hadn't she been dead wrong. The crying might not be a kid's best moment but sitting on a living room floor with one on her lap made her wonder if getting moments like these made all the others worth it.

Much to her surprise, Collin didn't jump up and run to his dad.

Grayson walked into the living room. His thick wet hair stuck up at odd angles, making him surprisingly more handsome. He had that fresh-from-the shower look, which had never looked so good on any other human. He wore pajama bottoms and a cotton T-shirt. Those had never looked sexier on a man either. Then again, Grayson's body was made for sinning.

"Hey, buddy," Grayson said. "How about that breakfast I promised you?"

Collin looked up at Abi with big blue eyes. "Will you stay?"

"For breakfast?" she asked with a smile. "Of course, I will."

The kid's smile melted what was left of her resolve as he let out a little yelp. He scrambled to his feet and then took hold of Grayson's hand.

Her heart couldn't take much more of this. Abi fought the urge to come up with an escape plan. Maybe all this was telling her was that she might be ready to open her life to someone. That having someone to go home to, to share her life with wasn't such an awful thing.

Of course, it would have to be the right person. Someone like Grayson. Now that she had the blueprint, it shouldn't be hard to find. Right?

Abi's heart said Grayson was one of a kind. The mold was broken after him. Hell's bells.

If she couldn't find another Grayson, there was no way she could settle for less now that she knew exactly what she was looking for.

Was being alone the worst thing? It had never seemed so in the past. Why now?

The answer came quickly. Life was short. She worked a dangerous job. And even if she didn't, there were no guarantees. The thought of dying without ever being loved suddenly sounded like the loneliest fate. The ache in her chest expanded.

Was there a slight chance Grayson felt the same way? If so, could she be brave enough to ask?

Chapter Nineteen

Grayson's heart nearly exploded out of his chest when he walked into the kitchen and heard his son ask Abi to be his Mommy. Did his son feel a tremendous void in the space where a mother's love would be?

Collin had to or he wouldn't have asked. And Grayson had never felt so inadequate or underprepared.

Seeing his son insist Abi sit next to him at the table warmed Grayson's heart. But the fact she was temporary in Collin's life needed to be kept in focus.

"Where do you live?" Collin asked as Grayson set down a bowl of cereal along with a banana. At least Collin's fever was down. Martha would be over in half an hour and Grayson could return to work with Abi.

"Far away but I grew up on a horse ranch about two hours from here," Abi supplied.

"What do you like for breakfast?" Grayson asked her. "I have hardboiled eggs, ham and a few tomatoes."

"Sounds perfect to me," she said.

Out of the blue, Collin exclaimed, "I like her." For a kid that had been sick with fever last night, he beamed today. Abi probably had something to do with it, but Grayson was relieved his son was feeling better. Kids bounced back at a surprising rate. Meanwhile, Grayson's joints liked to remind him of his age first thing when he got out of bed. He had to stretch before firing off a few pushups to get the blood pumping. He couldn't remember where he'd picked up the saying *Motion is lotion,* but it was true. His body was like the Tin Man from *The Wizard of Oz.*

After putting together twin plates, he made a pot of coffee.

"Can I help with anything?" Abi asked.

"You want to grab the plates?" Grayson responded as he filled two mugs.

She joined him in the kitchen, moved beside him so close he could smell the lavender bodywash from the guest bathroom. It had never smelled so good.

Shoulder to shoulder, she whispered, "I got a name of the ringleader at preschool who is bullying Collin. The little twerp's name is Rupert. Should we stop by the preschool and have a chat with Ms. Brown or go directly to the brat's parents?"

"You got a name?" Grayson asked. Collin never said any one individual was responsible. He always spoke generically.

"Sure did," Abi said, seemingly not realizing how monumental that felt to Grayson.

"Why doesn't he say anything to the teacher?" Grayson asked, figuring she might not know but it didn't hurt to go for broke.

"Doesn't want to be a narc," she stated.

"Do you think Ms. Brown will handle the situation?" Grayson asked. "Because I've been thinking of moving him to a new school."

"I can go with you if you want to set up a meeting," Abi offered. "Sometimes it helps to have an extra set of eyes and ears. A different perspective."

"You would do that?" Grayson was caught off guard with her eagerness to help.

"For Collin?" She paused. "I'd do anything legal for that kid. And it wouldn't be difficult to twist my arm to commit a misdemeanor if it got a bully off his back."

Abi grabbed the plates like nothing had just happened, twirled around and then headed back to the table. Meanwhile, the floor shifted underneath Grayson's feet. He had to grab hold of the bullnose edge of the counter to stay upright because he was floored.

"May I have some milk, Daddy?" Collin asked, bringing Grayson back to the present.

"Sure," he said, giving himself a moment to get back to reality. A mental headshake did the trick.

Grayson poured milk and balanced the cup along with a pair of mugs in his hands before setting them down on the table. Collin was right, though, Abi was amazing. Could his heart survive losing her once this case was closed?

ABI POLISHED OFF breakfast along with a cup of coffee in record time. She was always famished after a good night's sleep. There was something about this home that allowed her to relax.

"I should get dressed," she said after cleaning the dishes while Collin colored in a coloring book his dad brought to him at the end of the meal.

Since the pages were filled with Marvel superheroes and

Collin was allowed to set his figurines down on the table, he reluctantly gave up watching them on television.

By the time Abi returned, fully dressed and with her bag in hand, the babysitter had arrived. The older woman sat at the table with Collin, reading while he colored.

"Hi," Abi said as she entered the room.

"You must be Abi," the older woman said. She had a kind face and a pile of gray hair on top of her head tied in a loose bun. "Collin's been talking about you nonstop."

"He's a great kid," Abi said as moisture gathered in her eyes. What was that all about? The thought of never seeing him again? And since when had she become a crier?

Abi had no idea what was happening to her but assumed it had a lot to do with her grandparents.

Collin's smile widened. How was that even possible? The kid was already grinning ear to ear.

"I'm Martha, by the way," she said, studying Abi, who suddenly felt subconscious.

"Nice to meet you, Martha." She could feel the heat in her cheeks. She hadn't done anything to be embarrassed about. It dawned on Abi that she wanted Martha to like her because Martha was important to Collin and Grayson.

"I hope that I'm not being too forward when I say it would be neat to see you around again sometime soon," Martha said with a wink.

"I'd like that a lot," Abi admitted. Her cheeks were on fire now.

"What are you two talking about?" Grayson asked as he joined them.

"You," Abi teased, winking at Collin.

"Ms. Brown says you're not s'posed to tell a lie," Collin said with so much earnestness that Abi's heart squeezed.

"Your teacher is right," Abi said, figuring a qualifier that she was only joking would confuse the kid. His innocence was endearing. "We were talking about me," she said to Grayson.

"She wants to come back, Daddy," Collin supplied.

Abi needed to be careful around those little ears that seemed to catch everything. Were all kids like a sponge, like Collin?

Probably not. He was special. Sensitive.

"She's welcome anytime," Grayson said, his voice dropping an octave. The hitch was back.

Abi's cell buzzed. She fished it out of her handbag and checked the screen. One look at Grayson and he jumped into action.

"We have to go to work now," he said to Collin, who frowned.

"Can Abi come back with you?" Collin asked.

"We'll see," Grayson said, and Abi's heart gave a little flip.

"I'll see you soon," Abi said to the little boy.

"Promise?" Collin asked.

"Promise," she confirmed. Her answer seemed to satisfy him.

Grayson ruffled Collin's hair before planting a kiss on top of the boy's head. Abi turned away so no one could see the emotion once again gathering in her eyes. She cleared her throat, made a show of saying goodbye with a wave, and headed to the garage where the car was parked.

"Sandra Boylston didn't return to her dorm room last

night, according to her roommate," Abi supplied as they reclaimed their seats and the garage door opened. "The roommate's name is Chloe Sharp. Sandra fits the description that Reprehensible targets. Brown hair and eyes. And she always checks in with her roommate when she sleeps somewhere else. They have a pact."

"Which dorm?" he asked.

"Jester," she stated.

"What's the address of the party?" he asked.

"21st and Alamo," she supplied. "Second house on the right." She plugged the location into her phone's map feature. "We can be there in twenty-five minutes."

"Is there a good place to meet with the roommate near the party location?" Grayson asked. "The perp likes to stay nearby. We already know that. He'll be close. Sandra will be in a two-block range, if I had to guess."

"Alamo Pocket Park would be a good place to meet," she supplied after checking the area. "I'll request a meeting there to interview the roommate." Abi tapped out the message on her phone. Within a matter of minutes, the confirmation came through. "All set. She'll head there right now with her boyfriend."

"Good, I'm glad she's not going alone," he said.

"The task force received forty-two tips last night," Abi said. "This is one of three that seemed viable. One other checked in this morning, which leaves two."

"It's eight o'clock in the morning," he pointed out before falling silent.

"You don't think…?"

"That he will kill her immediately to satisfy what he

couldn't accomplish with Max?" Grayson asked. "I hope the hell not."

Abi checked the map. Eighteen minutes until they arrived but the perp would have had hours with Sandra by now.

"What about the other tip?" he asked.

"The missing person is blonde," she supplied. "Bleached, but that might not matter to our perp."

"Let me see if I can make it there in less than fifteen minutes," Grayson said, stepping harder on the gas pedal. "Put on the light and I'll go siren until we get close."

Abi did as requested.

They made it to the park in thirteen minutes. Her cell buzzed again. She checked the screen as Grayson parked on the street.

"Three possible locations have been pinned on the map being texted over," she said. She blew up each one. "All three have boarded-up windows, are within walking distance to the party, and neighbors would be used to and possibly even unaffected by rowdy neighbors. The one I think we should hit first is here." She tilted the screen so he could see it and pointed to the one two houses down from the corner. "It's a small duplex, but this side looks abandoned."

The area was gentrifying. A couple of new build homes were sprinkled in with mostly older homes, chain-link fences and boarded-up windows. The one she wanted to investigate first had an old, dirty towel pinned over the front window. The rag looked like it had been there for twenty years at a minimum.

"Let's meet with Chloe and then we can walk over," Grayson said. "Sound good?"

"I was just about to make the same suggestion," Abi admitted. They had no idea what kind of arsenal they would be walking into with this perp, which sent all kinds of tingles up her spine. "I'm sending a text to request Austin PD check out the other location. Time is the enemy. If this bastard has Sandra, we don't know how long he'll keep her alive."

Without another word, they exited the vehicle simultaneously. A college-age-looking female sat on her boyfriend's lap on the swing. They were the only ones at the park this early in the morning.

"She had a test tomorrow," Chloe began after they identified themselves and finished perfunctory introductions. "Has," Chloe corrected, catching herself talking about her roommate in the past tense. Bags underneath her eyes and her heavy expression said this was serious. Even if Sandra wasn't taken by the perp, something bad had happened to her in Chloe's view. Her friend's concern came across as heartfelt, genuine. "We were supposed to wake up early and study together, but one of her friends talked her into going to the party."

"What time did she leave?" Abi asked, taking the lead.

"Late," Chloe said. "Probably around eleven thirty."

"Had she been drinking?" Abi continued.

Chloe hesitated.

"No one is here to make any judgment or arrest for underage drinking," Abi quickly added in case the pause had to do with Sandra's age.

"I just turned twenty-one," Chloe said. "But Sandra had picked up a bottle of wine."

"How old is Sandra?" Abi asked.

"Nineteen," Chloe stated. She might be lying about who brought the alcohol into the dorm but ferreting out the truth about who supplied the alcohol wasn't the objective right now. Those details could be sorted out by Austin PD later.

Moving on.

Sandra fit the age the perp targeted.

"We were supposed to have a girls' night in, but Sandra's friend kept texting, said her boyfriend stood her up and she didn't want to be at the party alone," Chloe supplied.

"Does this friend have a name?" Abi asked.

"Jenn," Chloe supplied. "But I don't know her last name. She's someone Sandra met in class this semester."

"How much had Sandra had to drink before she left here?" Abi asked, figuring Sandra might have already been drunk or close to it before heading out. This could also be a false alarm as Sandra might have gone home with Jenn and forgotten to text because she was too drunk, and was currently sleeping it off.

"Most of the bottle," Chloe admitted. "I have a hard time waking up early if I drink more than a glass the night before."

Could be sugarcoating her own side of the story but she wasn't showing any tells of outright lying.

They needed to wrap this interview up and head to the residence in question.

"You didn't hear from Sandra for the rest of the evening, is that correct?" Abi continued, moving toward ending the conversation.

"No, ma'am," Chloe supplied with an exacerbated look. "And she didn't return any of my texts either."

"Phone battery could have died," Abi said.

"Sandra is militant about keeping a charge," Chloe said. "Even when she'd had way too much to drink, she texts."

"Does she overdrink often?" Abi asked.

"You know how it is first year," Chloe said honestly. "First taste of freedom."

"I'll take that as a yes," Abi said.

"Sandra is no worse than any other freshman, though," Chloe felt the need to clarify. It was good to see her being protective over her friend and roommate. "But, yes, she has been known to have a few too many."

"Agent Chisolm and I appreciate your honesty, Chloe," Abi stated. Sandra might be passed out somewhere, but she had someone looking out for her.

"She would do the same for me," Chloe said. "I just hope she's okay. I probably wouldn't have even called if not for all the alerts we've been getting." Chloe's eyes watered. "She's the right height and has the right hair color." She paused as if stopping herself from crying. "It scares me."

"Sandra is lucky to have you for a roommate," Abi pointed out. "We have a lot of resources on this. We'll do our best to find her." Abi had learned a long time ago not to make promises to folks no matter how much they needed reassurance. Time would tell when it came to Sandra. If the perp had abducted her, Abi could only pray they would find her alive. "Here's my information. I'd appreciate it if you contacted me the second you hear from Sandra."

"You can find her by tracking her phone, right?" Chloe asked, accepting the contact after giving her phone number.

"We're working on it," Abi noted. It took time to get a judge to sign off on invading someone's privacy. But approval was in the works and should come down any minute.

"Thank you," Chloe said. "For taking me seriously. For looking for Sandra. For being here so fast."

"You're welcome," Abi said. "Do me a favor?"

"Yes," Chloe said.

"As tempting as it might be, don't try to find Sandra on your own," Abi said. The last thing she needed was a young person to interfere with an ongoing investigation.

Chloe put her hands up, palms out. "I swear. It's the reason I called the tip line in the first place."

"You did the right thing," Abi reassured before ending the interview.

With that, she and Grayson headed away from the park, toward the duplex.

"What did you think?" she asked him once they were out of earshot.

"Chloe was honest," he supplied. "And we're running out of time."

The hairs on the back of Abi's neck pricked. An ominous feeling hung over her like a gray cloud before a storm.

Were they off track? Or about to come face-to-face with a monster?

Chapter Twenty

The home on the 2000 block of Alamo was a duplex three houses down from the corner. Other homes blocked the view of the park, but it was possible to see it from the backyard. The house to the left had rocks instead of grass and pots filled with indigenous plants. The home directly across the street had been torn down and rebuilt, painted in a dark hue with wood accents around the windows and door.

The neighborhood was an odd mix of old and new, with no master plan at work. The homes on both sides of the duplex were vacant. Its tree limbs tangled in overhead electric distribution wires. The front windows had makeshift coverings.

An icy chill gripped Abi's spine. This looked exactly like the kind of place she imagined Reprehensible would take a victim. The urge to barge in to save Sandra weighed heavily against the need to be safe and protect her and her partner.

Adrenaline surged through her as she drew her weapon while Grayson sent a message to inform the team they'd arrived on scene. Bursting through the door looked good in the movies but could cost Sandra her life. Plus, they needed probable cause. A hunch without cause didn't hold up in court.

Grayson made eye contact with Abi before indicating he would take the right-hand side. She nodded, then headed left. It was quarter to nine at this point. The sun was up on a partly cloudy morning. There was a chill in the air that caused her to wish she'd put on a coat instead of the blazer that normally did the trick. She wore the Kevlar vest that clearly marked her as a US marshal on the outside of her blazer.

Grayson had essentially the same vest marked with the letters FBI instead in bright yellow. There was no mistaking them for troublemakers or would-be squatters. Weapons leading the way, careful to duck underneath windows, she listened for any signs of life inside the home.

Was there any way to get a look inside without alerting the perp to their presence?

As she came around the corner in the backyard, Abi's cell buzzed. She paused long enough to check the screen.

Wrong address. Two doors down. Neighbor heard a scream. Go!

An image along with an address popped up next. Grayson got the same message because he was by her side in a heartbeat, urging her to move.

"We get there, and we go in immediately," Grayson said. "Deal?"

"I was just thinking the same thing," Abi admitted as they bolted to the address. She was a couple of steps ahead, being the faster runner.

At the front door, she could hear sounds of a struggle inside. It was enough for probable cause. Grayson caught up, took the opposite side of the door.

The no-knock, destroy-the-door entries were not at all fun to serve. They were hazardous for everyone involved. If Abi had her druthers, she would wait for the perp to come walking outside to get supplies from the pack he would have stashed nearby. In this scenario, she would be dressed in street clothes with a backpack on, happening by as she walked down the street like she might be a grad student, and then would say something casual before catching him off guard and then cuffing the bastard.

But that wasn't an option here. Not with Sandra's life on the line. She might be dead already except that Abi suspected the perp would have fled the scene with her limp body.

Although, he would have to wait for the cover of night. Not enough time had passed for him to pull a move like that one off successfully. If this perp was anything, he was calculating. He also knew his way around college campuses, understood the party scene well enough to blend in and somehow never get caught in the background in a picture.

A quick nod from Grayson, a moment of eye contact, and then she opened the screen so he could kick the door in. The second kick blasted the old wood.

"US marshal, put your hands up where I can see 'em," Abi demanded as she took the first step inside.

The victim, who fit Sandra's description, had wild eyes as she kicked like a banshee. She was flat on the floor on her side. Her long locks in a pile next to her, hair in a bowl cut.

The perp picked up a gun and aimed as Abi stepped outside onto the porch in search of cover. The bastard fired. A bullet pinged the wood not much more than an inch from her left ear at the entrance as she and Grayson hit the deck.

The man was tall and slim, runner's build. He had a head full of brown hair that was a little too long and unkempt. His eyes spoke pure disdain and evil, mixed with panic. Eyes like those said they'd rather die than go to prison.

There was no way they could lose this bastard. Not when they were this close.

Abi called it in, requesting all available resources to the 2000 block of Alamo. She gave the description of the killer: five feet ten inches, thin build. In her experience, guys like that could be wiry.

And then she and Grayson exchanged glances. They didn't need words. The look spoke volumes. They weren't letting this one get away.

Abi first ran inside to Sandra, who was gagged and crying. Her first move was to remove the gag and then the bindings forcing her arms behind her back.

Sandra cried hysterically as she tried to grab hold of Abi, like someone drowning would grip a ring buoy.

"I have to go," Abi said sternly, trying to shock the young woman out of her panic. "Help is on the way."

Sandra's eyes were unfocused. She reeked of alcohol, and she was still suffering the effects of sedation. There were bruises forming on her face, along with a nasty cut above her left cheekbone.

Abi's heart cracked in half at the desperation in the nineteen-year-old's eyes. But she couldn't stay.

The crack of a bullet split the air. *Grayson?*

Abi had to peel the young woman's arms off. "Help is coming. Stay right here."

Her legs were still bound but she would likely figure out how to remove the ropes. Would she stay put?

Abi couldn't stick around to find out. Grayson had already taken off after Reprehensible, and she needed to join the chase before he disappeared again. Striking this soon after Max was the equivalent of taunting law enforcement. It was saying, *I can do this right underneath your noses and you can't catch me.*

The man was smart. She would give him that much. He was a fast runner. There was no denying it. And now, she wondered if he was also a student. It would make it easier for him to blend in.

After peeling Sandra's arms off for the third time, Abi managed to break free from the desperate young woman. "I promise someone will be here in a matter of minutes."

Leaving was hard but had to be done. By the time Abi joined the chase, heading in the direction of the gunfire, she'd long lost any hope of visuals on Grayson and the perp.

A chopper overhead belonging to Austin PD was her best bet to locate them again, so she tracked to it.

Minutes had passed while she was interacting with Sandra, precious minutes. The gunfire could have been the perp firing a wild shot. The bullet could have slammed into Grayson. The image of Collin dressed in black standing at his father's gravesite fueled her to sprint even faster.

At this point, joggers were starting their mornings. Sidewalks were filling up. Austin was a twenty-four-hour city with all the college students and young professionals fighting for space. The college had more than 50,000 students, and that was UT alone. There were roughly 2.2 million residents coming from all walks of life, descending on the metro area and making it feel like being trapped in an ant farm.

With no word from Grayson, she could only pray that meant he was still giving chase and not lying on the street somewhere bleeding out with no way to contact her.

The thought of losing Grayson now that she'd finally found a friend almost caused her knees to buckle.

Another crack of a bullet split the air.

Tears streaked Abi's cheeks as she blasted through joggers on the sidewalk, praying she could find Grayson in time.

As she glanced up at the chopper, an idea came to her. Would it work? Could she afford to take a risk?

At this point, she might as well go for broke. Abi cut across the street and headed a block over. Would the move pay off? Or backfire in her face?

GRAYSON POPPED BEHIND a tree. A bullet came flying toward him, chipping off a piece of trunk. The perp was firing wild shots—shots that were getting dangerously close to hitting their mark...*him*.

He'd lost track of Abi, and the perp was a better runner than Grayson. She would have caught up to the bastard by now.

Using the massive oak tree to put some mass in between himself and the perp had kept a bullet out of him, but the killer was far enough away to disappear at any moment. Grayson couldn't let that happen.

As soon as the opportunity presented itself, Grayson made a run for it. This stretch of sidewalk had enough trees for him to run a zigzag pattern, providing at least some barrier.

The thought of being shot today crossed his mind. The last case omen?

His first thought, of course, was Collin. What would his kid do if he had to grow up without both parents? Grayson couldn't go there. Not even hypothetically. His second thought surprised him. Because it was about Abi.

Grayson had loved Michelle and he'd lost her. He'd never thought he would find that kind of love again. Lightning didn't strike twice and finding a soul mate seemed about that likely. He'd loved Michelle. However, Abi was his twin flame—a flame that burned even brighter than anything he'd known to expect.

Now Grayson had two reasons to ensure he made it home safe and alive.

Did Abi feel the same way about him? She'd been clear about not wanting kids. Would her friendship be enough?

Nearly face-planting after tripping on a root snapped his mind out of his reverie. The mind was a funny place. It went in all kinds of directions while facing danger. Grayson didn't normally allow his to wander in critical moments, which was another reason why he knew it was time to hang up his fieldwork in favor of sitting behind a desk.

The perp's legs had to be getting tired by now. Grayson's sure as hell were. His thighs burned.

He'd expected Abi to catch up to him by now, considering the speed with which she ran. Had she taken a different route? Would she stay with the victim?

The perp was almost a full block ahead of Grayson now.

The chopper overhead pulled away, banking right. Was the pilot called off the search?

Grayson didn't like that one bit. Because the other explanation was the chopper didn't have eyes on them. Stop to communicate, and Grayson could lose the perp altogether. Let this bastard slip away again and he was sure to kill again.

He couldn't allow that to happen. If this was going to be his last case in the field, he needed to stop the killings now.

Adrenaline gave him a boost of energy as his lungs clawed for air.

Pumping his arms helped him to keep on pace with the perp, who was still a block ahead. With no chopper, though, the guy could slip away.

Grayson focused on the image of Sandra locked inside that abandoned house, fighting for her life. He pumped his arms harder, closing a little bit of the gap between him and Reprehensible. At this point, he'd take the inches of gain.

The perp cut across the street, heading right. A cross street was ahead. Did he have another motorcycle stashed there?

Grayson bit back a curse. He would keep pushing until there was no point if that was the case. A motorcycle in Austin would make it even easier to blend in. The highway wasn't far. This guy chose his locations near quick getaways.

Austin traffic would work against them.

The perp disappeared around the corner.

Not again!

As Grayson pushed his legs as hard as they could go, he made it halfway up the block in record time. Frustration seethed because he was still a few seconds too late—he'd lost visual on the guy.

Could he stop long enough to make contact with Abi? Get a location on her?

The risk of letting the perp outdistance Grayson further stopped him from trying to contact Abi.

Where was she?

ABI MADE A sharp left, rounding the corner at the fastest pace she'd ever run. Adrenaline could be thanked for the extra boost, but also the thought of anything happening to Grayson made it unnecessary.

The second she had a clear view of the street, she saw him.

Reprehensible hopped on a motorcycle, facing the opposite direction. His face glued toward the direction in which he'd come. Grayson had to be close by because the perp had his gun aimed and ready to shoot as soon as the agent rounded the corner.

Abi stopped, hopping behind a tree. She fired a text to Grayson because she had to do something to stop him. After tucking her cell inside its case on her belt, she trained her weapon on Reprehensible. He was halfway down a short block.

A faster runner than Grayson, the perp was setting the agent up to be fired on. The perp had time, too. He sat there, heaving, as he switched hands in order to start the engine.

The motorcycle itself caught her eye. It dawned on her why no one had caught him on the scene of Max's attack. The motorcycle had a sidecar with a person inside. At least, it looked like a person. Was it, though?

As she crept up from behind, she realized the passenger in the sidecar was a life-size dummy. Everyone had been looking for a single motorcycle rider. Even a chopper would dismiss the bike with a sidecar, especially since the dummy appeared to be a real person who was strapped in. A decoy.

Smart.

And an almost surefire way to escape in plain sight.

Abi hoped she could get close enough to disarm the bastard before Grayson made it around the corner. The perp fully intended to shoot.

A door opened across the street. A young woman in pajamas stepped onto her porch, and then froze when her gaze landed on the perp. Abi cursed under her breath. Because the woman's gaze then shifted to her.

Abi waved her back inside her house. She complied but not before alerting Reprehensible that someone was creeping up from behind.

He immediately turned around and fired a wild shot.

Thankfully, Abi stepped behind a tree in time. "Halt! I'm a US marshal. Drop your weapon! Put your hands in the air where I can see them."

At that moment, Grayson came racing around the corner.

Attention shifting immediately to the agent who was closest to him, Reprehensible aimed and fired.

Chapter Twenty-One

Grayson was slammed back a step after the bullet struck him in the chest. Stunned, he dropped down to his knees. The moment of shock left him vulnerable to another shot. *Collin. Abi.*

The crack of a bullet split the air again as he dove for cover. This time, the bullet whizzed past his ear on the way down.

"I said put your hands in the air where I can see them!" Abi's demand was met with the perp turning to fire in her direction.

Was he determined to be shot and killed instead of serving time? How would justice be served if the bastard was dead?

Grayson couldn't allow it. Not as long as he had breath inside him.

The Sig Sauer P365 in his hands had a lower capacity of ten rounds. Grayson had no idea if he'd reloaded to full capacity after the attempt on Max. He'd lost count on how many rounds the bastard had fired so far.

Going at him would be taking a chance. Was it worth risking his life?

Abi moved toward the perp from behind. Was she enough of a distraction to allow Grayson to get close enough to disarm the man?

A determined criminal with nothing to lose wasn't the best guy to end a field career on, but here Grayson was. There was no going back now. His job was dangerous, but he was also a damn fine agent.

Would his skills be enough?

Not going home to Collin wasn't an option. So Grayson moved in the trees as Abi shouted and moved at a slower pace.

The motorcycle was parked in between two compact cars, providing little cover but a decent line of sight.

Reprehensible seemed to sense how close he was to losing his freedom because he started firing one after the other, narrowly missing Grayson's head with one of the wild shots.

Grayson was a car's length away when he heard the telltale click, no bullet.

Not wasting a second for the perp to reload, Grayson jumped from behind the tree and barreled into Reprehensible. The last-minute dive knocked the killer off balance. He flew off the bike as Grayson grabbed hold of his sweatshirt, landing on top of the bastard. The hard fall caused Grayson's elbow to smack concrete. Pain reverberated up his arm, exploding in his shoulder.

A flurry of desperate kicks and punches was like holding on to a tornado. Grayson took a knee where no man wanted to be hit.

"Freeze or I'll shoot," Abi said. Her voice was close enough to indicate she was standing roughly five feet away.

A glance in her direction revealed she was in an athletic

stance, the business end of her service weapon pointed at the two men.

The break in concentration cost Grayson an elbow to the throat. Arms flying every which way, trying to pin this bastard down was like trying to wrestle an alligator on crack.

The perp bucked, trying to break free of Grayson's grasp. The man must know Abi wouldn't shoot while Grayson was tangled up. She wouldn't risk shooting a fellow law enforcement agent.

Grayson doubled down on strength as he wrapped his arms around the man's torso in an attempt to pin his arms to his sides.

The move almost worked. A moment before Grayson was able to clasp his fingers together, the perp broke free. He rolled straight toward Abi, who delivered a kick hard enough to scramble the perp's brain.

It gave Grayson enough time to properly pin the bastard as a flood of footsteps arrived on the scene.

Just as Grayson felt himself losing his hold, Abi was there by his side. She helped wrangle Reprehensible's arms behind his back where an officer from Austin PD slapped cuffs on the guy's wrists.

Grayson rolled onto his back as the assailant was forced to his feet. A moment later, his legs were spread, his torso flat on the hood of a compact car, and he was being searched for any additional weapons.

But when he glanced up at Abi, his blood ran cold.

Time slowed to a stop, moving frame by frame. She mouthed two words that ripped his heart to shreds: "I'm sorry."

Abi dropped down to her knees as EMTs roared up to the scene.

And he shouted the words no law enforcement professional ever wanted to utter, "Officer down."

Blood dripped from her fingertips as she sat back on her heels, in shock.

Grayson was there to catch her before she hit her head on the pavement. "Stay with me. Look at me."

Abi's gaze fixed on him. There was blood pooled on the sidewalk. She was losing too much blood. Was she in shock?

Not two seconds later, an EMT was crouched down beside Grayson.

"What's your name, sweetheart?" the young man asked. His name tag read Charley.

Calling Abi sweetheart should have had fire coursing through her. Face pale, she nodded and then forced a word out. "Abi."

"Abi, you're going to be just fine," Charley said. "Do you hear me?"

Nothing.

"Nod if you can hear me," Charley said as he cut off her blazer from neck to end of sleeve. Blood pulsed from the base of her neck like a geyser.

Charley was on it with pads and pressure. "I need a cart here. Now!"

Grayson was no doctor, but he'd swear a bullet had hit her carotid artery. He muttered a string of curses that would make his grandmother disown him if she was still alive.

He bent down to her ear, "I can't lose you, Abi." Their "friendship" or whatever she wanted to call it was too special. Would the world be so cruel as to take away the only other woman he could see himself loving?

Correction, that he loved?

"Where are you taking her?" he asked Charley as an oxygen mask was placed over her mouth by a second EMT. Charley maintained pressure on her neck.

"Austin General," Charley shouted as she was being wheeled away.

Grayson recalled his government-issued sedan was parked a couple of blocks from here. An officer stepped into view as Grayson turned around.

"I thought you would want to know that the victim has been recovered," the Austin PD officer stated with a look of compassion. "She's already on her way to the same hospital as Marshal Remington and is being listed in stable condition."

"Thank you," Grayson said to the man.

"We'll keep the marshal in our thoughts," he said with a solemn expression. A service vehicle pulled up lights and sirens on. "Officer Perez volunteered to give you a ride to the hospital."

Grayson nodded, thanked the officer and prayed like hell Abi would survive. The only other time he'd felt this helpless was when he'd lost Michelle.

Would history repeat itself?

ABI'S MOUTH WAS as dry as Texas dirt in August. She couldn't summon enough saliva to spit if her life depended on it. She blinked through blurry eyes. Every piece of her had dried up. The cotton taste in her mouth made her want to drink a gallon of water.

"Hey," the familiar voice that had a way of sending warmth through her said.

The next sound was chair legs scraping against tile, moving toward her. She turned her head in time to see the most gorgeous face… Grayson's.

"How do you feel?" he asked, his voice heavy with concern.

"What time is it?" she asked, trying to sit up so she could have a civil conversation. She also needed to find water before her throat cracked from dryness.

"Tomorrow," he said with a smile that caused her insides to melt.

He placed the remote that controlled the bed in her hand.

"Water?" she managed to squeak out as the bed rose until she was in a comfortable sitting position.

The curtains were almost completely closed, allowing in a sliver of sunlight.

Grayson handed her a clear supersize carafe with blue markings to indicate the water level. The carafe must make it easier on the nurses to see how much water intake each patient managed without an IV.

Abi took a few sips before leaning her head back. "Better."

"Do you want me to call for a nurse?" Grayson asked. He was still in the same clothes as yesterday.

She shook her head, wanting a few more moments with just the two of them. He had a life to get back to, so he was probably waiting for her to wake up before he headed out. "Have you been here all night?"

She figured she knew the answer but asked anyway because what she wanted to tell him meant putting her heart on the line. And he needed to know how she felt about him.

"I'm not leaving your side, Abi."

A thrill of awareness shot through her at the sincerity

in his voice, combined with the way he looked at her when he said it.

"Sandra?"

Grayson took his seat again but kept a hand on her. The connection sent shivers racing up her arm while causing warmth to flood her.

"She was treated and released last night," he said. "Other than a cut on her right cheek that needed twenty-four stitches and several bruises, she is going to be fine physically."

That was a relief.

"She's being provided with a list of counseling services along with victim support group information," he continued. "Her parents arrived last night and promised to get her all the help she needed."

"That's good," she said as relief washed over her. She took a few more sips of water. "She'll need support to manage the emotional scars a horrific event like this leaves."

"The family is setting up a victims' rights fund in your name," Grayson supplied.

"Me?"

"You saved Sandra's life," he said. "You saved mine too, in more ways than one."

"It's my job," she countered. "It's what we do."

"You were amazing," he continued as she tried to not read too much into his last statement.

"Your sister was notified, by the way. She asked me to tell you that there's no change in your grandparents," he continued.

"You spoke to Crystal?"

"Yes," he confirmed. "Everyone has checked in, so I've spoken to Crystal and Duke. Your cousins Julie, Dalton and

Camden needed to hear that you were going to be okay directly from me or they threatened to walk off their jobs."

Abi smiled at the image of her clan charging into the hospital.

"Once they were reassured that you would be fine, they requested a call the minute you were up to talking," he said, handing over her phone. "They also requested an update the second your eyes opened. Should you do the honors?"

Staring at the phone in the palm of her hand, she fired off a quick message to ease everyone's concerns. With everything else going on with the family, she wanted to put their minds at ease as soon as possible.

"What about Reprehensible?" she asked, gripping the phone tighter. "By now you must know his story."

"The haircuts were the first indicator, but Nathan Cruz was dressing his victims to look like a male," Grayson began. "Nathan was a grad student who was kicked out due to aggressive behavior toward his students as a teaching assistant. Turns out, he spent his childhood being taunted and tortured by his half brother."

Abi cringed. There was no excuse for the pain and devastation Nathan had inflicted on individuals and their families, but the worst felons had stories that started with intense abuse at an early age.

"Nathan's mother was a single parent who was barely able to keep food on the table," Grayson continued. "She crossed the border into Reynosa to beg for money when she was in between jobs. The woman was doing everything she could to provide for the boys who came from different fathers."

"Families make such an impact on individuals," she surmised, grateful for the amazing siblings, cousins and grandparents who'd given her love and encouragement. She might have lost her mother and never had a father, but she'd been surrounded by love. It made all the difference.

Grayson nodded before continuing, "The perp's half brother came home after living out on a rig for years when he lost his temper on their mother, accidentally killing her before turning the gun on himself."

"That's awful," Abi said, unable to even begin to process what that might do to a young mind.

"Nathan is intelligent," Grayson pointed out. "Genius IQ, in fact."

"Most true geniuses can't tie their own shoelaces," she stated. "I always saw that kind of genius as being given extra in one area at the cost of having something taken away."

"I couldn't agree more," Grayson said. After a thoughtful pause, he continued, "Nathan became aggressive with any student who resembled his half brother following the tragedy."

"Since his half brother wasn't around to punish, he had to find other people to punish and make it look random," she surmised.

"That's right," Grayson confirmed.

A nurse interrupted the conversation. She took vitals, checked machines and then provided a menu. Before leaving, she told Abi how to request a meal.

Now that Grayson had made sure Abi was going to be fine, he had a life to get home to and a child waiting.

She set the menu down and took in a deep breath. What she had to say to Grayson couldn't wait. If he rejected her, she'd rather rip the Band-Aid off now.

Chapter Twenty-Two

"I guess we can finally put the case to rest," Abi said. Was that supposed to be Grayson's cue to leave?

Because what he had to say couldn't wait.

"I'm not planning on leaving," Grayson said to her. His heart thundered in his chest. His palms were suddenly soaked.

"What about Collin?" she asked.

"Martha is staying over for the time being," he confirmed. Finding the words to convey how he felt wasn't easy. Fear of being rejected knocked on the door.

But walking away without knowing if Abi felt the same way would be much worse even though this was a dead end. Abi didn't do kids. He had Collin.

"There's something I need to tell you," he said, after scrounging up the courage. "I've fallen in love with you even though I'm fully aware that nothing can ever come of it because I have a kid and, well, you've admitted several times to not being able to stand kids."

"That's where you're wrong, Grayson," she stated, giving him a tiny speck of hope. Was it dangerous? Because he couldn't put Collin through another loss like the one he'd suffered when Michelle died. "That little boy wriggled into my heart the moment I saw him sitting on the floor playing with his toys. Then, he talked to me and cemented the deal."

Warmth spread through Grayson's chest. Was it possible they could become a family?

"I know it's early and from the outside looking in it must seem like we barely know each other," she continued. "But I'm in love with you, Grayson. I've fallen hard and fast, and I don't want to be apart ever again." She paused before adding, "Is that too much, too soon?"

Grayson took her hand in his, "I never believed in love at first sight until you, Abi. And I've fallen hard." He was experienced enough to know the difference between infatuation and the real deal. This was it. His heart wanted Abi. "Abi Remington, I love you. And it's complicated but there's no one else in the world I want to figure life out with aside from you."

Tears streamed down Abi's cheeks as she nodded. "It's only ever been you. I never saw myself being in love with anyone let alone having a family. But I see those things with you, Grayson. I see a future that I never dreamed to imagine. I didn't think I had it in me but, it turns out, my heart was waiting for you."

He took a knee beside her bed. "Then, my next question comes easy. Will you become my equal partner in life? The person I can't wait to come home to every night? The person I'll sit on the porch and wait for until you come home every night?" He paused. "What I'm asking is…will you marry me?"

Abi's eyes sparkled as she smiled. "With all my heart, yes." And then a twinkle sparked in her eye. "I would very much like to be Collin's mother someday. I'll never replace Michelle, and I wouldn't want to, because I, of all people, know how important it is for Collin to hear the stories about Michelle. To grow up loving his mother with all his heart and, someday, understand the sacrifice she made to give him life."

Now tears welled in Grayson's eyes.

"My promise to Collin is to love him as though he is my own, but give him room to love his mother first," Abi said. "To keep her memory alive out of my love for him."

"You are an amazing person, Abi Remington," Grayson said. "And I'm the luckiest person in the world to get to be the one to love you."

The family Grayson had stopped believing would be possible was finally here. He would always have a special place in his heart for Michelle. A piece of him would always miss her. But he couldn't bring her back. Instead, she lived on in their son.

Collin would know his mother through pictures and stories. Abi had shown Grayson how important that was to a kid.

"Since we need Collin's approval to make this official, think we should have him come to the hospital?" Abi asked.

"I have an idea," he said, grabbing his cell. He made a call to Martha's voice using a video app. She answered on the second ring. "Do you mind putting Collin on the call?"

"Not a bit," Martha said.

A second later, his sweet face filled the screen.

"Hey, buddy," Grayson started. "Remember how you asked Abi to be your Mommy?"

"Yeah. Yeah." Collin chanted.

"I have great news," Grayson said through the excitement. "She said yes."

Collin lost his cool in the way only a kid could do. He jumped up and down. Excitement burst out of him.

When Martha finally had him settled again, it was her face on the screen next to his. "If I heard that correctly, I couldn't be happier for the both of you. Collin and I want to be the first to congratulate you."

"Thank you," Abi chimed in. More of those tears stained her cheeks.

Grayson ended the call before feathering kisses on her face. "I can't wait to start forever with you, Abi."

"Forever starts now," she said. "If you're up for the challenge, that is."

"I'm up for anything as long as you're with me," he quipped.

She shot him a mischievous look. "Oh, really? Because we have yet to tell my family the news."

"I hate to tell you, my love, but I asked for your hand in marriage before I proposed," he said with a grin.

"Well, then, we need to get me out of this hospital so we can start the honeymoon," Abi said with the kind of smile that wrapped him in love.

Together with Abi and Collin, he was ready to face the world—a world that finally gave him the family he'd never known he craved.

One week later

ABI SAT WITH her hands in her lap, tapping her foot on the tile in the headmistress's office.

Headmistress Evelyn Chin, an elegant woman, entered

the room and then took her seat across from Abi and Grayson. The office had framed pictures of various geniuses hung on the walls. The furniture was simple but sophisticated. Several impressive degrees were in frames to one side of the office. The color palette was calming, and the place had an inviting feel. Toys meant to evaluate intelligence were in the adjacent play area. Abi wondered if she would pass muster.

"Thank you for waiting," Dr. Chin said before clasping her hands and placing them on top of her desk.

"No problem, Dr. Chin," Abi conceded.

Waiting for Collin's evaluation results along with whether he would be accepted into the school had Abi's stomach churning. Grayson reached over and took Abi's hand. She realized he was just as nervous as she was.

Dr. Chin looked from Grayson to Abi and back. "I don't have to tell you how impressive your son's intelligence is."

No, she didn't. But it was a good place to start.

Playing it cool, Abi nodded and smiled.

"Collin is a loving child, who takes in the world with an inquisitive eye," Dr. Chin continued.

Was this her version of hyping them up before letting them down? Because the hype had Abi praying Collin was about to be given good news.

"After spending time with your son and allowing him a chance to shadow one of our students, I'm pleased to offer Collin a place in our school," Dr. Chin said. "There's a catch, though."

The brief moment of excitement died with the qualification.

"And that is?" Abi asked. Grayson's hand squeezed hers tighter.

"One of our students is moving and their spot is open next week," Dr. Chin. "If Collin can take it, his admission is guaranteed."

"Not a problem," Abi said as she felt the relief in Grayson's hand. "Collin can start tomorrow."

Dr. Chin stood up, smiled and offered a handshake. "Good. Because he indicated to one of the teachers that he never wanted to leave."

Abi couldn't hold back her smile. Collin was smart, inquisitive, and more than ready to leave his old school behind.

She couldn't wait for her and Grayson to tell him the news.

"Your son is waiting for you in the lobby with one of our student aides," Dr. Chin said.

Your son. Abi liked the sound of those words. Now that Collin's school situation was straightened out, she could head back to the hospital to be with her grandparents. And the hope they, too, would wake up soon.

* * * * *

STALKED THROUGH
THE MIST

CARLA CASSIDY

Prologue

Colette Broussard ran wildly through the swamp, gasps of pain and terror escaping her. She had to get away. She needed to escape from the madman who had held her captive for three long months. She had to get away from him before he finished killing her and there was no question in her mind that he would eventually kill her.

She ran, despite her dizziness and disorientation. The tree limbs and brush slapped against her and even the soft whisper of the Spanish moss against her bruised and broken body made her want to scream in pain. But she couldn't scream; if she did, then he might hear her and capture her again.

Time had no meaning as she pushed her body to gain as much distance as possible between her and the monster who had kidnapped her.

It was only when she reached the edge of the swamp that she completely collapsed, unable to push herself and her broken body any longer. She fell to her knees and then to the ground where she curled up into a fetal ball.

She closed her eyes, unable to hold them open. As she remained there, she became conscious of her heartbeat. It was slow and irregular. She was going to die here. The monster had killed her despite her escape from him.

That was her last thought before a wave of darkness called to her and she eagerly sought it to escape her pain.

Chapter One

The sunset glinted on the water and painted the entire swamp in a soft golden light. Birds sang their swan songs for the day from the tops of the cypress and tupelo trees that dripped with Spanish moss.

Angel Marchant used a push pole to guide her pirogue toward the back of her shanty. The fish she'd caught this evening would make a nice gift for her parents. Once she reached her shanty's back deck, she tied up the boat and then grabbed the stringer of fish to carry to her parents' place.

She moved through the swampland with ease, knowing from her twenty-seven years of living here exactly where to step and when to jump over the unexpected pools of water that appeared.

It didn't take her long to be at her parents' shanty. "Hey, Dad," she yelled in greeting as she crossed the wooden bridge that led to the front door of the small home on stilts.

The door opened and her father smiled at her. John Marchant had always been a tall man, but arthritis in his back bent him over slightly at the waist. Still, he was a handsome man with salt-and-pepper hair and dark eyes that gazed at her with obvious love. "Angel, what a pleasant surprise," he said and stepped aside to allow her entry.

Angel's mother, Maria, got up from the chair where she'd been sitting. Maria was still a beautiful woman with long black hair and dark green eyes. "Angel, we didn't expect to see you today," she said and kissed her daughter on the cheek.

Angel was very close to her parents, who had raised her with absolute and unconditional love and taught her love and respect for the swamp.

The shanty was three rooms. The living area and kitchen were small, as was the single bedroom and bathroom. During her years at home, Angel had slept on a cot next to the potbellied stove where her mother cooked all their meals.

"I brought you some fish," Angel said and handed her father the stringer. "There's several good catfish there."

"I see that. Looks like dinner to me, right, Mama?" John said as he carried the fish to the metal bin that served as a sink.

"Right," Maria agreed. "I'll fry them up here in just a few minutes. Thank you, Angel, you want to stay to eat with us?"

"Thanks, but no thanks. I'm actually thinking about getting some of my friends together tonight for a few beers. It's been a while since we've all been together," Angel replied.

"Why don't you sit a spell and visit," John said. "Have you heard about Colette Broussard?"

"No, was her body found?" Angel sank down on the sofa next to her father.

Colette Broussard was one of five people who had just disappeared without a trace from the swamp. Colette had been missing for over three months and most people had just assumed she, along with the others, were dead.

"What I heard in town this morning is that she was found half-naked and unconscious near Fisherman's Tree. She'd been beaten badly and had rope marks around her wrists and ankles," John said.

"That's horrible, but it gives me a little hope for the other people who have been missing," Angel replied. "Hopefully the others are still alive and she'll be able to lead Etienne to where they're all being held." A chill threatened to walk up her spine as she thought of the person who had been dubbed the Swamp Soul Stealer, a monster who made people disappear without a trace.

Etienne Savoie was not only the chief of police for the small town of Crystal Cove, but also for the swamp area that half surrounded the town. He was a good man who had been working hard on the missing persons cases.

"I don't know about that," John replied. "According to Louis at the grocery store, it's not a sure thing that she'll even survive."

"God bless her soul," Maria said as she sat back down in the chair facing the sofa. "I hope you're being very careful, Angel." She looked at her daughter worriedly.

"Don't worry, I'm very careful when I'm out and about," Angel assured her mother. "Besides, I take little sister with me whenever I leave my house."

"Little sister?" Angel's father looked at her curiously.

Angel pulled out the knife she carried in a sheath on a belt around her waist and beneath her clothes. It was a wickedly sharp fishing knife that could gut a man with a single thrust. She had started wearing it when the second person, a young man in her friend group named Luka Lurance, had gone missing.

"Don't be afraid to use it if need be," her father said.

"Don't worry. I take my own safety very seriously," Angel replied with a small laugh. "And on that note, I think I'll head back home before it gets any later." She stood and her father got up as well. "I'll see you in the next day or two. If you need anything, call me."

A few moments later Angel headed back down the bridge and then took off in the direction of her own shanty. She not only brought her parents fish occasionally, but she also fished for a living, selling what she caught to the local grocery store and the café in town.

As she slowly walked down the narrow trail that would lead her home, she drew in a deep breath of the scents that surrounded her. It was the scents of green things and various flowers and beneath that the faint smell of decay.

She loved living in the swamp. Some of her friends were working hard to save up enough money to leave the marshlands behind forever, but Angel had never wanted to live anyplace else. The swamp was in her blood...in her very soul.

Her thoughts turned to the people she was hoping to gather this evening for a little social time. Besides Angel, there were three women and three men who had run the swamp as young kids and grown to trust and rely on each other. Their friendship bond was tight and they were definitely ride or die for each other.

She hadn't gone far when she heard it—a deep cry for help coming from someplace off the trail she was on. Each and every muscle in her body tensed as she slowly followed the cries. Was this somehow a ruse? Did a man really need help or was he just pretending to in order to draw somebody close to him?

With the earlier talk about the Swamp Soul Stealer fresh in her head, she pulled the knife sheath out of the top of her jeans where the knife could be grabbed quickly by her if necessary.

She came to another narrow trail and the voice sounded closer. It was definitely a male and distress filled his deep voice. She continued to creep closer and then she saw him. He sat on the edge of the path. His dark hair gleamed in the dappled sunlight that cast through the trees and she could see his lower right leg was bloody.

He looked up at the sound of her approach and his blue eyes gazed at her in obvious relief. A jolt of electricity shot through her. Lordy, but the man was totally hot.

"Hi," he said. "Uh…my name is Nathan Merrick and I seem to have cut my leg pretty badly. Uh…is it possible you could just help me to get back up on my feet? Then I should be able to get to my car and to my motel room in town."

It was obvious this wasn't a ruse. The man's leg was definitely injured and appeared to still be bleeding badly. "I can help you up." She walked close enough to him and then saw he had in his hand a fancy-looking camera case. "Put that down," she instructed and held out both her hands toward him.

He placed the camera case on the side next to him and then reached out and grabbed her hands. Again, an electric tingle flooded through her. His hands were big and warm as they gripped hers.

She yanked on him and he rose to his feet, but instantly

groaned as he tried to put pressure on his injured leg. He listed heavily to his good leg as she picked up his camera case and handed it to him.

"Thank you," he said and then took a couple of limping steps forward that made the wound on his leg bleed even more.

"You're welcome, but I think you aren't going to make it all the way to your car and back into town the way that gash is bleeding. My shanty isn't far from here. Come with me and I'll bandage you up and then you can be on your way," she said.

"Really? Thank you so much. I can't tell you how much I would appreciate it." He winced again and she moved to his side so he could lean on her.

It was odd that despite his broad shoulders and solid build, she felt no real fear of him. Maybe it was because a man who groaned under his breath with each step he took didn't seem like much of a threat.

"Who do I send the thank-you flowers to?" he asked as they began to walk.

"What do you mean?" she asked.

"I mean when a lady walks you to her house and offers first-aid services, I should at least know her name," he replied. He gazed at her intently. God, the man had gorgeous eyes with long dark lashes. He smelled yummy, like what she'd always thought a fresh ocean breeze would smell like.

"Oh, I'm Angel… Angel Marchant," she replied.

"You're certainly my angel at the moment," he said with a friendly smile. "I was afraid I was going to be out there bleeding all night long."

"Do you know what you cut yourself on?" she asked.

"I don't have a clue," he replied. "I just took one step and something sharp cut me. I tried to look around to see what it was, but I couldn't find anything."

"That's my place just ahead," she said.

Her shanty lived on stilts like so many others in the swamp. It was larger than her parents' place, although it was also only three rooms. She had spent a lot of her money on the structure itself, making sure it was solidly built for a woman living alone.

She continued to help him across the bridge that led to her porch and then she unlocked her door. Once it was open, she guided him to the sofa and he sank down.

"Let me go get some supplies and I'll be right back," she said. She went into her bathroom, which held a tiny closet with shelves. On one of them was a first-aid kit and also a container with more injury supplies. She added in several wet washcloths and a tub full of water to clean up the blood.

Before she carried it out, she took a few moments to draw in several deep breaths. Finding an injured stranger was certainly not a common thing. Finding an injured totally hot man in the swamp had definitely never happened to her before.

As attractive as he was, she knew nothing about him and in any case, she just intended to bandage up his leg and then send him on his way. She needed to get to it before complete darkness fell.

He had the look of the city all over him, from the scent of his cologne to the make of the khaki shorts and the khaki-and-dark-green-patterned short-sleeved button-up shirt he wore. He didn't look like a man who would be comfortable finding his way out of the swamp in the dark.

With that thought in mind, she left the bathroom and returned to where he remained sitting on the sofa with his leg propped up on the coffee table.

"I normally don't put my feet up on the furniture, but I didn't want to bleed all over your sofa or the pretty rug on the floor," he said.

"Thank you for being thoughtful about that." She set her items on the coffee table next to his leg and then she sat on the table so she could minister to him. "I'm sorry, but I'm probably going to hurt you."

"I understand," he replied.

She felt his gaze on her as she began to wipe away the excess blood. Thankfully at some point the big gash had finally stopped bleeding. But it still oozed and it was definitely a nasty wound.

He only tensed up once and that was when she poured alcohol on the gash to clean it out. "If you don't mind my asking, what were you doing out in the swamp. You don't look like you belong here," she said as she began to bandage up the wound.

"Actually, I'm a biologist and I've been studying and photographing the flora and fauna here in the swamp. I've been commissioned to write a book about swamps. Unfortunately, I barely got started before this happened."

She looked up at him in surprise. A biologist? She'd never met anyone like him before. He smiled at her. "In other words, I'm a nerd...a science nerd."

She quickly looked back down at his leg. He certainly didn't look like a nerd. He was way too hot to be a nerd. "I think that will do it," she said as she finished wrapping the last of the bandage around his leg. "If I were you, I'd see a doctor in town first thing tomorrow."

"I will, and I can't thank you enough for everything you've done for me," he said.

"I couldn't very well walk away from you and let you bleed to death," she replied.

"Well, I'll just get out of your hair now." He went to stand up and instantly fell back on the sofa. He tried to stand again but it was obvious his leg was still weak and hurt too much to hold his weight.

She looked out the window where darkness had completely fallen. It was at least a fifteen-minute walk to get out of the swamp to where he'd probably parked his car. How could she just put him out in the dark when he could barely walk?

"It's obvious your leg is still hurting you badly," she said. "You can spend the night here on my sofa and hopefully you'll be well enough to walk out of here tomorrow."

He frowned, the gesture doing nothing to detract from his handsome features. "Are you sure that would be okay?"

"Positive," she replied. "I'll just go get you a pillow and a sheet to help you get comfortable."

She went into her bedroom and closed the door behind her. It was odd, but she felt no fear of him. Still, he was a stranger and she really knew nothing about him, and she was a woman all alone.

With these thoughts in mind, she pulled her cell phone out of her back pocket and quickly called one of her best friends, Shelby Santori. "Shelby, I need a big favor from you."

"What do you need?" Shelby asked.

"Can you spend the night here tonight? I know it's late notice, but I would really appreciate it."

"Sure…but why?"

"I discovered a man in the swamp. He has an injured leg and so I told him he could sleep on my sofa for tonight. But I'd feel far more comfortable if somebody else was here with me."

"I'll be there in fifteen or so," Shelby said without asking any more questions.

Angel gathered up the sleeping items for Nathan and then carried them back into the living room and set them all down on the chair that faced her sofa. She lit several lanterns in the room and then sank down on the sofa in the opposite corner from him.

"I can't believe you're going to so much trouble for me," he said.

"You needed help. Folks here in the swamp don't walk away from people who need help," she replied. "How does your leg feel now?"

"I could try to be a macho man and tell you it's feeling just fine, but the truth of the matter is it hurts like hell."

"I'm sorry I don't have anything to give you to help with the pain," she replied.

"That's okay. It should start feeling better with each hour that passes."

Once again, she could smell the totally awesome scent of him and his body heat warmed her in a distinctly pleasant way. Lordy, but she found the man attractive.

However, he was simply a stranger that was spending the night and would be gone tomorrow.

ANGEL WAS THE most beautiful woman Nathan had seen in years. Her black hair cascaded down her back in a curtain of richness. Her eyes were an interesting shade of green and rimmed with long dark lashes. Her features were delicate and amazingly attractive. However her mouth was wide and generous and her lips were plump and lush, only adding to her overall beauty.

She was clad in a pair of jeans that showcased her long legs and a fitted navy T-shirt that emphasized her slender waist and medium-sized breasts. God, but she was gorgeous.

"You have a nice place here," he said.

"Thank you, I love it here."

The room felt cozy with the sofa and chair and also a small potbellied stove. There was a small bookcase that held not only books, but also some knickknacks.

The kitchen area held a small table with four chairs and a sink and countertop. That was all he could see from his vantage point. The floors were a rich wood and covered by several braided rugs in vivid colors.

"You were born in the swamp?" he asked. He was interested in everything about her.

She nodded. "Not too far from here. I was born in the swamp as were my parents and my grandparents and so on," she replied.

"If you don't mind my asking, what do you do for a living out here?" He had no idea if he was getting too personal or not, but he was definitely curious about her and her life here.

"I fish for a living," she replied. "I sell the fish I catch to the grocery store and café in town." At that moment there was a knock on her door. "Excuse me," she said. "My friend and I had planned a sleepover for tonight and I haven't had a chance to call her to cancel."

"Please don't cancel your plans on my account. I'll just sit here and be quiet and try to disappear into the furniture," he replied.

She got up and went to the door. A woman swept in and stopped at the sight of him. She appeared to be about Angel's age and, while pretty, she didn't hold a candle to Angel. She carried with her a small overnight bag.

"Well, what a surprise," she said. "Hi, I'm Shelby Santori."

"I'm Nathan Merrick, and Angel rescued me when I cut my leg." He gestured toward his bandaged leg.

"That's our Angel, always ready to help anyone who needs it," Shelby replied. She looked at Angel. "So, are we still on for tonight?"

"Please, whatever the two of you had planned, don't cancel because of me," Nathan said.

"All we had planned was getting into Angel's bed and gossiping for half the night," Shelby replied with a laugh.

"Uh…before we do that, could I get you something to eat?" Angel asked him as she moved the pillow and sheet from the chair to one end of the sofa.

Despite the fact that it was getting late, Nathan had no appetite. Besides, out here in the swamp he doubted she could just whip something up for him without a lot of trouble and the last thing he wanted to do was cause her any more trouble.

"No, thanks. I'm really not hungry, although I wouldn't mind some water," he replied.

"Of course," she replied. She walked over to the kitchen

area and pulled a bottle of water from what appeared to be a built-in small refrigerator. She walked back over and handed it to him. "I'll leave the lamps burning for you and the bathroom is the doorway on the left. Is there anything else I can do for you?"

"No, you've done far more than enough. I'll never be able to thank you enough for your kindness," he replied. "I'll be fine here for tonight."

"Great," Shelby said and grabbed Angel by the arm. "Come on, girlfriend. We have a lot to talk about tonight."

"Good night, Nathan. I hope you sleep well," Angel said and then Shelby pulled her into a room he assumed was Angel's bedroom. The door closed behind them and then there was silence.

Except there wasn't complete silence as he became aware of bullfrogs croaking and water gently lapping against the stilts that held the shanty up.

He settled into the sofa with his head on the pillow and the sheet covering him. The pillow smelled like the woman... He'd noticed Angel's beguiling fragrance when she was supporting him on the walk to this place. It was the scent of mysterious flowers and spices...very alluring.

He was ridiculously drawn to her, but tomorrow he'd be leaving here and he doubted he'd ever see her again. His leg hurt badly, but with the rhythm of the frogs croaking and the water lapping, he fell asleep and into pleasant dreams about Angel.

Chapter Two

Nathan awakened around dawn. His leg still ached, but he managed to make it to the bathroom and then back to the sofa. He hadn't been sitting there too long when the bedroom door opened and Angel and Shelby came into the living room. Angel wore a pair of denim shorts and a red T-shirt and once again looked positively stunning.

"Good morning," both the women said to him at the same time.

"Good morning to you two," he replied.

"How is your leg feeling this morning?" Angel asked.

"It still hurts, but not quite as badly. I should be able to get out of your house this morning," he said.

"Let me make you some breakfast before you go," Angel said.

"And that's my cue to get out of here," Shelby said. "It was nice meeting you, Nathan. And girlfriend, I'll talk to you later." With that, Shelby left.

"I'm just going to go start up my generator, I'll be right back." Angel disappeared out a back door in the kitchen. He heard a faint thrum and then she came back in.

"So, you have a generator to give you electricity when you want it?" he asked.

"Yes, I use it to charge my phone and I have a two-burner electric cooktop for when I don't want to make a fire and cook on the potbellied stove," she explained.

She remained in the kitchen area. "I hope you like eggs and toast because that's what's on the menu this morning."

"That sounds great, but you really don't have to cook for me. You've already done more than enough."

"It's a rule of mine," she said and offered him a bright smile. "I never send a wounded man back out to the swamp without fixing him eggs and toast."

He returned her smile. "Far be it from me to be the man who makes you break your rule." From his vantage point, he couldn't really see what she was doing. "Do you mind if I come and sit at your table?"

"Not at all, in fact, I'm making a pot of coffee right now."

He was definitely looking forward to a cup of coffee, but even though he intended to leave here, she still intrigued him. Her lifestyle was so different from his. She was so different from any other woman he had ever known before.

He moved to the table and watched as she got a four-cup coffee maker out, plugged it into an outlet on the wall and then got it working. She then pulled out the two-burner stovetop and set it on the counter.

"Do you have a cell phone you want me to plug in?" she asked as she plugged in her own.

"I have a cell phone, but I don't have the charger with me and in any case, I can do that once I get back to the motel." He watched as she then pulled an iron skillet out of a lower cabinet.

"And now, for the most important question of the day…" she said and turned to look at him. "How do you like your eggs?"

"Any way you want to make them," he replied. The scent of fresh coffee filled the room and she poured him a cup and set it before him.

"Ah, thank you…the nectar of the gods," he said.

She laughed, the sound musical and very pleasant. "So, you're one of those," she said and raised one of her perfect dark eyebrows.

He laughed. "One of what?"

"One who likes to be fueled by caffeine."

He laughed again. "Actually, I'm a two-cup man in the morning and that's it. I much prefer sports drinks for the rest of the day."

"Well, I hope you like cheesy scrambled eggs because that's what I'm making."

"How did you know that that's my favorite breakfast?" he replied lightly.

She turned to look at him again. "Are you always so pleasant?"

"I try to be," he said more seriously. "I spend so much of my work time by myself either in my lab or in a field or a marsh that when I'm around people, I always try to be friendly and respectful."

"That's a nice way to be," she replied.

She grabbed a small container of milk, a bag of shredded cheese and a carton of eggs from the mini built-in refrigerator that blended in with her cabinets.

"How do you manage to keep your refrigerator running?

I know you just turned on your generator a little while ago," he asked.

"Oh, it's not a refrigerator, it's a cooler. About three times a week I go into town and buy blocks of ice for it." She pulled a toaster out of the cabinet and set it on the counter.

"Sorry I have so many questions, but I've never been in one of the shanties before and I find it all very interesting. In fact, yesterday was the first time I'd actually been in a swamp. I've studied them extensively by sitting at my desk, but I'd never actually been in one."

This time the look she gave him held a little bit of suspicion. "Then how on earth did you get commissioned for a book about swamps?"

A small laugh escaped him. "I wrote a proposal filled with my credentials and all the things I intended to deliver and much to my surprise, they offered me a contract. So, here I am."

She mixed together the eggs, milk and cheese and then poured it all into the awaiting skillet. She got out a loaf of bread and put four slices in the toaster. Finally, she pulled from the cooler a small container of soft butter.

"Why Crystal Cove?" she asked. "Out of all the swamps in the world, why here?"

"First of all, I live in New Orleans, so this was only five or so hours away. The second reason is I fell in love with the name, Crystal Cove. It just sounded so pleasant. The little town is big enough to have a decent motel, but small enough to have real character."

"The nice thing about it is for the most part the townspeople and swamp people get along and respect each other," she replied.

"That's a good thing. From what I've learned, it's not that way everywhere," he replied.

As she finished up the meal, he fell silent and just watched her. She moved with efficiency and grace. If he wasn't careful, he could become quite smitten with her.

It took only a few minutes and then the plates were on the table and she sat across from him. "Enjoy," she said.

"Thank you." He took a sip of the coffee. It was just the way he liked it…strong and black.

"There is one thing you need to be aware of as you go out and about in the swamp," she said.

"And what's that?"

Her eyes appeared to darken. "You need to have a weapon with you whenever you travel. There's somebody out there who is kidnapping people from the swamp and we don't know whether they have been murdered or are being held somewhere."

"Oh, yeah, I read a little bit about it in the paper. He's called the soul sucker or something like that?" He hadn't paid too much attention to the small story on the second page of the *Crystal Cove News*.

"The Swamp Soul Stealer has taken two men and three women. However, one woman who has been missing for three months turned up yesterday half dead from being beaten and bound. This monster is somebody everyone in the swamp should fear."

"What kind of weapon do you carry?" he asked.

"A fishing knife that could gut a man with a single thrust."

"And you could do that?"

"If it was to defend my life, damn right I could do that," she replied firmly. "Now, eat your eggs before they get cold."

He imagined she had to be an incredibly strong woman to live out here all alone. There weren't many conveniences in the swamp, so life out here had to be far more difficult than living in a city or town.

They ate for a few minutes in silence and then began to small-talk about the hot weather and the swamp. "I'll bet you know most of the plants here," he said.

She smiled and once again he was struck by her beauty. "I certainly don't know their fancy scientific names, but yes, I can identify a lot of the plants. My parents were very good teachers when it came to the plant and animal life here in the swamp."

"You said you fish for a living. How does that work?"

"I have some baited lines in the water that I check every morning and sometimes I sit on the bank and fish from there. I have a cage floating off my back porch where I put the fish until I have enough gathered up to make a trip into town," she explained.

"And you can make enough money doing that to survive?" he asked and immediately said, "I'm sorry, I might have gotten too personal."

"No, not at all. I make enough money to fill my basic needs. All I really require is ice for my cooler, gas for my generator and money for my cell phone bill. And at the end of the year, I pay some taxes on this place. I'm saving any extra money I get for some more updates to the shanty."

"And you love living here," he said.

"How do you know that?" She raised one eyebrow again.

"Because your eyes light up when you talk about the swamp and you become quite animated," he replied.

She laughed. "You read me right. And I'll bet I can read you fairly well, too."

"Go for it."

"You love what you do because your face lights up when you talk about your flora and fauna," she said, making him laugh. "But I can't read you about your personal life because you haven't told me anything about it. Are you married? Do you have children?"

"I'm single with no significant other and I have no children. I live in a house but rarely spend much time there. I teach classes at a small community college and if I'm not in the classroom, I'm in the lab or in the field."

"Out of all the flora and fauna in the world, why swamps?" She got up and carried their now-empty plates to the sink, and returned with the coffeepot.

"I've always been curious about swamps," he said. "Thanks," he added as she topped off his coffee. "Growing up in New Orleans, the marshes were part of the landscape. Did you know that swamps have a near perfect ecosystem? It's amazing how the plants all work together to support this system." He realized he was talking too much. "Sorry, I was about to go off on a tangent."

"It's okay, don't apologize for being passionate about your work," she replied.

He was really quite taken with her attractiveness. Her long dark hair begged him to run his fingers through it at the same time her lush lips looked ready for a wild, hot kiss.

Damn, what was wrong with him? It didn't matter how beautiful she was or how easy he found it to talk to her. It didn't matter that she was unique and intrigued him.

In minutes, he was going to walk out of here and would

never see her again unless… "Angel, would you be interested in working for me as a guide of sorts. I'll pay you daily." He mentioned a figure that he knew was a bit generous.

Her eyes widened slightly. "Are you serious?"

"Very serious. I'm sure you know this swamp very well and I don't know it at all. I could definitely use someone to help me get around. All you'd have to do is guide me while I take photographs. So, are you interested?"

"Uh… I don't know. I'd have to think about it."

He finished his coffee. "How long would you need to think about it?"

"I could have an answer for you tomorrow morning," she replied after a moment of hesitation.

"And how would I find you tomorrow morning?" he asked. He had no idea where this shanty was located.

"I'm assuming you parked your car in the lot in front of the swamp's main path in," she said. "It's a fairly big parking area that's used by most of the people who live here."

"Yes, that sounds right," he replied.

"Then I'll meet you there in the morning and I'll give you my answer," she replied.

"On that note, I've taken up enough of your time." He stood.

She also got up from the table. "I'll walk you out to your car."

He started to protest, but the truth was he needed her help to get back. He'd been in so much pain the day before when she'd helped him get here the last thing he'd been paying attention to was the paths they had taken. "Thank you, I'd really appreciate it."

He limped over to the coffee table and picked up his camera while she grabbed a key and her cell phone. Together they stepped out into the morning light.

The swamp was alive with birds singing from the tops of the trees and the sound of splashing coming from the water. The brush rustled with small animals scurrying about and insects whirred their own little songs.

"Sorry, I can't move too fast," he said as he followed her down the bridge and onto the trail.

"That's okay." She flashed him a smile over her shoulder. "I never mind a leisurely walk through the swamp."

She was virtually a stranger, albeit a very kind one, but that didn't explain the way her smile warmed him. He followed behind her and she did walk slow enough for him to keep up. His leg still hurt quite a bit, but not nearly as bad as it had the day before.

They didn't talk as they made their way through the jungle-like maze. It seemed to take forever, but finally they broke into the clearing where his car was parked.

"Angel, I know I've said this before, but I can't thank you enough for your kindness in helping me out," he said as she turned to look at him.

"You were a very easy houseguest," she replied.

"And about the job offer. I really hope you'll consider it."

"Why don't we do this. If I'm in, I'll meet you here tomorrow morning at seven thirty. If I'm not in, I won't be here. It was nice meeting you, Nathan." With that, she turned around and disappeared back into the tangled greenery of the swamp.

Nathan got into his car, but didn't start it up right away.

Instead he sat and thought about the woman who had just left him.

There was no question she was gorgeous, but aside from that, something nebulous drew him toward her. He wanted more of her. He wanted to know her better and he hadn't felt this kind of interest in a woman in a very long time.

He finally started his engine and pulled out of the parking lot. All he could hope for was that she'd be there in the morning.

THE NEXT MORNING around six Angel sat on the bank at her favorite fishing spot. But instead of thinking about catching fish, her thoughts were consumed with thoughts of Nathan Merrick.

There was no question she'd found him extremely attractive. It had been a long time since she'd been interested in a man.

Her last relationship had been four years ago. Jim Fortiner had been a townie and they had dated for a little over two years. She'd thought Jim was her forever man until she'd found out on the nights he wasn't with her, he was with another woman. His double life and utter betrayal had broken her and it had taken her a long time to finally get over it.

Now, at twenty-seven years old, she considered herself older and wiser and just because Nathan was a good-looking, seemingly nice guy, didn't mean she wanted anything more to do with him…or did she?

She'd gone back and forth in her head all night long about the offer to be his guide. When she'd talked to Shelby about it the day before, Shelby thought she'd be crazy not to do it.

"You could build that new deck you've been talking about

or buy a bigger, better generator with the kind of money he's offering you. Seriously, Angel, why on earth wouldn't you do it?" Shelby had said. "It's perfect for you."

Why not, indeed. Maybe she was hesitant because she'd felt an unexpected spark with him, an attraction that she hadn't felt in a very long time. She had a feeling spending more time with him would only draw her closer to him and what was the point of that?

He lived in New Orleans, a four-and-a-half-hour drive from here. He was a scientist who was highly educated. She'd been homeschooled by her mother. They couldn't be more different from each other. Of course he hadn't said anything to indicate to her that he had any interest in her other than her knowledge of the swamp.

And it was far too soon for her to know if she liked him or not. He may be a jerk at heart. Just because he'd been pleasant to her for a night and a morning, didn't mean she would find him pleasant if she knew him better.

At seven o'clock she packed up her fishing supplies and headed home. She left the items on her back deck and then headed toward the parking area.

She hadn't even realized she'd made up her mind to take him up on the offer until she was on her way. She had no idea how long he might want to use her as a guide, but there was no question the money he had offered her could be put to good use.

It didn't take her long to get to the parking area. He was already there standing outside his car. "Angel," he said with a big smile that warmed her more than the morning sun. "You came."

She couldn't help but return his smile. He looked so handsome clad in a royal blue polo that matched the color of his eyes and emphasized his broad shoulders. He also had on a pair of dark blue shorts with a fresh bandage on his calf.

"You offered me a job with pay that I couldn't resist so I decided to come," she replied. Ultimately that's why she was here. Not because Nathan was superhot or that she was somehow drawn to him. This was strictly a business relationship and nothing more.

"So, the first thing we need to hash out is how you want to be paid. I'm assuming you want cash. Do you want to be paid daily? Weekly?"

"Daily," she replied. The *weekly* had thrown her off a little bit. "Uh, how long do you expect this all to take?"

"To be honest, I don't have a real answer. It will take as long as it takes…until I have all the photos I feel like I need to complete the book."

"Do you want to get started today?" she asked.

"Sure, that would be great," he agreed.

"Then let's get started," she replied. She watched as he opened his car door and retrieved his camera. He took the cap off the lens and then nodded.

"How's your leg this morning?" she asked as they entered into the swamp on the path.

"Still hurting, but a bit better," he replied.

"Where exactly would you like to go or what would you like to focus on for the day?" She paused and turned to face him. He stood close enough to her that she could smell the scent of shaving cream mingling with his attractive, slightly spicy and fresh cologne.

"Maybe today we could focus on some of the animals who live here," he said. "Would that be possible?"

"Sure, we can do that," she replied. "I know where the gators lurk and the turtles snap. I also know where the wild boars stay. Keep your camera handy because there are a lot of animals here."

"Just give me a minute. I think I need to change my lens." She watched with interest as he took off the one that had been on the camera and replaced it with a longer one. He grinned at her. "This way I can take photos from far away so a gator doesn't get a chance to eat me."

When he grinned like that, it gave him a new attractiveness that created a warmth deep in the pit of her stomach. "I also added a stun gun to my collection of toys this morning so that soul sucker fellow won't get me."

She laughed. "That helps, but I think we're safe in numbers and during the daylight. In any case, you can stun him and then I'll gut him."

"We're definitely a dangerous duo, so bad guys beware," he replied. For a moment their eye contact held. Oh, she could fall into the depths of his beautiful blue eyes.

She quickly turned around. "Follow me," she said. "I'll take you to some of the gators first."

They walked in silence. She didn't want to get to know him better because she was afraid she might like him too much. *Strictly business*, she reminded herself.

Tonight she planned to be with the people she belonged with…her fellow swamp friends. She certainly didn't belong with somebody like Nathan. She realized she was probably overthinking things. He hadn't shown her any indication he felt the same attraction toward her that she felt toward him.

"You doing okay?" she asked as the path narrowed and they walked deeper into the swamp.

"I'm fine," he replied.

She could move pretty soundlessly through the swamp, but there was no way they were going to sneak up on anything with him making so much noise as he followed behind her. She could tell he was heavily favoring his good leg.

There was a part of her that admired his determination to do his job despite the injury that still had to hurt badly. "Are you under some sort of a deadline?" she asked.

"Not a real firm deadline, but I'd like to have the photos taken in the next month or so," he replied.

A month, and then he'd be gone. All the more reason to keep things strictly professional between them, she told herself. She continued to lead him toward the deep pool of water that several big gators called home.

"We talked about my personal life, but I don't know much about yours. Do you have a significant other?" he asked.

"No, there's nobody special in my life right now," she replied.

"Your friend Shelby seemed very nice," he said.

"She's the best. We've been friends since we were about six. Our parents were friends. She's only one of my friends here in the swamp. In fact, I'm planning on getting them all together tonight for drinks. If you'd like to come, you're more than welcome. It will probably be around seven." What was she doing inviting him to spend time with her after hours?

"Thanks for the invite," he replied. "I'd love to meet your friends."

"We can talk about it more later," she replied, vaguely surprised by his answer. Of course he was a stranger in town.

Maybe he just needed a little social time. That certainly didn't explain why she had invited him in the first place.

By that time they had reached a small cove. Cypress and tupelo trees with their complicated root structures rose up out of the water and dripped with Spanish moss.

There was a quiet, almost mysterious hush here and a pristine, primitive beauty. Nathan stepped up next to her and began to snap photos of the trees. His camera clicked and whirred over and over again.

The sound drew the gators from their resting places. Dark eyes and snouts appeared in the water, obviously curious about this new noise.

Nathan continued to snap photos, quietly gasping as one of the kings of the swamp showed his entire massive body. He took a step closer and his foot slipped, sending him into the water. He gasped, yet managed to hold his camera up over his head and Angel quickly leaned over and grabbed it from him.

She set it on the ground. The loud splash of him falling into the water had called the gators even closer. As he tried to climb back up onto the bank, he slipped down once again. A slight panic lit his eyes and it wasn't until Angel grabbed his hand that he managed to get up out of the water and back on shore.

He rose up directly in front of her, so close she could feel his breath on her face and see the tiny shards of silver in the irises of his eyes.

For a moment she was breathless and her body didn't get her brain's command to step back from him. He remained unmoving as well. His eyes sparked with something that looked like desire and that made her feet move backward and away from him.

"Thanks for helping me out," he finally said, further breaking the awkward moment. "I almost became that big guy's breakfast."

"I should have warned you how slick the bank's edge was," she said.

"Well again, thanks for hauling me out of there."

"No problem. I'm not a big fan of watching gators eat photographers."

He laughed. "Thank God. I'm not a big fan of getting eaten by a gator." He bent over and picked up his camera. "Thank goodness this stayed dry, but since I'm soaking wet, I think this is going to be a very short day. Of course I'll certainly pay you for a full day."

"I'm not worried about that. If fact, since this was such a short day, you don't have to pay me at all."

"We'll see about that," he replied.

She led him back to where his car was parked. Despite his clothes being soaked, he stopped along the way to take more pictures of the plants they passed.

They were silent on the walk back to his car. When they finally reached it, he opened the car door and put his camera inside and then turned to face her. He began to pull his wallet out of his wet pants, but she waved her hands to stop him.

"Really, you don't owe me anything for today," she said emphatically.

"Are you sure? I took up much of your morning."

She smiled. "I've had worse things take up my mornings."

"Is the invite still good for tonight?" he asked.

"Definitely," she replied. "Maybe we should exchange

cell phone numbers just in case things don't work out with my friends tonight."

"We should probably do that anyway since we're working together," he agreed. "Hang on, my cell phone is in my glove box." He slid into the driver's seat, retrieved the phone and then got back out of the car.

It took them only moments to exchange numbers. "If we're on for tonight, I'll just meet you here around six," she said. "And if things don't work out for tonight, I'll give you a call."

"Sounds good to me." He smiled at her and once again an inexplicable warmth swept through her. "Then hopefully I'll see you later this evening."

She stepped back from his car and watched as he pulled out of the parking lot. It was only when his car disappeared from sight that she turned and headed back to her shanty.

She wasn't sure exactly what to make of Nathan Merrick. She especially wasn't sure what to make of her crazy attraction to him. There had been that moment when she'd helped him out of the water that she irrationally thought he might kiss her. What was even more irrational was that she might have welcomed it.

The only thing she did know for sure was she couldn't wait for the evening to come.

Chapter Three

Nathan was thrilled not to get a call canceling the evening plans. He was looking forward to seeing Angel with her friends. The morning with her had been rather awkward. He'd been self-conscious and the unexpected dip in the swamp hadn't helped matters any. He'd been embarrassed by his own clumsiness and needing her to rescue him by pulling him out of the water.

It had been years since he'd had any kind of a relationship or been on a date. He certainly wasn't looking for anything like that with Angel. He only knew he found her vastly attractive and he wanted to get to know her better. Hopefully this evening he would get that opportunity.

When he'd gotten back to the motel room, he'd changed out of his wet clothes and had also changed his bandage. He'd found a walk-in clinic located in the pharmacy and had had his leg checked out by the nurse on duty.

She had given him a tetanus shot and a tube of antibiotic cream to keep on it. She told him he'd probably needed stitches but since the wound was already closed up and healing, he'd been good to go. At about four o'clock he left his motel again and drove through a burger place called The Big D. He took his burger and fries back to his room and ate.

He showered and shaved and changed the bandage on his leg once again and then dressed in a pair of jeans and another blue polo shirt. He added a couple sprays of his favorite cologne. A glance at the clock told him it was almost time to leave and meet Angel for the evening.

Minutes later, when he got into his car, he was surprised to feel a flutter of nerves rush through his veins. It was the anxiety of meeting new people…people who were very different from him. And truth be told, he wanted to impress Angel, and for her friends to like him.

There had been a minute after she'd pulled him out of the water when they'd stood so close together that he could feel her body heat radiating toward him. He could smell the wonderful scent of her and saw a slight flare in the depths of her green eyes.

In that moment he'd wanted to kiss her. He'd wanted to wrap his arms around her, pull her tight against him and explore those lush, inviting lips of hers. Of course he hadn't done that, but it surprised him that he'd even wanted to.

He was about fifteen minutes early arriving at the parking lot. He sat in his car and stared at the swamp ahead of him. It looked primeval and mysteriously beautiful, like the woman it had spawned.

Even though it had been a short morning, he had snapped dozens of good photos today, capturing a number of plants indigenous to the swamp. He'd also gotten several of the alligators. All in all, it had been a good start to his mission.

At that moment Angel appeared in the clearing. Clad in a pair of black jeans and a dark green tank top, and with her dark hair loose around her shoulders, she looked like part of the surroundings. She appeared as mysteriously beautiful and a bit wild, like the mystifying swamp she came from.

He got out of his car and when she smiled at him, he felt a ridiculous amount of warmth explode in the pit of his stomach. Did her beautiful smile affect all men that way or was it just him?

"Hello, Nathan," she greeted him.

"Hi, Angel."

"Glad you could make it this evening," she said.

"I appreciate the invite. The motel room can get fairly lonely at times."

"Well, you won't be lonely tonight. I've got six of my good friends coming over."

"Sounds like fun to me," he replied.

"Then just follow me and I'll take you to my place." She turned and headed up the path. He followed closely behind her, paying careful attention to the directions as they walked.

"How was the rest of your day today?" he asked.

"Good, how was yours?"

"Once I cleaned the swamp water and embarrassment of my own clumsiness off me, it was fine," he replied.

She laughed and flashed a quick glance back at him. "You had no reason to feel embarrassed. I really should have warned you that the bank was slippery."

From the main path they took a smaller trail to the left and followed that until they came to another fork and she took another left. They didn't go far before her shanty came into view.

He hadn't noticed much about it when she'd brought him

here with his injured leg. It looked like an enchanted cabin rising up from the glistening water that surrounded it. It was finished in a dark brown wood but had a cheerful yellow trim around the windows and doorway. He already knew the inside was cozy and surprisingly nice.

They crossed the bridge that led to her porch and then she unlocked her door and ushered him inside.

"Make yourself at home," she said. "The others should trickle in here in the next few minutes. In the meantime beer is on the menu for tonight when it comes to alcoholic drinks. Would you like one?"

"Are you having one?" he asked as he eased down onto one corner of the sofa.

"I am," she replied. She went into the kitchen area, opened her cooler and pulled out two beers. She handed him one and then sat in the chair facing the sofa.

They unscrewed the tops of the bottles at the same time and then she held hers up. "Cheers," she said.

He raised his bottle toward her. "Cheers back at you." He took a drink and then set the bottle on a coaster on the coffee table. "So, you want to tell me about the people I'll be meeting here tonight?"

She took a drink of her beer and then set it on the little end table next to the chair. "You already know Shelby and she'll be here. Then there's Rosemary Fantiour, she's twenty-three and the baby of the group."

A knock fell on the door. It opened and a tall, physically fit man walked in. He had bold features with high cheekbones. His long dark hair was tied at the nape of his neck with a piece of rawhide and he was clad in a pair of jeans and a navy T-shirt.

Nathan immediately got to his feet and held out a hand to him. "Nathan Merrick," he said.

The man grabbed his hand in a firm shake. "Louis Mignot."

Within minutes everyone had arrived. Along with Shelby, there was Rosemary Fantiour and Marianne LaCroix to round out the women and Beau Gustave and Jacques Augustin to round out the men.

All the men were dark-haired, dark-eyed and in great physical shape. The women were also dark-haired and pretty, although none of them held a candle to Angel.

Nathan offered his place on the sofa to the women, but they all declined. Instead kitchen chairs were pulled in and a couple of the men sprawled on the floor.

Angel brought them all beers and then she settled back in the chair that had remained vacant. Initially the talk was of swamp matters...what fish was biting where and where a new sounder of boars was located. There was a lot of teasing among the group and it was obvious they all cared deeply about each other.

Nathan remained quiet, listening and observing the group dynamics. It was obvious they all respected Angel and he suspected most of the men might have a crush on her. And why wouldn't they?

She wasn't just beautiful, but with her friends she was also witty and fun. Nathan enjoyed seeing her this way, relaxed and having a good time. She put out a platter of cheese and crackers and they all began to graze on the offering, and then she lit kerosene lanterns against the encroaching darkness. The lanterns' light created a warm glow in the room.

It wasn't long before the conversation turned to him. "So,

I hear you offered Angel some kind of a job," Louis said, his dark eyes sharp and filled with more than a touch of suspicion.

"Yes, I have. It didn't take me long to realize I needed somebody who knows the swamp well to guide me around, so I offered that job to Angel and she accepted."

"And you're getting pictures for a book?" Rosemary asked. She struck a pose. "You can take pictures of me for a book anytime. You can title them fiercest animal in the swamp."

Everyone laughed, including Nathan. The young woman looked about as fierce as a caterpillar. "Tell us exactly what the book is about," Jacques said.

Nathan spent the next few minutes explaining he was a biologist and had scored a book deal based on his studies of plant and animal life in the swamp.

"I've studied swamp life extensively from my desk but had never actually been in a swamp," he explained. "So, I'm here to see things up close and personal and take photos to go along with my writings."

They asked him more questions about where he lived and how long he intended to be there. "I'm planning on being here about a month or so," he replied to that question. "It should take me about that long to get all the photos I need."

"And you're planning on tying up Angel's time for that long?" Beau asked. "You might not realize this, but she has other responsibilities here. She takes care of her parents by bringing them fish and the supplies they might need."

"Beau, I can take care of myself," Angel said.

"I just don't want to see you overdoing things," Beau replied. There was a softness in the man's eyes when he gazed at Angel. Nathan didn't know if Angel knew it or not, but Nathan believed Beau just might be in love with her.

The evening was pleasant, although Beau and Louis continued to eye him with more than a bit of suspicion. Nathan really couldn't blame them. He was a virtual stranger to them and they were just looking out for Angel's welfare.

He learned that Marianne worked as a waitress at the local café. Rosemary had an online business selling potions and notions from the swamp and Shelby worked as a clerk in one of the shops. Louis, along with Beau caught gators for a living and Jacques was also a fisherman. Nathan found them all to be utterly fascinating.

At about ten thirty everyone began to leave. "Nathan, I'm sure we'll be seeing a lot of you," Shelby said to him.

"I hope so. I really enjoyed meeting you all this evening," he replied.

"Yeah, it was nice for you to meet the gang. We bark at each other, but we never bite," Rosemary said.

Nathan laughed. "It reminded me of some of my friends back home."

Within ten more minutes everyone was gone. Nathan carried what was left of the cheese and crackers into the kitchen and set the platter on the countertop while Angel picked up random empty beer bottles left around the room.

"I love my friends, but they're all pigs when it comes to picking up after themselves," Angel said.

Nathan laughed once again. "I get it. I have the same kinds of friends."

She began to put the cheese back into the cooler. "Do you hang out with a bunch of other scientist types?" she asked.

"Actually, I do. I have two good friends who are both

biologists and we hang out together when we can. One is married, one is divorced and then there's me."

"It's nice to have good friends," she replied. "By the way, did you get your leg checked out by a doctor today?"

"I used the walk-in clinic at the pharmacy. I got a tetanus shot and she told me I might have needed stitches, but you did such a great job of wrapping it that it would heal nicely without them."

"Oh, that's good news. Now, are you ready to head back to your car?"

"Whenever you're ready." He was still a bit uneasy about finding the parking lot in the dark.

"Then let's take off." As they left her cabin, she locked the door. Today he'd noticed she not only had a regular lock on her front door, but she also had a hasp lock for extra security when she was inside the shanty. Definitely smart for a woman who lived all alone.

He was grateful she'd grabbed a flashlight on the way out. He was relatively sure she didn't need it, but he was grateful that she lit his path as the night was deep and dark.

It didn't take them long to get back to his car. He hadn't wanted the night to end. The more time he spent around her, the more intrigued and attracted he was to her.

"Would you like to have breakfast with me at the café in the morning before we start work for the day?" he asked on impulse.

To his surprise and pleasure, she tipped her head upward to look at him and then nodded. "Sure, that would be nice," she replied. "I never get breakfast out."

"Then why don't I pick you up here at around seven

thirty in the morning," he said, ridiculously pleased she had agreed.

"Okay, I'll be here," she replied. "'Night, Nathan."

"Good night, Angel. Thanks again for tonight. I really enjoyed your friends."

"I'm glad." She turned and quickly melted into the darkness of the night. He got into his car and wondered what in the hell he was doing. Nothing good could come out of him spending extra time with Angel. In a month he'd be gone from here and back to his life in New Orleans. After breakfast in the morning, it was important he keep things strictly professional between them.

SHE HAD NO idea why she had agreed to go to breakfast with him. Angel got home and locked up and then curled up on the sofa to think about the night that had just passed.

She'd been pleasantly surprised by how well Nathan had gotten along with her friends. He'd been friendly and open and she'd thought he'd even won over Louis and Beau by the end of the night, and they were like two tough, overly protective brothers to her.

The next morning, she was at the parking lot early. She loved daybreak when the sun was just rising and painted everything with its gilded glow.

The air smelled fresh and so…green. It was an impossible scent to describe but it fed her very soul. It was definitely the smell of home.

She heard the crunch of his tires before his car came into sight. Her heart did a slight flip in her chest as he parked and stepped out of the car.

"Good morning," he said with a wide smile. "Are you ready for some breakfast?"

"Definitely," she replied.

He quickly walked around to the passenger door and opened it to usher her into his car. She slid in and watched as he walked back around to the driver's side.

The man definitely rocked a pair of jeans. They fit his long legs and firm butt to perfection. The black polo shirt he wore emphasized his broad shoulders and the darkness of his hair.

He got into the car and started the engine, then turned and smiled at her. "You look quite pretty this morning. Pink is definitely a good color on you."

"Thank you," she replied as a rush of warmth filled her. She'd particularly chosen to wear the pink sleeveless blouse this morning because she knew it looked good on her. She'd also put on a bit of mascara, something she rarely did.

"I enjoyed getting to meet your friends last night," he said once they were on their way to the café.

"They all enjoyed meeting you," she replied. "They're a nice bunch, although Beau and Louis have always been a bit overly protective. Jacques is the quieter one of the three."

"Yeah, I noticed."

"I hope you didn't take offense to them and their hundreds of questions."

He shot her a quick smile. "No offense was taken. It's obvious they all care about you very much."

"And I care about all of them," she replied. "So, have you become familiar with the town yet?"

"I know where the hamburger drive-through is located,

and the little donut shop. And of course I know where the café is," he replied.

"Ah, I'm sensing a theme here," she said teasingly.

He laughed, the deep rumble resounding in the pit of her stomach. He had such a wonderful laugh. "I do love food. What about you? Do you pick like a bird or do you enjoy a nice big meal?"

"I definitely like to eat," she replied.

They entered the city limits of Crystal Cove. It was a charming place with storefronts painted in pink and yellow and turquoise. There was a grocery store, a dress shop and the official city offices.

There was also a thrift shore and various other little shops that kept the town thriving. Even though the place rarely saw tourists, there was a nice six-unit motel where she knew Nathan was staying. She also knew there were several people who lived full-time at the motel.

As they drove, they talked about the hot, humid weather that always ruled this area in July and small-talked about the people he had met the night before.

It didn't take him long to arrive at the café. He found a place in the café's parking lot and then together they got out of the car and headed for the front door.

The café was always busy in the mornings and even though it was Wednesday, it was no different. Silverware clattered and people talked and laughed as they visited with neighbors and family.

The scents of frying bacon and fresh coffee filled the air, along with the fragrance of cooking eggs, grilling vegetables and yeasty biscuits and bakery goods.

They managed to find an empty booth toward the back

and settled in. Almost immediately Marianne arrived to wait on them. "Fancy seeing you two here this morning," she said with a bright smile.

"We decided to catch some breakfast together before we get to work," Nathan said.

"Well, you've certainly come to the right place," Marianne replied. "What can I get for you two?"

Nathan ordered a number four special with two eggs, bacon, toast and hash browns and she ordered French toast with bacon. They both ordered coffee and orange juice.

"This is really a nice place," Nathan said once Marianne had left their booth. "I've enjoyed eating my dinners here since I got into town."

"It's owned by a woman named Antoinette LeBlanc. She opened it about twenty years ago and she still very much runs the place and is the main cook."

"The decorations are very nice," he said. "I like the homey feel of it."

It was true that Antoinette had decorated it to feel comfortable and without any nods to the swamp or the town. Hanging on the beige walls were antique kitchen instruments. There was also an oversized wooden fork and spoon painted in copper colors that took up most of one wall.

"It's definitely the most popular place in town. The food is excellent and the prices are reasonable," she replied.

"I've learned that in the past couple of nights when I've had dinner here," he said.

At that moment Marianne returned with their coffee and orange juice and then left them once more to check on her other tables and booths.

"So, tell me more about Angel Marchant," he said.

"What do you want to know?" She took a drink of her coffee.

"I don't know…let's start with this. Where do you see yourself in five years?"

She blinked in surprise. She'd expected an easier question from him. "Oh, I don't know. I'd like to be married and have a baby or two by then. What about you?"

"The same," he replied. "I definitely want a family in the next couple of years."

"How many children would you like?" she asked.

"Two…maybe three."

The conversation was interrupted by Marianne bringing their food. "Thanks, Marianne," Angel said.

"Yes, thanks. This all looks delicious," Nathan added.

"Enjoy," Marianne said as she once again moved away.

"I guess we should dive in while it's hot," Nathan said.

"Definitely," Angel agreed. She grabbed the bottle of syrup and liberally doused her French toast with it while he cut into his over-easy eggs.

"Breakfast is my favorite meal of the day," he said. "I hope you don't mind that I'm a dipper." He picked up his toast and dipped it into the runny egg yolk.

She smiled at him. "I don't mind at all. I say go for it."

They ate for a few minutes in silence. Angel was the one who broke the quiet. "So, is there anything in particular you'd like to see today?"

"No, nothing in particular. I need to take more pictures of the plants. That's what's going to be the most time-consuming," he replied. "There are so many wonderful plants and they each serve a function to keep the swamp healthy.

I've got everything written up on them. I'm just lacking the photos."

"I heard you tell the gang last night that you expect this all to take about a month," she said.

"Yes, and while I'd like you to guide me for the period of time I'm here, I certainly understand if you have other responsibilities, especially if those responsibilities revolve around taking care of elderly parents."

"Don't pay attention to what Beau said last night. My parents are perfectly capable of taking care of themselves. However, I do things now to try to make their lives a little easier," she replied.

"So, you're close with your parents. That's nice," he replied.

"I'm very close with them. What about you? Are you close with yours?" she asked curiously.

His eyes appeared to darken in hue. "Unfortunately, my father passed away ten years ago from a heart attack and about eight years ago my mother remarried and she and her new husband moved to Kansas City. We try to stay in touch by phone, but it's just not the same."

"I'm sorry about your father and the way things turned out." There was a sadness in his eyes and Angel fought against the unexpected desire to reach across the table and cover his hand with hers.

"Hey, Angel." Mac Singleton appeared at the side of the booth.

"Hi, Mac," she said and introduced Mac to Nathan. "Mac is the guy I sell all my fish to at the grocery store," she explained. Mac was about Angel's age. He had dark blond hair and hazel eyes and was a pleasant-looking man. Angel had felt for some time that he had a bit of a crush on her, but he'd never asked her out.

"And I've missed seeing you for the last couple of days," Mac replied.

"Don't worry, I've got a basketful of fish to bring in to you tomorrow evening," she replied.

"Good, I'm glad you're coming in tomorrow night and not tonight as today is my day off," he replied. "And now I'll just let you two finish up your breakfast. It was nice meeting you, Nathan." He left their booth and returned to his seat across the room.

"He seems nice," Nathan said.

She nodded. "He's a very nice guy."

Their meals were finished and he gestured to Marianne for their check. "Breakfast is on me," he said as he pulled his wallet from his back pocket.

"Oh, no, I like to pay my own way," she replied in protest.

"Please, allow me to get the tab this morning," he insisted.

"Okay, just this once," she relented, deciding not to argue with him.

Together they left the café and headed back to the swamp. The morning passed quickly as they walked through the thicket and he took pictures.

They small-talked as they walked and she learned he had no siblings, loved fried chicken and also loved the outdoors. As he took his pictures, he explained the plants to her that she'd always taken for granted. He also told her their official scientific names, which she found interesting but knew she'd never remember.

However, there was a wild energy between her and Nathan. Whenever his body accidentally came into contact with hers, she felt a flame clear down to her toes. And she had a feeling he felt it, too. There were several times when their gazes had caught and held for a moment too long.

What was it about this man? Was it just a matter of racing hormones? Was it just because she hadn't been around a man she was attracted to in a very long time? Somehow, it felt deeper than that, but since she'd never felt this way about a man before, she didn't know exactly what to call it.

They knocked off at about four o'clock and made plans for her to meet him in the parking lot the next morning at seven thirty.

She watched him drive away and then turned to head back to her shanty. It was early enough that she could get a little evening fishing in. Maybe sitting on the bank with a fishing pole would give her more clarity about the crazy pull she felt toward Nathan.

She frowned as she walked over her bridge. Something was hanging from her doorknob. As she drew closer, her frown deepened. When she reached her door, she stared at the object.

What in the world? It was a voodoo doll with long dark hair, big green eyes and a tiny knife shoved through its heart. She grabbed it from the doorknob, and then looked around her shanty as chills raced up her back.

Seeing nothing and nobody around, she quickly unlocked her door, went inside and then closed and locked the door behind her. She sank down on the sofa and placed the doll before her on the coffee table.

She didn't believe in voodoo curses, but there were some in the swamp who did. She knew Rosemary made the dolls and sold them from her online store as novelties. But Rosemary certainly hadn't left this for her.

So, who had? And why? All she knew for sure was that it couldn't mean anything good.

Chapter Four

Nathan sat in his motel room and went through the latest photos he had taken. He and Angel had spent the last week together and he'd captured many images of the swamp's beauty.

Each day he spent with Angel he got to know her better and he was having emotions about her he'd never felt before. He lusted for her and every day his lust for her grew hotter and more intense.

But his emotions toward her went much deeper than his lust. He wanted to know about her childhood. He would like to know what made her laugh and cry. He wanted to know all her hopes and dreams.

There was no question in his mind he wasn't falling in love with her. He just wanted to know her better as they were work partners and she was such a unique, strong woman.

Hopefully he would learn some of the things he wanted to know about her tonight. She'd surprised him today by calling him and inviting him to dinner at her place. She said it was to pay him back for the breakfast he'd bought her the other day.

He was definitely looking forward to the evening with

her where they wouldn't be focused on anything swamp and could instead focus on each other.

They hadn't worked today. He couldn't expect her to work with him seven days a week, so they'd agreed to take the day off and meet for dinner at six.

He packed his camera away as he realized it was almost time to leave to meet her at her shanty. Tonight he was walking in on his own without her to guide him. Over the last week he'd paid special attention to the trails and now believed he could make it to her place without her bringing him in.

He'd already showered and shaved and dressed for the evening. When five thirty arrived, he got into his car to drive to the parking lot in front of the main trail.

Each time before he knew he was going to see her, a wave of anticipation coupled with a bit of anxiety swept through him. The anticipation was self-explanatory but the anxiety was more complex.

It was the apprehension of a young man going on his first date, of a man who wanted to please the woman he was with. Finally it was Nathan wanting Angel to like him.

There had been moments over the past week that he'd wanted to point his camera at her. When she'd bent down beneath the Spanish moss, he'd wanted to capture her image. With her green eyes and her long dark hair falling around her shoulders, she'd looked primitive and beautifully wild.

She appeared so strong, so unafraid, and he'd love to capture her beauty and spirit on film. But he would not take a photo of her without her permission and so far he hadn't worked up the nerve to ask her for one.

He arrived at the parking lot and left his car. He had his

phone and a small flashlight tucked into his back pocket; the flashlight was for when he left her place later. He also carried with him the stun gun he had bought to protect himself after hearing about the Swamp Soul Stealer.

At least it wasn't dark yet and so it was easier for him to keep his bearings. Entering the swamp was like entering the belly of an unknown beast. It wouldn't be long before nighttime creatures awakened and the daytime animals went to sleep.

The gash on his leg had almost healed up, although he was still using antibiotic ointment and bandaging it, making sure it stayed clean. It didn't hurt anymore, which was a good thing.

He tried to walk slowly, not wanting to arrive at her shanty too early. But the sweet anticipation of spending time with her in her home moved his footsteps faster and faster.

He was ridiculously proud of himself for remembering the directions when her shanty came into view. As he crossed the bridge, he heard the sound of her generator running and smelled something delicious wafting outward.

She answered his knock on the door and greeted him with one of her bright smiles. "Come on in, Nathan," she said and opened the door wider to usher him inside.

"Something smells amazing," he said. Not only did something smell amazing, but as usual she looked incredible. She wore black jeans and a red blouse. The outfit showcased her incredible figure and the color of the blouse looked gorgeous with her dark hair and green eyes.

"Fried chicken. Come sit in the kitchen so I can finish it up," she replied.

"You made fried chicken for me?" He followed her into

the kitchen area where the table was set for two. He took a seat there while she moved to the counter where an iron skillet sat on one of the two-top electric burners.

"You told me it was your favorite, so I decided to make it for you and see how mine stacks up to others you've eaten. Want a beer?"

"Sure." He was oddly touched that she'd not only remembered him telling her that fried chicken was his favorite, but that she'd actually gone to the trouble of making it for him.

She pulled a beer from the cooler and handed it to him. "How was your day?" she asked.

"Quiet," he replied. "I had a late breakfast at the café and then spent the rest of the day going through the photos I've taken so far."

"Were you happy with what you had?" She flipped over a couple pieces of the frying chicken and then turned to look at him.

"I'm very happy with most of them. There were a few bad ones in the bunch," he replied and then grinned at her. "That just means I'm not perfect all the time."

She laughed. "Who is? So, what other mistakes have you made in your life besides taking the occasional bad photo?"

He was going to make a joke, but he decided to answer the question seriously. "I fell in love with the wrong woman," he replied.

"Tell me more," she said and then turned back around and began to take the chicken out of the skillet and place the pieces on an awaiting plate.

"There isn't a whole lot to tell. I met her in graduate school and we dated for about seven months. I thought she was my person and we'd get married and start our family together. Then one evening she sat me down and told me she cared deeply about me. She loved me, but she wasn't in love with me and that was the end of that."

She placed the chicken on the table and then paused to gaze at him. "Was your heart broken?"

"Yeah, for a while it was," he admitted. She held his gaze for another long moment and then went to the cooler and retrieved a bowl of coleslaw and a tub of butter and added that to the table. She placed several pieces of bread on a saucer and then sat across the table from him. "Help yourself," she said.

"What about you? Any heartbreaks in your past?" he asked as he got a crispy thigh from the plate.

"I fell in love with the wrong man," she replied.

"Tell me more," he said, echoing back to her what she'd said to him.

She grinned. "Quid pro quo, right?" She paused a moment to take a leg and put it on her plate and then looked back at him. "He lives in town and I dated him for about two years. I thought he was my person and I was expecting a proposal, but instead I found out that on the nights he wasn't here with me, he was with another woman. He was basically leading a double life."

Although her tone was fairly light, he saw a flash of hurt deep in her eyes. "I'm so sorry that happened to you. I'm sure that broke your heart," he said.

"Yeah, it did for a while. Now let's eat up before it gets cold," she said.

He added a heaping spoonful of the coleslaw to his plate and then buttered a slice of bread. Finally he bit into the chicken thigh and an explosion of flavor shot off in his mouth.

"Oh, my God, this chicken is beyond delicious," he said.

Her features lit up. "I'm so glad you like it. The coating is my own recipe. I use it for chicken and some fish."

"Well, whatever it is, it's really good," he replied.

As they ate, they chatted about the places they had been in the swamp and where they planned to go next. The talk turned more humorous as he told her some of his most embarrassing moments when he'd entered the dating pool again. He made her laugh over and over again.

There was something quite intimate about laughing together. He felt more drawn to her than ever. In turn, she told him funny stories about her and her friend group growing up in the swamp.

With the stories came a new depth to their relationship, whatever that was at the moment. All he knew was he liked Angel. He liked her a lot and the more he learned about her, the more taken he was with her.

When dinner was over, he insisted he help her with the cleanup and then they both got fresh beers and went into the living room where she sat next to him on the sofa.

"Thank you so much for the amazing dinner," he said.

"No problem," she replied. "Did you hear that another woman has disappeared from the swamp and it's suspected she was taken by the Soul Stealer?"

"Yeah, I read that in the paper this morning. Did you know her?"

"Yes, although I didn't know her well. She was a bit younger than me and lived at home with her parents. From what I heard today, she had spent an evening with a friend but never made it back home."

"And the police have no clue who this Swamp Soul Stealer is?" he asked.

She shook her head. "None and I heard today in town that the only person who might be able to help identify him has been placed in a medical coma."

"Colette Broussard, right?"

"Right." She looked at him in surprise.

"I've been doing my homework, and having meals at the café is like being at news central."

She laughed. "Keep in mind not everything you hear at the café is always true."

"I take it all in with a grain of salt, but the one thing I do believe is the Swamp Soul Stealer is dangerous and I worry about you going out and about on your own," he replied.

She released a small dry laugh. "I don't worry so much about the Swamp Soul Stealer right now. I'm more concerned about something a little closer to home."

"What's that?" he asked curiously.

She got up from the sofa and went to the bookcase where she grabbed something off the bottom shelf and carried it back with her. "This was left on my door a few days ago."

She handed him a primitive doll, with long dark yarn for hair and big green eyes. A little knife was stabbed through the heart. He looked up at her with shock.

"This is a nasty piece of work. Do you have any idea who left it for you or why?" he asked.

"Not a clue."

He set the doll on the coffee table and then moved closer to her. "It looks like a threat of some kind," he said.

"I know, but at least nothing else has happened since I got that," she replied. "I asked Rosemary if it was one of hers because she sells the dolls on her online store, but she said it definitely wasn't one of hers. In fact, I asked all my friends about it, but they couldn't figure out who might have left it for me."

"You have to tell me if anything else like this happens," he said.

"Why, what are you going to do about it?" she asked.

"I don't know, but I do know that even though I haven't known you for very long, I care about you," he replied.

"It's funny you say that because I feel the same way about you," she replied and a dusting of pink filled her cheeks. "But of course we need to keep things strictly business between us."

"Of course," he replied and held her gaze. "But I have to confess that I really want to kiss you right now."

A flame appeared to kindle in the depths of her eyes and the tip of her tongue dipped out to dampen her lower lip. A hot fire flickered to life inside him as their gazes remained locked.

"Nathan, I… I really want you to kiss me right now," she said half-breathlessly.

He moved closer to her, tucked a strand of her soft silky hair behind her ear and then lightly touched his lips to hers. He intended the kiss to be brief and soft, but his lips didn't get the memo.

He consumed her mouth with his and when she opened up to him, he dove his tongue in to dance with hers. Her arms encircled his shoulders as he leaned into her.

She tasted of warm beer and hot desire and he would

have kissed her forever, but as he felt himself getting very aroused, he reluctantly ended the kiss.

She dropped her arms from around him and sat back. "Do all male scientists kiss as well as you do?" she asked.

He laughed. "I don't know. I've never kissed one. Do all the women in the swamp kiss as well as you do?" He was grateful nothing felt awkward between them.

"I don't know. I've never kissed one," she replied. "Okay, we kissed, and now things need to go back to strictly business between us."

"Of course," he agreed. "And I need to get out of your hair." He stood and picked up his empty beer bottle to carry it to the trash in the kitchen, but she stopped him.

"Leave it, I'll get it," she said as she also stood.

Together they walked to her door. "Thank you so much for the delicious dinner tonight."

"No problem," she replied. "I'm glad you enjoyed it. Do you need me to walk you out to the parking lot?"

"No, I think I've got it. Are we on for tomorrow morning?" he asked.

"Definitely, same time, same place?"

He nodded. For a long moment they remained close, their gazes locked and a tension building once again between them. "Since we've kind of already blurred the line between strictly business and personal tonight, I wouldn't mind if you wanted to kiss me good-night," she said.

"I would love to kiss you good-night," he replied, surprised by her invitation.

He drew her into his arms and stole her lips with his. Her arms went up around his neck as he pulled her closer and closer against him.

Her body fit perfectly against his own. She opened her mouth to him and their tongues met and swirled together in a deep kiss. He was lost in her. Her scent…her warmth and her lips all combined to dizzy his senses.

He was fully aroused with his want of her. But she had only invited a good-night kiss. With that in mind, he reluctantly pulled his mouth back from hers to end the kiss.

"Good night, Angel," he said as he dropped his arms from around her.

She stepped back from him. "Good night, Nathan. And tomorrow, it's back to strictly business."

"Understood," he replied, and with that he stepped out into the darkness of the night and she closed her door.

He clicked on his flashlight and began the trek back to his car. They could pretend that things were going to be strictly business between them, but he had a feeling with tonight's kisses everything had changed and he was excited to see how those changes played out.

SHE HAD NEVER been that forward with a man before. After Nathan left, Angel sank down on her sofa with her lips still feeling the burning imprint of his.

What on earth had possessed her tonight? Why had she asked him for that second kiss at the door? She could pretend to be confused about it, but the bottom line was she'd just wanted another one of his kisses. Being held in his arms for that brief period of time had felt so good. It had been forever since she'd been held in a man's arms.

There was no question she felt something different with Nathan, something exciting and electrifying. It wasn't just a physical pull, but it was an emotional one as well. He was so easy to talk to and he had a great sense of humor. Her feelings toward him scared her more than a little bit because it had heartbreak written all over it.

She got up and took the voodoo doll back to her bookshelf. As she did, a shiver walked up her back. She wished she knew who had left it for her and why. Even though nothing else had happened, every time she thought about the voodoo doll she felt as if she was holding her breath, just waiting for something else to occur.

She finally went to bed and awakened just before dawn. She took her pirogue out to run her fish lines as she intended to take the fish she'd caught all week to the café and the grocery store that evening.

Once she was finished with that, she ate a quick breakfast and then at a little after seven o'clock she headed toward the parking lot to meet with Nathan.

She hoped things weren't awkward between them this morning. If she was really smart, she'd cut her losses, quit the tour guide job and never see him again. But the idea of doing that made her heart hurt. She was so enjoying her time with him.

Besides, she told herself it was all about the money. With the cash he was paying her and the savings she'd managed to squirrel away, by the end of this she would have enough to build a bigger, better deck around the shanty and that had been a goal of hers for months.

It's all about the money, she reminded herself as she reached the parking lot. Nathan was already parked there and at the sight of her, he got out of his car with his camera and a bright smile.

Damn him for being so handsome…for looking so fine in

his jeans and a navy T-shirt. Damn his blue eyes for being so bright and his smile for being so wonderfully inviting and warm.

"Good morning, oh, faithful tour guide," he said to her.

"Good morning to you, biologist photographer," she replied.

"Now that we know who we are, shall we get started?"

"Follow me," she replied. "I'm going to take you on some new trails this morning."

"Sounds good to me," he said. "I've got my camera ready for anything." They walked for a bit in silence. Thankfully it wasn't an uncomfortable one, but rather a companionable one.

"Did you sleep well last night?" hc asked, breaking the silence.

"I did, but I pretty much always sleep well," she replied.

"The one night I stayed at your place it was the croak of the frogs and the water lapping against your stilts that made me sleep like a baby."

"For me, that's the rhythmic lullaby sounds of home," she replied.

"I could definitely get used to that."

"Stick around long enough and you'll fall in love with the swamp," she replied.

"I'm already halfway there," he admitted.

She was grateful that their conversations continued to be light and easy with no talk about what they had shared the night before.

They spoke a little more about the latest news of the woman who had disappeared and was a suspected victim of the Swamp Soul Stealer. There was no more news on the case, and she was still missing.

"Isn't it sad that potentially the most dangerous thing in the swamp is a man," he said when they stopped so he could take photos of the duckweed plants floating in a still pond.

"It's tragic," she replied. "I know Etienne, the chief of police, and his officers have combed the swamp looking for the victims and whoever has them, but the swamp is so dense and vast."

"It would be like looking for a needle in a haystack," he replied. He raised his camera and leaned closer to her to capture images of the frond-like plants. His nearness to her evoked a desire inside her.

It was the desire to touch his warm skin and to feel his lips on hers once again. It was the wish to know all the hopes and dreams in his heart and to share hers with him.

She released a deep sigh as he finished taking photos and straightened up. What was wrong with her? She realized she was in trouble. She was on the verge of being absolutely crazy about a man who would probably only be here for another two or three weeks.

It was wild, she'd known him less than two weeks and yet there was a part of her that felt as if she'd known him forever.

She knew she should stop the free fall, but there was another part of her that wanted to embrace all that was Nathan while he was here and deal later with the potential heartache she might have when he was gone.

That day she showed him a group of wild boars, which he explained to her weren't indigenous to the area. Still, he took photos of the animals along with several other smaller animals that scurried about.

There was nutria, large river rats with Cheetos-orange front teeth and plenty of turtles. They also saw a couple of otters and beavers busily building their homes. All in all, the day was a huge success for him as he got plenty of pictures.

It was late afternoon when they decided to head back. "Angel, I've wanted to ask you something for the last couple of days," he said when they were nearly back to the parking lot.

She stopped and turned to look at him, curious. "What's that?" she asked.

"I was wondering if you'd let me take a couple pictures of you."

She gazed at him in surprise. "Why would you want to do that?"

He smiled, that warm gesture that always made her feel special. "Because you're absolutely beautiful and I'd like to have a few photos to remember my time here with you. In fact, I wouldn't mind including a photo in the book of my intrepid swamp tour guide if you'd allow me to do that."

She frowned at him. "I don't know about being in a book, but if you want to take a few photos of me, I guess I wouldn't mind, but only on one condition."

"And what's that?"

"That you allow me to take a couple pictures of you for me to remember your time here," she replied.

"Sure, if that's what you want," he replied easily.

"Then when do you want to do this?" she asked.

"How about right now?" He raised his camera and began

to snap pictures while she stood still, feeling awkward about the whole thing.

After he had taken several, he lowered his camera and smiled at her. "Thank you, you make a lovely model."

"Thanks, now it's my turn." She pulled her phone from her back pocket and took several pictures of him.

When she was finished, she returned her phone to her pocket and they continued their trek back to the parking lot. After telling him goodbye and agreeing to meet the next morning, she headed back to her shanty.

As she walked, all kinds of thoughts tumbled around in her head, all of them concerning Nathan. Each and every moment she spent with him only made her like him more. He seemed to be such a kind, good man and that definitely drew her closer to him. Then there was their physical chemistry. It was definitely off the charts.

She nearly stumbled as a new thought crossed her mind. Was it possible that he was only drawn to her because she was a swamp woman? Something unique and different to be studied? Was it possible she was really nothing more to him than a specimen to be analyzed?

As she reached her bridge, her heart sank as she saw a piece of paper taped on her front door. Now what? She reached the door and pulled off the note.

STAY AWAY FROM THE SCIENCE MAN!

The words were written in bold red marker. She looked around as icy chills crept up her spine. Who had left this for her? Had somebody been watching her and Nathan together? Was somebody watching her right now?

She quickly went inside and locked her door behind her. First the voodoo doll and now the note. Who didn't want to see her around Nathan? And what would happen if she didn't stop seeing him?

Chapter Five

For the first time in a long time, Angel hadn't slept well. The note had unsettled her more than she wanted to admit. Was it merely somebody trying to look out for her or was it a threat of some kind? Coupled with the voodoo doll, it definitely felt more like a threat, but from whom?

She hadn't told Nathan about the note when she'd met him that morning. She knew instinctively that if she did, he would make the decision to stop seeing her for her own safety. And she was the only one who got to make that decision for herself.

It was now almost six in the evening and her lack of sleep weighed heavy on her, but she still intended to make a trip into town to sell the fish she'd caught over the last week. Hopefully that wouldn't take too long so she could catch up on her sleep tonight.

"Angel, you home?" The deep voice came across Angel's bridge and she opened her door to see Jacques, Beau and Louis approaching.

"I'm here," she replied and opened her door wider to allow the men inside.

It wasn't unusual for the three to show up unexpectedly

for a visit. "What's happening?" Louis asked as he sank down on the sofa.

"Nothing much," she said. "I was just starting to get things together for a trip into town."

"You taking a haul in tonight?" Jacques asked.

"I am. What are you three doing, besides looking for trouble?" she asked teasingly.

"We just thought we'd check in on you. Have you heard that another woman is missing?" Beau asked.

"I have." Angel sank down in the chair facing the men on the sofa. "And you know that it isn't just women at risk, right? Two men have also disappeared. We're all at risk whenever we go out alone."

"We're big and strong enough to take care of ourselves," Louis said.

"Luka was big and strong, too," she reminded them, referring to their friend who had disappeared. "And he disappeared."

"Yeah, but we worry about you more because you aren't exactly a physical threat to anyone," Beau said.

"I appreciate all the concern, but I can take care of myself," she retorted firmly. "Besides, I'm not spending all that much time alone in the swamp right now."

"What's that photographer guy going to do to protect you? Take a picture of the Swamp Soul Stealer?" Jacques asked, making the other two men snicker.

"He has a name and he's making somebody nervous," she replied. She got up from her chair and went to the bookcase where she had placed the note next to the voodoo doll. She picked it up and showed it to her friends.

"Do any of you know anything about this?" she asked.

They all shook their heads. "I don't like this," Beau said. "You don't have any idea who left that?"

"None," she replied.

"What about Remy Theriot?" Louis asked. "We all know he's had a crush on you forever."

Remy lived deeper in the swamp. He was an odd young man who Angel had befriended several years ago. "I haven't seen Remy for months. I doubt very seriously if he's somewhere out there spying on my social life and that he left that note for me."

"Maybe you should take the note's advice," Louis suggested.

She looked at the big handsome man. "Louis Mignot, when has anyone been able to tell me what to do? I'm enjoying my time with Nathan and I'm making good money. I'm not about to do what some damned anonymous person wants me to do."

"Whoa." Louis held his hands up in a gesture of surrender. "It was just a thought."

"Well, think again." She returned the note to the bookcase and then looked at the men. "Now, I'd love to sit and visit with you all, but I need to get my fish ready to take into town."

"We'll help you with that," Jacques replied.

It took a half hour to get the fish on stringers off her back deck and carry them to her pickup truck. In the back of the truck was a very large cooler that she'd already put water in so the fish would stay fresh to go to market.

Normally it would take her much longer to do everything, but tonight with the men's help, it went much smoother and was done all in one trip.

"Thanks, guys," she said when she was ready to get into the truck and take off.

"Hey, I'm sorry if I made you mad earlier," Louis said.

She smiled. "Don't worry, I forgive you."

"He just said out loud what we were all thinking," Beau added. "None of us like the idea of somebody warning or threatening you in any way."

"I appreciate all of you and now I need to get going so I can get back home." She got into the truck, waved a quick goodbye and then took off.

As she drove, she thought of the three men she had just left. She adored them all and would trust any one of them with her life. It was funny, they were all nice-looking but she'd never felt a single romantic spark with any of them.

Despite the note's advice, she had spent much of the day in the swamp with Nathan. He took more photographs as they talked about anything and everything that came to mind. As usual she had completely enjoyed her time with him and the last thing she wanted to mention to him was the note.

There had been several times when the tension between them had been palpable, when their gazes had locked and she had a feeling he was remembering the very hot kisses they had shared. Still, the note bothered her more than she wanted to admit.

She shoved away thoughts of him and the note and within minutes she was at the grocery store. She parked by the loading dock at the back of the building and then went into the door that led her right next to the butcher's glass enclosure.

Not seeing anyone, she rang the bell that would summon

somebody from the back room. Mac Singleton appeared behind the glass and immediately stepped out of the enclosure to greet her.

"You just caught me," he said. "I get off work in a half hour."

"Then I'm glad I came when I did," she replied. "Are you ready to go see some fish?"

"Definitely. My fish supply has gotten low. Let me go find Joey and get my cooler and I'll meet you out by your truck," he said. Joey was a young kid who also worked in the meat and seafood department.

Angel went back outside where the shadows of night were quickly encroaching. She lowered the tailgate of her truck and sat on it to await the men.

It was a beautiful night with a near-full moon rising. The temperature had cooled off enough to be almost pleasant. As she waited, her thoughts once again turned to Nathan.

She still didn't know how she'd come to be so close and to have such feelings for a man in so little time. But something about him had crawled deep into her heart. How was it that when she wasn't with him, she missed him? She'd never felt that about a man before, not even her ex-boyfriend.

She was pulled from her thoughts as Mac and Joey came outside carrying a large cooler. She opened up hers so Mac could see the fish inside.

"Ah, I see you brought me some beauties," he said as he began transferring the fish from her cooler to his.

"Only the best for you, Mac," she replied teasingly.

"Ha, I know you probably have the best of the bunch stashed away to sell to Antoinette at the café," he said with a laugh. "So, how is life treating you these days? I hear through the grapevine that you're spending a lot of time with that Nathan guy." He talked while he worked, picking out fish and handing them to Joey, who put them in the store cooler.

"I have been spending quite a bit of time with him," she replied as she mentally kept track of the fish he was taking.

"I heard you were working with him. Is it strictly a business relationship?"

"Business and a little more," she confessed.

He straightened up and looked at her intently. "Do you really think it's wise to get into any kind of relationship with him? From what I hear, he isn't going to be in town for long."

She gazed at him in surprise. Mac had never gotten so personal with her before. "No, it's probably not wise," she replied honestly.

"I would just hate to see you get hurt by him."

"That's not going to happen." It was a little white lie. She already knew she was going to be hurt when her time with Nathan was over. Not that she was in love with him or anything that deep, but she would certainly miss their time together.

By that time, Mac had the fish he needed and they negotiated a price. Minutes later she was on her way to the café with plenty of fish left to sell to Antoinette, who was always the bigger buyer.

She'd been surprised by Mac's not-so-subtle probing of her relationship with Nathan. Was it possible she and Nathan were gossip fodder at the café? She supposed it was possible. During the past week she and Nathan had shared another breakfast together at the café before heading into the swamp for work.

She pulled into the alley behind the café where a door was open and a young man, who was obviously on a break, stood smoking. "Will you let Antoinette know that Angel is here?" she asked him.

"Sure." He dropped the last of his cigarette and stepped on it to grind it out. He then disappeared back into the café's kitchen.

A few moments later Antoinette stepped outside. She was a short, squat woman with silver hair pulled into a large bun at the nape of her neck. She was reputed to run a tight ship while being a fair, good employer. She was followed out the door by a tall buff man carrying a large cooler.

"What have you brought for me tonight?" she asked Angel. Despite her age and physical condition, she showed her spryness by jumping up into the bed of the truck.

"You can see for yourself there's a nice variety in there," Angel replied.

"Sam, bring that cooler up here," she said. The big man got into the truck and Antoinette began to pick her fish. When she finished, the two dickered with each other about price. Antoinette was a tough cookie, but Angel was certainly no pushover. They finally came to an agreement. Angel got paid and both parties were satisfied.

Darkness had fallen and Angel was now eager to get home. She hadn't eaten any dinner before she'd left, so she was hungry and tired. Her cooler was now empty and her business was done for the day.

She finally reached home and once she was locked inside, she made herself some fried fish and ate it with a piece of bread and butter.

As she ate, she thought about the day and then the note

that had been left for her. Was it possible Mac had left it for her? He'd certainly seemed very concerned about her relationship with Nathan.

Or was it possible one of her friends had left it on her door? Did one of those three men have a secret thing for her? A thing that had become oppressive and controlling?

When she crawled into bed that night, she felt very alone. As the frogs began to croak and the sound of the water lapped outside, she realized she didn't know whom to trust…and that scared her.

NATHAN SAT IN the café and waited for his order to be delivered. He hated eating alone. He hated feeling so lonely. He hated to admit it but he was lonely whenever he wasn't with Angel.

It was more than just being in a town where he didn't really know anyone. It was about his growing feelings for the woman who had helped him when he'd been hurt, for the woman who brightened his days and stirred an intense flame inside him he'd never felt before.

With each day that passed, with each click of his camera, he was getting closer and closer to the end of his time here. There was a touch of sadness growing in him whenever he thought of packing up and leaving Crystal Cove, the swamp and Angel behind.

"Here you go, handsome." Dana Albright was an older woman who almost always waited on him at dinnertime. She set his platter of fried shrimp and mac and cheese before him.

"Thanks, Dana," he replied with a smile. Most evenings he just ordered a burger and fries, but tonight he'd opted for something different.

"Can I top off your iced tea for you?"

"No, I'm good right now."

"Just holler for me if you need anything," she replied and then she left his table.

He was about halfway through his meal when a familiar face greeted him. "Hey, Nathan…mind if I sit with you for a few minutes?" Beau Gustave asked.

"No, I don't mind a bit," Nathan replied.

"So, how are you doing with all your picture-taking?" Beau asked. The man was clad in a dark pair of jeans and a black T-shirt. His dark hair was brushed back from his face, exposing his bold strong features.

"It's all going really well," Nathan replied. At that moment Dana returned to the table.

"Can I get you anything, Beau?" she asked.

"I wouldn't mind a cup of coffee," he replied and then looked back at Nathan. "As long as you don't mind me hanging out here for a few minutes."

"No, in fact I welcome the company," Nathan replied with friendliness.

"Got it, be right back," Dana said.

"Anyway, I've been getting tons of good photos to use in the book," Nathan said, picking back up the conversation. His mind immediately went to the four photos he'd managed to get of Angel. He'd been grateful that they had come out beautifully.

"That's good," Beau replied.

"Angel has been a very good guide for me. I've been grateful for her help."

"How much more time you think you have here?" Beau asked.

"Maybe a couple more weeks."

Once again, the conversation was interrupted as Dana returned with Beau's coffee. "There you go, honey," she said as she set the cup of dark brew down.

"Thanks, Dana."

"So, then things are going well with our girl, Angel?" Beau asked.

"Things are going great. At this point, I don't know what I'd do without her."

Beau took a drink of his coffee and eyed Nathan over the top of his cup. He lowered his cup slowly but his gaze still held Nathan's intently. "Don't hurt her."

Nathan sat back in his seat, surprised by what sounded like a veiled threat. "Trust me, that's the last thing I'd ever want to do," he replied.

"She's a very special woman and we all love her," Beau said.

"I could see that the night we were all together. Look, Angel has been a godsend to me as far as guiding me around in the swamp, but we both know I'll be leaving here in a couple of weeks."

Beau took another sip of his coffee and then smiled. "As long as you don't intend to take advantage of her in any way, then we're good."

Nathan nodded and held the man's gaze. "We're good."

"Then I'll just let you get back to your meal," Beau said. He stood and without saying another word, he headed for the café's exit.

Nathan watched him go and then picked up his spoon to finish his mac and cheese. As he continued with his meal, he thought about the conversation that had just occurred.

There was no question in his mind now that Beau might have feelings for Angel and he saw Nathan as a threat. But Nathan couldn't be a threat because his time here was limited.

Nathan knew he was more than a little charmed with Angel, but he wasn't sure what she felt about him. Oh, there was no question there was an intense physical attraction between them. He knew she liked him, but it likely was nothing deeper than that.

He'd told Beau the truth; the last thing he wanted was to hurt Angel. But, just like Nathan wasn't in charge of Angel's feelings, neither was Beau. She was a grown woman and surely if she felt uncomfortable with Nathan and the time they were spending together, she would stop seeing him.

It didn't take him long to finish his meal. He told the waitress to add Beau's coffee on his tab. Once he'd paid, he headed back to the motel room. At seven thirty the next morning he was in the parking lot to meet Angel.

He couldn't help the burst of warmth that swept through him at the sight of her. Today she was clad in a pair of jeans and a bright yellow tank top that looked gorgeous against her tanned skin and dark hair. She looked like a beautiful ray of sunshine.

"Good morning," he said.

"Back at you," she replied.

"Are you ready for more exploring today?" he asked as he grabbed his camera and then joined her at the edge of the swampland.

"Always ready," she assured him with one of her bright smiles.

Together they took off, making small talk about the

weather, the food in the café and her fish run into town the night before.

As they talked and walked, he snapped pictures along the way. He didn't mention his dinner companion from the night before. He hadn't yet decided if he'd tell her about the conversation with Beau or not.

"How about I take you to my special fishing place and we sit and rest for a few minutes," she said when it was around noon.

"That sounds like a great plan," he agreed. They had been moving pretty much nonstop through the morning and he was ready for a break. "Besides, I'd like to see your special fishing place."

He followed her up another trail and then another and then they broke into a clearing where the bank was a bit high and dry over a quiet small cove of water.

Knobby cypress and tupelo trees rose up all around the shore, dripping with lacy Spanish moss. Insects and fish kissed the surface of the water and birds sang like a melodious choir from the tops of the trees. It was a tranquil place of enormous beauty.

She sank down on the ground and he did the same, sitting close enough that he could smell the wonderful, slightly spicy and mysterious scent of her. "It's really nice here," he said.

"This isn't only my fishing place. Sometimes I come here to sit and think or just to relax."

"It definitely feels like a nice, relaxing place," he replied.

She looked at him curiously. "Do you have a place in New Orleans where you go to just sit and think or relax?"

"Not anywhere as splendid as this. I sometimes go to a little ice-cream shop not far from my place."

"You're an ice-cream man?"

He grinned at her. "Oh, definitely."

"What flavor?"

"Anything caramel. What about you?"

"Chocolate."

"Now you've made me hungry for it. Why don't we go to the ice-cream place in town this evening? We could go to the café for dinner and then have ice cream for dessert."

"That sounds like fun," she agreed, her eyes shining brightly.

"Then I'll pick you up for dinner around six. Will that work?" he asked.

"That will work," she replied with a smile.

"Do you know that your friend Beau is possibly in love with you?" The words blurted out of him before he realized he was going to say them.

"Talk about an abrupt change of subject," she said with a small laugh. "And I don't know where you get your information from, but Beau and I are just good friends. I don't have any kind of romantic feelings toward him."

"I believe he definitely has romantic feelings for you." He went on to tell her about the conversation he'd had with the man the night before in the café. He recognized that he should tell her about the encounter in case she heard something about it from Beau. "In fact, if I was to guess, all three of those men are more than half in love with you."

She laughed again. "And I think you are more than half crazy. Those men love me as friends, but they aren't in love with me."

"Then we'll agree to disagree on that point," he replied easily. Why wouldn't any of those men be half in love with her? Nathan had only known her for less than two weeks and he had feelings for her that he was finding confusing.

The realization of the depths of his feeling for Angel surprised him. He'd known he was growing closer to her with each day that passed, but it had nothing to do with love. He couldn't fall in love with her because it wouldn't go anywhere. If he loved her, then he was only setting himself up for heartache.

No, he wasn't anywhere near in love with her, he just liked her a lot and wouldn't mind having her in his bed. Friends with benefits; he definitely wouldn't mind that with her.

If he was smart, he'd tell her he didn't need her anymore and he'd stop seeing her. But he wasn't willing to deprive himself of her company and she was a terrific guide through the many trails in the swamp. Apparently on this subject he wasn't a very smart man.

"Shall we get going?" she said after they had been sitting for several minutes in silence.

"Ready." He got to his feet and then held out a hand to her. She took his hand and he pulled her up to her feet. Close... so close, they stood together.

He fought against the wild desire to pull her into his arms and kiss her until the sun set in the sky. Instead, he quickly took a step back from her. "Thanks for sharing your special fishing, thinking and relaxing spot with me," he said in an effort to break the tension that had risen up with their nearness to one another.

"No problem," she replied and then turned and led him

back into the tangled trail where he began to once again take photos.

They worked until three and then called it a day. She walked with him to the parking lot where he tossed his camera on the seat and then turned to look at her. He pulled his wallet out and paid her for the day. It was still business when it came to paying her for her services. She quickly tucked the bills into her back pocket.

"I'll meet you back here at six," he said. "And I'm really looking forward to it," he couldn't help adding.

"I'll be here, and I'm really looking forward to it, too," she replied and then as always she turned and quickly disappeared into the swamp.

Chapter Six

Angel returned home and sank down on her sofa, her head filled with a million thoughts. Was it possible Beau really had feelings for her? The whole idea seemed crazy to her. They had been friends forever and he had never made any indication that he wanted anything more from her than her friendship.

Was he overly protective of her? Definitely, as were Louis and Jacques. Ever since she'd moved out on her own, the men had become fierce warriors who watched out for her and her safety.

Surely Nathan had been wrong about Beau. He'd mistaken Beau's overprotectiveness as love. What was more confusing was her feelings toward Nathan.

She didn't want to fall in love with Nathan, but there was no question her feelings for him deepened each and every time they were together. Their conversations were so easy and she loved their shared laughter.

She felt giddy when she was with him, much like she had once felt with her ex. Nothing good had come out of that and nothing good would come out of her falling in love with Nathan.

Still, that didn't stop her from wanting to continue to see him. She wanted to spend as much time as she could with him. At least she would have wonderful memories of him when he was gone from here.

At five forty, she checked her appearance in her mirror. She wore jeans that she knew fit her like a glove and a coral-colored sleeveless button-up blouse that tied at the waist.

She'd pulled her long hair into a high pony and small gold hoop earrings danced on her ears. Her makeup was minimal, just a little blush and some mascara.

She knew she looked good as she left to go meet Nathan. As she was walking there, she couldn't help but think about the note and the voodoo doll.

STAY AWAY FROM THE SCIENCE MAN!

Who had written it? She certainly wasn't taking the advice and didn't intend to. Still, she felt as if she was holding her breath, waiting for something else to happen. And she had no idea what or where it would come from.

But she lived her own life and made her own decisions and nothing and nobody was going to stop her from what she wanted to do. Life in the swamp could be hard enough without this kind of drama.

When she reached the parking lot, Nathan was waiting for her. He got out of the car with a wide smile. He looked wonderfully handsome in a pair of jeans and a light blue button-up short-sleeved shirt that did amazing things to his eyes and showcased his strong biceps.

"Hi," he said. "You look absolutely gorgeous."

"Thanks, you clean up nicely yourself."

He walked around to the passenger side and opened the door. "Your chariot awaits," he said.

She slid into the seat and then watched as he walked around to get behind the wheel. Part of Nathan's charm was she didn't think he realized just how hot he was. He seemed totally oblivious to the fact.

"Are you hungry?" he asked when he got in the car.

"Always," she said with a laugh.

"I like that about you," he replied. "My ex was one of those women who only picked at her food and made me feel guilty for what I was eating."

"You'll never have that problem with me. As you know, I love food and I encourage you to eat however much of whatever you want," she replied.

"Like I said, I definitely like that about you." He shot her a quick smile. "So, anything new since last time I saw you?"

"I can report that nothing new happened in the last two hours. I sat on the sofa for a while and then started to get ready to go out," she replied. "What about you?"

"Also nothing new to report. I watched television for about an hour and then I started getting ready to pick you up."

"Are we getting boring?" she asked teasingly.

"That's us…just a boring old couple going to dinner together."

"Actually, in all the time I've spent with you, I've never found you boring," she admitted.

"I can say the same. I find everything about you and your lifestyle here in the swamp interesting."

Once again she wondered if she was just another swamp specimen to be studied by him. Did he really see her for the woman she was or as a foreign species to be analyzed? She hoped it wasn't that, but she couldn't know for sure what went on in his head.

She shoved the troubling thought aside, intent on just enjoying the evening with him. It didn't take them long to get to the café and be seated at a booth toward the back.

As usual the place buzzed with conversations and people laughing and eating. It smelled like a cornucopia of different mouthwatering flavors.

"I've eaten here most every night and have yet to get a bad meal," he said as he offered her a menu and then took one for himself.

"I haven't eaten here very often but everyone always raves about the food."

"Most nights I just get a burger and fries, although I do like the fried shrimp, too. But I'm thinking of something different tonight," he said.

For a moment they both studied the menus in silence and then he closed his. She looked at hers for a moment longer and then also closed hers.

At that moment a pleasant older woman Angel didn't know came up to the side of the table. "Evening, Nathan," she said in greeting and offered Angel a friendly smile.

"Evening, Dana," he replied and then looked at Angel. "Angel, this is Dana Albright, waitress extraordinaire. And Dana, this is Angel Marchant."

"Nice to meet you, Angel," she replied. "Now, what can I get for you two this evening?"

"I'd like the fish platter," Angel said.

"And I'll take the chicken fried steak," Nathan added. They both ordered iced tea and then Dana left their booth.

"Even with all the options on the menu, you still choose to have fish," he said.

She smiled. "What can I say? I love fish."

"So, you can take the fisherwoman out of the swamp, but you can't take the fish out of her mouth."

She laughed. "I think you just butchered that saying."

He grinned, that special grin of his that always made her heart beat just a little bit faster. "I think you're right."

Dinner was very pleasant. They talked about the things they'd seen in the swamp that day and about some of the charming stores in town.

"How does Rosemary manage to work an online shop from the swamp?" he asked, curious. "Does she have a generator big enough to run a computer?"

"No, there's a little shop off Main Street that offers internet services for a small daily fee. There are several people from the swamp who work from there," she explained.

"Interesting."

As dinner continued, he made her laugh with more stories of his time as a young teacher and biologist, and she returned with more funny stories about growing up in the swamp with her friends.

The food was delicious and all too quickly the meal was done. "I hope you saved plenty of room for ice cream," he said as he motioned to Dana for their check.

"Definitely," she replied as she opened her purse.

"I don't know what you think you're doing, but stop it right now," he said with mock sternness.

"I've told you before that I like to pay my own way," she protested.

"Angel, I invited you to dinner and for ice cream tonight, so I pay. If you want to repay me, then cook me another meal."

She closed her purse. "Okay, you got it. Tomorrow night plan on dinner at my place."

"Sounds perfect," he replied with one of the smiles that warmed her down to her very toes.

Minutes later they walked out of the café. Although warm and humid as usual, it was a nice clear night. The sinking sun left behind a faint hue of pink and orange that added to the beauty of the skies.

"You want to drive to the ice-cream shop or should we walk?" he asked.

"We can just walk. It's only a block away. That is if you can walk after that huge meal you just scarfed down," she said teasingly.

"Ha, I noticed you cleaned your plate, too."

Together they began to leisurely walk side by side. They had only taken a couple of steps when he reached out and took her hand in his. "Do you mind?"

She smiled at him. "I don't mind at all." His hand was big and strong around hers and it just felt right.

They walked at a leisurely pace, noting the businesses they passed along the way. "I spent way too much money in that place," he said as they walked by a clothing store. "They had some really nice shirts and slacks that I decided I couldn't live without."

He looked at her. "You don't strike me as a woman who cares much about always buying new clothes, although the blouse you're wearing tonight looks beautiful on you."

She felt her cheeks warm. It had been a very long time since a man had complimented her and it felt wonderful.

"Thanks, and no, I don't care too much about buying new clothes. I have some nice things in my closet if I need them, but there aren't too many places to go in the swamp where you need to be dressed up."

"You look great in just your jeans and a tank top," he said.

"My, my, Mr. Merrick, careful or you're going to swell my head with all your compliments," she said with a small laugh.

By that time they had reached Bella's Ice Cream Parlor. It was a small shop with a long counter, behind which there were round cartons of all flavors of ice cream. There were four small high-top round tables and also a small counter against one wall for customers to sit. The only customers inside at the moment were a teenage boy and girl seated at one of the tables.

"Hi, welcome to Bella's," a petite blonde greeted them from behind the counter with a cheerful smile. "What can I get for you folks this evening?"

"I'd like chocolate ice cream in a waffle cone," Angel said.

"And I'd like the caramel drizzle in a cup with caramel sauce on top," Nathan said.

It didn't take them long to get their treats and settle in at one of the tables. "Now this is a way to finish up an evening," she said.

"I totally agree," he replied as he dug his spoon into his cup. "Do you treat yourself to ice cream often?"

"Almost never," she replied. "I'll occasionally buy one of those little cups at the grocery store, but it's too hard to keep in the ice cooler for long."

"And I imagine it would be far too expensive to run a generator and a refrigerator full-time."

"Yes. Unfortunately that's one drawback of living in the swamp, but I get by fine with my cooler."

His gaze held hers for a long moment. "And you would never consider moving out of the swamp?"

"Never. The swamp is in my blood, in my very soul. I'm where I belong and where I'll always be," she replied firmly, wondering why he'd even asked the question.

They finished their ice cream and then headed back to his car. The darkness of night had fallen and stars twinkled in the skies.

Once again, he took her hand in his as they walked back. It didn't feel like business with him, rather it felt as if they were a couple exploring a more personal relationship. And she didn't want it to stop.

She was almost disappointed when they reached his car and she knew their night together was coming to an end. "Is there anything in particular you'd like on the menu for tomorrow night?" she asked when they were almost back to the parking lot.

"Whatever you want to make. I'm sure whatever it is, it will be delicious."

"Keep those high hopes, young man," she replied, making him laugh. Oh, she loved the sound of his deep laughter. She'd like to have her ear on his bare chest when he laughed. She could only imagine the deliciously deep and rumbling noise it would make.

Within minutes they were back at the parking lot. They both got out of the car and he walked with her to the beginning of the trail into the swamp.

"I really enjoyed this evening," he said as he stepped closer to her.

"I really enjoyed it, too. Does six o'clock sound good for tomorrow night?" She felt a little breathless by his nearness and the glowing shine in his eyes that was visible in the moonlight.

"That sounds perfect," he replied. "Angel, can I kiss you good-night?"

"I'd like that." Her entire body tingled as he took her into his arms. His lips captured hers and she immediately opened her mouth to invite him to deepen the kiss.

When he did, chills of delight danced through her. Kissing and being kissed by Nathan was a special kind of magic. A hot, sweet desire rose up inside her. It was the desire for him to touch her bare skin, for her to touch his.

At that moment he broke the kiss and dropped his arms from around her. "Since you're cooking for me tomorrow night, maybe you'd like to take tomorrow off."

"Are you sure that's okay with you?"

"It's more than fine with me. I can take the time to go through the photos I've taken in the last week or so. I'll just see you tomorrow night," he replied. "Good night, Angel."

"'Night, Nathan," she replied as she tamped down the desire that had risen up so quickly inside her with the kiss. She turned and headed up the trail that would eventually take her home. She heard the sound of Nathan's car driving off and thought about the desire that had kicked up so high in her at his kiss.

Did she want to make love with him? Absolutely. Was it a good idea for her to make love with Nathan? Absolutely not. She had a feeling all she'd have to do was give him a little more encouragement and he'd be in her bed. She'd tasted his desire for her in the kisses they had shared.

She stopped in her tracks as she heard a loud crashing coming from someplace behind her. She turned in her tracks and gazed behind her. In a shaft of moonlight casting down amid the leaves overhead, she saw a man clad all in black and wearing a ski mask and rushing toward her.

Wha...what the hell? Acting purely on survival instinct, she turned and ran, at the same time fumbling at her waist for her little sister. A loud roar of what sounded like pure rage bellowed from the man. Animals scurried away from the trails as sheer terror gripped Angel.

With her knife gripped tightly in her hand, she ran blindly through the trails. The back of her throat threatened to close up and deep gasps escaped her as she raced for her very life.

Tree limbs tried to grab at her and the Spanish moss half blinded her as she sped ahead. None of that mattered as the crashing noise continued to follow her.

Who was it? Who was chasing her and why? Questions flew frantically through her brain. Oh, God, was it the Swamp Soul Stealer trying to make her his next victim? Would Nathan show up in the morning only to realize she had disappeared...vanished without a trace?

It didn't really matter who it was; the fact that he wore a ski mask meant he intended harm. The last thing she wanted was to lead the person to her shanty and so she raced in the opposite direction.

Her breaths became deep pants and she struggled to keep the screams that wanted to be released inside her. She could feel him getting closer and closer. She imagined she could feel his hot breath whispering on the back of her neck.

She was afraid she couldn't run fast enough to stay in front of him and instead she began to frantically look around for a place to hide. If she could just lose him for a minute… just long enough so she could dive into a thicket and pray he wouldn't find her there.

The deeper she ran into the swamp the less moonlight was able to pierce through the thick foliage overhead. At the moment the darkness was her friend and when she got the opportunity where she didn't believe he could see her, she dove into a thick tangle of woods and vines. She pulled herself into the smallest ball she could make and sat perfectly still.

Desperately she tried not to move, to not even breathe. Her hand gripped her little sister tightly. She didn't want to have to use it. The last thing she wanted was a personal confrontation with whoever was after her. Why? Why was this happening? Who could it be?

Her muscles remained tense, ready to spring into action in a second if necessary. There was a sudden stillness. Although she couldn't see him, she heard him. His deep ragged breathing filled the air, letting her know he was very close to where she hid.

Her body wanted to shiver in sheer terror, but she squeezed her eyes closed and suppressed it, knowing that any kind of involuntary movement or sound meant he would find her. And then what? Oh, God, what did he want? What did he intend to do to her if he did find her?

Move away! she screamed inside her head. *Please, move away!* He was so close to her. He was just standing on the trail as if waiting for her to do something to show herself.

After several agonizing minutes, he continued to crash

through the trail away from her. He roared once again, the animalistic sound raising the hairs on the nape of her neck and along her arms.

As he continued to move away from her, she rose from her position and ran toward her shanty. Even though she tried to run as quietly as possible, deep sobs began to escape her. She stuffed the back of her hand into her mouth in an effort to staunch them.

Still, the sobs continued as she finally reached the bridge that carried her to her front porch. She unlocked the front door with trembling fingers and then flew inside, quickly locking the door after her.

She still gripped her knife tightly in her hand as she went to her front window and gazed out into the night. Would he find her here? Did he know where she lived? Sobs continued to escape her, along with deep pants for air.

She had no idea how long she remained at her window with sheer terror a living, breathing thing inside her. Finally, as the minutes ticked by and her breathing started to return to normal, the horror began to ebb somewhat. But it certainly didn't go away.

Had it been the Swamp Soul Stealer after her tonight? Or did this have something to do with the voodoo doll and the note?

At this point it didn't matter. All she knew was she'd never been so afraid in her life. It felt as if a rageful animal had been unleashed in the swamp and she'd been the target. Why? And who had it been?

She remained awake for a very long time and then finally fell into a troubled sleep on her sofa with her little sister still gripped in her hand.

HE RAN THROUGH the swamp toward his home, his rage an animal bursting from his veins, from the very heart of him. The bitch. He'd watched her and the intruder kiss. He'd seen the way she'd leaned into him and he'd pulled her intimately close to him. The traitorous bitch.

The minute he'd seen them, a sharp, wild anger had risen up inside him. He'd already warned her. He'd left her the voodoo doll and the note to warn her away from the man.

Had she forgotten she was swamp? He loved her. He'd been in love with her for a while and she was supposed to be his. They had always been destined to be together. She had even promised she was his girl forever.

But now his love for her had turned to complete disgust… to absolute hatred. A new rage roared through him as he thought of her and the science man kissing so intimately. She was not worthy of his love.

He wasn't sure what he would have done to her tonight if he'd caught up with her, but it wouldn't have been good. He could have shown up at her shanty and made her pay for her disloyalty, but he'd give her one last chance to change her ways and if she didn't, then she would die in the swamp she professed to love.

Chapter Seven

Angel awakened later than usual the next morning and for the first time in years she'd decided not to do a fish run. She hated to admit it but the fear from the night before still had a firm grip on her.

She went outside to take a shower in the structure she'd built on the back deck. She collected rainwater for the showers she took and the system worked out quite well. At least the back deck couldn't be reached unless somebody came through her shanty or approached by water, so she felt safe there.

After the shower, she pulled on fresh clothes and then placed her knife back in the sheath around her waist. She then made herself breakfast and as she picked at the eggs she had made, her thoughts raced with the horrifying events of the night before.

Who had chased her? Who was the man beneath the ski mask? His deep roars of rage had made the entire swamp shiver in fear. Did the monster come out in the daytime or only at night?

She had a feeling he needed the darkness to completely hide his identity, although if he wanted to kill her or make her disappear, then her knowing his identity wouldn't have mattered.

Too bad Colette Broussard was still in her coma. She was potentially the only person who might be able to identify the Swamp Soul Stealer.

Angel certainly couldn't identify the person who had chased her last night. Between the darkness and the ski mask, it had been completely impossible. She wasn't even sure she could give a good description of his body type. In the terror of the night, he'd seemed huge…bigger than life.

Should she call Etienne and make a report of what had happened? At this point, what could the lawman do about it? She had no real description of the man, and it was over now. She turned it over for several minutes in her mind and in the end she decided not to call the police.

She spent the morning dusting and cleaning up the place. At least Nathan would be here this evening and she always felt safe when she was with him.

Just after noon she was about to head out to go into town when Shelby and Rosemary dropped in. "Hey, girlfriend, it's been a while since we've checked in with each other," Shelby said as she sank down on the sofa.

"Yeah, you've been so busy with your new boyfriend," Rosemary added with a sly grin.

"Nathan's not my boyfriend," Angel protested with a small laugh. She sat in the chair facing her friends. "But I'm really enjoying working with him and I am making him dinner tonight," she confessed.

"Just say it, Angel," Shelby said. "You're crazy about the man. It's evident every time you even just say his name."

"What difference does it make how I feel about him. He'll

be gone in two weeks or so." A wave of depression threatened to sweep through Angel. She didn't even want to think about when it came time to say goodbye to him. He'd filled her days with so much laughter and good conversation.

"That totally stinks," Rosemary said softly.

"It is what it is. I knew the timeline all along," Angel replied.

"So, what's on the menu for tonight?" Shelby asked.

"I don't know yet, I need to make a trip into town and go to the grocery store."

"Those smothered pork chops you make are totally yummy," Shelby said.

"Thanks, maybe I'll make those for him," she replied.

"Angel...what's up with you? You don't have your normal energy level or cheerful smiles today," Rosemary observed.

"I had a rough night," Angel confessed, and then told her friends about being chased through the swamp the night before.

"Oh, my God," Shelby said once Angel was finished. "You must have been absolutely terrified."

"I was." Angel fought off a shiver that threatened to creep up her spine at the memory of just how terrified she had been. "I was terrified."

"Do you think it was the Swamp Soul Stealer?" Rosemary asked, her eyes wide.

"Either that or it was the person who left the voodoo doll and the note for me," Angel replied.

"The note? What note," Shelby asked, curious.

Angel got up and grabbed the note from the bookcase and then set it on the coffee table for them both to see.

"When did you get this?" Shelby asked.

"It was left on my door a few nights ago."

"Have you talked to Etienne about all this?" Rosemary asked.

Angel shook her head. "With everything else he has on his plate, I really didn't want to bother him with this. Besides, all I can tell him is I was chased through the darkness by an unknown man. What can he do about that?"

"Then what are you going to do?" Shelby said, her concern rife in her voice.

Angel shrugged her shoulders. "What can I do about it? I'll just have to be careful when I go out and about, especially after dark."

"Why don't you invite one of the men to stay here with you for a while?" Rosemary asked. "You know any one of them would drop everything and do that for you."

"I know that, but I don't want any of them here in my personal space," Angel replied. She didn't want to say that she wasn't sure she trusted them anymore.

"I understand that," Shelby replied. "I love all of them, but I wouldn't want to spend 24/7 with any of them."

"I wouldn't mind spending that kind of time with Beau," Rosemary said with a sigh.

Both Angel and Shelby looked at her in surprise. "You have a thing for Beau?" Shelby asked.

Rosemary nodded. "I've had a thing for him for a long time now."

"Have you let him know how you feel?" Shelby asked.

"No. I'm still trying to get my nerve up," Rosemary replied. "Eventually I'll pick the time and place to let him know."

"You should tell him how you feel about him soon,"

Angel replied. "Now, what are you two doing out and about today?" Angel asked.

"We're both off work today and so we decided to go into town and have lunch at the café. We stopped by to see if you wanted to go with us, but I guess that's a firm no," Shelby said.

"That's definitely a no," Angel replied. "Next time," she added.

The three continued to talk for about another half hour or so and then they left. Angel walked out with them to head into town.

She breathed a sigh of relief as she reached her pickup. The swamp once again felt friendly this afternoon. She now knew she needed to make sure she got everything done that needed to be done during the daylight hours whenever possible.

When darkness fell, the swamp was not her friend. She wasn't sure what she'd do about taking her fish into town to sell. Both Mac and Antoinette preferred she come later in the evenings to meet with them. But she couldn't think about that right now. In fact she refused to think at all about the night that had just passed.

All she wanted to focus on was the fact that Nathan would be at her place this evening and she wanted to cook him a great meal. Twenty minutes later she pulled up and parked at the grocery store.

She picked up a small bag of potatoes, then added a can of corn to her basket. She then went to the dairy section and grabbed a small bottle of milk. She had decided she'd make the pork chops that Shelby had mentioned, along with mashed potatoes and corn.

Hopefully Nathan liked pork. She knew from some of the conversations they'd shared that he was a man who liked almost everything when it came to food. The only thing she'd heard him say that he didn't like was brussels sprouts, and she was in total agreement with him on that. She didn't like them, either.

The last place she went in the store was to the butcher area. Mac saw her through the glass and stepped out to greet her.

"Aren't you looking pretty this afternoon," he said in greeting.

"Thanks, Mac," she replied with vague surprise. It was the first time he'd ever said something about the way she looked.

"Is there anything in particular you're looking for today?" he asked.

"I need three nice-looking thick pork chops," she replied. She'd decided to buy three in case Nathan could eat more than one.

"Three, huh. That's a big order for you," he observed.

"I'm having a guest tonight for dinner."

"Let me guess, you're having that city, science man for dinner," Mac said with a faint hint of disgust in his voice.

"That's right," she replied.

Mac held her gaze intently. "Just don't forget where you came from, Angel."

"Don't worry about me, Mac." What she wanted to tell him was to stay in his own lane and mind his own business, but she didn't because she did sell to him and she wanted to maintain that relationship.

"Let me look in the back and see if I can find you three

nice pork chops." He disappeared into the butcher area behind the glass.

Angel released a deep sigh. Why did anyone care that she was spending her time with Nathan? They all knew he would only be here for a short amount of time and it wasn't like she was going with him when he left. She was just enjoying his company while he was here and that was her right and her choice.

It hadn't been lost on her that Mac had called Nathan that "science man." Those were the very same words that had been left on the note she received.

Was it possible Mac had left the note for her? Even though Mac had an apartment in town, he had grown up in the swamp and certainly knew his way around there.

How pathetic was it that she would even suspect the butcher she'd done business with for years of putting a warning note on her front door? It proved to her that she really had no idea who to trust. Except Nathan. She completely trusted him.

"Here we go," Mac said as he returned to where she waited. He handed her a package of three nice thick pork chops.

"Thanks, Mac. These look really great." She placed them in her basket. "I'll see you later."

"Angel, be careful when you're out and about," he said.

"I always try to be," she replied, once again unsettled by him.

She finished up the shopping and the last thing she did was buy a block of ice for her cooler. She loaded everything up and then headed for home.

The inability to know whom to trust was almost as frightening as her race through the swamp last night. Equally as unsettling was the fact that the one man she trusted, the one man she felt safe with would be gone in a very short period of time and she would be all alone.

AS USUAL, as Nathan got ready to go to Angel's for the evening, a sweet anticipation rushed through him. If somebody had told him six months ago that he would have such deep feelings for a woman from the swamp, he would have told them they were crazy.

Angel had been such a surprise to him. With the end of his time here quickly approaching, along with the anticipation of seeing her again, there was a growing sadness inside him as well.

He was definitely going to miss her when he left. He would miss her smiles and her laughter. He would miss the conversations they had about anything and nothing. He didn't know how long he would mourn for what might have been if they hadn't been from two such very different worlds. He would definitely mourn for the deep friendship they had built.

He parked in the lot just before five thirty. Knowing he was early, he decided to sit and wait about ten minutes before walking into her shanty.

There was no question he'd grown to love this beautiful yet potentially dangerous place. The beauty of the swamp was apparent no matter where you looked. It was only when you delved deeper beneath the surface that you recognized the dangers.

Along with the gators that hid in dark waters, there were also lots of snakes, some harmless and some poisonous. But he knew how to stay away from both dangers and so for him the beauty far outweighed the dangers.

There was also a real peace inside Angel's shanty, a peace he'd never felt before. It was as if the world outside didn't exist. Time stood still when he was with her in her cozy home. Suddenly he couldn't wait any longer. He grabbed the bouquet of flowers he'd bought for her off the passenger seat and then got out of his car.

He'd been in the grocery store buying a couple of bags of chips for snacks in his motel room when he'd seen the bright, colorful bouquet of daisies. The flowers were dyed a hot pink, bright yellow, turquoise and neon green.

It had been an impulse buy because they had instantly reminded him of Angel. Bright and vivid and fun... He just hoped she liked them and understood it wasn't a romantic gesture from him. He quickened his steps as her shanty came into view.

He headed across her bridge and then knocked on her door. She answered almost immediately and he held out the bouquet. "I saw these today in the floral section of the grocery store and I immediately thought of you."

"Oh, Nathan. Thank you, I absolutely love them." She took the bouquet from him and opened the door wider. Once he was inside, she closed and locked the door behind him. "Let me just get something to put these in."

"Something smells absolutely delicious in here," he said and followed her into the kitchen area.

"That would be your dinner," she replied. She placed the flowers on the table where no plate was set and then looked under the sink. She pulled out a tall clean jelly jar.

"I don't have any real vases. Nobody has ever bought me flowers before."

"Really? Now that's a real sin," he replied, genuinely surprised.

"Have a seat," she said and gestured to the table. "Dinner will be ready in about fifteen...twenty minutes." She got a pair of heavy-duty scissors from a drawer and then began to trim down the long-stem flowers and arrange them in the jelly jar.

It took her only minutes and then she added water and set the arrangement in the center of the table. "They look beautiful. Thank you again, Nathan."

"It's my pleasure," he replied.

She threw away the stems she had cut and then moved to her stovetop burner where a covered skillet was on one burner and potatoes were boiling on the other one. As usual, Angel looked beautiful.

She wore jeans and a sleeveless button-up pink-and-white-flowered blouse. Her hair was a rich dark curtain around her shoulders and his fingers itched to lose themselves in it.

However, something seemed a little off with her this evening. The smiles she offered him as they talked moved her lips upward, but didn't quite reach her eyes the way they normally did.

He sensed something was wrong but didn't think it was his place to probe. Hopefully she would tell him if it was something important and she thought he needed to know. In the meantime, all he could do was try to bring out more real smiles from her.

"Genuine mashed potatoes? I'm so impressed," he said as she began to beat the potatoes with butter and milk.

"Is there any other kind?" she asked.

"I usually get the ones in a package that you add to boiled water."

She looked at him and turned up her nose. "Ugh, that sounds positively awful."

He laughed. "Actually, they aren't that bad, but nothing beats the real deal."

She opened a can of corn, poured it into a saucepan and then put it on the burner where the potatoes had been. She then opened the lid to the skillet and stirred whatever was inside.

"So, how has your day been?" he asked.

"Okay. Shelby and Rosemary came by to get me to go to lunch with them at the café, but I declined. I knew I had an important dinner to cook tonight."

"You do realize you could have simply served me buttered bread and I would have enjoyed it as long as we were eating it together."

She smiled and this time the sparkle was back in the depths of her eyes. "I would at least put a piece of bologna on the buttered bread, but tonight smothered pork chops are on the menu."

"How did you know that's a favorite of mine," he replied with a grin.

She laughed. "It's funny how everything I cook for you is your favorite. I hope you're hungry because I made plenty."

"I'm hungry. I skipped lunch today because I knew I'd be eating well tonight."

She grabbed the plates off the table and began putting

the food on them. Once they were both ready, she set one plate in front of him and then sat opposite him at the table with a plate before her.

"This looks absolutely delicious," he said.

"I hope it tastes as good as it looks."

"I'm sure it will." It took him only a couple of bites to taste how good it was. The pork chop was tender and flavorful with the gravy that covered it. "You are really a good cook, Angel," he said.

"Thanks. I don't cook much but I owe everything I know about it to my mother, who cooked good meals for my father every evening."

"How are your parents doing?" he asked.

"They're doing okay. I haven't been by to see them lately, but I've spoken to them on the phone a couple of times."

"That's good, and by the way, I didn't tell you how pretty you look tonight."

She smiled at him. As always, the smile warmed his heart. "Nathan, you're very good for a girl's ego."

He returned her smile. "I just call them like I see them."

As they ate, the conversation flowed easily, as it always did when they were together. As the meal continued and they laughed about a variety of things, her smiles were more normal as her eyes sparkled with her amusement.

Whatever was bothering her didn't seem to be bothering her anymore and he was grateful for that. He wound up eating two of the pork chops along with plenty of mashed potatoes and corn.

"I'm absolutely stuffed," he said as he got up from the table to help her with the cleanup. "You might have to roll me out of here when it's time for me to leave tonight."

"Ha, there's nothing round about you," she replied.

They continued to talk as they finished up with the dishes. As he stood next to her and helped her, he wished he could do this every night. Just the simple task done together was a pleasure.

She grabbed them a couple of beers and then they moved into the living room where they sat down on the sofa. Immediately he felt her energy change. The sparkle was once again gone from her eyes and she released a deep sigh.

"What's going on, Angel?" he asked softly.

"Oh, nothing." She took a drink of her beer and averted her gaze from him.

"Angel, don't tell me nothing when there's obviously something bothering you. You should know by now that you can tell me anything." He scooted closer to her. "Talk to me, honey."

She set her beer down on the coffee table and then looked at him, her beautiful green eyes appearing darker than usual. "Last night when I left you, I was chased through the swamp by a man dressed all in black and wearing a ski mask."

He stared at her in growing horror as she continued to tell him about the howls of rage and her frantic run to escape the person.

"I was so scared," she said as her eyes welled up with tears. "Nathan, I… I've never been so terrified in my entire life."

He reached for her and she came willingly into his arms. He held her tight as she began to cry in earnest. He stroked up and down her back while murmuring reassuring words.

"It's okay. You're safe now," he said.

She nodded and clung to him, still weeping against his

neck. Meanwhile, as he soothed her, his mind raced. Had it been the Swamp Soul Stealer who had chased her the night before?

Who else could it have been? He couldn't imagine Angel having any enemies in the swamp. It had to have been the monster that everyone feared.

Had she simply been a convenient target walking home in the dark? Or had she been specifically targeted? This thought shot fear for her straight through his heart and soul. Thank God she had gotten away. Thank God she was here and relatively unharmed.

"I… I'm sorry. I'm s-so sorry." She finally pulled away from him and swiped her cheeks in obvious embarrassment.

"Please don't apologize. You obviously needed that cry," he replied gently. He reached out and tucked a strand of her hair behind her ear so he could better see her features.

"I guess I did," she replied with a half laugh.

"Have you told anyone else about this?" he asked. "Did you call the police?"

She shook her head. "No, I know there's really nothing Etienne can do about it now, but I did tell Shelby and Rosemary about it when they stopped by earlier."

"And I'm sure they were very worried about you," he replied.

"They were, but it's over and done with now and as you said, I'm safe and that's all that matters." Her eyes still appeared dark and haunted with residual fear.

"I have a suggestion for you," he began.

"And what's that?" She looked at him curiously.

"You let me move in here with you so you never have to be out in the dark alone again for as long as I'm in town." He held his breath as her eyes widened in stunned surprise.

Chapter Eight

Angel stared at Nathan, shocked not only by his suggestion, but also by the fact that she was actually considering it.

"Think about it, Angel," he continued as he leaned forward. "I can sleep here on the sofa and I'd try to stay out of your way as much as possible. But I'd be here when you have to go out. You said yourself that there was safety in numbers and I don't feel right leaving you here all alone and so vulnerable right now."

He was definitely making a hard sell. What she also thought about was she'd never have to tell him goodbye at the end of the day. She could enjoy his company all the time. Of course, he would sleep on the sofa, but he'd be here with her throughout the darkness of the night.

It would probably make it all the more difficult when he had to leave for good, but she didn't want to think about that right now. With the terror of the night before still deep in the back of her throat, she slowly nodded her head.

"Okay," she said.

"Really? You'll let me be here for you?"

"Nathan, I've never needed anyone in my entire life," she said. "But I have to admit having you here will make me feel better…safer. Hopefully my fear will pass soon and I'll be fine on my own once again. Still, I know there will be times I have to be out after dark, mostly on the evenings when I make fish runs."

"From now on I'll be by your side on those nights and on any other nights you have to be out," he replied. His eyes shone with the light that always made her feel special. "Angel, I actually feel honored that you'll allow me to do this for you."

She laughed as an enormous relief rushed through her. "You won't feel so honored when you see me first thing in the morning after I've just rolled out of bed."

His eyes sparked with something dangerous and delicious. "I actually look forward to that." She broke eye contact with him as a wave of heat swept through her. This was about her safety, not about her hormones.

"So, when do you want me to make the move here?" he asked.

She gazed at him once again. "How about sometime tomorrow?"

"Okay, shall we say about noon? It won't take me long to pack my bags and check out of the motel."

"That sounds perfect." Now that she'd agreed to let him be here, she couldn't wait for it to happen as soon as possible.

"Now, I'd better get out of here before you change your mind about me staying here with you." He stood and finished the last of his beer.

She got up as well to walk him to the door. When they reached it, a sudden fear for him gripped her. "Do you have your stun gun with you?"

He pulled it out of his pocket. "I never travel without it."

"Keep it out until you get back safely to your car."

He leaned closer to her. "Now that my leg is pretty much healed up, I can definitely run like hell. Don't worry about me, Angel. I'll be fine and I'll be here at noon tomorrow. Now, can I kiss you good-night?"

"I'd like that," she replied. She wanted to be held in his arms just one last time before he left for the night.

He gathered her close, but instead of the hot kisses they had shared in the past, his kiss was gentle and infinitely filled with a caring and warmth she hadn't even known she needed.

"I'll see you tomorrow," he said as he released her. "And don't go outside tonight."

"Don't worry. I have no plans to be out tonight," she assured him.

It was only when he was gone that she realized she still hadn't shown him the note she had received. She sank down on her sofa and grabbed her beer.

It was odd to her that she hadn't wanted any of the men she had grown up with to be here with her, but rather she wanted a man she'd only known for a couple of weeks. It spoke of the distrust she had with all the men right now and the fact that she absolutely trusted Nathan with her life.

She took a drink of the beer, her thoughts on what she'd just agreed to. She'd never lived with a man before. Jim had never lived with her. He'd always spent the evening with her and then had gone back to his apartment in town. She should be feeling nervous about this new experience, but she had a feeling Nathan would be a very easy man to live with.

She finished the beer, checked to make sure both of her doors were double-locked and then she went into her bedroom to get ready for bed.

As she changed into her nightgown, another huge sense of relief swept through her. With Nathan here, she would feel safe and secure. She wouldn't have to be so frightened of the dark. Hopefully her fear of the swamp in the dark would pass with each day that went by.

She slept well that night and got up early the next morning. She was surprised by the sweet anticipation that filled her at the thought that Nathan would be there at noon.

One of the first things they would have to do was go to the grocery store. She didn't keep food for two and her cooler was fairly empty. She hoped Nathan wouldn't mind, but if he wanted to eat, then the trip was necessary.

She had no idea what her friends would think about this arrangement. Her women friends would probably just be glad that she had somebody to be with her and keep her safe. She had a feeling that Louis, Jacques and Beau would have a much bigger problem with it.

They would probably be angry and upset that she hadn't depended on one of them. But she just couldn't right now. Somebody had left that note and the voodoo doll for her and unfortunately those men were all at the top of her suspect list.

She spent the morning getting things ready for Nathan. She cleaned and made sure she had fresh sheets for the sofa. She had to go into town to do laundry at the local Laundromat, but thankfully she had done that recently enough that she had plenty of clean bedding for him.

She also made space in her closet for his things. It was

all a new experience for her, thinking about sharing her space with a man full-time. She cleared out a drawer in her dresser and then cleaned off a shelf in the bathroom closet so he could put his toiletries there.

It's all only temporary, she reminded herself. Nothing had changed about his timeline for leaving Crystal Cove. He had a life to get back to in New Orleans, and that day would be here far too soon.

But she didn't want to dwell on that right now. All she cared about was he wanted to be her hero and for now she was going to let him. In truth, she needed a hero right now.

Surely with a little time away from the terror in the swamp, she would be okay going out on her own again after dark. At least the monster, if it had been the Swamp Soul Stealer, obviously hadn't found her shanty and she was definitely grateful for that. However, she didn't believe the Swamp Soul Stealer had left her the voodoo doll and the note, and whoever that person was, he definitely knew where she lived. But she didn't want to think about that right now.

The morning flew by and at precisely noon his footsteps sounded on her bridge outside. She opened the door and smiled at him. His camera case was slung around his neck and each of his hands held a medium-sized duffel bag.

"Permission to come aboard," he said with a boyish grin.

"Permission granted," she replied and opened the door wider to allow him and his bags entry. He walked past her and she smelled the delicious scent of him. It smelled like safety.

He set the bags down and took off the camera and placed

it on the sofa. "Haven't changed your mind about all this, have you?" he asked.

"No, and I can see by your bags that you haven't changed your mind, either."

"Speaking of bags, where do you want me to put these things?" he asked. His eyes held a sparkle that warmed her from the top of her head to the very tips of her toes.

"I made room for your hanging clothes in my closet and cleared a drawer for you in the dresser. There's also an empty shelf for your toiletries in the bathroom closet."

"You obviously went to a lot of trouble," he replied with a frown. "You do realize I could have just lived out of my bags."

"Nonsense and it was no problem at all. Why don't you get unpacked and settled in and then we need to make a trip to the grocery store. I don't usually keep enough food for two."

"Sounds like a plan," he replied agreeably. He carried both his bags into her bedroom and she sat on the edge of the bed and they talked while he unpacked.

The setting was intimate. It had been years since she'd had a man in her bedroom for anything. At least her nightstands were neat and clean and her bed was made up with the bright pink spread that she loved. There were also several white and pink decorative pillows tossed on there as well.

Still, as he hung his clothes and then tucked things into the drawer she'd had ready for him, it was far too easy to imagine him on the bed with her and between her sheets. The desire she had for this man was completely insane.

Thankfully, it didn't take him long and once he'd stowed his toiletries in the bathroom, they headed out for the grocery store. The fresh air outside cooled the crazy thoughts that had momentarily flowed through her head about him being in her bed.

"Is there anything in particular you're hungry for?" she asked. She was seated in the passenger seat as he had insisted he would drive.

"No, nothing in particular, but we'll share the cooking duties so you aren't always cooking for me," he replied.

She cast him a grin of amusement. "Can you cook?"

"I love food so much I had to learn to cook, so the short answer is yes. I can definitely make a mean burger."

"Then I look forward to having one," she replied.

They continued to talk about cooking until they arrived at the grocery store. Once inside, he grabbed one of the carts and she walked beside him while they shopped.

She had been on a bit of a sexual burn since they'd been together in her bedroom and her desire for him only increased as they shopped and laughed together.

He looked so handsome in a pair of black slacks and a gray short-sleeved button-up shirt. His hair had grown out a bit and the slightly shaggy style only emphasized his strong features and beautiful blue eyes.

They were in the produce department, playfully arguing about a bag of shredded lettuce versus a whole head of lettuce when she realized she wanted him in her bed. Maybe not tonight or tomorrow night. But before he left town, she wanted to make love with Nathan Merrick.

She suddenly recognized that she'd invited a different kind of danger into her home. She was afraid of physical harm outside and she now had to worry about heartbreak on the inside.

IT TOOK THEM about an hour in the grocery store to get everything they would need for several days. Their time together was off to a great start with plenty of laughter. He'd tried to pay for the groceries but she'd insisted she pay half, so he told her she could work a day for free instead. She finally agreed to that.

He'd been surprised she had agreed to his offer to stay with her. He knew her to be a strong, independent woman, but it was obvious her experience being chased through the swamp had truly shaken her up.

Hell, it had shaken him up when she'd told him about it. He couldn't even imagine the terror she must have experienced. He was just happy that she'd agreed to allow him to stay with her. He wanted to keep her safe for as long as he was here in Crystal Cove. He didn't even want to think about what could happen when he left. Hopefully by that time the Swamp Soul Stealer would be behind bars and everyone could breathe a big sigh of relief.

They got back to her place and between the two of them, carried all the groceries inside in one trip. Once in the shanty, they placed the bags on the kitchen table and then he handed each item to her and she put it away.

It was such a mundane task and yet he thoroughly enjoyed it. As they worked, they talked about all the meals they could make with what they had bought.

"Don't forget, we can always fish for our dinner," she said. Today she looked like another ray of sunshine in jeans and a bright yellow T-shirt. Her smiles were bright and her eyes sparkled. The tears from the night before appeared gone and he was grateful she seemed back to her normal, cheerful self.

"It's nice to know that if all the grocery stores around the world shut down, you could still feed me fish," he replied teasingly.

"You don't fish?" she asked.

"I've never been fishing in my life," he admitted.

"Then we definitely need to remedy that." She picked up several cans of vegetables and stored them in a cabinet. "You have to learn to fish so you can feed me."

"I wouldn't mind learning to fish so I can support you in the manner to which you've become accustomed," he replied.

"Now that's what I'm talking about," she replied with a laugh.

They finished putting all the groceries away and then he looked at her expectantly. "What do you normally do in the afternoons when we aren't out in the swamp working?"

"I usually just chill. I enjoy reading and I always have a couple of library books on hand."

"Hmm, that explains it," he said.

She looked at him curiously. "That explains what?"

"The fact that you're so intelligent."

She laughed, that musical sound that he loved to hear. "I don't know about how intelligent I am, but part of it is due to my mother who homeschooled me. She had me study a wide variety of subjects and she was a tough taskmaster. There were plenty of days I would have much rather been out running in the swamp, but study time always came first."

"Good for your mother," he replied. "Still, reading definitely makes people smarter and wiser. And now I'll just go sit on the sofa and stay out of your way."

He sank down on one side of the sofa, noticing on the

other end was a pillow and a folded sheet and blanket. His bedding for the night.

Her bed had looked damn inviting when he'd been in her bedroom, but that wasn't part of their deal. He would be a gentleman and sleep on the sofa…unless she invited him into the bedroom.

Before any steamy visions of that happening could fill his head, he picked up his camera. He always had photos to edit and decide which picture would go best with what text for the book. He certainly couldn't forget the reason he was here.

As he got to work, Angel grabbed a book off the bookshelf and sank down in the chair facing him. The next couple of hours were peaceful, although he found himself gazing at her again and again. Her presence wasn't very conducive to him getting his work done.

Still, with the lapping of the water outside and Angel's presence inside, there was a peace in his heart, the peace that at least for the moment all was right in the world.

It was about four thirty when she closed the book and stood. She stretched by bending first one way and then the other. He tried not to look at her smooth skin that was exposed where the T-shirt she wore pulled up with her stretching. "Are you hungry?" she asked.

"Definitely getting there," he replied and began to put his camera away. "I didn't eat any lunch today."

"I didn't, either."

"How about I fry up a couple of those burgers I told you about? The buns we bought are fresh today and it won't take me long."

"That sounds great," she replied. "And this way I can see if your burgers are really all that."

"Be prepared to be amazed." He finished putting his camera away and then stood.

Minutes later he stood at the kitchen counter ready to make his hamburger patties. He'd bought the specific spices he needed and he now mixed them altogether with the hamburger in a bowl.

She sat at the table watching him and laughed as he tried to hide his spices from her view. She had gotten out the cooktop for him and he had a skillet and a saucepan for a can of baked beans they had bought.

"I'm not used to somebody cooking dinner for me," she said as he began to form the meat into patties and placed each one into the skillet.

"I'm not used to cooking dinner for somebody," he replied. He grabbed the can opener and opened the can of beans, then dumped them into the saucepan to warm. He then turned and grinned at her. "I'm not used to it, but I could definitely get used to it."

"Me, too," she replied with a laugh. Oh, her eyes sparkled so brightly and despite the rising smell of cooking hamburger, he could still smell the alluring scent of her. It had been a constant all afternoon and it drew him to her like a bee to honey.

Twenty minutes later they sat at the table to eat. Besides the hamburgers and beans, they also had potato chips to round out the meal.

"Okay, it's the moment of truth," he said as she picked up the burger. He watched intently as she took her first bite.

She chewed and swallowed and then quickly chased it down with a big drink of water. She then gazed at him soberly.

"You don't like it," he said in dismay. "Maybe I put in too much seasoning, or maybe I didn't use quite enough."

She grinned at him then, an impish grin that immediately shot through to his heart. "Actually, it's very good and I love it."

"Woman, you're going to age me long before my time," he said. "So, is it the best burger you've ever had?"

"I do love the Big D's burgers, but I have to admit this one tops theirs hands down."

"And that's exactly what I wanted to hear," he replied.

Their lighthearted banter continued as they ate. Once they were finished eating, she helped him with the cleanup and then they moved back into the living room where they both sank down on the sofa.

As darkness began to fall, she lit the lanterns in the room, giving it all a cozy glow. "I'd say the first day of this experiment has gone very well," she said.

He raised a brow at her. "You consider this an experiment?"

"In a way, yes. I've never lived with a man before, so this is all new to me."

"You didn't live together with the boyfriend who broke your heart?" he asked.

"No, he always lived in town and I lived here. In fact, he never spent the night here. So, I don't know how to live with a man in the house."

"At least you think today went well."

She cast him a soft smile. "You're just an easy man to be around."

"Thanks, I feel the same way about you." She looked so

lovely in the lantern light. The glow emphasized her high cheekbones and illuminated her olive skin tone. Her eyes shone like those of a wild animal in the jungle and his blood heated up inside him.

They continued to talk as the night deepened and the sound of throaty bullfrogs came from outside. It was about nine o'clock when she stood up from the sofa.

"I think it's my bedtime," she said. He got up from the sofa as well.

"What are the plans for tomorrow?"

"What do you think about having your first fishing lesson early in the morning?"

"Can you make sure I don't slip in the water and get eaten by an alligator?" he asked.

"I'll make sure you don't get eaten," she replied. "After we do a little fishing, then we can do our usual thing exploring the swamp so you can get more of the photos you need."

"Do you feel comfortable doing that?" He took a step closer to her.

"During the daylight and with you, I feel very comfortable. Besides, if it really was the Swamp Soul Stealer, then as far as I know, he's only taken people after dark."

She took a step closer to him. "So, I guess I'll just say good-night now." Still, she didn't make a move to leave the room or step back from him.

"Would you like a good-night kiss?" he asked, his body heating up once again.

She smiled at him impishly. "How did you know?"

He took another step toward her and then gathered her into his arms. He intended the kiss to be short and sweet, but as always, the moment his lips took hers, he was lost in her. Their tongues swirled together in a dance of hot desire.

Her arms tightened around his neck as she leaned into him. Did he want to make love to her in that moment? Absolutely, and he had a feeling she would have let him…even encouraged him to do so.

But he was also aware that her fear still might be weighing heavy in her heart and she might make a decision tonight that she would regret in the morning when she was thinking more clearly.

With this thought in mind, he reluctantly broke the kiss and stepped back from her. "Good night, Angel."

She looked at him for a long moment and then slowly nodded. "Good night, Nathan." She turned and headed into her bedroom. He heard the door close and then he made up his bed on the sofa and stretched out.

As the fire of his desire for her slowly ebbed away, he released a deep sigh. Living here with her was going to be much harder than he'd anticipated. His desire for her was a living, breathing animal inside him and he knew she felt the same way about him.

Surely that's all it was with Angel. It had nothing to do with love or anything like that. He loved her company. He loved her laughter. He loved so many things about her, but that didn't mean he was actually in love with her.

He didn't want to be in love with her. While he would miss her when he left here, he refused to walk away from here with a broken heart.

He knew the bitter taste of a broken heart. He remembered the absolute searing pain and he never wanted to experience that again. He would be leaving here soon, so as much as he desired Angel, he would never allow himself to fall in love with her.

Chapter Nine

She would have slept with him last night. Angel awakened the next morning with that single thought playing in her mind. She'd wanted to take him by the hand, bring him into her bedroom and make sweet, fiery love with him.

As he'd kissed her, she'd tasted his desire for her and knew he wanted her, too. However, before anything more could happen, he'd broken the kiss and stepped back from her, allowing the moment between them to pass. She now rolled over on her back and released a deep sigh. She should probably be grateful he'd broken up the moment.

It was very early in the morning. The sun wasn't even beginning to peek over the horizon and so she remained in bed and gave her thoughts free rein.

During the years after she and her ex had broken up, there had been plenty of men who had asked her out. She'd rejected each and every offer. After the pain and betrayal of Jim, she hadn't wanted to open her heart up to any man. She had her friends and that had been enough for her.

Until Nathan.

Either he had changed her or she'd grown from the past heartache because she'd opened her heart up to him completely. How foolish was she to pin her heart to a man who was unavailable for a real, lasting relationship.

It wouldn't be long before she'd rouse him to go fishing with her. She knew it would be fun to teach him and they'd have a great time together, as they usually did. Then they'd once again go exploring in the swamp so he could continue to take the pictures he needed.

Once he had the last of the photos he wanted, then he'd be leaving. He would take her heart with him. As much as she'd fought against it, she realized now she was completely and madly in love with Nathan Merrick.

She loved him far more than she'd ever loved Jim. Her love for Nathan was different than it had been with Jim. It was deeper and richer. But in the end, it couldn't…wouldn't last.

Yes, she had been an utter fool. When she'd felt herself falling for him so deeply, she should have stopped being his guide and never seen him again. She should have protected her heart more carefully, but she hadn't and now it was too late. She'd just have to deal with her emotions after he left.

Releasing another deep sigh, she got out of bed. Quietly she crept across the hallway and into the bathroom. She washed her face and brushed her hair, then captured the long tresses into a big silver barrette at the nape of her neck.

Once that was done, she returned to her bedroom to dress for the day. She pulled on a pair of jeans and then a plain light pink T-shirt.

By that time the sun had peeked up over the horizon and it was time to wake up Nathan. If they were going to catch fish, early morning was the very best time.

She walked into the living room, surprised to find him

sitting on the edge of the sofa. The lanterns in the room were still burning and in the lamp's illumination he looked sexy as hell.

He wore only a pair of black boxers and his hair was slightly mussed. His bare shoulders were wide and his chest showed muscles she hadn't even known he possessed. Almost instantly a rush of heat infused her.

"Good morning," he said with a smile.

"Good morning to you." She looked at him with a frown. "I didn't expect you to be awake yet. Did you not sleep well?"

"On the contrary, I slept so well that I woke up a few minutes ago feeling refreshed and ready to catch some fish," he replied.

"Then while you get dressed, I'll get the poles ready to go," she replied. She needed him to get dressed as soon as possible, before she snatched him up off the sofa and pulled him into her bedroom.

"Great," he replied. As he stood, she quickly turned and headed for the back door.

Once outside, she drew in a deep breath of the air that didn't smell like Nathan. She gathered the fishing items, which were two poles and a tackle box. She then went to a small tank filled with dirt that contained the earthworms she used as bait. She grabbed a handful of them and then placed them in a small plastic container to take with them.

Once she had everything together, she carried it all into the living room and placed it by the front door. Nathan was obviously in her bedroom getting dressed.

She started to sit on the sofa, but at that moment he came

out. Dressed in a pair of jeans and a gray T-shirt, he also brought with him a big grin.

"I've been thinking about this fishing thing," he said.

"And?"

"And I think I'm going to kick your butt by catching way more fish than you do."

"Ha! Is that a challenge I smell in the air?" she replied.

"I believe it is," he said. "How about loser has to cook dinner tonight."

"You're on, loser." With a grin, she handed him the poles to carry while she grabbed the tackle box and worms. Together they stepped out into the golden light of dawn.

"I assume we're going to your favorite fishing spot," he said as he followed behind her across her bridge.

"That's exactly where we're going," she replied.

"You do realize that gives you a slight advantage over me."

She laughed. "Are you already regretting your challenge to me?"

"Not a chance," he replied. "Even though you might have a personal relationship with all the fish in your favorite fishing spot, I'm still going to catch more than you."

She laughed once again. "Time will tell."

It took them fifteen minutes to reach the place where she usually fished from the bank. She opened her tackle box, removed the lid from the container of worms and then took one of the poles from him.

"Okay, first you need to bait your hook." She took one of the wiggly worms and got it on the hook.

He watched her and then did the same thing with his.

"This is going to be a piece of cake," he said once he was finished.

She grinned at him. "And this is how you cast out into the water." She showed him how to throw the baited hook and line into the water.

He raised the pole over his head and then threw his line out. It landed in the water about three feet in front of the bank.

"Uh, you might want to try that again," she suggested, trying not to laugh. "The farther out you are in the water, the better the odds of getting a fish on the line."

"I know. That was just my practice shot," he replied. He reeled the line in and then threw it back out, this time getting it out far enough.

"Now we wait for a bite." She sank down to the ground and he did the same, sitting far too close to her for her peace of mind.

As they waited, they small-talked about what kinds of photos he still needed to get. As he told her what he needed, she realized there weren't that many left. And once he had those, he'd be gone.

He was the first one to jump up as the tip of his pole bent. "Set the hook," she said. "Give it a quick jerk and then reel it in as fast as you can."

He did as she said and reeled in a nice-sized catfish. He crowed with his success and did a silly dance. "Who's the boss now, baby?"

She laughed at his antics. "Our deal wasn't who caught the first fish, it's who catches the most fish." She got up and helped him get the fish off the hook and then showed him how to place it on a stringer. He then rebaited his hook and cast it out in the water once again.

"Sunrise is beautiful here," he observed.

"I love it at this time of the day when the first rays of the sun shimmers golden on the water and birds sing their morning songs from the trees."

"I know living in the swamp is hard, but there is a lot to be said for it," he said thoughtfully.

"I agree that it can be difficult, but there's a much slower pace here than I imagine there is anywhere else. We work hard but we also relax hard. I find such peace here. Of course, I don't know anything different than this."

He smiled, but before he could say anything else, the tip of his pole dipped again with another bite and he jumped back up to his feet.

They fished for about another hour or so and by that time she had caught four and he had two. "Ready to head back?" she asked.

"I hate to go home as a loser, but I admit you beat me fair and square this morning," he replied.

"I can almost smell the scent of dinner cooking," she said with a small grin.

"Oh, so you're a bad winner and will be crowing about your success all afternoon long," he said as they put their equipment away.

"Are you a bad loser and going to pout all day?" she returned.

He laughed. "I don't think I've ever pouted a day in my life."

"Then I like that about you," she replied.

They walked a few minutes in silence. "Maybe we need

to go into town and buy a few board games to help pass the afternoons," he said.

"Board games? Like what do you have in mind?" she asked.

"Have you ever played chess before?"

"Yes, I have. My dad taught me years ago and we would often play together. He has a board and the pieces. I'm sure we could borrow it from him. It's time for me to check in with them, anyway. I'll bring them some of the fish we caught this morning and you could meet them."

"I'd love to meet them. Why don't we put off our usual trek through the swamp for today."

"Would you be okay with that?"

"I'm fine with it," he replied.

She could imagine introducing her parents to the man she loved, the man she was going to marry and build a life with, but instead she would introduce him as the biologist friend she'd been working for.

It didn't take them long to get back to the shanty where she put two of the biggest catfish on a stringer to take to her parents and tossed the other four into her floating cage. Then they left to head to her parents' place.

"I'd prefer we not say anything about you staying with me," she said as they walked. "I don't want to outright lie to them, but I haven't mentioned anything about what's going on in my life right now because I don't want them to worry about me."

"Got it," he replied. "I have to admit, I'm ridiculously nervous to meet your parents," he added.

She flashed a quick backward glance at him. "Why?"

"Because they have to be awesome people to have created a woman like you."

"There you go again, Mr. Merrick, turning my head with all your flattery and charm."

"I'm serious, Angel. You are an amazing woman."

Then love me and stay here with me forever, her heart cried out. But she knew the whole idea of him staying and living in the swamp with her for the rest of his life was ridiculous.

He was a biologist, not a fisherman. He was a teacher and a respected person in his community. Besides, despite all the flattery she got from him, in spite of the fact that there was a wild sexual chemistry between them, he certainly hadn't indicated that he was in love with her.

Maybe it was a good thing he'd stopped kissing her last night and they hadn't gone to her bedroom. She was so confused about what she wanted in her life right now.

Did she want to throw all caution to the wind and make love with Nathan? Did she want to act on the crazy sexual desire she felt for him? She knew without doubt if she gave him an open invitation into her bed, he would take it.

Did she want to carry that memory with her when he was gone? Or did she not want to have that memory at all to taunt and torment her when he left?

NATHAN THOROUGHLY ENJOYED meeting Angel's parents, who seemed like wonderfully kind and good people. It was obvious they adored their only child and he could easily see where Angel got both her confidence and sense of loyalty and compassion.

It was also obvious her parents still adored one another.

It was in their tone of voice when they spoke to each other and in the way they looked at each other.

It made him envious. He wanted that in his own life. He wanted a woman to grow old with and continue to love through the years. He wanted to grow a family with a special woman who he knew would make an amazing mother.

They visited for about half an hour and then left her mother and father the fish Angel had caught and walked out with a box that held the chessboard and pieces inside.

"I'm now looking forward to a challenging game of chess," he said as he followed her home. "I couldn't beat you at fishing this morning, but I'm pretty sure I'll kick your butt at chess."

"Ha, pretty full of yourself, aren't you?" she replied with a laugh.

"Nah, just warning you about what's going to happen."

"The first thing I want to do when we get back is take a nice, refreshing shower," she said.

The day was unusually humid and just walking had him sweating more than a little bit. "I wouldn't mind taking one myself," he replied.

Instantly his mind filled with visions of them showering together. He would be able to slide the bar of soap across her breasts and down her belly, then he'd pull her close against him as the water played on their heads. He snapped the very hot vision out of his brain before it could go any further.

"I'll let you shower first since you have dinner duty and then I'll shower."

"Works for me," he agreed. So, there would be no shower for two.

They were silent for the rest of the walk. Once they got

back to her place, she set the chess game on the coffee table and grinned at him. "I hope you're prepared to get *your* butt handed to you when we play chess."

"Ha, that's not going to happen." He loved it when she grinned at him so teasingly. "I let you beat me at fishing this morning, but I'm not going to let you beat me at chess."

"Oh, you *let* me beat you at fishing? You're a funny man. And now I'll just go grab you a towel for your shower."

She went into the bathroom and returned with a large bath towel. She handed it to him and then gestured for him to follow her outside.

He was surprised by the structure she had built for showering. It was a small wooden enclosure with a large bucket overhead and plastic tubing leading to a showerhead.

"I imagine this looks fairly primitive to you, but it works," she replied.

"Actually, I find it quite brilliant," he replied.

"Thanks. There's soap in the dish and a bottle of shampoo on the floor inside there and all you have to do is open the plastic tubing clip to get the water to run."

"Got it," he replied.

Five minutes later he stood beneath the spray of water. The soap was fresh-scented and he worked quickly, not knowing how much liquid was in the bucket. The water was a bit cool and completely refreshing.

When he was finished, he squeezed the clip to stop the water flow and then dried off. He wrapped the towel around himself and then stepped back into the house.

Angel was seated on the sofa and setting up the chessboard. "Mind if I duck into your room for my clothes."

"Nathan, feel free to go into my room anytime you need

anything of yours," she replied. "And while you're dressing, I'll go take my own shower."

He went into the bathroom first and grabbed his deodorant. He then went into her bedroom and took out a clean pair of jeans and a light blue polo. Within minutes he was dressed and then went back into the bathroom.

As he put away his deodorant and spritzed on some of his cologne, he tried to keep all thoughts of Angel taking her shower out of his head. Just imagining it was something he didn't need.

He went into the living room and sank down on the sofa in front of the chessboard. He hadn't realized until now that the board, along with the pieces, appeared to be hand-carved from wood. They were positively stunning.

The water outside stopped and a few minutes later she stepped back inside. A big red towel was wrapped around her body, but the sexy vision of her made him momentarily tongue-tied.

"I'll be out in just a few minutes," she said and then disappeared into the bedroom.

He released a deep shuddery sigh. He wanted her so badly it hurt inside him. Being around her and not touching her was an exquisite form of torture. He didn't love her, but he definitely wanted her far more than he could ever remember wanting a woman before.

She came back into the living room a few minutes later clad in a red-and-white housedress. It was fitted at the top and then swung out from her waist and hips. It looked cool and relaxing and she smelled of the alluring scent that he loved. Every muscle in his body tensed with his desire for her.

"So, are you ready?" She gestured toward the chessboard. "I think we have time for a couple of games before you have to cook dinner."

"I'm ready," he replied and picked up one of the pieces. "Do you know who made this set? These look hand-carved."

"They are. My father made it. He likes to whittle a little in his spare time." She went into the kitchen and grabbed one of the chairs at the table.

"He's very talented," he replied.

She set the chair opposite to where he sat on the sofa and straightened the chessboard between them. "It's just something he enjoys doing." She sat in the chair. She cast him one of her impish smiles. "I'm so confident I'll even let you make the first move."

"Okay, then."

She was smart as a whip and knew the game well. He had to really concentrate on the moves he was making and that was difficult with her beautiful presence seated right across from him.

They played three games. He won two and she won one. By that time, he needed to start dinner. They both moved into the kitchen where she sat at the table and he opened the cooler to see what he could prepare.

"What do you think about smothered hamburger patties and mashed potatoes?" he asked.

"Sounds good to me. At least I can help you by peeling the potatoes." She got up and pulled the bag of potatoes out of the lower cabinet.

"Okay, then while you do that, I'll put together some awesome patties." He took the pound of hamburger out of the cooler and then grabbed a bowl to put it all together in.

As he gathered up breadcrumbs and various spices, she began to peel the potatoes. Once again, he thought about how nice it was to be working together in the kitchen. It felt natural and right and he wanted this kind of relationship in his life.

Of course it wouldn't be with Angel. It couldn't be with her, but when he got back home, he intended to open himself up fully to the dating game. It was time. He now realized he was ready for a wife, somebody who would fill his days with laughter and conversation like Angel had these last couple weeks.

He also wanted a woman who filled his heart with healthy lust, a lust they could explore every night of his life. He wanted a woman who would rival the lust he felt toward the woman who was now peeling the potatoes.

As they worked, they talked more about her parents. "How did they meet?" he asked.

"Their parents were good friends and often got together to visit. They're the same age and Dad always says when they were both thirteen, he knew he wanted to marry Mom."

"Is that the way lots of relationships form here? With parents being friends?" he asked, curious.

"It's definitely one way that young people meet. But a lot of them just meet when they are going about their lives in the swamp."

Once the potatoes were boiling and the patties were cooking, she sat back down while he manned the burners.

Their conversation moved on to the chess games they had played. "You do realize I let you win the first one so your male pride wouldn't be hurt," she said with a teasing lilt to her voice.

"You're a funny woman," he replied with a laugh. "Actually, I let you win the second game so you wouldn't pout if I beat you in all three games."

"Ha, and you're a funny man," she replied. "And I'm definitely not a pouter."

"And I like that about you," he said, throwing her words back at her. He went to the cabinet of canned goods and pulled out two cans of brown gravy he had bought from the store. He drained the grease off the patties into a coffee can she kept specifically for that purpose and then added the gravy to the patties. He turned down the heat beneath it and covered the pan with a lid.

He then turned his attention to the potatoes. It didn't take long after that to get the meal on the table. They lightly bantered with each other as they ate and then they cleaned the kitchen together.

Once that was done, they settled back into the living room for a couple more games of chess before bedtime. Once again, he found her to be very distracting.

Her green eyes appeared to glow as her gaze went from him to the chessboard. Her scent made it difficult for him to concentrate and her long silky hair begged his fingers to tangle in it while he kissed her until they were both mindless.

He also found her natural intelligence hot as hell, and he was on a slow burn the entire time they played. As darkness descended, she lit the lanterns that were positioned around the room, the soft glow loving her beautiful features.

By the time they decided to call it a night, they were tied. She'd won the first game and he'd won the second. He stood and began putting the pieces back in the box where they belonged while she returned her chair to the kitchen.

"First thing in the morning I'm going to take the pirogue out and do a fish run," she said. "You don't have to come with me. I'll be perfectly safe out on the water."

He frowned. "Are you sure?"

"I'm positive. I don't even have to step a foot on the shore so I'll be completely safe. Besides, the pirogue is a one-person boat."

"And I'm not a fan of dangling in the water and holding onto the side of a little boat," he replied. "As long as you're sure you'll be safe, that's all I care about."

"And I appreciate that. Now, I think I'll call it a night because I like to do the fish runs early," she said. Like last night, she didn't make a move to leave the room. In fact, she took a step toward him. "Do I get a good-night kiss from you?" she asked.

"Absolutely," he replied, even knowing it was going to be sheer torture for him to kiss her and then let her go.

He stepped toward her and she met him halfway. He didn't intend to take her into his arms, but when she wrapped her arms around his neck, he couldn't help himself.

He pulled her shapely body tightly against him and took her mouth with his. She immediately opened her mouth and danced her tongue with his. Hot flames of desire whipped up inside him, creating an inferno.

She was on fire, too. He could tell by how hungrily she kissed him and how she moved her hips against his. He was already aroused, and with her hips rubbing against him, it only intensified.

He finally broke the kiss and stepped back from her. She reached out and took his hand in hers. Her eyes blazed with a deep emerald fire. "Come into my bedroom, Nathan. Come with me and make love to me."

He stared at her for several long moments, looking for any hint of hesitation or regret from her. He saw none. All he saw was open fiery hunger.

She tugged on his hand. "Nathan, make love to me," she whispered urgently. "You know it's what we both want."

With that, he allowed her to lead him into the bedroom, his heart pounding wildly in his chest. He knew on some level this was all wrong, but his want for her in this moment was far greater than anything else.

Chapter Ten

Angel knew she might regret this in the morning, but it felt like she'd wanted Nathan since the moment she first met him when he was sitting on the side of the trail and looked up at her with his dazzling blue eyes.

The fire inside her burned hot and bright and she wasn't going to deny herself this pleasure any longer. And she knew without doubt it would be a pleasure. Once they were in her bedroom, she lit a lantern, creating a soft glow around the bed.

Then she turned and reached out for him once again. He gathered her back into his arms and his mouth took hers, and at the same time his hands slid from the middle of her back and down across her buttocks. He pulled her even closer to him, close enough that she could feel his arousal and she was quickly lost in him.

His familiar scent stirred her and the feel of his body so close to hers caused her blood to heat to liquid fire as it rushed through her veins.

She didn't know how long they kissed as time didn't matter. They were hungry kisses…fiery ones that only increased her incredible desire for him. Her nipples were erect beneath her housedress and it wasn't long before she wanted more.

She plucked at the bottom of his shirt and he took the cue, stepping back from her so that he could remove his shirt. The lantern's glow played on his muscled chest and she moved close to him once again so she could stroke her hands down his warm bare flesh.

His eyes burned with a brightness she'd never seen before and she wanted to fall into the blue depths and stay there forever. His gaze made love to her long before he'd even touched her body.

She rained kisses across his chest and then stepped back and swept her housedress off and tossed it next to the bed. She was now clad only in a wispy pair of red panties.

"Oh, Angel, you are so beautiful," he said, his voice deeper than usual as his gaze swept down the length of her.

"So are you," she replied. She slid into her sheets while he took off his shoes and socks and then kicked off his jeans, leaving him clad only in a pair of navy boxers.

His body was magnificent. His shoulders were broad and his waist was slim. His legs were firmly muscled and athletic-looking and the sight of him nearly naked stirred everything inside her.

He joined her in the bed and once again pulled her into his arms and captured her mouth with his. His half-naked body against her own felt incredible.

She loved his skin. It was so smooth and warm and tasted slightly of salt. He rolled her over on her back and then slid his hands down her neck and across her collarbone. She held her breath in sweet anticipation and then he touched her breasts.

His hands cupped them for a moment and then his fingers rolled and toyed with her erect nipples. They hardened even more and ached in sweet torment beneath his touch.

She'd dreamed of him touching her like this and in reality it was so much better than she could have ever imagined. His lips slid down the path of his hands, nibbling along her collarbone and then capturing one of her nipples in his hot mouth.

Electrical currents shot off inside her, running from her nipples to the very core of her. Her body was moist and ready for him and when one of his hands slid downward from her breasts, she opened her legs to him.

But he continued to torment and tease her, running his fingers back and forth across her lower abdomen and then her hips, but not touching her where she wanted...where she needed him to touch her the most. At the same time his lips once again plied hers with heated kisses.

She clung to him, her fingers biting into his shoulders as she opened her legs even wider. She gasped as his fingers finally touched her intimately at her core. They danced against her slowly at first. It was a new source of pleasure and sweet torment.

He began to move his fingers faster and faster in a dance that beckoned a rising tension inside her. Higher and higher she flew on a wave of such heightened desire it stole her breath away.

And then she was there, spiraling completely out of control and shaking with the force of her climax. For a moment afterward she was utterly boneless and unable to move, but once that moment passed, she began to caress his chest.

As she slid her hands down his muscles, she followed

it with nipping, teasing kisses. She licked and kissed his nipples and then worked her way down his body, down his flat abdomen and then took his hard erection into one of her hands.

He tangled his fingers in her hair and moaned her name as she slid her hand up and down his velvety hardness. He only allowed her to caress him for a moment or two and then he pushed her away and positioned himself between her thighs.

"Yes," she hissed softly as he slowly entered her. He eased halfway in and then paused, as if afraid he might rush her in some way. She grabbed him by his buttocks and raised her legs around him, plunging him deeper and more fully inside her.

He moaned deep in his throat and the sound of his pleasure only increased her own. He moved his hips, slow at first with long strokes in and out of her. Her desire spiraled upward again as he increased his pace.

Their gasping filled the air, along with plenty of moans. She clung to his shoulders as he drove into her faster and faster. Then she was there, once again flying over the moon and then crashing down to earth with her orgasm. She shuddered against him and at the same time he climaxed, groaning her name over and over again.

When it was all finished, he rolled over on his back next to her and for a few moments they remained still, just trying to catch their ragged breaths.

"That was…" he began.

"Explosive," she replied.

"Amazing," he added.

"Incredible."

"Earth-shattering."

She laughed, filled with a joy she'd never felt before.

"Don't tell me it was funny. That would definitely destroy my male ego."

"Oh, it wasn't funny… We're funny," she replied.

He raised up on one elbow and gazed down at her. "We are funny, but you know what isn't? We went into this without any birth control."

"Don't worry, I'm on the pill and I can assure you I'm clean. I haven't been with anyone for a very long time," she replied.

"It's been years since I've been with anyone." He bent down and kissed her softly on the cheek. "Thank you for sharing yourself with me."

"I thank you for the same," she replied. "I've wanted you for a long time, Nathan."

"You couldn't have wanted me as much as I've wanted you," he replied. "Angel, you have been a beautiful torment for me. Every time we touched, I wanted to pull you down and make love with you."

"I have felt the same way," she replied.

"And now, I think I need to get up." He slid out of the bed and grabbed his clothing from the floor.

"Nathan, if you want, you can come back in here to sleep tonight."

He smiled. "I would love to do that," he replied and then left her room. As he went into the bathroom, she stared up at the ceiling where the lantern's light flickered and danced.

Making love with him had probably been a huge mistake and she'd just compounded it by inviting him to share her bed for the rest of the night.

At this current moment she didn't care about anything. Her body still tingled with the feel of his touch and she couldn't think of anything better than falling asleep in his arms.

It would be a memory she would cherish long after he was gone. But she also didn't want to dwell on him leaving right now or how big of a fool she had been in falling in love with the man.

Right now her plan was to enjoy each and every moment of the time she had left with him. She could entertain all her regrets, and there would be plenty, when he was gone from here forever.

When he came back into the room, she rolled out of the bed and headed for the bathroom. Once there she cleaned up and then pulled on the nightgown that hung from a hook on the back of the door.

When she went into the bedroom again, Nathan was already back in the bed. He looked like he belonged there and her heart squeezed tight. She slid into the bed next to him and he immediately drew her close to him, spooning around her with his big strong body.

He rose up and kissed her on her cheek. "Good night, my sweet Angel," he whispered in her ear.

"Good night, my sweet Nathan," she replied softly. She closed her eyes, happier than she'd been in years.

She knew the moment he fell asleep, but she remained awake for a little while just reveling in the sound of his soft rhythmic breathing and in the embrace of his arm around her waist and his body around her back.

She must have fallen asleep because the next thing she knew it was just before dawn. At some point during the night, they had physically separated so thankfully she could ease out of the bed without awakening him.

And thankfully the lantern was still burning so she was able to grab some clothes without fumbling around in the dark. She looked at Nathan one last time. Even in sleep, he was so handsome and looked like he belonged in her bed. He was probably sleeping far better there than on the sofa.

She left the room and went into the bathroom to wash her face, brush her teeth and hair and then dress. Once she was ready, she left the bathroom and headed to the backdoor.

It took her only minutes to be out on the water, using the push pole to guide her to her fishing lines. The sun was just peeking over the horizon, as always painting the swamp in a golden glow.

The real glow this morning was deep in her heart. Making love with Nathan had been beyond wonderful and it had been magical falling asleep in his arms the night before. She had felt a peace, a security she'd never felt before. He had completed her life in ways she'd never expected.

Would he miss her when he was gone from here…from her? When he returned to his life in New Orleans, would he even think about the woman from the swamp who had entertained him for a month?

Now that they'd explored their lust for each other, would his interest in her wane? Certainly that wasn't the case for her. She still wanted him, and her love for him had only grown with their physical intimacy.

Dammit. How had she allowed this to happen? How had she fallen in love with a man who was completely unavailable to have a life with her? Why couldn't she have fallen in love with one of the three men who had been by her side since they were kids? Things would have been so much easier that way.

She shoved all these thoughts aside, determined to just enjoy the beauty and peace of sunrise on the water in the swamp she loved.

This would give her strength when Nathan was gone. She'd always have the swamp to sustain her. She didn't need a man to complete her. She was more than enough on her own.

She still had her parents and her women friends. Eventually she might find a man to love…to marry. However she still suspected that one of her men friends had been behind the voodoo doll and the note.

What she wasn't sure of was if it had been the Swamp Soul Stealer who had chased her through the night or if it had been one of the three men who professed to care about her. If it had been one of them, then why hadn't they come to her shanty? Had the person merely wanted to terrorize her so she'd turn to them for help and protection?

With these troubling thoughts starting to bubble up in her mind, she was grateful to reach her fish lines and gather the fish she had caught. As she got them all up, she baited the hooks once again and then started toward home.

There was a peace in the swamp this morning, but somewhere a monster crept and Angel didn't know if there was just one monster or another one who had her in his sights.

NATHAN AWAKENED AS Angel was leaving to do her fish run. He remained in bed for several minutes, thinking of the night they had shared.

She'd been an amazing lover. She'd been so passionate

and she'd driven him half mad with her hot kisses and fevered strokes against his bare skin. She'd met his intense desire with her own and that had been incredibly hot.

Even though he'd been completely sated last night, he wanted to repeat making love with her as soon as possible. His desire to have her again was as fevered this morning as it had been the day before. He'd never experienced this kind of heightened desire for any woman before. What made it even hotter was how much he liked her.

He finally got out of bed and got washed and dressed for the day. He went into the living room and sank down on the sofa to await her return. The shanty felt lonely without her. It was crazy that he felt lonely when she wasn't with him.

His gaze landed on the voodoo doll in the bookcase and he got up to get the doll. Next to the doll was a folded piece of paper and out of curiosity he opened it.

STAY AWAY FROM THE SCIENCE MAN!

The words screamed from the page in bold red ink. He stared at it in stunned surprise. When had Angel received this? And why hadn't she told him about it?

He left the doll on her bookcase and carried the note back to the sofa. He laid it out on the coffee table and stared at it. He believed there had been no secrets between him and Angel. She'd shown him the voodoo doll, so why hadn't she shown him this note, which definitely had the feel of a threat to it?

A touch of anger rose up inside him. He was angry at whoever had left the note for her and almost as equally angry at Angel for not telling him about it.

So who had written it and was it possible that person had terrified her by chasing her through the swamp? The first name that jumped into his mind was Beau. There was no doubt in Nathan's mind that the man was in love with Angel, no matter what Angel felt on the matter. That meant Beau had to have seen Nathan as a threat.

He ruminated on the mystery of the voodoo doll and the note-writer until the sound of the back door opening and closing pulled him from his thoughts.

"Good morning," she said cheerfully as she walked in. Even though it was early morning, as always, she looked amazing. She wore jeans and a fitted light blue T-shirt.

"Not so much," he replied.

She frowned. "Did you not sleep well?" She stepped closer to him and her gaze fell on the note.

"When did you receive this?" he asked.

Her shoulders stiffened. "What are you doing? Sneaking around in my stuff?"

"Don't deflect, Angel. I hardly had to sneak around to find this," he replied. "So, when did you get this and why didn't you tell me about it right away?"

She sank down on the opposite side of the sofa from him and stared down at the note. "I got it about a week ago and I didn't tell you because I was afraid you'd immediately fire me from my job working for you."

"I probably would have," he admitted. "This definitely seems like a threat, Angel. I would never forgive myself if something happened to you because of me."

"I wasn't about to allow an anonymous note left on my door dictate what I do and don't do," she replied with a stubborn lift of her chin.

"Still, you should have told me about this. I should have known about it."

"Yes, I probably should have told you," she finally admitted. "But to be honest, Nathan, I was enjoying our time together and I didn't want it to end."

Her words, coupled with the look of misery that crossed her features, made any anger he'd felt toward her melt away. "Come here," he said and gestured her into his arms.

He held her for a long moment and then released her. "So, who do you think wrote it?" he asked.

She shrugged. "I don't know, but I think it has to be one of the men I thought I could trust with my life."

"My first suspect would be Beau. No matter what you think, Angel, I believe the man is in love with you and would see me as a threat. He wouldn't want you hanging around me. He wouldn't know that we're not in love with each other and that when I leave here, he'll still have an opportunity to woo you."

"I don't have any romantic feelings toward any of those men, and I never will. To me, this is more the style of Jacques or Louis. They are far more hotheaded than Beau," she replied.

"Looking back on that night when you were chased through the swamp, is it possible it was one of those men and it wasn't the Swamp Soul Stealer?" he asked.

A line danced across the center of her forehead as she frowned. "Yes, I suppose that's possible. The only thing that made me believe otherwise was the fact that the person didn't come to my home. All the men know where I live, so if it was one of them chasing me, then why didn't they just show up here?"

"Maybe it was just an attempt to scare you so you'd turn to them for comfort and safety," he suggested. "Maybe whoever it was believed that they would be here with you instead of me."

"Maybe. I'd thought about that, but instead I turned to the one man I trust in all this and that is you." She released a deep sigh. "I don't want to talk about all this anymore. Why don't we head out so you can get more of your pictures?"

"I've got to say this, Angel, you are one strong, independent woman. Most women who received a note like that would have stopped seeing me immediately."

She offered him a small smile. "You should know by now that I am not most women." She got up from the sofa and he did as well. "So, do you forgive me for not telling you?"

He couldn't help but smile back at her. "You're forgiven, but I don't want you to keep anything else like this from me, deal?"

"Deal," she replied.

Aside from his physical lust for her, he also had a lot of admiration for her. "Then let's go get some photos." He picked up his camera from where it rested at the side of the sofa.

He double-checked that he had his stun gun in his pocket and then they took off. In truth he now had almost all the photos he needed, but he was reluctant to tell her goodbye.

He couldn't leave now while she was so vulnerable. If it had been one of her male friends who had chased her through the swamp, then it had been an evil thing to do. If one of those men had romantic feelings for her, then why hadn't they just spoken to her about them?

They stayed out in the swamp until almost dinnertime

with him taking mostly unnecessary photos. She fried up a pan of catfish for dinner and afterward they played a couple games of chess.

"I think it's a wise idea for you and I to go into town in the morning and talk to the chief of police," he said when they had finished their last game and he was putting the pieces away in the box.

She looked at him in surprise. "Why? I'm sure there's nothing he can do about any of this."

"I think he should at least know about what's been going on with you," he said. "Angel, I think it's really important. So can we go into town tomorrow?"

She sighed and stood from the chair where she had been sitting for the chess games. "Okay. If you really think it's necessary, then how about we plan on going around nine in the morning?"

"That sounds fine." He stood as she pulled the kitchen chair back to where it belonged.

She came back into the living room. "I guess I'll just say good-night, then." She didn't wait around for a kiss but instead turned to head into her bedroom.

"Good night, Angel."

She flashed a quick smile over her shoulder. "Good night, Nathan." She then disappeared into her bedroom and closed the door behind her.

Nathan made out his bed on the sofa, sorry that he wasn't sharing hers. Aside from the delicious pleasure of making love to her, he'd loved having her warm sweet-smelling body to spoon around. The cuddle afterward had been almost as good as the sex.

Tonight it would just be him and the bullfrogs and the

gentle lap of the water. It was a far cry from the sound of car horns honking and sirens blaring that he was accustomed to being jarred by when he was trying to fall asleep in New Orleans.

It was odd, but the noise of the swamp had begun to sound like home. But, of course, that was impossible. This wasn't his home and it never would be. Still, once he left here, he would retain the sounds of the swamp at night and the memory of a beautiful woman to lull him to sleep.

THE NEXT MORNING at nine o'clock they were in his car and headed into town. She held both the voodoo doll and the note in her lap and she was very quiet.

"Are you nervous?" he finally asked.

"No, not exactly nervous, but I do hate to bother Etienne with all this," she replied.

"I still think he should know about it. If I'd known about the note, I would have encouraged you to talk to him immediately after you received it."

She released a deep sigh and fell silent once again. It was impossible for him to know what was going on in her mind. He knew how difficult this all had been for her and he wished he had the words to make it all go away.

But he didn't and so he didn't try to find any words and instead allowed her to have her silence. The police station was in a fairly large one-story building. It was painted turquoise and had two large plateglass windows in the front.

He parked and together they got out of the car and he ushered her into a lobby. There were half a dozen chairs in front of the windows and a reception window, which a uniformed officer stood behind.

He opened a window in the glass front of his area. "Hey, folks." He greeted them with a friendly smile. "What can I do for you two this morning?"

"We'd like to speak to Chief Savoie," Nathan said.

"Can I just get your names?"

Nathan told them who they were. "Okay, just have a seat and I'll see if he's available right now," the officer replied. He closed the window and left the desk through a back doorway.

Nathan and Angel sat side by side in the gray plastic chairs in front of the windows. She clutched the voodoo doll and note close to her chest with one hand and he reached out to hold her other hand.

She not only allowed him to but she also squeezed his hand tightly, as if needing his support in this moment. "You know there's nothing to be nervous about," he said softly. "You're the innocent victim here."

"Like I said before, I'm not exactly nervous. It's just that showing all this to Etienne makes it all so real."

"It is real, honey, and that's why we need to be here."

At that moment the officer returned to the front window. "If you two want to go through the doorway on the right, I'll take you back to the chief."

They followed him into a long hallway and he stopped at the second door on the right. He knocked on the door and then opened it. "Chief, they're right here." He then opened the door wider to allow the two of them inside.

Nathan had never met the chief of police before. He was younger than Nathan had expected. His dark slightly curly hair looked like it was weeks past a haircut, but his gray eyes appeared sharp with intelligence.

He rose from his desk as they entered the room and he held out a hand to Nathan. "I know Angel, but I don't believe we've met before," he said.

"I'm Nathan Merrick," Nathan replied as he gave the chief's hand a firm shake.

"Nice to meet you, Mr. Merrick. Please, have a seat," he said and gestured toward the two chairs that were directly in front of his desk. Once they were all settled, Chief Savoie smiled at them. "Now, what can I do for you both this morning?"

"There's probably nothing you can do to help the situation I find myself in, but Nathan insisted it was important for me to speak to you about it," Angel said.

"Okay, so tell me what's been going on," Chief Savoie replied.

Angel began telling him, starting from when she had found the voodoo doll on her door. She handed him the doll and he examined it carefully and then set it aside on his desk.

She then showed him the note and once again he looked at it closely and set it next to the voodoo doll. Finally she told him about being chased through the swamp. As she recounted the horrifying event, her voice rose slightly in pitch and tears filled her eyes. Once again Nathan reached for her hand and held it tight.

"Well, it's obvious you didn't heed the note's warning, because the two of you are here together now," Etienne said.

"You know me, Etienne, I don't take well to people telling me what to do," Angel replied.

"Actually, I've moved in with Angel for her protection

but I'm only going to be in town for a short while so I'm hoping this somehow gets resolved quickly."

The chief frowned. "The first thing we need to do is get your fingerprints so they can be excluded when we dust this note." He looked at Angel. "Is there anyone you've been having problems with? Have you had words with anyone?"

Angel shook her head. "No, nobody."

"Do you have any suspects in mind?"

She hesitated a long moment and then nodded. "Louis Mignot, Beau Gustave and Jacques Augustin and maybe Mac Singleton from the grocery store." The names fell from her lips as if released from under an enormous pressure.

Etienne wrote down the names and then looked back up at her. "And why do you suspect these men in particular?"

She explained her reasons, specifically the fact that they were the only four men consistently in her life. "Mac has always given me the impression he has a small crush on me and as for the others, I've just lost all trust in any of them because somebody left me those things and they're the only men in my life."

"Is it possible a woman left these for you?" Etienne asked and turned his attention to Nathan. "Has any woman expressed an interest in you since you've been in town? Maybe somebody who would be jealous of your time with Angel?"

"No, there's been nobody," Nathan replied firmly. "However, I do believe Beau is in love with Angel, and he would certainly see me as a threat and wouldn't want Angel having anything to do with me," Nathan added.

"I'll bring them all in for questioning," Etienne said.

"I didn't want to add to your workload," Angel replied

miserably. "I know you have your hands full with the Swamp Soul Stealer."

"Speaking of that, I think that you can rule him out as the one who chased you through the swamp," Etienne said.

Angel frowned. "Why?"

"You said the man who chased you roared loudly several times with rage. In all the instances of the disappearances of people, on the nights they were taken, not a single sound was heard. And believe me, my men asked dozens of people if they heard anything. Our belief is he sneaks up on his victims silently."

Angel stared at him for a long moment. "So, then it was probably one of the men I mentioned to you. He is either a person I call my good friend or a man I've done business with for years."

"Unless the Swamp Soul Stealer has changed his ways, which I highly doubt, then yes it was probably one of the men closest to you. Angel, I swear I'm going to do everything I can to get to the bottom of this."

"We would appreciate it," Nathan said. "Unfortunately I'll be leaving Crystal Cover in a matter of weeks and when I leave here, I want to know that Angel is safe."

"The thing that concerns me is there is a definite escalation at play," Etienne said. "First the doll, then the note and then the chase through the swamp." A deep frown cut across his forehead. "My concern for you is what happens now? If the escalation continues, then what is this person's next move?"

Angel's hand grew cold in Nathan's as Etienne's question hung heavy in the air. What, indeed, might happen next?

Chapter Eleven

A wave of depression swept through Angel as they walked out of the police station. Her discouragement had begun the day before when Nathan had told her that Beau couldn't know she and Nathan weren't in love with each other.

It had been a stark reality check that he could so easily say he wasn't in love with her. She wasn't sure what exactly she'd hoped for, but she'd definitely hoped for a little more from him considering all they had shared.

Now to compound things, she had to face the fact that one of her "friends" may have left her the note and the voodoo doll. One of those "friends" may have chased her through the swamp roaring like a wild animal and scaring her half to death. What kind of a friend did something like that to a vulnerable woman he supposedly cared about?

She cast a look at the man in the car's driver seat. As if he sensed her gaze, he turned and offered her a small smile. "Are you okay?" he asked, his soft voice like a caress against her ear.

"I will be," she replied.

"There's no doubt in my mind that you will be," he replied. "I can imagine all the thoughts and emotions that are flying around inside your head after speaking to the chief."

That's only the half of it, she thought. Thank God at this point she hadn't spoken to him of her love for him, even though it had and still shouted loudly in her head.

She released a sigh and stared out the passenger window. It was time for her to start distancing herself from Nathan. Although she wasn't fool enough to kick him out of her home. She still needed his safety and protection and if she looked deep within herself, she still wanted to enjoy his company until the final day when he left here.

But there would be no more hot kisses between them, no more tumbles into her bed. She had to start protecting herself from the crazy love he had evoked in her.

"Are you ready to head out for more picture-taking?" she asked as he parked the car.

"Do you really feel like doing that today?" he asked.

"Why not? We've taken care of the police business of the day, so we might as well get to your work now."

"Okay, then I'm all in," he agreed.

They got out of the car and once they were at her shanty, he grabbed his camera and they took off. As usual, his camera stayed busy as they went first up one trail and then another.

They talked a little bit, but she just really wasn't in the mood to chat about inane things. The reality that one of her friends, one of the men she had known since childhood had possibly chased her through the swamp suddenly hit her hard.

As they continued their trek through the trails, she recognized Nathan was working hard to put her in a better mood and she forced herself to try to get there.

Surprisingly, by the time they knocked off for the day around four o'clock, she was in a better frame of mind. She still had a big, strong man staying with her and Etienne had promised to do some investigating into the matter. Besides, she'd never been one to entertain a foul mood for very long.

When they got back to the shanty, they each took a shower and then she started on dinner preparations. They decided to keep it simple. She fried up some fish and made a box of mac and cheese.

"Want to play some chess after we eat?" he asked when the two of them were at the table.

"Sure, I wouldn't mind beating you a few more games before bedtime," she replied.

"Ha, you're always crowing before but you'll be crying afterward," he replied with those teasing eyes of his.

"We'll see who is crying afterward," she replied with mock confidence.

This was part of what she enjoyed—their easy banter and playful competition with each other. That continued through their meal, and once the cleanup was complete, they moved into the living room and set up the chess game.

They had just started playing when a knock fell on the door. "Hey, Angel," Beau's voice cried out.

A sudden tension gripped her as she got up to answer. It was all three of the men… Louis, Beau and Jacques. "Hi," she said and opened the door to allow them all in. They brought with them what felt like an angry energy and Nathan immediately stood up from the sofa.

"Well, doesn't this look like fun," Jacques said as he

gazed at the chessboard. "Angel, apparently, you're a woman of many hidden talents. I didn't know you could play chess, and I definitely never suspected you of throwing your friends under the bus."

The tension inside her increased. "Why don't you all have a seat," she said, uncomfortable with them all standing and glaring at her.

Beau took the chair she had been sitting in to play chess. Louis stalked into the kitchen to grab a chair and brought it in and sat, while Jacques threw himself on the opposite end of the sofa from Nathan. She sank down in the chair where she usually sat when they all came over.

Finally they were all seated, but their obvious displeasure with her still stood tall in the room. "Why in the hell would you even bring up our names to Etienne? Do you really think that any one of us is responsible for that voodoo doll or note?" Louis asked, his dark eyes searching her features.

"I'll be perfectly honest," she replied. "Aside from the note and the doll, a few nights ago somebody also chased me through the swamp and terrified me."

Beau sat back in his chair, appearing surprised by this news. "I hadn't heard about you being chased. Are you sure it wasn't the Swamp Soul Stealer?"

"According to what Etienne told me this morning, it's doubtful," she replied.

"And you believe it was one of us?" Jacques asked. He shot a narrowed gaze at Nathan. "Have you considered that it might have been him? Looks like it got him a pretty cozy setup here."

She stared at Jacques and she couldn't help the burst

of laughter that escaped her at the very idea of Nathan being the one who had chased her in the darkness through the swamp.

She sobered quickly. "There's no way it was Nathan. The man who chased me knew the swamp very well."

"Personally, I was shocked when I got word that the chief of police wanted to interview me," Louis said. "I figured he wanted to talk to me about gator poaching, but when he asked me about my relationship with you, I was very surprised that you had put my name in his mouth."

Angel released a deep sigh. "I'm sorry, my intention wasn't to hurt any of you, but somebody is doing these things to me and I don't know who and I don't know why. I went to Etienne because I'm afraid, and I have Nathan here with me for the same reason. I... I don't know who to trust anymore."

Beau released a string of curses. "I can't believe what I'm hearing. Angel, I can't believe you don't know that you can trust me with your very life. I would never ever do anything to harm you."

"I wouldn't, either," Jacques added.

"I agree," Louis said. "Angel, you're barking up the wrong tree by suspecting any of us."

"But you have to understand the position I'm in," she replied. Angel was grateful that the anger the men had brought in with them seemed to have dissipated some. "Etienne asked me what men were in my life and so I told him. The three of you weren't the only names I gave him."

"It's time for us to go," Jacques said abruptly and rose from the sofa. He looked at the other two men. "We've told her how we feel and there's nothing more to say here."

Beau and Louis moved the chairs back into the kitchen and then the three of them walked to the door. Angel got up from her chair and opened the door for them.

"Good night Angel... Nathan," Jacques said and then the three of them left.

Angel locked the door behind them and then returned to the easy chair opposite the sofa. She released a deep sigh. "I don't know why but I didn't expect that."

"I certainly didn't expect it so soon," Nathan replied. "Chief Savoie must be taking this quite seriously and I'm glad for that."

Angel wrapped her arms around herself as a chill suffused her. "I just didn't think this through. I'm almost sorry I gave Etienne their names."

"Angel, you had to tell Etienne their names," Nathan said in protest. "This isn't a game, honey. Somebody is terrorizing you."

"Did you get any feeling about them? Did one of them appear guilty to you?" She searched his features, wishing he held the answer for her.

He shook his head. "I watched each one of them closely and unfortunately as far as I'm concerned it could be any one of the three. One of them is a very good liar."

"Unless it's Mac from the grocery store."

He frowned at her. "Do you really believe Mac is the guilty party?"

She released a deep sigh. "Not really. In my heart of hearts, I believe it's one of the men who just left here. What worries me is now whoever it is knows Etienne is investigating and I'm really afraid about what's going to happen next."

HE STEPPED INTO his shanty and roared as a new rage nearly drove him to his knees. The bitch. He'd warned her to stay away from the science man and now she'd moved the bastard in with her.

He'd been watching her…watching them. He'd seen the day Nathan moved his duffel bags into her house and then he'd never left.

Slamming his fist into the back of his recliner, he thought about the two of them in bed together. The visions of them making love made him absolutely sick. That photographer was getting what was rightfully his.

She was a disloyal bitch and Nathan Merrick was an interloper who didn't belong here. However, he couldn't really blame Nathan for becoming besotted with Angel. She'd probably seduced him with her dark green eyes and perfect body. The poor city boy hadn't stood a chance against the very hot swamp woman.

It was Angel he blamed, and it was Angel who would pay. She was the one who had forgotten where she came from and she was the one who had forgotten she belonged to him.

He'd continue to watch and wait for the perfect opportunity. Sooner or later she would have to pay and this time it would be with her life. Only with her death would he finally be free of her.

FOR THE NEXT four days Angel and Nathan fell back into an easy routine. In the early mornings she took her pirogue out to do her fish runs and when she returned, they ate breakfast and then took off into the swamp.

Nathan continued to take more photos he didn't really need. He'd pretty much gotten everything he needed for his book and then some. However he still wasn't ready to leave without things being more settled for Angel.

Like her, he worried about what escalation would look like. There had been no more visits from the men, but Nathan was relatively sure one of them was the guilty party. He just didn't know which one and he didn't know what might happen next for Angel.

There was no way he could just bail on her now. He cared far too deeply about her to leave right away. He was hoping Chief Savoie would find the answer and get the guilty man behind bars in a relatively short period of time.

Tonight they were planning on her making a fish run into town and this time he would be by her side. He now looked across the room where she was curled up in her chair reading a book.

She really was the most beautiful woman he'd ever met. There was no question he was going to miss her a lot when he left. There had been no more lovemaking between them, no kisses or any other kind of physical touching since the night they last made love.

His desire for her hadn't waned at all, but she'd made it clear nothing was going to happen between them again. Each night she told him a quick good-night and then just as quickly went to her room and closed the door behind her.

There had been a hundred times over the past few days that he'd wanted to touch a strand of her long hair and tuck it behind her ear, kiss the cheek he'd expose and then run his lips across to capture hers with his. But instead he'd given her space because that's obviously what she wanted.

Still, one of the things he was going to miss about her was the deep friendship they had built. She'd been not only a good friend, but also a confidante in the time he'd spent here with her.

He had shared all kinds of things with her about his personal life and about his past. She'd shared with him as well. He felt like she knew him better than any woman had ever known him before.

She finally closed her book and got up from the chair. "We'll eat a quick dinner before we go since the fish run usually takes about two hours or so."

"Sounds good to me." He put his camera away while she went into the kitchen.

Hot dogs and chips were on the menu for that night and it was about four o'clock when they sat down to eat. "I love a good hot dog," he said.

She laughed. "You love a good anything if it's fit to be eaten."

"This is true," he replied with a grin.

"We'll need to make another trip into the grocery store tomorrow. It's time to restock the cooler."

"We can do that," he replied. "And maybe it's time we stop in at the ice-cream place again."

"That would be nice," she replied and smiled.

Her smiles—he was definitely going to miss those when he left here. They were so bright and beautiful. "Then we have a plan, a fish run tonight and then ice cream tomorrow night."

"I like that plan."

She ate two hot dogs and he ate three. The dinner cleanup was a breeze and by that time it was after five o'clock. He helped her get her fish together to take into town. It was a big job and took them two trips from her back deck to the cooler in her truck. She went back into the shanty to light some of the lanterns for when they returned after dark.

"I can't believe you do this all by yourself on a regular basis," he said when they were ready to leave.

"I'm used to it," she replied. "It's my work…my life." She got into the driver's side of the truck and he got into the passenger's side.

It was a cloudy gray evening providing a false early twilight. "Looks like we might get some rain," he said.

"That wouldn't be a bad thing," she replied. "I always like it to fill up my rainwater barrels."

"I would think the humidity would help with that."

"It helps, but a little rain never hurts things. Besides, I love the way the air smells after a good rain. Why? Are you going to melt?" she asked teasingly.

"Not at all, in fact I like to dance in the rain. Maybe we can have a jig or two later."

She laughed. "You are a bit of a goofball, Nathan, but I like that about you."

"And I think you have a little goofball in you, and I like that about you, too." He released a small sigh. It was moments like these that he would miss with her.

She was exactly the kind of woman he wanted to find to fill his days and nights. When he got back to New Orleans, that's who he'd be looking for, a woman just like Angel.

"So, where do we go first?" he asked as they entered the small town.

"The grocery store."

He heard a faint rise of tension in her voice. "Are you nervous to see Mac?"

"Maybe a little. I'm not afraid of him, but I'm sure it's

going to be more than a bit awkward if Etienne has already interviewed him."

"Will it affect your business dealings with the store?" Nathan asked curiously.

"I don't think so. Mac has always been a professional when it comes to business. At least I'm hoping that doesn't change. The store pretty much depends on me to keep them stocked in fish and I depend on them to sell my fish to."

"Then hopefully this will all go okay," he replied as she pulled up behind the grocery store at a loading dock. "I need to go inside to get Mac to come out."

"I'll go with you," he replied and together they got out of her truck. He felt tension wafting off her as they went up the loading ramp and in the back door that brought them out next to the meat and fish area.

Mac came out from behind the glass enclosure. He nodded at Nathan and then gazed somberly at Angel. "Chief Savoie had a chat with me this afternoon," he said. "Angel, I hope you know I would never do anything to hurt or scare you."

"Mac, I'm sorry but Etienne asked me about my male friends and associates," Angel replied.

"I had no idea about what's been going on in your life, and I'm so sorry to hear you've had problems, but, Angel, I'm not one of them," he said.

He appeared completely earnest to Nathan. He didn't believe Mac was the guilty party. He still believed it was one of the three men who had come to her house and acted so outraged about being interviewed by Chief Savoie.

"Shall we go look at some fish?" Mac asked.

"Absolutely," Angel replied, relief in her tone.

"Let me go grab Joey and the cooler and we'll meet you outside," Mac said.

"I don't think he's the one," Nathan said as the two of them stepped outside the store.

"I don't, either," she replied. "And thankfully that went far better than I expected."

They had just reached her truck when Mac and a young kid came out carrying a large cooler. Angel got up into the bed of the truck as did Mac and the teenage boy.

Nathan stood next to the back gate and watched with interest as Mac picked from the variety of fish Angel had provided. The whole transaction didn't take long.

As they drove toward the café, the dark clouds overhead had thickened even more, turning the last gasp of day into the darkness of night.

"The stop at the café always takes a little bit longer," Angel said. "Antoinette likes to bicker over prices."

"And I'm sure you aren't a pushover," he observed.

"Ha, not hardly, however I let her believe she's getting one over on me so she walks away happy," she replied.

"And that's what makes you a savvy business woman." Thankfully he could tell the tension that had gripped her before they'd gone into the grocery store was gone. She now appeared completely relaxed and in her element.

She drove up the alley behind the café and once again they got out of the truck. She asked a kid hanging out by the back door to go get Antoinette.

Moments later the older sturdy woman came out with a big guy carrying a cooler. "Nathan, this is Antoinette LeBlanc, the owner of the café. Antoinette, this is my friend, Nathan Merrick."

"He likes my burgers and fries," Antoinette said, surprising him that she even knew what he ate when he was inside the café.

"Nice to meet you and yes, I definitely like your burgers and fries," Nathan replied.

"Now, let's talk fish," she replied. To Nathan's surprise the short round woman easily jumped up into the bed of the truck. She was followed by the man with the cooler and then Angel.

Once again Nathan watched the transaction with interest. This was a large part of Angel's life and if he stayed here, it would become a part of his.

Whoa, where had that thought come from? He wasn't staying here. He had a life in New Orleans to get back to. As much as he had come to love many things about the swamp and the lifestyle here, he certainly wasn't staying.

As the wrangling began between Antoinette and Angel, he admired Angel's skills. The two women went back and forth until finally they both appeared satisfied with the transaction.

"Mission accomplished," he said when they were both back in the truck and headed home.

She flashed him a smile. "It was nice having your support tonight."

"I didn't do anything," he protested.

"But you were here with me, and I just want you to know that I really appreciate it," she replied. "I have to admit, Nathan, I'm really going to miss you when you're gone."

It was the first time she had mentioned his leaving. "I'll miss you, too. I'll miss so many things about this place," he admitted.

"If you remember, I told you once that if you stuck around long enough, you'd fall in love with the swamp," she replied. She pulled into the parking lot and stopped the engine. She unbuckled her seat belt and then instead of getting out she turned to gaze at him.

The lights on the truck were still on, so he could see her lovely features in the illumination from the dashboard. "Nathan," she said as a frown danced across her forehead. "I need you to know that I don't want you to stay here just for my benefit and safety. Once you have all your photos, then I want you to leave just as you'd planned. You aren't responsible for me."

"Trying to get rid of me?" he asked in an effort to lighten the suddenly sober mood.

"Not at all, at least not until you have what you need for your book. I just want you to know that you don't owe me anything when your work is finished here."

"I recognize that, but I still have some more photos to take," he replied. It was a tiny white lie. She didn't have to know he had all the photos he needed. "You're probably just afraid I'll beat you in more chess games."

A small smile erased the line across her forehead. "You are something else, Nathan Merrick." She turned out the truck lights and then they both got out.

"Maybe tomorrow morning I could try to beat you at fishing," he said as they started up the trail with her in the lead.

"You could try to beat me," she replied with a laugh.

When he left here, he would carry the memory of her laughter deep in his heart. It wasn't just the sound of humor, but it was filled with such a vibrancy and a lust for life.

They were about halfway to the shanty when he heard

a rustle behind him. He started to turn to see what it was, but before he could, something crashed down on the back of his head.

The tremendous blow sent him straight to the ground, pain screaming through his skull. He gasped for air and tried to fight against the bright stars that swam in his brain.

The last thing he heard before complete darkness descended was a rumble of thunder and Angel's scream.

Chapter Twelve

There was a loud rustle on the trail behind her and Angel turned to see what was going on with Nathan. For a brief moment she was confused as her brain tried to make sense of the scene before her. Nathan was on the ground and not moving. Had he fallen?

Then her gaze focused on the man standing over Nathan. He was clad all in black and wore a ski mask. He held in his hand a short thick leafless branch. She screamed and then turned and ran.

Terror gripped her by the heart, squeezing so tight she could scarcely draw a breath. It wasn't just fear for herself, but for Nathan as well.

Was Nathan dead? Oh, God, if he was, then it was all her fault. He shouldn't have been here with her. She'd known there was danger around her and she'd invited him into the danger. And now he might be gone forever.

Deep sobs escaped her as she continued to race through the darkness and thick foliage. A deep roar resounded from behind her. It was the roar of unbridled rage.

It came from too close behind her. She tried to increase

her speed, gasping and fighting to get some distance from the person who chased her.

As she ran, she fumbled at her waist to get her little sister out. She tried to staunch her cries, hoping that she could lose the man and hide from him like she had the last time.

Hopefully then she could circle back and help Nathan, if help was possible for him. Her heart ached for him, but she couldn't help him unless she got away.

She tore through the Spanish moss and tried to push through the vines and limbs that threatened to slow her down. Once again the man bellowed, the frightening, horrendous sound shooting icy chills through her.

Lightning rent the night sky and thunder rumbled overhead, only adding to the madness of the night. Her brain raced with questions. Who was the man chasing her? Was it one of the men she called her friend?

Maybe she should just stop running, turn and confront him. If it truly was one of her friends, then maybe she could talk some sense into him.

But what if it wasn't one of those men? Perhaps she could lose him and run to her shanty for safety. She could hole up there while he continued to hunt the swamp for her. Or maybe she just needed to dive in somewhere and hope she stayed hidden until he moved away from her.

All she knew for sure was he was gaining on her. She had to make a decision about what to do before he caught up with her. Her tears had stopped, unable to be sustained as she raced for her life.

She finally dove into a tangle of vines and thick undergrowth. As she had the last time, she pulled herself into the tightest ball she could make and then she tried to stop breathing so he wouldn't hear her.

It took only moments before he was on the trail near her. The sound of his ragged breathing as he paused nearby only made her fear intensify.

Lightning once again flashed across the sky. *Don't let him see me. Please don't let him find me*, she prayed. She had to survive this so she could help Nathan.

Please let Nathan be okay. Please, please don't let him be dead. She squeezed her eyes tightly closed as hot tears burned there. He didn't deserve any of this. A loud boom of thunder reverberated and once again the man chasing her released a roar to rival nature's sound.

Angel couldn't help the tremors that shot through her body. The leaves around her shook slightly and her pursuer moved closer to her hiding place. With a willpower she didn't know she possessed, she suppressed any more shivers that might give away her hiding place.

Seconds ticked by…long minutes passed with him standing so close to her she thought she could reach out and touch him. Who was it? And what did he want from her?

Thankfully the man moved on down the trail.

A shudder worked through her and she remained hiding for several long minutes. She heard him roar again, but he was far enough away that she felt relatively safe and rose from her position. She waited another few minutes and then she headed for her shanty. She'd hide out there for a little while to make sure the hunter was really gone and then she'd go to Nathan. He had to be okay. He just had to be.

She crept through the various trails as quietly as possible. She could no longer hear the sounds of her pursuer. As she got closer to her shanty, she began to run. She needed to be inside where hopefully the man chasing her didn't know where she lived. Or, in the case of her friends, the person wouldn't come to her front door.

As she reached her bridge, deep sobs began to escape her once again. She cried because she didn't know if Nathan was dead or alive, and she wept from the sheer terror of the night's chase. Lightning continued to slash the darkness of the skies and it was followed by loud rumbles of thunder.

She finally got inside, and she closed and locked the door after her. She collapsed on her sofa and tried to catch her breath and stop crying. Dammit, who had been after her? And what had he done to Nathan?

The thought of Nathan on the ground and not moving brought new tears to her eyes. Had Nathan been stabbed? Had he been bludgeoned by the thick wooden baton the man had carried? What was Nathan's condition and how much longer should she wait before she went back outside?

A loud boom sounded on her front door, pulling a new scream from the very depths of her. She jumped up from the sofa with her knife held tight in her hands.

Another violent bang on the door sounded. Before she could react, her front window exploded inward. Glass and wood crashed to the ground inside. The man in the ski mask hurtled through the opening and into the room. He waved the big baton-like stick in his hand.

"Who are you?" Angel screamed as she backed up from him. "Who are you and what do you want from me?"

"I want you dead," he yelled. "I'm going to beat your beautiful face in until you no longer exist."

She stared at the masked man in disbelief. She knew that voice. "Louis?"

He took a step toward her and pulled the ski mask up and off his head. He threw it down next to him and then glared at her. In the glow from the lanterns, she saw that his features were twisted with an anger she'd never seen before.

"Louis, what's going on? Why are you doing this?" She took another step back from him. "Why?" She looked at his angry features searchingly.

"You belong to me, Angel. I tried to warn you to stay away from him."

"So, it was you who left me the voodoo doll and the note," she replied as she slid backward another step.

He gave a quick nod. "You were supposed to be mine. You belong to me and yet you invited Nathan into your bed." His dark eyes simmered with his rage.

"What do you mean? I never belonged to you. I belong to nobody," she replied.

"That's not true," he replied angrily. "We talked about getting married. We talked about being together forever. Dammit, Angel, you belong to me."

She continued to stare at him. She searched her brain, trying to remember a time when they'd ever spoken about marriage. She finally remembered. "Louis, I was ten years old when we talked about it," she replied incredulously. "Louis, we were just kids."

"It doesn't matter," he screamed, his features twisted with his anger. "I loved you, but I don't love you anymore. I hate you, Angel. You allowed that man to kiss you, to touch you and now I completely hate you."

"But, Louis, you're my friend," she implored, trying to

reach the man who had cared about her, the man she believed would never hurt her.

"You aren't my friend. You're nothing but a nasty slut and sluts need to die." He raised the wooden stick and advanced toward her. He swung at her. She managed to duck and the blow missed her.

When he swung the second time, he struck her on the shoulder. She gasped as the painful blow momentarily stole her breath away. "Louis, please…you hurt me," she managed to gasp.

"Don't you get it, Angel, I want to hurt you. I'm going to enjoy killing you," he replied, and then he bellowed, the sound seeming to rattle the entire structure of her shanty.

Before she could recover from the painful blow to her shoulder, he hit her again. This time the strike hit the back of her hand and knocked her knife to the floor. "Die, you bitch," he yelled.

She began to scream and cry as she now knew Louis meant to kill her. There was no way to reach the man who had been her friend. He was gone, usurped by the monster who stood before her.

Tears blurred her vision as she dove for her knife and grabbed it. As she quickly turned over on her back, Louis leaped on top of her.

He apparently hadn't realized she had the knife in her hand. She felt it sink deep into his stomach and saw the widening of his eyes. "You bitch," he hissed. He raised the stick, but before he could hit her with it, she twisted the knife in his belly.

His arm fell to the side and with a deep moan, his eyes

closed. With deep sobs racking her body, she shoved at him to get him off her.

She managed to push him over and she scooted backward on the floor like a crab as she stared at him. Blood. Oh, God, there was so much of it. It covered the front of her. It covered her hands.

Horror swept through her as she continued to grapple with everything that had just happened. She'd killed her friend, although the man who had been in her shanty...the one who now was dead on the floor, hadn't been the Louis she knew. This man had been a monster, apparently twisted by what he'd believed was love for her.

She wasn't sure how long she sat there when she heard Nathan shouting her name from outside. She jumped to her feet and ran to her door. She quickly unlocked and opened it and threw herself into his arms.

"Thank God you're okay," she cried as he wrapped his arms tightly around her. "I was so scared."

"I'm okay, and thank God you're okay," he replied.

She looked up at him. "It... It was Louis and I stabbed him and I... I think I killed him." Her sobs overwhelmed her as she clung to Nathan and wept into the front of his shirt. "He was going to b-beat me to death. He...he said I was a slut and I needed to die. I... I killed him, Nathan."

"Shh, it's okay, Angel. You did what you had to do," Nathan replied. "Come into the bedroom. We need to call Chief Savoie."

On trembling legs, she allowed Nathan to lead her into the bedroom where she collapsed on the edge of the bed while he remained standing. "I'll be right back," he said.

"Wait...where are you going?" she asked in a panic.

"I just need to check on Louis," he replied. "I want to see if we should call for an ambulance."

He walked out of the room and she stared after him, her brain still working to make sense of everything that had just happened. She couldn't believe that Louis had hung on to the words she'd spoken as a young girl.

She had said she'd marry Louis when she grew up, but she'd only been a kid at the time. Around that same time she'd told Beau and Jacques that she'd marry them, too.

She looked up at the sound of Nathan coming back in the room. "No ambulance is necessary. He's gone."

She buried her face in her hands and began to weep once again as she thought of the man she had stabbed…the man who had been her close friend since childhood. She'd had no choice but to protect herself but she mourned deeply for how badly things had gone.

Nathan made the call to get Chief Savoie to the shanty and then he went back into the bedroom and sat next to Angel, who was still softly weeping.

He threw his arm around her shoulder and pulled her tight against him. She leaned into him and slowly began to pull herself together. She drew in deep gulps of air and finally straightened up.

She gazed up at him and her eyes widened. "Oh, Nathan, I haven't even thought to ask you if you're okay." She grabbed his hand and her eyes once again filled with tears. "The last time I saw you, you were on the ground and not moving."

"I'M OKAY," he assured her, although his head still ached. "The bastard hit me over the head from behind and knocked me out cold." He squeezed her hand. "At least I have a hard head, and when I came to, all I could think about was getting to you. Thank God you're okay, Angel. That's all I wanted. I needed you to be okay."

He'd been so afraid for her. When he'd regained consciousness, he'd been so terrified for her safety. He'd heard her screams coming from her shanty and he'd run as fast as he could to get to her.

Thankfully she was alive and even though he'd thought one of the men was the guilty party, it had still been a shock to see Louis sprawled out on her floor.

He couldn't even imagine what was going on in Angel's head right now. Not only were Louis's actions a deep betrayal, but she had also killed the man.

She was quiet and gravely pale as they sat silently side by side on the bed to wait for law enforcement to arrive. He held her hand tightly, knowing that she needed all the support he could give her.

Still, deep in his mind as he sat next to her, he realized it was finally over. She was no longer in danger and he would be free to leave here and go home. But he didn't want to think about that right now. He wouldn't leave until he knew for sure that Angel was going to be okay, both physically and mentally.

"Angel… Nathan," Chief Savoie's voice called out. They both got off the bed and Angel leaned heavily against Nathan as they left the bedroom.

Within minutes there were police officers working the scene and rain had begun to patter on the roof. Chief Savoie grabbed a kitchen chair and carried it into the bedroom and then gestured for Nathan and Angel to follow him there.

Once again the two of them sat on the bed while Chief Savioe sat on the chair facing them with a mini tape recorder in his hand. "First of all, do either of you need any medical attention?"

"I don't," Angel replied.

"And I don't, either," Nathan replied, even though he suspected he suffered from a mild concussion.

"I need to get statements from you both. Do either of you mind if I record this conversation?" the lawman asked.

They both indicated they didn't mind and then Nathan began to give his statement. He started with the fish runs. "Everything went fine and then we started walking back here from the parking lot. We hadn't gone far when I was hit on the head from behind. I was immediately knocked unconscious."

Angel picked it up from there. As Nathan heard what had transpired in the shanty between her and Louis, his blood ran cold. If she hadn't had her knife, there was no doubt in Nathan's mind she would have been killed by Louis.

"It was obviously a case of self-defense," Chief Savoie said when they'd finished. "Unfortunately, Angel, you're going to have to find another place to stay for the night while we finish things up here."

"I'll take her to the motel with me," Nathan replied. "Can we pack an overnight bag?"

"Of course. I'll be in the other room when you're ready to leave." The chief picked up the kitchen chair and left the bedroom, and Nathan got to his feet.

"I could go stay at my parents' place for the night," she said, not moving from the bed.

"Is that what you want to do?" he asked.

She released a deep shuddery sigh. "Not really. I... I don't feel like I'm in the right frame of mind to go to them."

He crouched down in front of her and pushed a strand of her hair behind her ear. "Then come to the motel with me. You can be in whatever frame of mind you need to be in."

Her beautiful green eyes held his gaze. "Are you sure you don't mind? I'd get my own room but I really don't feel like being alone right now."

"Angel, I want you to stay with me." He rose to his feet once again. "Now, let's pack our bags and leave this all to Chief Savoie."

It took them only minutes to get bags together and then they left the bedroom. Angel immediately faced the front door with her back to Louis's body on the floor.

"We're just waiting for the coroner to get here," Chief Savoie said. "But I have everything I need from you two right now, so you can go ahead and leave."

"We'll be at the motel if you do need us for anything," Nathan replied, then he guided Angel out the door.

The rain had turned to a fine drizzle and they were both quiet as they made their way to his car in the parking lot. He walked close behind her and wondered what she was thinking.

She'd been through a horrible trauma tonight and despite the fact she was a strong woman, something like this would be too much for anyone. It would break anyone.

She remained quiet on the ride to the motel and he didn't attempt to make her talk. He wondered if she was in some sort of daze. If she was, and it was a daze of self-protection, then he was grateful for it. But sooner or later she'd have to process what had gone down tonight.

They reached the motel and Angel sat in the car while he went into the office and got them a room. He returned to the car and drove them down to the room number.

"You go on inside," he said and handed her the room key. "I'll grab the bags."

They both got out of the car and he popped the trunk to retrieve the two bags while she disappeared into the room. A few minutes later he placed the bags on the floor next to one of the beds. He'd gotten a room with two double beds, not knowing what she needed or wanted from him.

She sat on the edge of one bed, looking achingly vulnerable. Her T-shirt held the violence of the night in blood streaks and her face was still unnaturally pale.

"I need a shower," she said and rose to her feet.

"Are you hungry? Do you want me to get you anything? I could order in or go run to get something."

She shook her head and grabbed her bag. "No, I'm not a bit hungry, but if you are, then feel free to get yourself something." With that, she disappeared into the bathroom.

Nathan sank down on the bed closest to the door. He wasn't hungry, either. His head still ached and now that he knew it was over and Angel was safe, he was exhausted.

The shower spray sounded from the bathroom and he got back up and opened his bag. He hung the shirt he had brought with him and then pulled out his toiletries and a clean pair of boxers. He then turned on the lamp next to his bed and closed the curtain over the front window. Once Angel was finished, he'd jump in the shower.

He remained stretched out on the bed until Angel came into the room. She was dressed in a sleeveless pink nightie. He had no time to dwell on how beautiful she looked for what caught his attention was a huge dark bruise on her shoulder.

He jumped up off the bed and approached her. "Oh, Angel. Is that what Louis did to you?"

"Yes, he hit me there before I could duck away," she replied.

"I wish I could touch it with magical fingers and make it disappear. I wish that somehow I could kiss it and make it all better," he said fervently. It was definitely a nasty bruise

She smiled. "And I like that about you." The smile immediately disappeared. "It will be okay. It's just going to take some time to heal."

"I would have killed him for you," he said softly. It was true. He would have done whatever was necessary to protect her.

"I know," she replied.

For a long moment they merely gazed at each other. He was grateful to see that some of the color had returned to her face.

She sank down on the edge of the bed closest to the bathroom with her hairbrush in her hand.

"I'm going to pop in for a quick shower," he said. He grabbed the boxers and bag of toiletries and went into the bathroom.

The whole night felt like a nightmare and even though it was over, it wasn't over yet for Angel. He knew without a doubt that she would replay this night in her mind for a while to come. It would be the stuff of nightmares.

He figured he'd stick around for another few days and then it would be time for him to go home. The thought brought him no real happiness but rather it was just something that was going to happen, something that had to happen.

He got out of the shower, pulled on his boxers and then even though he needed to shave, it was far more important that he get back in the room with Angel.

When he came out of the bathroom, she was already in bed with the sheet pulled up tightly around her. It was obvious she wanted to sleep alone.

"Are you tired?" he asked as he pulled down the blankets on the other bed.

"I'm utterly exhausted."

"So am I," he admitted. He got into bed. "Are you ready for the light to go out?"

"Ready," she replied.

He turned off the lamp, dousing the room into darkness except for where a faint shaft of light danced out of the bathroom. He'd left the light on in there in case either of them got up in the middle of the night.

"Good night, Angel."

"Good night, Nathan," she replied.

The room was quiet, with just the monotonous hum of the air conditioner's fan blowing. He stretched out on his back and stared up at the dark ceiling. All his thoughts were on the woman in the bed next to him.

She had shown very little emotion since it all had ended. Was she really that strong? It was definitely going to take him a while to unwind and actually go to sleep. He wasn't going to easily forget the vision of Louis dead on the floor and Angel covered in his blood.

He didn't know how long it was before she softly called

his name. "Nathan, would you mind just coming over here and holding me for a little while?"

"Honey, I can definitely do that." He immediately got out of his bed and slid into hers. He took her into his arms and he could feel the frantic beat of her heart against his.

With the scent of her filling his head and the warm curves of her body in his arms, this felt right. It felt right that he was here with her in this moment...to comfort her in her hour of need.

She began to cry. They were soft but deep sobs as she clung to him. He didn't ask her any questions or speak to her in any way other than in soft whispers meant to soothe.

She cried for a while and then the sobs slowly stopped. He could feel her utter exhaustion now and knew the best thing for her was to get some sleep.

He spooned himself around her back and then pulled her tight against him with his arm around her waist. He knew the moment she fell asleep once her breathing became deep and rhythmic. It was only then that he allowed himself to fall asleep as well.

Chapter Thirteen

Angel had no idea what time it was when she awakened. The room was dark but she sensed it was way past sunrise. Nathan was in the bed next to her and for several minutes she just listened to the sounds of his deep even breaths.

She was grateful he'd been there for her through the night as she'd tried to process everything that had happened. She'd tried to figure out if she'd had any other option rather than killing Louis. Her brain had worked around difference scenarios but at the end of each one the end result was the same.

The man who had burst into her shanty hadn't been her good friend. There had been nothing of Louis in the monster who had confronted her and she'd had no choice but to protect herself. If she forgot that, she had the aching pain in her shoulder to remind her.

It was going to take time for her to get over everything that had happened. And the one thing she knew for sure was her time with Nathan was at an end.

She'd suspected for the past couple of days Nathan had been taking pictures he didn't need. She knew he'd just been sticking around for her protection. Now she no longer needed his protection. The danger had passed and she was safe.

Tears burned hot at her eyes as she thought about telling him goodbye. It was going to be the most difficult thing she'd ever done in her life.

She had only herself to blame for the pain. She'd allowed herself to fall deeply in love with him. When she'd first started feeling so much for him, she should have stopped things. But instead she had encouraged them, knowing that at the end of it all was heartbreak.

Unable to stay in bed any longer, she quietly got up, grabbed her overnight bag and then went into the bathroom. She washed up, brushed her hair and then put on the jeans and T-shirt she'd brought with her.

She then stepped out of the bathroom. "Good morning," Nathan said and sat up.

"Oh, I hope I didn't wake you," she replied. The sight of him with his hair charmingly mussed from sleep and his bare chest gleaming in the light from the bathroom caused her heart to squeeze tightly.

"No, you didn't wake me," he replied. "How are you doing this morning?" The look he gave her was filled with such caring.

"I'm okay." She sank down on the bed that hadn't been slept in.

"Why don't I get dressed and we go to the café for some breakfast, and while we're there we can check in with Chief Savoie."

She frowned. "Breakfast at the café?"

"Angel, you might as well face it all now. You know everyone will have heard what happened last night. You need to show people that you're okay."

She sighed, knowing he was probably right. Besides, she wasn't even sure they could return to her place yet, so they might as well get some breakfast.

"Far be it from me to stand between a man and his morning meal," she replied, forcing a lightness to her tone.

He grinned at her. "That's my girl. Give me fifteen minutes or so and I'll be ready to go." He got out of the bed, grabbed the shirt that was hanging and his bag and then disappeared into the bathroom.

She got up and opened the curtains, allowing the morning light to fill the room. A look at her phone let her know that it was just after nine. She couldn't remember ever sleeping so late.

True to his words, about fifteen minutes later Nathan came out of the bathroom. He was dressed in a pair of jeans and a navy button-up, short-sleeved shirt. "Make sure we have all our things out of here and I'll check us out on the way out," he said.

"I have all my things," she said and grabbed her bag.

"Okay, then let's head to the car," he replied.

Minutes later they were checked out of the room and on their way to the café. "Are you hungry?" he asked.

"Maybe a little bit." She was definitely hungry for things she couldn't have. She hungered for his love. She wanted him to stay here with her forever. But each moment she spent with him now only led to their goodbye.

She steeled herself as he pulled up in front of the café and parked. As usual the place was packed and she suspected most of the morning conversations were probably about her and what had happened the night before.

Nathan gripped her elbow firmly as they walked in. She felt the curious gazes that followed them as they took a booth toward the back. Marianne greeted them and immediately pulled Angel to her for a tight hug.

"Girlfriend, I'm so glad you're okay," she said when she finally released Angel. "I can't believe it was Louis. I'm not going to say anything more right now, but, Angel, you know you have your girlfriends to lean on. We're all here for you."

"And I appreciate that," Angel replied and then slid into the booth opposite Nathan. She knew she could count on her friends. But she wasn't sure what to expect from Beau and Jacques. The three men had been thick as thieves. How would they feel about her now? She'd killed their friend. Would they understand that it had been self-defense? That she'd loved Louis until he'd tried to kill her?

Marianne took their orders and minutes later they both had coffee. "How are you doing?" Nathan asked, his gaze soft on her. "I seem to be asking you that a lot."

"I'm okay," she replied and broke eye contact with him. She had to start distancing herself from him. If she gazed at him for too long, she'd start to cry and that was the last thing she wanted to do.

They were halfway through their meal when Beau and Jacques came in and immediately beelined to their booth. Angel steeled herself, not knowing what to expect from them.

"Mind if we sit?" Beau asked. He didn't wait for an answer as he slid in next to Nathan and Jacques sat next to her. "I'm so glad we found you here. Angel… We didn't know."

"We had no idea it was Louis who was terrorizing you," Jacques said.

"And we understand that you only did what you had to do," Beau said, his dark eyes simmering. "Angel, I would have killed him myself for what he put you through."

Once again tears pressed against her eyelids. She was so very lucky to have friends to support her through all this. She'd been worried about how these two men would react to her, but she realized they cared about her enough to be okay with the choice she'd had to make.

The two stayed only a few minutes more and then left. "Feel better?" Nathan asked.

"Much better," she admitted. "I was so worried about how they would feel about things."

"You have a great support system around you."

"I know, I'm very lucky," she replied. She was a very lucky woman to have survived what she had and to have wonderful friends around her. But in one area of life, she was very unlucky because the man she loved didn't love her back.

ONCE THEY FINISHED up breakfast, Nathan called Chief Savoie, who told him the investigation was complete and they were free to return to the shanty.

As they drove toward the parking place, he shot several glances toward Angel. After the men had left the café, she had grown quiet and distant.

As always, he couldn't begin to guess what was going through her mind. Did she dread returning to her home? Had the peace she'd always had there now been forever tainted by the violence that had occurred there? For her sake, he hoped that wasn't the case.

He wanted to support her however he could, but he wasn't sure what to do for her in this moment. Time... It would just take time for her to heal. He planned on sticking around for another week or two so he could be her support and make sure she was healing.

They reached the parking lot where he stopped the car and took off his seat belt. She made no move to get out. She stared straight ahead for several long moments, then released a sigh and took off her own seat belt.

"Are you dreading this?" he asked.

She turned to look at him and her beautiful eyes simmered with emotion. "A little bit. I just wonder how the police left it." She sighed again. "I've never been nervous about going home before."

He reached out and took her hand in his. What he really wanted to do was wrap her in his arms and hold her until she was okay. "At least you don't have to worry about being in danger anymore."

She squeezed his hand and then withdrew it from his. "Thank God there is that. Okay, let's head in." He grabbed their bags and together they got out of the car.

He followed behind her as they walked through the trails to get to her shanty. The swamp was alive all around them with birdcalls and rustling brush as little animals scurried to go about their morning business.

Her shanty came into view and the first thing he saw was that the broken window had been boarded up. It was a nice thing for the police to do before they left and it gave him hope for what they'd find inside. Hopefully there were no blood stains left behind for her to clean up.

When they reached the front door, Angel pulled her house key out of her pocket and unlocked the door. He heard the audible breath she took and then she opened the door and they went inside.

It was a bit dark inside with the only light coming from the window in the kitchen. But even in the dim light he could see that thankfully, other than the board on the window, there was no indication that anything had happened here. Chief Savoie and his men were to be commended for the total cleanup that had taken place.

He could feel Angel's relief as she walked around the room. "Are you okay?" he asked.

She stopped walking and turned to face him. "There you go, asking me again. I'm okay. It's all going to be fine." She lit a couple of the lanterns and then sank down in her chair as he sat on the sofa.

"Who do you have to talk to in order to get a new window?" he asked.

"Brett Mayfield. He's a handyman and one of the few people who will come in and do work in the swamp. I'll call him later today," she replied.

"What do you want to do this afternoon? Are you up to going to your fishing spot and doing a little fishing?"

"No." She stared at him for a long moment. "What I am up for is you leaving here today. It's time you pack your bags and go home."

He gazed at her in stunned surprise. He wasn't ready to leave here...to leave her. "Angel, are you sure that's what you want?"

She looked away and nodded her head. "It's what I want. I'm safe now and it's past time for you to go back to your own life." She gazed at him once again. "I need you to go, Nathan. I'm ready to be alone again."

He swore he saw a glint of tears in her eyes that belied what her words were saying to him. "Angel, I... I don't know what to say. My plan was to stay here with you a little while longer."

"Cancel that plan," she said. "Pack your bags and go." She got up from the chair and he rose as well.

There was a bite of anger in her tone, an anger he didn't understand. "Angel, have I done something wrong?"

She released a deep sigh. "No, you've done everything very right, Nathan. You've made me laugh and you've made me think. You've made me feel safe and you've filled up my life in a way I never thought was possible."

The words fell out of her quickly, as if released from under an enormous pressure. But they certainly didn't explain why she was asking him to leave now or the sharpness in her tone.

"In fact," she continued, "you've done everything so right that I've fallen in love with you. I'm in love with you, Nathan, and every moment I spend with you now is sheer torture for me."

Once again he stared at her in stunned surprise. She was in love with him? He hadn't seen this coming and his heart squeezed and tightened his chest.

"I... I don't know what to say," he finally replied.

"Then don't say anything. I thank you for everything you've done for me, but please just pack your bags and go. I'll be out on the back deck."

He watched as she walked through the kitchen area and then disappeared out the back door. She was in love with him? Surely she was mistaking friendship for love. He'd been here with her through the rough times and she was confusing gratitude for love.

He went into the bedroom and began to pack up his things. She might be mistaken about a lot of things, but she'd been very clear she wanted him gone.

His heart ached with a depth of emotion he didn't want to examine right now. All he knew was he hadn't been ready to tell her goodbye yet. He'd just wanted a little more time with her.

It didn't take him long to gather his things. He set his two bags and his camera by the front door and then headed for the back door.

He couldn't leave here without saying goodbye. She'd been such an important part of his life for the past five weeks. He loved her deeply, but he wasn't in love with her. He couldn't be because he had to go back home.

He stepped out on the back deck where she stood at the railing looking out on the water. She turned at the sound of him and her eyes were filled with tears.

His heart squeezed even tighter, making it difficult for him to breathe. God, he hated to see her pain…pain that apparently he was causing her. He'd never meant for this to happen. She'd known from the very beginning he wouldn't be staying here with her.

"Angel… I'm so sorry," he said. "The last thing I ever wanted was to hurt you."

"I know." She swiped a tear off her cheek. "This isn't

your problem, Nathan. It's mine. I hope your book is an amazing success."

"Thanks. So, I guess this is goodbye?" Dammit, he didn't want it to be. Even now he wanted to draw her into his arms and hold her body against his. He wanted to feel her heart-beat and smell the scent of her. But, of course, he didn't do that. He knew in this moment she wouldn't want any kind of touch from him.

"Goodbye, Nathan," she said softly and turned her back to him. This was it. It was time for him to leave.

"Goodbye, Angel." There was nothing left to say…nothing left for him to do except abide by her wishes and go. She remained on the deck while he went back into the shanty and grabbed his things.

As he walked down the bridge away from her, he couldn't even begin to sort out all the emotions that rushed through him. It was over. It was done. He had what he needed to finish his book and it was time to go home.

ANGEL SAT AT her favorite fishing place and waited for a bite. It had been a week since Nathan had left and the pain of his absence still ached deep inside her.

She missed the sound of his laughter, so deep and robust. She missed their conversations and that silly little grin of his when he was teasing her. She even missed the click of his camera.

She had a feeling she would never ever again love as deeply, as completely as she'd loved Nathan. He'd left an imprint in her heart that would never go away.

But life went on. The window in her shanty was fixed and she'd fallen back into her usual routine. Her friends had been wonderfully supportive and she told herself she was fine despite the tears that often overwhelmed her at unexpected times.

With the week that had gone by, her tears were coming less frequently now even though the pain of loss still resided deep inside her.

She jumped to her feet as the end of her pole dipped. She jerked to set the hook and then reeled in a nice-sized catfish. As she took it off the hook, she couldn't help but remember the last time she'd been here with Nathan.

They'd had such fun fishing together. He'd made her laugh so hard with his antics and his desire to beat her at catching more fish than her.

She rebaited her hook and then cast it back out in the water and sat once again. At least she had the swamp and she no longer had to worry about it holding a monster who was after her.

The Swamp Soul Stealer still continued to dominate the news but there had been no leads in the cases. Colette Broussard remained in a coma and Angel had heard through the grapevine that Etienne often spent late nights sitting in her hospital room.

"Angel." The deep familiar voice came from behind her. Was she so lovesick she was imagining Nathan's voice?

She jumped to her feet, whirled around and gasped as she saw him standing in the small clearing. "Nathan," she exclaimed in stunned surprise. Was this some kind of dream? Was he just an imaginary mirage created by the desire in her mind?

"I was hoping I'd find you here," he said and took a step closer to her.

"Nathan, wha…what are you doing here?" Had he forgotten something? Had he left something important at the shanty? She hadn't found anything of his.

It was sheer torture to see him again. He wore jeans and a royal blue shirt that did amazing things to his eyes. Oh, he had such beautiful eyes.

"I went home from here and got settled back into my life and I thought I was going to be just fine, but I haven't been fine. I missed the sounds of the swamp at night and walking leisurely through the trails, but more than anything I missed you, Angel." He took another step closer to her.

"Before I left here, I told myself that I loved the sound of your laughter and the conversations we had. I convinced myself that I loved absolutely everything about you, but I wasn't in love with you. I was wrong, Angel. I was only fooling myself. I'm totally and madly in love with you and I can't imagine my life without you."

He stepped forward and drew her into his arms and her love for him exploded through her heart and soul. He loved her. The words rang through her with happiness. It was all she'd wanted but…how could it possibly work between them?

"I'll tell you something else," he continued before she could say anything. "I have fallen in love with this wild and beautiful place. I want to spend my days here and fall asleep with you in my arms and the sounds of the swamp lulling me to sleep."

"But what about your work?" she asked.

"I realized I could do much of it, including teaching classes, by utilizing the place in town you told me about. I can make my life work for me just fine from here. So, I have a question for you." He pulled her more tightly against him. "Is there room in your shanty for a biologist nerd who loves you with all his heart?"

"Oh, Nathan," she replied breathlessly. "Of course there's room for you."

"So does that mean you're going to marry me and have my babies?"

"Yes...yes, I'll marry you and have your babies." She barely got the words out of her mouth and then his lips were on hers kissing her with a love and caring she could taste.

When the kiss ended, he gazed at her with those beautiful eyes of his. "I'm deeply in love with you, Angel Marchant."

She smiled up at him. "I like that about you, and I'm deeply in love with you, Nathan Merrick."

He laughed, that deep rumble of joy she loved to hear. "And I like that about you."

She frowned up at him. "Are you sure you really want to do this, Nathan? Are you really ready to leave New Orleans for a life here in the swamp?"

"I'm more than sure. I can easily leave the city behind for the life and love I've found here with you." That boyish grin she loved so much danced to his lips. "And I'm still determined to beat you by catching more fish than you."

She laughed and as he kissed her once again, she knew that her life with him was going to be filled with laughter and fun and love forever more.

Epilogue

Etienne sat in the hospital room where Colette Broussard slept in her coma. Machines clicked and whirred in an effort to sustain her life.

He vaguely remembered seeing her around town before she'd been kidnapped. She'd been a pretty woman with her long hair and dark eyes. Now that beauty had been marred by whatever hell she had been through at the hands of her captor.

She'd been malnourished and it had shown in her skinny frame and gaunt face. She'd had three broken ribs and a fractured arm, along with too many bruises to count.

The intravenous feeding tube had managed to put a little weight on her now but she still appeared ill and too thin. The bruises had also begun to heal and her arm had been set in a cast.

Everything that could be done was being done in an effort to help her. Etienne needed her to wake up. He hoped and prayed that she would lead him to the man...the monster dubbed the Swamp Soul Stealer.

The fact that she'd been found alive gave him hope for the others who had been kidnapped. He'd thought they were all dead, but Colette was proof the others might still be alive.

He liked ending his nights here with her. He hoped that in some crazy way his presence might soothe and comfort her, that he might give her the strength to fight through the darkness she was in. He fought the impulse to draw her hand into his.

Her parents had been killed two years ago in an accident with a drunk driver, and Colette had been their only child. So there were no family members vying for time with her. She was alone except for Etienne.

The doctors had told him that one day next week they were going to begin to bring her out of the medically induced coma. Hopefully at that time she would be strong enough to wake up and be able to help him find the monster who had done this to her.

Who had starved her and beaten her to within an inch of her life? Who was the monster who walked the swamp and kidnapped both women and men? She had to wake up and help him find the Swamp Soul Stealer. At this point she was all Etienne had to solve the mystery and get a human monster behind bars.

* * * * *

COMING SOON!

We really hope you enjoyed reading this book.
If you're looking for more romance
be sure to head to the shops when
new books are available on

Thursday 24th
April

MILLS & BOON

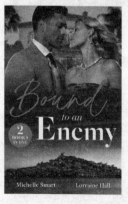
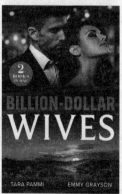

LET'S TALK

Romance

For exclusive extracts, competitions and special offers, find us online:

- **f** MillsandBoon
- **X** @MillsandBoon
- **◉** @MillsandBoonUK
- **♪** @MillsandBoonUK

Get in touch on 01413 063 232